If the magic had died—

But it hadn't. Beneath her hand, the mirror thrummed. In the reflection of her eyes, the first flickers of green fire sparked, and following those flickers, the long, bright flashes, and in the back of her mind, the low, heavy roll of thunder building in the distance—

—and then the resistance of the glass vanished from beneath the weight of her palm and Lauren tightened her grip on her son, leaned over, and picked up her picnic basket. And stepped through.

A moment in which sound died, in which she and Jake were utterly engulfed in cool, energizing, electrifying green flame, when every cell in her body felt both separate and vibrantly alive. In that moment she felt Brian beside her, and felt his lips brush the nape of her neck, and heard him whisper, *"I told you I'd never leave you."*

HOLLY LISLE

Memory of Fire

BOOK ONE OF THE WORLD GATES

An Imprint of HarperCollins*Publishers*

EOS
An Imprint of HarperCollins*Publishers*
10 East 53rd Street
New York, New York 10022-5299

Copyright © 2002 by Holly Lisle
Excerpt from *The Fresco* copyright © 2000 by Sheri S. Tepper
Excerpt from *Destiny* copyright © 2002 by Sharon Green
ISBN: 0-380-81837-X
www.eosbooks.com

First Eos paperback printing: May 2002

Eos Trademark Reg. U.S. Pat. Off. and in Other Countries, Marca Registrada, Hecho en U.S.A.
HarperCollins® is a trademark of HarperCollins Publishers Inc.

Printed in the U.S.A.

10 9 8 7 6 5 4 3 2 1

For Matthew

Acknowledgments

Thanks to:

Russ Galen, for spot-on worldbuilding critiques and for pointing out what was really good about the initial concept, and for helping me strip away what wasn't;

Bob Billing, for gracious assistance in researching British beer;

The readers of the Sneak Peeks board at http://hollylisle.com for comments and queries about the first several chapters of the first draft, which helped point me in the best direction for the rest of the book;

Sarah Jane Elliott, Jim Mills, Beth Adele Long, Doug Dandridge, Chris Hughes, Jennifer St. Clair, Ron Brown, Teresa Hopper, Lazette Gifford, and Sheila (S.L.) Viehl, for reading and commenting on the finished first draft;

And for my family, who are my first readers and my assistants, excellent critics and wonderful companions . . . and who love me even when I am unlovable, which is a real plus.

Memory of Fire

CHAPTER 1

Ballahara, Nuue, Oria

MOLLY MCCOLL WOKE to darkness—and to men dragging her from her bed toward her bedroom door. The door glowed with a terrifying green light.

She didn't waste her breath screaming; she attacked. She kicked upward, and felt like she'd kicked a rock—but she heard the satisfying crack of bone under foot, and the resulting shriek of pain. She snapped her right elbow back into ribs and gut, and her hand broke free from the thin, hot, strong fingers that clutched at it. She twisted and bit down on the fingers holding her left wrist, and was rewarded with a scream. She clawed at eyes, she kneed groins, she bit and kicked and fought with every trick at her disposal, with every ounce of her strength and every bit of her fear and rage.

But they had her outnumbered, and even though she could make out the outlines of the ones she'd hurt curled on the floor, the rest of her assailants still dragged her into that wall of fire. She screamed, but as the cluster of tall men around her forced her into the flames, her scream—and all other sounds—died.

No pain. No heat. The flames that brushed against her didn't hurt at all—instead, the cold fire felt wonderful, energizing, life-giving; as her kidnappers dragged her clawing and kicking onto the curving, pulsing tunnel, something in her mind whispered "yes." For the instant—or the eternity—in which she hung suspended in that place, no one held her, no one was trying to hurt her, and for the first time in a long time, all the pain in her body fell away.

She had no idea what was going on; on the one hand she felt like she was fighting for her life, and on the other hand like she was moving into something wonderful.

And then, out of the tunnel of green fire, she erupted into a world of ice and snow and darkness, and all doubts vanished. The men still held her captive, and one of them shouted, "Get ropes and a wagon—she hurt Paith and Kevrad and Tajaro. We're going to have to tie her." She was in trouble—nothing good would come of this.

"It's only two leagues to Copper House."

"She'll kill one of us in that distance. Tie her."

"But the Imallin said she's not to be hurt."

Other hands were grabbing her now—catching at her feet, locking on to her elbows and wrists, knees and calves.

"Don't *hurt* her," said the one closest to her head. "Just *tie* her so she can't hurt us, damnall. And where's that useless Gateman the Imallin found to make the gate? We still have people back there! Send someone to get them out before he closes it!"

Molly fought as hard as she could, but the men—thin and tall, but strong—forced her forward, adding hands to hands on her arms and legs until she simply couldn't move.

When she couldn't fight, Molly relaxed her body completely. First, she wasn't going to waste energy uselessly. Second, if she stopped fighting, she might catch them off guard and be able to escape.

"Gateman—can you hold it?" someone was shouting behind her. "We're going back for the others!"

"He's worthless," one of her captors muttered. "This was as close to the city as he could get us—a good Gateman could have put the thing almost in the courtyard."

"I don't like the feel of the forest tonight, either," the one closest to her said. "Keep the guards in tight."

Molly's bare feet stood on packed snow, and she wore nothing but flannel pajamas—when she stopped fighting, that fact plunged into her consciousness with shocking speed.

"If you don't get me some boots, and a coat, and maybe a hat and some gloves, you aren't going to have to worry about getting me where you're going—because I'm going to freeze to death right here."

Someone dragged a big, snorting animal through the dark toward her, and rattling behind the animal was a big wooden farm-type wagon. But what the hell was the thing pulling it? It wasn't a horse and it wasn't any variety of cow—it had a bit of a moose shape to it, and a hint of caribou, and some angles that suggested bones where bones didn't belong in any beast of burden Molly had ever seen. And its eyes glowed hell-red in the darkness.

"You can do without the shoes and the coat," the one who had done most of the talking said to her. "You'll ride in the back of the hay-wagon, covered with a few blankets—if you decide you want to try to escape, you can do it in your bare feet in the snow."

"You can't talk to the Vodi like that," one of the other men said.

"No one knows if she's the Vodi yet. Right now, she's the creature who crushed Byarriall's chest and snapped Loein's leg in two. What sort of Vodi would do things like that?"

Molly didn't know what a Vodi was. She didn't care. "How about one that got kidnapped from her bed in the middle of the night?" she said, but they no longer seemed to be listening to her. The mob picked her up and shoved her into the back of the wagon, and most of them clambered up there with her—bending down to twist soft rope around her ankles, and then around her wrists. When they had her bound, they wrapped blankets around her, and tucked her deep into bales of straw. Instantly, she was warmer. Hell, she was warm. But as the wagon lurched and creaked and began to rattle forward, she heard lines of marching feet forming on either side of the wagon. She knew the creak of boots and pack straps, the soft bitching, the sound of feet moving in rhythm while weighted down by gear and weapons. She remembered basic training all too well—and if Air Force basic was pretty easy compared to the Army or the Marines, she'd still got enough of marching to know the drill. She had a military escort.

What the hell was going on?

But the people who had come to get her weren't soldiers. They were too unprepared for resistance, too sure of themselves. Soldiers knew that trouble could be anywhere, and took precautions. More than that, though, she couldn't get over the feel of those hands on her—hot, thin, dry hands.

She decided she wasn't going to just wait for them to haul her where they were going and then . . . do things to her. She'd learned in the Air Force that the best way to survive a hostage situation was to not be a hostage. She started to work on the rope on her wrists, and managed by dint of persistence and a high pain tolerance to free her hands. She'd done some damage—she could feel rope burns and scratches from metal embedded beneath the soft outer strands, and the heat and wetness where a bit of her own blood trickled down her hand—but she wasn't worried about any of that.

Fold and wrap a blanket around each foot and bind it in place with the rope, she thought. It won't make great boots, but it will get me home. Turn the other blankets into a poncho, get the hell out of this place and back home. She could follow the tracks in the snow.

Except there were the niggling details she hadn't let herself think about while she was fighting, while she was getting her hands and then her feet untied, while she was folding boots out of blankets and tying them in place. She hadn't heard an engine since she came out of the tunnel of fire; she hadn't heard a car pass, or seen anything that might even be mistaken for an electric light; nor had she heard a plane fly over. In the darkness, she could make out the vague outlines of trees overhead, but not much else—not a star shone in the sky, which felt close and pregnant with more snow.

She suspected that if she managed to escape the soldiers that marched to either side of the wagon and succeeded in tracing the wagon tracks back to the place where she'd come through the tunnel of fire, that tunnel wouldn't be there anymore. And she was very, very afraid that there would be no other way to get home.

She listened to the speech of the men who drove the wagons, and she could understand it flawlessly—but if she forced herself to listen to the words, they were vowel-rich and liquid, and they didn't have the shape of English. The hands on her arms had felt wrong in ways besides their heat, their dryness, their thinness. When she closed her eyes and stilled her breath and forced herself to remember, those hands had gripped her with too many fingers. And when she'd been fighting, her elbows had jammed into ribs where ribs weren't supposed to be.

When the sun came up or they got to a place with lights, Molly had a feeling that she wasn't going to like getting her first clear look at her kidnappers. Because when she let herself really think about it, she had the feeling that she wasn't on Earth anymore—and that her captors weren't human.

She had her makeshift boots in place, her blanket poncho wrapped and knotted. But she wasn't going anywhere. Not yet. She was ready to run when she got the chance—but not into a cold, dark, trackless forest with a snowstorm going on and no signs of civilization anywhere.

She leaned back into the straw, and let the warmth and the rocking of the cart and the voices all around her lull her into a near-sleep.

The sound of someone running and voices raised in anger snapped her out of her half-doze. An argument—she wished she had someplace to run because an argument would make perfect cover for her to slip away into darkness. But then someone jumped into the back of the cart with her.

Someone pulled the covers away from her face. Darkness unrelieved by moon, by stars, or by any form of man-made light offered her nothing that she hadn't been able to see under the blanket. Snow blew into her face and her hair with a steadiness that suggested a pending blizzard.

"Vodi—oh Vodi—I bring you my child," he said. He knelt

in the straw by Molly's side, and she made out the outline of a white-wrapped bundle in his arms. Small. Still. Silent.

He laid this bundle beside Molly, and pressed his forehead to the straw-covered floor of the cart. "She dies, Vodi," he said. "You can save her with a word. With a single touch."

Molly could have said nothing. She could have turned her face away. But sudden fury enveloped her, and she shouted, "You people have kidnapped me; bound me; kept me prisoner in the back of this cold cart without food or water all day and part of the night! And you ask me to help you? Who's going to help me?"

The man said nothing. Instead, he reached out to her and with trembling fingers touched her hand. "My other four children are dead these last three days. Ewilla is my last. A word from you is all I ask. A single word to heal her, to save her, that my mate and I will not lose everything we love. Curse me and I will bear the weight of your curse gladly— even if it be death. But spare a single word for a dying child."

Molly's gut twisted. One side of her raged with her own fear and fury, but on the other side lay the knowledge that this was what she did, that this was who she was.

She held out her hand, and the man passed the unmoving child to her. Molly touched the dry skin of Ewilla's face and felt terrible fever and an unyielding tightness of flesh over bone that felt already dead. What she did not feel—what she had always felt before in the presence of the sick, the dying, the tortured—was the pain of the sufferer. She felt only her own cheek pressed close to the child's nose and mouth, and the rapid hot breaths that blew against her skin that convinced her Ewilla still lived.

"I can't feel her sickness," Molly said.

"She is sick. She is very near death."

"You don't understand. I can't feel her pain. If I can't feel what she feels, I don't know that I can help her."

"Please. Oh, please. She's all that her mother and I have left."

Molly closed her eyes, and her fingers, still pressed to Ewilla's cheek, trembled. Since childhood, Molly had helped the sick by taking the razor blades and jagged glass of their sickness and pending death into her own body, and feeling their terror as it flowed through her. Now she felt nothing; some empathy for the father, yes. Some fury at her own situation, yes. But no pain. No fear. No . . . no poison.

"Be well," she whispered, without any real hope, any real expectation that what she did would do any good; with only a vague determination that if she could help, she would. She touched the child's face.

At the point where her fingers touched Ewilla's skin, green-white fire glowed in a tiny point that quickly spread. It was the fire of the tunnel that had carried her to this place, and it both shocked and scared her. Molly yanked her hand back, but the connection remained; she could feel the cool, energizing rush of a current powerful as a river at flood pouring through both her and the child, washing around them, and then driving into the child and changing her. Changing Ewilla, cell by cell, molecule by molecule, replacing sick with well, weak with strong, dying with healthy; rinsing her free of death as if death were nothing more than a loosely attached surface stain, and filling the child with life as pure and vibrant and electric as the moment of creation. Molly, riveted by this impossible power, this insane magic, couldn't catch her breath. She felt that out of thin air she had summoned a whirlwind, had called forth both gods and devils and told them to dance, and had seen them obey her. Intoxicated, she basked in the power that embraced and caressed her. And then she looked, truly looked, at the child who lay in her arms, bathed in green fire, illuminated like the heart of an alien sun.

And all her fears were made reality by the sight of that face.

It wasn't just sickness, and it wasn't deformity; Molly could not look at the little creature and think that she had been twisted in the womb. She was a beautiful creature. But she was not, and had never been, human. Her eyes, slanted like a Siamese cat's and large as lemons, were emerald-green from corner to corner, without sclerae, without pupils, without irises. They were two cabochon gems set into a

high-cheekboned, feather-browed face, lovely and terrifying. The child's tiny hand, poking free of the soft blanket
that swaddled her, had too many fingers, and each finger had
too many joints. When Molly looked up at the face of the father, those same eyes, those same pointed, off-angled, alien
features stared back at her.

Then the last of the poison washed out of the little girl,
and the fire that flowed through Molly, no longer needed,
flowed back to the heart of the universe that had spawned it,
and the light died.

The child sat up, looked around, and in the liquid sounds
that Molly's mind knew, uttered a stream of protests at incredible speed. She struggled away from Molly and held out
her arms to her father.

Molly could hear the father weeping. His voice sounded
reedy, and had she heard a human sobbing that way, she
might have mistaken the sound for choking. But Molly understood. The child's father wrapped his daughter in his
arms, clutching her to him as if to pull her through his chest
and into his heart. Through his sobs, he said, "I have to get
her home—out of this cold." He pulled back from his daughter for just an instant, and said, "When you need me most, I
will be here for you. I swear it."

Molly, in shock, stared at her hands as if they didn't belong to her. Green fire had come from her touch, and some
alien monstrosity swore himself to her service. She wanted
to hide. She wanted to scream, or to faint. Instead, she whispered to him, "Take me home."

"You are among friends," he told her. "You must trust us.
You go now to your castle. You will be a goddess, Vodi. And
if ever you need me, simply speak my name. Say 'Yaner,
Yaner,' and will your wish, and I will come to you." He
pulled his daughter close and dropped off the back of the
wagon. And then he ran away.

Molly lay back in the straw, too numb to do anything but
stare at nothing, too numb even to cover herself with the
blanket again. She'd suspected the truth, but discovered that
knowing this particular truth was far more distressing than
merely considering it as a possibility. She wasn't in some

third-world country, a political prisoner, a hostage for some terrorist's ideological crusade.

She had felt the green fire, but she had felt no pain.

Molly McColl stared at her hands and tried to understand what was happening to her. The tunnel of green light, the aliens.

Above the peculiar muffled hiss of snow falling, Molly suddenly heard a sound out of place. A baseball bat hitting a leather jacket, but slowly. And from overhead.

With no more warning than that, people grabbed her and began running through the woods with her, as silently as if they were ghosts. Behind her, she heard the eruption of hell, and screams of, "Rrôn, rrôn!"

The sudden leathery thunder of enormous wings, and roars that shook the snow from the trees and deafened her— the clash of metal, the screams of dead and dying, the stink of shit and blood.

Her rescuers dropped her on the ground, then squeezed in tightly on either side of her. "No sound," a voice whispered in her ear, but whoever offered this advice need not have spared breath or chanced even the risk of a whisper; she could hear the hell behind her, and she would no more vol- untarily call that down upon herself than she would throw herself in front of live fire to see what might happen. She did what she could to help her own survival; she breathed through her mouth because that made less noise than breath- ing through her nose, and she forced all of her muscles to re- lax, and she tried to think of anything she might do to save her own life if she and her rescuers were discovered. She wouldn't be able to do much. With an M-16 and a thousand rounds, she bet she'd be able to make a positive contribution to the fight, but all she had to offer were two blanket- wrapped feet, two bare hands, and no weapons of any sort.

And whatever had landed on the caravan was big. Really big.

She could feel the creatures to either side of her trem- bling. The roars had words in them, though not words she could understand. Trees shattered with cannon booms and carts and cart beasts came sailing through the air to land in the forest all around the place where she and her kidnappers hid. Men shouted, and fought, and died, and Molly heard screams, and then fewer screams, and then no screams at all.

And then the thunder of leather wings filled the air again, and the roaring stopped.

Silence.

The hiss of snow falling on snow, the rattle of branches one against another in the frozen forest, and not so much as a moan, a whisper, the sob of someone begging salvation or release.

For a long time, she lay unmoving between the two who had taken her away from the wagon caravan. Then she felt them move, and she sat up, slowly, shook the blanket away from her face so that she could see, and looked from one to the other.

"Rrôn," the one to her left said in the softest of voices. "They felt the healing. They came."

The other one said, "You will have to walk now. No wagons will be left. Stay with us, though, for the rrôn may check the road—you do not want them to find you."

"What about helping the survivors?" she asked. "The injured?"

"The rrôn would not leave survivors. The injured are dead."

"Others like us, then?"

"If any hid instead of fighting to protect you, better they throw themselves on the mercy of the rrôn than ever return to Copper House."

One checked her feet and discovered her no longer barefoot and bound—then checked her wrists. She heard breath hiss out of him, and felt his steady gaze on her. After a moment, he said, "There are only two of us left. Will you come with us?"

Molly cleared her throat and said, "yeah." She was quiet for a moment.

"How many died?" she asked at last, as her two captors pointed her away from the road, deeper into the forest.

"More than a hundred. Others of our . . . unit . . . will

come tomorrow to retrieve the bodies, before the yaresh haul them off to sell. Or eat."

Molly decided she would not try an escape tonight. Maybe not for a long while.

Cat Creek, North Carolina

Lauren Dane finished scraping the last of the black paint from the antique mirror's glass. She swore a final time at the unknown vandal who had painted it over, then sighed and stood. Her legs ached from crouching for so long—she stretched, hearing the creaking in her knees and feeling the cracking in her spine, and she reflected that thirty-five was a lot harder than twenty-five had been. She was pretty sure she was getting smarter, but she figured she was falling apart at about the same rate. By the time she was seventy, she ought to be both brilliant and too decrepit to make any use of her hard-won knowledge.

But at least now the mirror looked good. Reaching from floor to ceiling at the back of the foyer—ten feet high, framed by one of those ornate carved dark wood frames that collected dust in the crevices but looked so pretty when rubbed with oil—it seemed a little out of place, too grand to be at the back of the foyer in the old Southern farmhouse. But the mirror had always been there. Lauren remembered being terrified of it when she was little—of refusing to walk past it in the dark, and of staring into it in the daylight, certain that she could see ghosts moving within its silvered depths.

She smiled at her childishness and liked the look of the smile on her reflected image. She couldn't resist a little primping—this particular mirror had always been fairly kind with the images it reflected, unlike the closet mirror in her old apartment, which had put twenty pounds on her and made her skin look green no matter the lighting or the time of day. She thought she still looked decent for her age. No gray in her hair yet, no real lines on her face—though she could see where she'd have crow's-feet at the corners of her eyes in a few more years—and when she stood sideways, her stomach was flat enough and her butt still looked good in her jeans. The last year had been rough on the inside, but it hadn't done much to the outside.

She looked into her reflected eyes, and saw the faintest flash of green light shining back at her. Her heart skipped a beat, and she smiled nervously, and turned and looked down the hall to see where the light had come from. But the beveled-glass sidelights to either side of the front door showed nothing unusual outside. A North Carolina afternoon in mid-November, the scrub oaks still clinging to their brown leaves, the river birches bare, the leathery leaves of the magnolias so deep a green they were almost black. The bright, pale sky wore a few mares' tails high up, and to the west she saw the fish-scaled clouds her father had called mackerel sky. Nothing moved except a bluejay; he sat on top of the cedar bird feeder she'd hung out the day she moved in and glared at her as if he questioned his right to the corn and sunflower seeds inside.

The street lay empty; the house across the street was still; and no kids full of after-school rambunctiousness dotted the neighborhood yards yet.

No green light. She felt the slight stirring of hairs at the back of her neck, and shivered. She turned around again, but averted her eyes from the mirror as she had when she was a little girl . . . and she caught herself doing it, and she shook her head and forced herself to look in her reflection's eyes again.

The green flash. Just a spark, a sparkle, but it seemed to come from within the mirror.

And she thought, of course, the coatings on these old mirrors tarnish and flake off, and one of the flakes is catching the light oddly. If I move . . . here, I won't get that little—

A single tendril of green fire flickered from behind her reflection's head off to the left, looking like a slow flash of lightning. Her heart raced and her mouth went dry and she

took a step back. That hadn't been caused by a bit of tar-
nished silvering.

The mirror seemed to tug at her; she stepped nearer, even
though she was as suddenly and completely frightened as
she had ever been as a child, and she stared deep into her
own eyes, and within their reflections she saw green fire
play. Light licked out from her reflection, hypnotic and
beautiful and somehow welcoming. She reached one hand
forward, and beneath her splayed fingertips she felt the cool
glass hum and vibrate and grow warm.

Memories flowed around her—a memory of fire that embraced but did not burn, of images that danced within the
soft green glow shimmering through the gentle flames: a
meadow that spread to the end of sight in all directions, with
flowers chin high that rolled away like a sea of crimson and
white; a woman, young and brown-haired, her dress white
and full-skirted and covered with huge red poppies, her high
heels white with sharply pointed toes; high-pitched laughing
voices calling her to come play come play come play; and
on the back of her neck, Brian's lips pressing a kiss, and
Brian's soft deep voice in her ear, promising her he'd be
home soon.

Out in the living room, Jake woke screaming.

Lauren jerked away from the mirror, the spell broken.
Tears ran down her cheeks and burned in the back of her
throat; the woman who stared back at her from the other side
of the mirror looked lost and dazed and bereft, as if she'd
been stolen away from heaven within sight of its gates.

Lauren turned and fled—raced into the living room to
gather Jake into her arms; she held him and patted his back
and crooned at him that everything was okay, okay, okay,
okay until her own racing heart quieted and her own trembling hands steadied and she could breathe again.

She carried Jake up to his new room to change his diaper,
but she went the long way—through the dining room and the
kitchen and the side hall and up the back steps, past stacks
and stacks of boxes waiting to be unpacked, so that she did
not walk by the mirror with him in her arms.

Silly superstitions, she told herself as she carried the two-year-old up the steep, narrow stairs. Childish behavior. She had no reason not to carry Jake up the front stairs. None. Exhaustion from a long move, from big changes finally made, from uncertain chances finally taken as challenges instead of obstacles—all of those had left her fragile and vulnerable and weary. Suggestible. She'd remembered the mirror, had remembered her childhood fear of it, and in her tired state her mind had played a trick on her. The next time she looked at her reflection in the mirror, she would see nothing out of the ordinary. A thirty-five-year-old mother with her father's black hair and her mother's green eyes; the foyer of her childhood home; light reflected from out of doors.

In the back of her mind, thunder rumbled and green lightning flickered across a land like no place on Earth, and high-pitched voices called to her called to her called to her to come and play.

And Brian waited. Somewhere.

"Mama. Please—biteys?" Jake, grown tired of pounding on pots with wooden spoons, now stood behind her with a hopeful expression on his round face. "Please—broccoli?" Which came out with each syllable carefully enunciated, and all three stressed the same. Bra Cole Lee. "Please—cookie-biteys?"

She pushed up from the half-unpacked box of glassware and brushed the hair from her forehead with the back of a dusty hand. She glanced from habit to the spot above the sink where her mother's clock used to hang, but of course it was gone, along with everything else that had been in the house ten years ago. Still, a look out the window told her what she needed to know—it was already dark outside, and the time when she should have had supper done for the two of them had come and gone long ago.

"Okay. Biteys it is, monkey-boy. Want to help me?"

He grinned at her. "No." He started backing away, ready to run should she decide to push the issue.

Ah, two. The age when everything was a test, and the only person who could fail was Mom. Lauren had heard other mothers telling horror stories about their two-year-old children and had assumed that such misbehavior merely reflected the poor parenting skills of the teller.

God got even with people who entertained thoughts of that sort—he gave them kids like Jake, and said, "Go to it, bright girl."

She smiled down at Jake and said, "Good boy. Go get me the broccoli from the refrigerator," as if he'd said "yes," and turned her back on him. After an instant she heard the refrigerator open and a moment later he was holding up two stalks of broccoli for her.

"Thank you," she said. "Now I need for you to sweep the floor for me. Go get the broom and the dustpan." She needed the floor swept by Jake about as much as she needed the house repainted by him—he'd do equally as good a job at either. But he *liked* to sweep, and would happily push dirt around the floor all day if she also let him try to use the dustpan. If he knocked over a few things in the process—well, that was why she didn't store anything breakable less than six feet from the floor.

He yelled, "S'eep!" and took off to find the broom.

She heard his sneakered feet thudding on old linoleum. Then the change when he hit wood. More wood. The baby gate would keep him from going up the front steps, she could see the back steps, and she hadn't unpacked anything in any of the rooms yet that he shouldn't touch. So she let him run. She got out the steamer and put the broccoli in it with a cup of water in the bottom, covered the pan, put it on the back burner.

Different range than had been in the house when her parents lived there, she thought; one of those fancy white-on-white models that matched fridge and microwave and dishwasher and the new bleached-wood glass-fronted cabinets that had replaced her mother's homey pine ones. Granted it wasn't avocado, which the old one had been, and that was a good thing, but it wasn't familiar either.

Even though she would have had to live with ancient avocado appliances, she wished the people who had owned
the house last hadn't remodeled the kitchen. She was so
glad they'd had to move before they could change anything else.

Jake was being awfully quiet.

"Jake—broom!" she yelled, but she didn't hear any footsteps.

Which meant that he'd found something to get into. Probably had decided to climb into another of the empty boxes
she had stacked by the front door. Unlike her, Jake so far
seemed to adore moving.

Then she remembered she'd left both broom and dustpan
beside the mirror in the foyer. She'd been sweeping up the
paint flakes as she scraped them from the glass so that they
wouldn't become embedded in the old wood floor. Something cold and terrifying crawled down her spine, and she
yelled, "Jake, *come here!*"

And she heard him laugh, and say, "Hi!"

She jumped boxes, skidded over the slick wooden floor in
her stocking feet, and careened around the corner to find him
staring into that darkened mirror, smiling, reaching toward
something that he saw within with one chubby starfish hand.

She shrieked, "*NO*, Jake!" and lunged for him, and he
turned toward her, scared not by the mirror but by her sudden insane eruption from the kitchen, and his face crumpled
and he began to wail.

"Baby," he sobbed, pointing to the mirror. "Baby."

She looked in the mirror. No green lightning. No monsters. No fields of red and white flowers, no pretty woman in
a Jackie Kennedy dress and summer shoes, no Brian. Just an
idiot in jeans and a gray sweatshirt holding a baby.

Jake liked the baby in the mirror. He *always* liked to talk
to the baby in the mirror.

She swung him around so that he was riding on her hip,
and picked up the broom and the dustpan and with shaking
hands and her heart thudding in her throat, she carried baby
and cleaning supplies into the kitchen. On impulse, she hit
the light switch with her elbow on the way around the corner

into the kitchen, and behind her the foyer flooded with light.

To keep Jake from falling in the dark and getting hurt, she told herself.

Right.

CHAPTER 2

Ballahara

THE DEAD LAY SCATTERED along the road like mangled toys flung by a ruthless child. On the white snow, in the darkness barely tinged by dawn, the blood still crusted black. Shattered wagons; slaughtered beasts; weapons broken and twisted from unimaginably violent forces. Molly had never been in battle; she had seen the dead, but never the dead who lay as they had fallen, corpses still steaming in the cold. This face of death stunned her, pressed the breath from her chest, and sent the sweat trickling down her spine in spite of the bitter cold.

"Why did this happen?" she whispered. "Who did this, and why?"

The guard to her left, taller than Molly by two feet, wrapped in robes that swirled as he moved along the line of devastation looking for she knew not what, did not turn his face toward her as he said, "The rrôn feel magic, and they hunt down and destroy its sources."

Magic. Her healing of the child?

"So when I took away the child's death . . ."

"The rrôn felt you. Yes."

"Why didn't someone stop me? Why didn't someone stop the child's father?"

"The rrôn are not always nearby. Besides, we believed we were protected—we carry copper, each of us wears copper, you wear copper. Your attempt at magic should have had no result."

Molly frowned. "Not to be disagreeable, but I'm not wearing copper."

"You were. Your hands were bound—we *thought*—with rope threaded with it; this was to protect you, to protect us, to get you safely to Copper House. No one thought your will or your power would be stronger than copper."

But she had taken off the ropes, and a hundred soldiers had died.

"Did the child and her father get safely away?" she asked, and as soon as she did, feared that she did not want to know the answer.

But her captor, the only one so far to speak to her, said "Yes."

Good. That, at least, was good. "The other people in this caravan? They were civilians?"

"We were *all* soldiers." He added, "We all volunteered. We knew the risks when we offered our services to the Imallin."

The other guard said, "You are the Vodi—you stole a child from death, and the Vodi-fire came to your summons. This is the miracle we have awaited, and you have already proven yourself to be everything the Imallin promised. We all saw this; that is why all of them"—he waved a hand at the scattered bodies—"died for you, and that is why Birra and I kept you safe."

Her guards fell silent. The three of them walked along the line of ruin. As well they were silent; she did not feel like talking anymore. The corpses in the forest weren't human, but they had died to save her from something terrible, something that chilled her blood in her veins and made her flesh crawl. She'd *felt* the things that had come after her; their hunger and their rage and their watchfulness still echoed in her gut, as if from a distance they still sought her.

She did not understand the guards' comments about copper. She couldn't grasp the reality of their inhuman faces, their oddly accented voices, their almost reverent words to her juxtaposed with the fact that they'd kidnapped her, tied her up, and dumped her in the back of a hay wagon. She couldn't quite surrender to a complete belief that what she'd just gone through had really happened. Except for the bodies by the side of the road, the iron-hard blood-stink in the air, the eyes opened in terror and staring at nothing and turning dull and white in the cold, the faces twisted in grimaces of pain that resonated beyond race or species, she might have convinced herself that this was a bad dream.

She walked between her guards, shuddering at the carnage. She'd never wanted anyone to die for her.

Human and veyâr stood atop the parapets of a well-built quarried-stone castle that overlooked vast forests, a fine, cold, rocky river, and wild meadows. The veyâr said, "Is this what you had in mind?"

"Aside from the problem with the mice, it will do. And it comes with the land?"

The veyâr nodded. "The district rolls are short, but annual taxes provide enough income in crops and herds to support a reasonable household. And as you can see, you'll have more than enough wood, and the waters of both the river and the small lake to the south are rich with fish. If you decide you want to do this, I'll provide you with the tax rolls, and for the first year or two, with an accountant who can help you make sense of them and guarantee that you'll receive your tithes in an accurate and timely manner."

The human rested both hands against the parapet. "You want a lot."

"I do. But as you can see, I'm willing to offer a great deal in return."

"And the people here would accept humans as the master of this land."

"You are of the Old Gods. They would serve with complete obedience."

The human laughed. "I know all about that complete obedience once it comes down to 'it's your turn Sunday to bring the roast.' Doesn't matter, I guess. The land and the castle will work for what I intend." A mouse crept along the inner wall of the parapet, body flat, and the human frowned and pointed a finger at it. For a moment green fire enveloped the mouse. Then the glow died away, and with a tiny squeak the mouse raced away, no longer attempting stealth.

"I thought you'd killed it," the veyâr said.

The human shrugged. "Killing one mouse would be a complete waste of time."

"True. That's why there are cats, I suppose." He shrugged and gestured to the castle and the lands beyond. "So—you'll do this?"

"I'll give you want you want."

"When I have them in my hands, all in good condition, you'll receive the castle and a fully trained staff to serve you. The only staff member that won't be permanent will be the accountant, but I'll make sure you have time to train your own before I take mine back."

"Then we have a deal." The human turned to go, then said, "Perhaps you'd best show me out. I'm afraid I'll require a bit of time to learn all the passageways of this place."

Molly did not fight the blindfold her captors put over her eyes. She'd caught a glimpse of the edge of a wall, and she'd heard sounds in the quiet predawn air that sounded like the waking of a small town. If she was near warmth, near shelter, near a place that could protect her from those monstrous flapping nightmares that dived screaming from the sky, she would bide her time and see what happened before she decided what steps to take.

Her captors led her, blind, toward something that rattled and clanked—she thought "drawbridge" and questioned her first impression, and then found herself walking across booming metal, while beneath her feet water rushed, moving too fast to freeze even in this bitter cold.

"Almost there," one of her guards said, and she stumbled along an uneven street, then heard a heavy metal door open and someone whisper—and she moved at last from cold air into warm. Next the footsteps thudded over stone, and now they rang on metal.

"We're very sorry, Vodi," one of the creatures said, as they settled her onto a comfortable seat. She heard doors clanging behind her, bars falling into place, locks clicking shut. Metal, metal, and metal, and she thought—I'm in a jail cell. A prison. Perhaps she should have attempted escape when they tried to blindfold her—except that she didn't know yet where she would run. Where could she find safety? She had no idea how to get home, because her problem lay deeper than what country she was lost in. She could not even guess her world.

And one of her captors said, "We have done everything within our power to make this place comfortable for you. You will want for nothing; you will suffer no discomfort and no harm."

Her head was still covered. She thought of pictures she'd seen of American captives held in foreign prisons, tied to chairs with hoods over their heads, and she thought if they kept her like that, she'd lose her mind. Air Force hostage training had taught her a lot about herself. But the hostage training had been based on the assumption that the captive would have some idea of where he was in the world, of who held him, of why he had been taken. She knew none of these things, and the slipperiness of her predicament left her with nothing to grasp.

One of her captors removed her blindfold, and for a moment the light blinded her. Then she got her first clear look at her captors.

Three of the creatures stared down at her. Their pastel-tinted flesh ranged from creamy yellow-gold on the one who'd removed the blindfold to soft green on the one who stood by the door to pale blue for the one who knelt by her side, holding a beautiful bowl of steaming, scented water and a thick, soft cloth so that she could wash her hands and face. Their long, thick hair was in darker tones of their skin colors, so that they reminded her suddenly of tremendously tall, skinny chicks dyed for Easter. They wore their hair bound back in intricate braids and knots, and their huge almond-shaped emerald-green eyes—which in this light did have pupils, but still no visible sclerae—watched her with unnerving, unblinking intensity. All three wore gorgeous robes of velvet heavily embroidered with satin thread and gold and silver braid, with hems and sleeves turned back to display layered undergarments of embroidered silk. Pretty fancy for kidnappers. All three wore intricate facial tattoos.

They belonged in the room in which she found herself—but it wasn't a room. It was a suite, and a world away from her single-wide back in Cat Creek. From where she sat, on the edge of an intricately carved wooden bed, she could see vaulted copper ceilings that rose to five-sided points; from the peak of each point a silver lamp hung, the many flames casting a warm glow. Pillars, also copper and formed to look like smooth-barked trees, reached branches upward along each arch, and each branch was hung with thousands of silver leaves that jingled softly with every faint movement of air. The copper panels of the ceiling and the frames around each door bore brilliant enameled leaves, flowers, fruits, and vegetables. The copper floor had been hammered to mimic tiles.

Only walls, ceiling, doors, and floor were made of copper, however; the furnishings were of inlaid woods, oiled to a soft sheen, while the appointments—lanterns, plates, cups, and dinnerware—were of polished silver. On the bed, silk blankets and embroidered bed curtains. On the cushioned couch and behind it, tapestry that would have fit well in a king's castle. Heavy lace curtains at the windows.

Nice place. Nice *prison*. But Molly didn't want to be a prisoner, and her guards were sloppy. She knocked the basin of water from the hands of the yellow one, wrapped her arm around his neck, and twisted his head back until he was forced to come to his feet, back arched nearly in a bow, to keep his neck from snapping.

"I want to go home," she said. "I don't know what you people are, and I don't know what you want from me . . . and I don't want to find out. You get the guy who made the green tunnel, and get him to make another one, and do it now or I'm going to break this skinny bastard's neck. You understand me?"

The creature she held did not fight. He stared at her with sad, willing eyes, and said, "If I must give my life to have you here, it is yours."

And the other two nodded. "We would each have died for you in the forest. He would die for you now. If you feel you must kill him, you will do so—but we cannot take you back to your home yet. Not yet. Not until you understand why we have paid such a terrible price to bring you to us."

And how the hell were you supposed to argue with that? She didn't want to kill the yellow guy. She just wanted leverage—and she didn't have any. If she killed her captive—if she killed all three creatures in this copper room—she would still not be on her way home. She wouldn't know anything more than she knew at that moment.

The distance between the world she knew, the world where things made sense, and this place beyond reason and understanding ached in her bones. She yearned for a sign. For something that she could hold on to.

She let her captive go and looked from one tall, tattoo-faced creature to the next. She took a deep breath to keep her voice from trembling, and said, "What are you?"

"I am named Birra."

"No—not your name. I mean . . . *what* are you. Aliens? Elves? Doctors in a psych ward? Have I gone crazy? It feels like it."

Birra laughed. An odd sound, dry and papery. "None of those things. We are the people of this world. Your new world. Your true home."

"My home is in Cat Creek, North Carolina. People don't have to be kidnapped into their true home."

"We brought you here to save you . . . and to save us."

"I'm perfectly capable of saving myself—most of the time, at least. So spare me your self-congratulatory odes to the praise of my jail cell." She looked around her. "Pretty though it is. Just tell me what you want, who you want it from, and what it has to do with me. I don't have rich friends, I don't know anyone in a position of power, and I can't affect political or military policy." She rested her hands on her knees, and said, "So what is going to happen is, you're going to tell me that you took me to get some sort of leverage, I'm going to tell you that having me in your cell won't give you any leverage, and then you're going to say you're sorry and take me back home."

Birra was shaking his head. "Your world was hurting you—it was destroying you. Why do you so want to go back to it? Here you will have the love and appreciation you deserve. You belong here, Molly. You belong with us."

Molly stood up and brushed past the three of them; she stalked to the window and stared out of it. Love and appreciation sounded good, of course, but there would be a catch. And it wasn't going to be a good catch, either, because her windows had bars on them. And though they were lovely bars—thick copper grilles done in elaborate curving diamonds—bars told her at some point she was going to want to leave enough that she'd consider going out by the window.

Down the side of a smooth-as-glass tower. At *least* five stories.

Things could be a whole lot worse than they looked even at first glance.

Or maybe the bars were there to keep out the . . . what had her captors called them? The rrôn?

She shuddered just thinking about that possibility, and immediately pushed it out of her mind.

If this was such a great place and she was such an honored guest, why hadn't they simply invited her? Why kidnap her, tie her up, and dump her in the back of a hay wagon? Why not be more forthcoming with the information?

She turned away from the window and saw the three of them huddled by the one door she was sure led out of her cell. They watched her the way three baby songbirds would watch a snake crawling through their tree. The hell with them—she turned her back on them and started searching through the several generous rooms of her cell; along with the huge, elaborate bedchamber, she had a salon, a small pantry, a lovely dining room, a closet filled with elaborate clothing that looked like it would fit her, and a fine bathroom. And thank God for that—she'd thought she would explode if she didn't find one soon.

No kitchen, no cooking staples. So she would be dependent on her captors for meals. But in the pantry she found dried fruits and jarred delicacies that could be eaten as they were, and large stocks of two of her favorite foods—Peter Pan peanut butter and semisweet Dove chocolate. That gave her the shivers; semisweet Dove chocolate was one of her favorite things in the world, but she'd not bought any for herself in—six months? Eight months? Maybe longer. So how long had they been spying on her before they grabbed her, and how much did they know about her? In the salon she found a fine selection of knitting wools in rainbow colors, all sizes of knitting needles, and good watercolor supplies and an easel. A twelve-string Gibson acoustic guitar stood in a corner of the bedroom, beside a beautiful solid-wood music stand that looked hand-carved and very old. Tablature paper—that gave her the creeps, too. Bad enough that they knew she played guitar, even worse they knew that she played a twelve string, when she had never played for anyone but herself in the privacy of her trailer living room. Worst of all that they'd watched her so closely that they knew she couldn't read music and had to do all of her compositions in tab.

They kidnapped her, they tied her up and blindfolded her and locked her in a fancy jail cell, they died in droves to save her from monsters, they wanted to be nice to her. Schizophrenic bastards. All being nice meant was that they wanted something from her—something she had the power to withhold. The healing magic? Of course. She would be asked to sacrifice. They would demand that she eat death, devour pain. That long caged nightmare would begin again.

And perhaps they wanted something else, too. Something she would be even less inclined to give freely.

Clearly these creatures were not her friends. She'd learn more, though, before she decided what sort of enemies they were.

Cat Creek

In the dream, Lauren was still in the house. Thunder rumbled across the horizon, and when she looked outside, black storm clouds approached across a broad, golden plain that was nothing like what she could see from her windows when she was awake; the clouds scudded near the earth, blowing dust and dervishes of paper and other debris before them. Initially the dream was silent save for the growling of the thunder; then the first lightning appeared—green and glowing as a neon sign—and as it crackled to the ground, she began to hear wind, too.

As she watched, the clouds birthed the first of the tornadoes. A point descended like a python dropping from a low tree, whipped to the ground, and began moving toward her, writhing sinuously. Then another, and another, and another, until the mass moved at her like Medusa's hair, and she felt herself as turned to stone by dread as any mythological warrior had ever been.

Twenty tornadoes or more whipped across the ground, all tearing straight toward her and the house, and finally, in the painful slow-motion run of dreamtime, she pulled herself away from the window and fled toward Jake, but when at last she reached him, they had nowhere to go.

Then she heard Brian's voice, telling her to run for the mirror—that she and Jake would be safe in the mirror.

Yes. The mirror.

She felt the echoes of the green lightning in it—but the tornadoes were of this place and this time, and from the here and the now; at least, the mirror offered safety. Clutching Jake, she raced down the steps and stood before the tall old mirror; she was not frightened that she could not see her reflection. Somehow that seemed right. She pressed her hand to the glass. And it opened, as a door would open, and she ran through into darkness.

The darkness wasn't right. She'd made a mistake, done something wrong. Brian was still calling to her, but she couldn't find him, and suddenly she realized Jake was gone, too; she'd left him in the house with the tornadoes bearing down on him. She'd abandoned him. But when she turned to go back to get him, the darkness trapped her. She could see no place to go, no doorway, and she began screaming Jake's name, and Brian's—

She woke, sat up in the bed with her heart racing, and in the back of her mind, the thunder still rumbled, nearer, ominous, and tornadoes still threatened. She looked out the bedroom window, but of course there were no thunderheads, no tornadoes. It was November, and light from the full moon sparkled on the frost-covered ground, and the stars glittered against the black-velvet backdrop of the sky. No thunder, except in her mind. No lightning.

She went down the hall to Jake's room and peeked in. He was sound asleep in his big-boy bed, arm around the giant white rabbit that had been an Easter present from Brian the year Jake was born. Jake seemed to know that it was special, though he couldn't remember Brian. That tragedy broke her heart—his father had loved him more than life itself. And Jake was a beautiful child; when she looked at him, she saw Brian—he was everything she had left of Brian.

She bit her lip and fought back tears. She'd been doing so much better lately. She didn't think she would survive Brian's death, but Jake had kept her going, and then she'd discovered her childhood home on the market at the same time that Brian's SGLI—Servicemen's Group Life Insurance—paid out, and it had seemed like a sign. Get away from Pope, from all the wives whose husbands still came home, from all the friends suddenly made awkward and distant by the widow in their midst, as if her widowhood might be a catching disease. Get away to someplace safe, familiar, to the last place in her life that had really made sense until Brian. Take

Jake home—to the only home she had ever known that didn't include Brian.

It had seemed like a good idea at the time.

Now? Now she didn't know.

But at least the nightmare hadn't been some subliminal distress signal about Jake. Reassured that he was fine, she carefully closed his door again and went down the hall. When she reached the door to her own room, though, she couldn't make herself go back in. That wall of tornadoes still bore down on her, backlit by the green fire of otherworldly lightning, the dream's intensity not fading even though she was awake. She wasn't going to be able to sleep. Not a chance.

And Brian's voice was still clear in her mind, telling her to go to the mirror.

She went down the front stairs, wondering what she was doing even as she did it. She was an adult woman and she had no reason to be afraid of the mirror, but neither did she have any reason to pay it a visit at three o'clock in the morning.

She tugged her bathrobe tight and for just an instant saw the woman in the white dress with the giant poppies again— she saw the way the sleeveless top zipped up the back, and how carefully fitted the bodice was, and how the skirt was full and held out by a crinoline slip, and how the poppies seemed so pure and wholesome. Pure sixties-housewife glamour, she thought. The woman was wearing nylons—and though it felt odd, Lauren was sure the term nylons was precisely right. Was wearing high heels, too, and her dark hair was short and curly and had about it the faintest scent of hair spray.

Then the memory vanished, and Lauren shook her head. So odd—she couldn't remember anyone who had a dress like that, and it was the sort of dress that would stick in a child's mind. Those huge red flowers . . .

She smiled faintly; moving into the home she'd lived in as a child, she should have anticipated the visitation of a few of the Spirits of Times Past. She could just be grateful the spirits were in the form of little snatches of memory, and not something really frightening, like Physically Manifesting Old Boyfriends. Cat Creek no doubt still had one or two of those tucked away; she hoped they were all happily married with dozens of children, wherever they might be.

And then she was face-to-face with the mirror again. In the dark, she couldn't see much of her own reflection. The moonlight outside lit up the beveled-glass sidelights and threw enough light down the hall that she became nothing more than a black form, shapeless in her bathrobe, without facial features or identifying detail. The mirror reflected the beveled glass, the silver world beyond the front door, the black-and-white film-noir interior of the entryway, with its scattered moonbeams and shadows. Not seeing herself clearly brought the nightmare closer. She shivered, and told herself the shiver was because the foyer was so cold.

It was just a mirror.

But even in the dark, even when she couldn't see her face, she could still feel the storm behind that old silvered glass. It called to her, as storms had always called to her, drawing her out to the front porch when she was a child to watch the wind whip through the trees and feel the rain slash against her bare legs as they dangled just within reach of the monster, to hear the dance of water on the tin roof—she had shivered with delight as the thunder roared just overhead, as the lightning slammed into the ground near enough that she could feel the earth tremble with the strike. She had sucked the storm air into her lungs with greedy intensity, though it was almost too wet to breathe and so close it seemed ready to swallow her; still, it was so fresh, so pure, so alive that she wondered how she would ever breathe again when it was gone; and then her poor mother, terrified of thunderstorms, saw her out there and raced outside shrieking to drag her protesting into the house, away from the wild beauty of the world that danced just at the edge of chaos.

Within the mirror, that storm waited for her.

What an odd conceit.

She reached out to touch the glass, and felt something thrum as her fingers neared its surface, and she hesitated, barely breathing. She could feel the rain on her legs, the stinging spray that the wind blew in gusts into her eyes and up her nose; she could smell the ozone in the air, and tannins and dust and wet earth.

My storm. *My* storm.

Her hand hovered, merest millimeters above the glass, and the thrumming grew stronger, and suddenly she knew— *knew*—that she'd feared the mirror for a reason. She'd been an imaginative kid, but not subject to unreasonable fears; she'd needed neither a night-light nor someone to check her closets for monsters. She'd been perfectly comfortable in enclosed spaces, loved heights, took to the water like a fish, and had no more than the usual anxieties upon starting school, and those she had alleviated by punching the first bully who thought she looked like an easy target. She'd had a reputation in grade school as a hellcat. A smart hellcat, but a girl, nonetheless, whose pigtails were not to be pulled. And yet throughout her childhood, she had come in the house through the kitchen door and used the back stairs rather than go anywhere near the mirror.

I was not a stupid kid, she thought.

She stared into the mirror's depths and again caught just that faintest, briefest flash of green fire. No wash of memories this time—no Brian, no voices, no lady in poppies. But the fire flickered far away, deep inside the mirror, and her hand moved closer, closer, feeling the pull, feeling an indescribable, eerie hunger for something her body remembered but her mind refused to acknowledge. Something to do with the mirror.

She pressed palm to glass, and the thrum intensified, and the lightning flickered faster, moved closer, and she could begin to make out shapes within the darkness—a horizon, trees, a single lonely house boarded shut and abandoned, its architecture oddly rounded and both too tall and too narrow, but somehow, she was certain, also right. The glass was warm—as warm as a living thing, as warm as a petted cat lying in a beam of sunlight—and in the part of her mind that still held on to *here* and *now* and *how this is supposed to work*, she knew that was wrong, that the glass should be cold. The hall was cold—her bare feet on the hardwood floor were freezing and her nose tingled with chill. The glass should have felt like ice. A separate part of her was saying, "I ought to be afraid now," but she wasn't afraid. And the knowledge that she wasn't afraid and should be was more unnerving than what was happening with the mirror, because some part of her had known about the mirror.

The green fire reached her—kissed her palm and spread between her fingers and then rippled outward, and the entire surface of the mirror began to glow. She was staring into the fire and through it, and on the other side, she saw clearly, as if looking through green daylight, a massive hardwood forest covered by snow, the trees bare-branched and lacy; the clearing, starting to look overgrown, in which the lonely little house sat, with not a footstep in the snow to indicate that anyone ever gave it a thought anymore; and then she was looking inside the house at dusty floors and cobwebbed ceilings and windows boarded shut through which a little light nonetheless managed to leak, and she saw a round table in the center of the floor, and suddenly, impossibly, she remembered sitting beneath that table with a crayon, writing her name on the underside when her mother wasn't looking.

My storm. My storm.

And her hand slipped through the glass, all the way up to her elbow, and she could feel the pull of the place, calling her in. A single step—through the mirror. She had been there before, years before. Had been through the mirror, and had somehow forgotten, but now she was back. *Almost* back. This belonged to her; a forgotten birthright rediscovered, magic that had been stolen from her but was now nearly recovered, just within reach, almost hers again if she would just . . . step . . . through. . . .

And she found something more there, too. She could feel Brian's hand close around hers, his fingers meshing with hers as they had when the two of them had walked through the North Carolina woods together. She could feel him—feel his warmth, his strength, the reassurance of his presence as surely as if he were alive, in the room. As surely as if he had never left her. She could not see him, but she could feel him.

If she stepped through, would she find him there? Was he whole, well, simply waiting for her on the other side of magic?

She almost stepped through then. She would have walked through hell to get to Brian again—she would step through a mirror without question.

But at that instant she remembered the other part of her nightmare—the part where she'd become separated from Jake. Her body went rigid, and the mirror lost part of its hold on her.

She might find Brian on the other side, but she might not. Probably would not. Almost certainly would not, no matter what. Nor did she know where that house was. She didn't know how she could get back to Cat Creek once she was there—and she knew wherever that other house was, it wasn't in Cat Creek. She couldn't leave Jake sleeping in the bed upstairs and go away to an unknown house in a strange forest.

She would step through the mirror. She had to go. She had to see if Brian still lived somewhere; she had to reclaim the part of herself that she just discovered she had been missing. This birthright of magic, this touch of wonder—she needed it, she knew. She hungered for it. It was the answer to the question that had driven her entire peripatetic, rootless life. But she would not go without Jake.

With her right arm pushed through thrumming glass into green fire, with her body telling her "Go on! Go on!" she stopped. It was like being nineteen again and half-naked in the backseat of a Chevy Nova, and saying, "Um, wait." In fact, in retrospect, the business in the Chevy had been more pleasant. But that was what being a grown-up was all about, wasn't it?

She withdrew her arm, and saw that the glass continued to glow. It was waiting for her.

Yes, she thought. It's supposed to do that. But how did she *know*?

In the back of her mind, her father's voice. "Once you open a gate, it stays open until one of two things happens. Either something will cross through it—either from here to there or from there to here—or it will crash. Never, never leave a gate standing open."

Another shiver—this one hard and teeth-rattling. She looked through at that snowy vista, at the boarded-up house, and thought perhaps she shouldn't go through in bare feet and pajamas, either. Warm clothes. Boots. Hat. Gloves. Be a grown-up, Lauren.

But if she really wanted to act like an adult, maybe she shouldn't go through at all. Certainly the sensible thing to do would be to go upstairs to bed and hire somebody to come in and take the mirror away first thing tomorrow morning. It would be tough to move, but not impossible, she thought. And she bet she could get good money for a ten-foot-tall antique mirror.

But being an adult did *not* mean eliminating sudden magic from one's life. It meant taking reasoned risks, using fail-safes where possible, thinking things through before jumping to find the best way to jump. It did not mean avoiding risk altogether—*that* was the definition for being dead. And parts of her life that she hadn't even suspected were linked to that mirror, and to whatever lay beyond it. She was going to *have* to go through. But she was going to do it with warm clothes and a packed hamper of food, and she was going to have to decide what to do about Jake, too. Leave him with a safe sitter? Take him through the mirror?

Two schools of thought existed on what parents in uncertain situations were supposed to do with kids. She'd had years to hear both. Her mother's sister Caroline and Caroline's husband, Ed, had gotten Jesus in a big way—so big they'd decided what they really needed to do was move into a series of third-world hell-holes to convince the people living in squalor and semistarvation there that starving with Jesus was better than starving without him. When they did their jaunt for Jesus, they took their kids.

Lauren got to watch the slides every time they came back on furlough. "Here we are being attacked by a water buffalo; Jimmy, you remember that big water buffalo? And here we are with the guerrillas who held us up in the mountains— they only agreed not to shoot us after we told them we were reporters for *Rolling Stone*. Thank God Katie had a copy of *Rolling Stone* with her. Didn't you save that magazine, honey? Oh, that's right, it got burned with the rest of the things in the house. Here we are during the native insurrection, when they were burning the houses of foreigners. That was our house right there on the right—the really tall flames. Yep, that one. My, that was exciting. Here's the new house we built. It is pretty, isn't it? And here's a picture of it just after the earthquake—Dad had to pull Jimmy out of the wreckage from that one—his bedroom fell in on top of him. Remember, Jimmy?"

Those slide shows had held Lauren transfixed. She lived in Cat Creek and never went anywhere or did anything (and in the back of her mind, something whispered, "Even when you were little, you knew better than that.") and her cousins were facing down water buffaloes and guerrillas with machine guns and earthquakes and God alone knew what else. Lauren's parents had been supportive of Caroline and Ed— "Whatever you do, keep the kids with you. The worst thing I can think of would be to have them separated from you with no way to get back together."

Her parents' friends had been appalled. "Why don't they send those poor children to boarding school? All those terrible things will scar them for life."

Lauren thought about it. She'd had plenty of time to see how her aunt and uncle's experiment with including their children in their adventures had turned out. Jim was a freelance photographer—he did a lot of work for *National Geographic* and *Rolling Stone*, actually. Wild animals, guys with machine guns in third-world countries, disasters. If he'd been scarred, he'd managed to turn it into a nice living. Kate was a multilingual fashion buyer for Sak's Fifth Avenue, traveling around the world in search of the perfect cocktail dress. Different set of wild animals, Lauren supposed, not so many guys with guns, disasters of an entirely different scope and nature—but she'd seemed happy, too. Neither of them had followed the path of Jesus, which left their parents bent out of shape, but as far as Lauren knew, neither Jim nor Kate had turned into psychopaths or serial killers.

And in the back of her mind, her mother's soft voice talking to Caroline—"Whatever you do, keep the kids with you. The worst thing I can think of would be to have them separated from you with no way to get back together." And Lauren thought, How true, Mom. To be in that giant forest and to not be able to get back—to have me there and Jake here . . . No.

So Jake would go with her. It would be . . . educational. Yes. That's what Caroline and Ed always said—they'd given their kids an education that money couldn't buy. And, years later, it looked like they'd been right.

Which left the matter of the opened gate to be decided, and quickly. "Never, never leave a gate standing open," her father had said, and—easygoing mailman, civil servant questing for a pension—he hadn't been particularly emphatic about most things in his life.

She couldn't remember when he'd said that, actually, or why he might have said it to her. She couldn't remember anything, really, and the more she tried, the stranger the blank spaces in her past began to feel. But she did know he'd said it. And though she didn't know what she had to fear, she knew she didn't want to find out.

She got a chair from the living room, since it was the closest to the hall, carried it into the foyer, and, without thinking too hard about what she was doing, shoved the chair through the surface of the mirror. It vanished with a soft, sucking pop, and the green fire flickered and shimmered and swirled in on itself, spiraling tighter and smaller and dimmer, like glowing water going down a drain.

She didn't let herself look too closely at her actions—she felt like two people, one who knew what she was doing and one who was clueless, and the only thing she could figure out was that someone had left the clueless part in charge of most of her life. Now she was getting hints that she'd been missing something—something big—and the part who knew what was going on wasn't telling, and the clueless part was scared to death to ask any questions because she knew she wasn't going to like the answers.

On-the-Ball was thinking, "I just shoved a chair through a mirror into another world so monsters won't get into the house while we're sleeping," and Clueless was whistling loudly so as not to hear such frightening thoughts. While they fought it out with each other, Lauren tuned out both sides of her mind and listened instead to the voice of reason, which reminded her that her energetic two-year-old would be waking up and ready for action in a very short time. If she didn't get some sleep, he'd run all over her. So she pretended she hadn't seen anything out of the ordinary and went up to bed.

Cat Creek

"Eric? Sorry to call at this godforsaken hour, but we had another blip. A bad one this time."

Eric MacAvery rolled over and stared at his alarm clock. Three-thirty in the morning. He sat up but didn't turn on the lights. Maybe he'd be able to go back to bed. "How bad?"

"Every gate in the circle shimmied. From the size of the blip, we only have a few options, and most of them don't make sense. Either something came in from upworld—"

"Not a chance."

"—or something blew open a gate from downworld—"

"*Blew* open a gate . . . ?"

"—or someone just blasted through a locked gate or ripped us a new one."

"Shit." Eric rubbed his eyes and tucked the phone against his shoulder so he could talk and fish for clothes along the side of his bed at the same time. "You said 'blip.' You said 'shimmy.' To me, a 'blip' is a tiny event that goes away without doing anything, and 'shimmy' implies a *wee* fluctuation in the gate flow. They don't belong in the same sentence as 'blasted through' or 'blew open.' "

Tom Watson, who was young and earnest and hadn't been doing night watch all that long, sounded chastened. "Well, maybe blip wasn't quite what I felt—and I guess the gates didn't exactly . . . shimmy. The Tubbses's gate crashed. George Mercer's gate is so wobbly he's already called Willie over to restructure it. The rest of them have pretty much gone back to normal now . . . as far as I can tell from reading the circle . . . but whatever hit was big. I was in the circle at the time, and oh, mama . . ."

Eric had started swearing softly with "The Tubbses's gate crashed" and by the time Tom got to "oh, mama," he had pulled on the first pair of pants he found in the pile of acceptably used clothes and the first shirt and the first two socks, even though he could tell when he pulled them up that they didn't match, and he was fishing for shoes. "Directionals?"

"Yes, I got . . . sort of . . . well. That gate opening hit me so hard I . . . got kind of muddled. I thought you put me on the night shift because it was so slow, and when everything happened, I . . . it took me a minute or two to get my head straight. . . . The hit came from in town. I'm sorry. I can't do better than that."

"Not a circle gate."

"No."

"It's got to be related to the one yesterday."

"Not really. I mean, yesterday's could still be natural gateflux. We don't have any real proof that something took Molly McColl downworld. She might still show up. She's been a bit . . . flaky . . . since she moved to town."

"Tom—" Eric located two work shoes. He hoped they were from a matching pair, but if they weren't, he'd live with

it. People in small towns got used to the sheriff showing up
looking like he just woke up and got dressed in the dark.
Frequently he did. "You're at the watchpoint, right?"

"Yes."

"Stay put. Get back in the circle, keep your feelers out for
any changes. I'm going to pick up Willie Locklear—I'm
guessing he'll be either at George's place or on the way, and
then I'll be *right there*. If you get any directionals at all . . .
anything . . . mark them immediately. I don't care if they're
weak, if you're not sure . . . I want no excuses. This is two
gate disturbances in two days, and we have a woman missing. You got me?"

"Yessir." Tom, when yelled at with sufficient volume, always got very polite. That never ceased to amaze Eric, whose
reaction to the same stimulus was exactly the opposite.

He slammed down the phone and ran out the door, not
even bothering to lock the place up first. There was sheriff's
business, after all, which in Cat Creek could generally be
done at a walk, and sometimes even from a hammock. And
then there was Sentinel business. And this was the latter.

Willie was already at George's and hard at work when
Eric skidded into the drive. George came out to the front
porch when the headlights flashed across the front of the
house, his bathrobe flapping around him like rags on a scare-
crow—his skinny legs, knobby knees and bony feet in their
floppy slippers looked oddly vulnerable. He peered near-
sightedly at Eric through thick, rimless glasses, and at the
look on Eric's face, said "I'll get him," and ran back inside
without Eric having said a word.

When Willie came out, he seemed to float on a private sea
of calm. "Wasn't bad," he said, and saw Eric's face. He
chuckled, an action that involved his whole body from
white-bearded face to broad shoulders to ample belly. He
ran one massive hand through still-thick white hair and said,
"Tom got you all riled up, didn't he? That boy's been itching
for some excitement since we brought him in—he got some
flitters tonight, and my guess is he damn near shit his
britches—"

"More than flitters," Eric said, waving a hand. "Anyone reach you yet to let you know the Tubbses's gate went down?"

"Crashed?"

"So I'm told."

"Well—that's pretty serious. Both good stable gates; George tends his like it was his own newborn baby, and I don't think Ernest and Nancine have ever had a crash. . . ."

"And Tom suggested that the rest of the circle had the shimmies, though he says everything seems to have leveled out now."

"One crashed . . . one twisted . . . and the whole circle shaken . . . ?"

"Yes."

Willie was quiet for a long time, but that was Willie. Eric had always figured thoughts took a long time to bore through hair and beard and that placid wall of calm to the place where work actually got done. Finally, Willie said, "I was wrong then," though he still maintained his aura of unshakable self-assuredness. He was the oldest of the Sentinels—at seventy, he'd seen more of everything than the rest of them, and he'd always said it was his lot in life to be the voice of serenity when everyone else panicked. "Eric, I reckon you need to get everyone together."

"George can call them and have them meet us at the watchpoint. I want both of us to get out there right away."

George looked at Eric. Eric nodded.

George, wide-eyed, said, "I'll start calling everyone then," and hurried off the porch.

Eric watched him go, thoughtful.

"Still . . . might find out something interesting by paying everyone a surprise visit," Willie offered.

Eric gave him a long sideways look. "Might. And might not find a damn thing, and then we've lost anything we could hope to get from the circle while the disturbance is still fresh."

Willie set his bag of tools on the porch and rubbed his back thoughtfully.

"You hurt it?"

Willie glanced at him, realized what he was doing, and seemed a little surprised. "The back? Just the price of age, son. The price of age." He picked up his tools again and hefted them with the ease of long practice. "You're thinking it might be one of us, though, aren't you?"

"Hell, Willie, you know I *have* to think that. But if we have somebody who's turned, I'll find him soon enough. If we have something breaking through from Oria, though, or some sort of . . . rogue . . . or, God, I don't even know what my worst nightmare is here. What I'm saying is, we at least need to find out right now what this isn't. When we've narrowed down our possibilities, we'll figure out what the hell it is."

"Let's go then."

NEW FLU HITS HARD
By Lisa Bannister, Staff Writer
(Richmond County Daily Journal, Rockingham, NC)

Flu patients between the ages of twenty and forty have filled Richmond Memorial Hospital to overflowing, in what RMH spokesman Rick Press called "the worst outbreak of influenza we've seen in Richmond County since 1918." County doctors are recommending that anyone who has not had a flu shot this year should have one immediately. Richmond County doctors all agree that they've seen a sudden sharp rise in new flu cases, and that these new cases are severe. Symptoms include sudden headaches and intense body aches followed by fevers that run as high as 105°, and respiratory symptoms that begin with sneezing, coughing, and difficulty breathing.

"It's the respiratory distress that's the big thing with this new flu," states Dr. Wilson Tilley, chief of staff at Richmond Memorial. "People's lungs fill up very fast with it; one minute they're coughing and wheezing and the next they're drowning. And this isn't hitting the usual flu sector—the very old and the

very young. Our sickest patients are people in their
twenties and thirties."

Dr. Tilley and other area doctors recommend. . . .
(continued on page B-8)

Cat Creek

By the time the last arrivals hid their cars behind Nancine
Tubbs's flower shop, Daisies and Dahlias, the scene had
the look of an old Abbott and Costello routine. What it
lacked, Eric thought, was the humor. No matter how he ran
this through his mind, it still came out reading disaster.
He'd gotten a call the previous night from June Bug Tate,
telling him that unexpected motion had hit the circle—she
read it as a quick gate-open-and-close. Nothing big, she
said, and it might have been a natural gate that just happened to intersect the circle—but Eric had always known
that the size of the problem didn't necessarily have anything to do with the size of the ripples it caused. It was
like . . . stealth submarines and Great White sharks, he
thought. They didn't leave much of a wake, but they
packed a hell of a punch.

And midway through the day, someone had gone looking for Molly McColl and hadn't found her. The door to her
trailer had been open, and all her lights were on, and the
lady had called, sounding kind of nervous. So Eric had
done a walk-through of the trailer, noticing that nothing
seemed disturbed and nothing seemed to be missing. Except, of course, for Molly. He'd tried the speed-dial numbers on her phone and discovered that her priorities in life
were delivered pizza, delivered Chinese food, and delivered fried chicken, all from up in Laurinburg, and that she
didn't have a single personal number in the bunch. That
seemed scary to him.

He'd known the girl to look at her, but in a town of just
over a thousand he would have had to be either stupid or re-
miss not to have known her name and face. His comfortable

assurance that he was on top of things in Cat Creek got a bad shaking when he had to look deeper than the surface, though. He realized he had no idea what she did for a living, who her friends were, who her family was, or how to find anyone who might be able to clear things up for him.

He couldn't say for sure that something bad had happened to her—his gut told him she'd run into trouble, but she did have a reputation for eccentricity. For being a loner. People in the town didn't know her and didn't seem to care to, but in the three years she'd lived in the town, he'd never heard anyone say anything bad about her. No one seemed to say much about her at all.

He'd worked on her disappearance all day because it was the only thing happening all day. When Pete Stark, his lone deputy, came in to relieve him, he didn't have much to give him. And of course he couldn't give Pete the truth, or what he suspected to be the truth—that the girl had either gone through to Oria on her own or been kidnapped there. The Sentinels weren't the business of the Sheriff's Department. Couldn't be, if anyone cared to have the planet continue in its more-or-less-healthy rotation.

He'd kept his suspicions to himself. But the girl's trailer was neat. Carefully kept up, bed made, laundry in a hamper, no mess in the kitchen, food carefully stored in the tiny pantry, spices in alphabetical order. No sign of struggle.

And the door left unlocked, and unlatched, which didn't fit in his book with the sort of person who took the time to put Chives ahead of Cinnamon and behind Cayenne. The door had looked closed from a distance, the woman who called in the report had said, but when she went up to it to knock, it had just been hanging open. She'd poked her head in and yelled when no one answered her knock, then peeked in to see if there was a body on the floor, but she hadn't actually stepped inside. To her, that open door had said trouble.

To Eric, too. And two troubles within the span of two days that touched on—perhaps threatened—the Sentinels and their work was too much of a coincidence for Eric to buy. They would run the circle—check for directionals, check for ties or leaks or anchors, wait for anything that didn't belong there to move through the flow again. They would find the problem, he told himself, and then they would correct it. The beginning of the end would not fall on his watch.

CHAPTER 3

Copper House, Ballahara

THROUGH THE WINDOW GRILLE of her lovely
prison, Molly watched the start of her second day in this
new world. Her captors had appeared before first light and
laid out clothing for her and brought her a hearty meal. She
got up then, which seemed to surprise them; her years in the
military had left her used to early mornings. She tried out
the tub, put on the complicated clothing, and then she
waited.

Mostly, she found herself waiting for the other shoe to
drop. She grew more certain with every passing minute that
when it did, it was going to be elephantine.

They'd barred the grand doors from the outside. She'd
given both the front one and the back one a solid shove, and
nothing short of dynamite would move either of them. They
felt like they weighed a ton apiece, and she thought that in
all fairness, if they were of solid metal and as thick as they
appeared—she'd looked through the gap between door and
frame and estimated thickness—they could easily weigh
twice or three times that. The hinges were on the outside, of
course; no sense designing a prison and leaving the prisoner
even the flimsiest of keys. Had she been able to pull the
hinge pins, she thought her luck would have been to crush
herself when the door fell free on top of her, so she was
probably fortunate that she couldn't get at them. But she
hated being in a position where all she could do was wait.

Her captors had given her all of the day before to rest

and eat and wander about in her cage, but she didn't believe they would keep her waiting much longer. They would be impatient to start seeing returns on their considerable investment—they would want her to start healing their sick, making their lame to walk, making their blind to see.

Her lot in life was to never be able to escape the sick and the dying. Her bitterly resented talent had scarred and maimed and twisted every facet of her existence from childhood on. She felt the pain of others as if it was her own—she hadn't been able to walk through a grocery store without getting the by-blast of every arthritis twinge and groin pull and throbbing hernia and creeping cancer that came down the aisle. All her life, she'd been a magnet for everyone else's agony—and when she discovered that she could touch the sufferer and take the agony into her own body and thus relieve them both of it, things got worse instead of better.

When she learned how to eat death, she also learned that she had a limited appetite, but that death spread an endless banquet. Her body would only take so much—she could help one person who was dying, or a few who were terribly sick, or many who were merely ill, but when she reached her limit, she collapsed. She couldn't move again until her body did whatever it did with the horror it had swallowed. She lay where she fell, wracked with pain, poisoned by death not her own, for hours on top of hours, until her body gradually washed the stranger-death out of her and sent it . . . elsewhere.

She had always felt the pain of others—Jimmy and Betty McColl, her adoptive parents, had wearied themselves of taking her to the doctor for sudden fits of screaming and vomiting and diarrhea before she was even old enough to speak. By the time she was six, they had debated for the thousandth time giving her to a children's home—but they kept her, in the same way and with the same grudging spirit that they kept the puppy they got from the pound to play with her, the puppy that turned out to be too nervous and stupid to be housebroken.

Then, when she was seven, everything changed. She had
felt the nightmare pain of the old woman sitting next to her
on the pew in church. She doubled over in agony but kept
quiet, because by the age of seven she had learned that there
were worse things than sharing the suffering of those
nearby. Screaming in church was worse, because the pain
and the humiliation *that* brought her came when she got
home, where no strangers could see how furiously her adoptive parents punished her.

So instead of crying out, she had rested her hand on the
old woman's hand, and she had wished the woman's pain
would stop—had thought she would do anything to make
that pain stop. And the pain and the death that were devouring the old woman had listened. They poured into Molly's
young body through the old woman's hand—heart failure
and kidney failure and arthritis and inoperable stomach cancer. Molly didn't remember what happened right after that;
her adoptive parents told her later that she had turned the
most terrible shade of gray and fainted. The old woman,
they said, stood up shouting, "I've been healed, I've been
healed," and ran from the church.

Jimmy and Betty McColl scooped the child up and took
her home, wondering at the odd coincidence of Molly passing out at the same moment that the old woman sitting beside her suddenly went crazy and believed herself
miraculously healed. But Molly had been sick so often in
her short life with things that had never amounted to anything that they didn't make the connection until days later,
when Molly was better again and they heard that the woman
had been cured—truly cured—and that her doctors were
mystified.

A short season of experimentation had followed, while
Molly learned to eat death by being presented with a steady
diet of it. Jimmy and Betty McColl had looked like good
people on the surface, but beneath the veneer, they were
nightmares; they found within the person of their adoptive
daughter an unexpected gold mine, and their relative poverty
coupled with the potential for vast wealth proved more of a
temptation than their surface niceties could survive. They

began offering Molly's services underground; they developed her healing as a cash-only black-market commodity, and they grew very rich from her pain.

She ran away when she was fifteen, but Jimmy found her and brought her back, and she became a virtual prisoner. Her next chance to flee didn't come until she turned eighteen, when Jimmy and Betty were trying to decide how to keep her in the house now that she had reached her majority; after all, they had a lifestyle to support. She moved heaven and earth and got herself to a recruiting station and joined the Air Force. That was the day she said good-bye to eating boozer death. Said to hell with the drinkers, the pill-poppers, the gorgers, the bingers, the pukers, the mainliners, and the rest of the hide-from-the-world horde. Those who bought their own poison could keep its sting. She couldn't save the world and she wouldn't try.

She used her time in the military and almost every penny she earned trying to find her real parents. She succeeded after four years, but what she learned was that they had died in a car crash when she was fifteen. She visited their graves, and found she liked the town where they had lived and died. It was tiny, it was quiet, and she found the people there easy to avoid. When she finished her second tour of duty, she bought herself a little trailer in Cat Creek and she made herself hard to find.

But not hard enough, apparently.

She paced through the lovely suite, restless, full of energy. These creatures would want her to heal. They would keep her in this cage, as Jimmy and Betty had kept her in a cage—they would profit from her talent, and use her until she dropped, and then wait until she could get herself up so that they could use her some more.

No matter how reverent her guards, no matter how pretty her cage, that was what this was all about. They would come with their pain and their death, and because there was no end to pain and death, once they started coming, they would never stop. Nothing she did would ever be enough. They would set her before the ocean with a thimble and demand that she empty it, and as she had done before, she would empty herself trying. Unless she could find her way to freedom.

She heard soft voices through the glass, and glanced out the window. Far below she saw creatures like her captors lining up across a stone courtyard. Some held babes or children in their arms. Some supported infirm elders. Some hobbled along on crutches; some limped; some coughed. And behind her she heard the ring of footsteps in the metal hallway outside her doors. They were coming for her—coming to make her drain the first few drops of her ocean. She bit her lip and waited for the sting of the waves.

Six guards came—beautifully dressed, kind-voiced, patient. They led her from the suite, and she did not fight them. Not yet. She needed to get the lay of this place first. She would pretend compliance until she knew enough to get herself safely home.

The guards were wary—they bore no weapons that Molly could see, but they had the gait and stance of martial artists and the edginess of the deservedly paranoid. They'd heard about her stunt with the blue guard; they clearly weren't hoping for a repeat performance.

They took her into a vast stone room decorated with tapestries and covered with rich, deep blue carpets, and they sat her on a chair that she could only think of as a throne—a tall, wide chair cushioned with velvet but otherwise made either of gold or covered in a thick layer of it. She sat when they told her to sit, all the while figuring a plan of attack should this get bad enough that she needed to flee, and she watched as the first of the supplicants, the seekers of healing and release, crept across the floor to her, heads down, afraid.

She waited for the pain to come, for the first touches of the poisons that were destroying the one who approached her to touch her, to bite her flesh and make her want to scream. But the creature—the woman—reached her and knelt before her and murmured a few words in her own language, and Molly felt nothing. No hurt. No suffering. No death. It was like the child brought to her when she rode in the wagon.

"She says," the guard at her right side translated, "that a

great snake eats through her belly, and she cannot eat or sleep, and she fears that she dies."

No pain. No pain—Molly felt only the beating of her own heart, the movement of air through her own lungs, the smooth working of her own flesh. Tentatively she reached a hand forward and touched the woman and saw as a quick flash in the back of her mind, the twisting white tendrils of a huge cancer that knotted its way through the woman's bowels and vital organs, strangling them. The flash of insight vanished, and she willed that many-limbed octopus to oblivion, and she said, "Be well."

The green fire that she had seen when she touched the little girl leapt from her fingers and spread into the woman's body from the contact point at her shoulder. The woman gasped, but the gasp was not of pain. Molly had seen that sudden joyous release before, but only through eyes blurred with agony. Now she watched the miracle as if she were merely an observer.

The fire burned and burned and burned—and then it died. And the woman, her face radiant and suddenly, with her pain removed, years younger, threw herself at Molly's feet and babbled something that even the guards seemed to find incoherent. Two of them helped the healed woman to her feet and led her to the door that exited the chamber; the guard at Molly's right said, "She wished to thank you."

"I guessed that," Molly said. Her mind was not on the woman she had helped, though. She was thinking about herself.

She felt good. Strong. Alive. Filled with energy, as if she could run a hundred miles, as if she could fly. She had healed, but the fire that flowed through the dying woman had poured through her, too, and left her stronger than she had been before.

Another woman approached, this one carrying a child. A boy, Molly guessed. A young boy. He was the size of a human eight-year-old. That, Molly knew, meant nothing, for she had no idea how these people aged, or how quickly they grew from childhood to adulthood, but something about his

size and the way he lay in his mother's arms triggered a
memory that Molly would have given anything to have forgotten forever.

While she was stationed at Pope, she'd house-sat for
friends for a couple of weeks. She relished time off base and
away from her dorm, especially on the weekends when both
her roommate and many of her dorm mates drank endlessly
and she got hit with their hangovers. But off base, she wasn't
protected; no gate and no guards stood between her and the
people who knew who and what she was. Someone who
knew her from her days with the McColls had spotted her—
in a grocery store or at a bookstore, maybe—and had followed her. And had passed on her whereabouts.

And in the middle of the night, Molly opened the door to
a child, and to a mother with hollow eyes and lips drawn thin
and bloodless by the constant helpless watching of her
child's pain. The butchers and the poisoners had been at the
boy with their radiation and their chemotherapy, even
though they'd told the poor mother her son's type of cancer
rarely got better with either chemo or radiation. They'd
turned the child into a skeleton—a puking, hairless, aching
skeleton—and when they were sure he hadn't the strength to
enjoy another breath, when they were sure he was too weak
and too broken ever to walk or laugh again, then they said,
"We can't do anything more for him."

The mother had no other hope, so she came—in the dark,
in a car fifteen years old with peeling paint and a wrecked
right fender. She stood in that doorway with her son in her
arms, a boy who would have reached to her shoulder had he
been able to stand on his own, but so thin she lifted him
without seeming to notice.

The second Molly opened the door, the boy's pain hit her
like nails rammed through every organ of her body from the
inside out and all at once. Molly looked at the kid and doubled over right there and started throwing up, and she
couldn't stop until she was on her hands and knees with her
head hanging almost to the floor.

The kid had looked at her with sad, beautiful eyes, and

she had hated him—hated him for the pain he was going to put her through, hated him for looking at her with such regret and such hope, hated him for wanting her to suffer so that he could live—and she had told the mother, "I'm too sick to see him tonight. Bring him back after my shift. Five. I'll see you at five."

The mother didn't come back. Her son died in the middle of the night.

Molly could have saved him. A touch, a word, and his poison would have been hers for a while, and then he would have lived.

The world was full of people she *could* save, and she had fought her way to terms with the fact that she couldn't save them all. But she should have saved him. She tried to tell herself that he wasn't her responsibility just because he'd shown up at her door on the last night of his life, but his ghost rode on her back and whispered in her ear, "If you had touched me, I would still be alive today." He was heavier by far in death than he had ever been in life.

She didn't even know his name.

She touched the child in front of her, and said, "Be well," and the green flame flickered through and over his body, and he was well. I do this in payment for the one I didn't save, she told herself. In penance. But she felt no pain—the death that was devouring this gaunt, green-haired child couldn't touch her, and somehow she knew that she could not pay penance for that long-ago moment of callousness if she felt no pain and made no sacrifice. She would never escape that ghost, perhaps.

But this child, at least, she had saved. He hugged Molly and ran away, his weeping mother hurrying behind him in a desperate attempt to keep up.

And another hope-filled supplicant approached.

Perhaps she was still trying to empty the sea with a thimble, Molly thought. Perhaps here she could no more fend off all death and pain than she could have in her own world. But here, at least, the thimble was not her own body. Energy filled her to the bursting point. Perhaps she could shed her dark memories here—forget her past. She could find good in the curse bestowed on her at birth. At that moment, joy and pleasure bubbled through her veins and sang beneath her skin. Any residual weariness she had felt when she entered the chamber had fled, vanquished by this glorious suffusion of magic.

A line of the sick and the crippled, the twisted and the maimed and the dying stretched as far as she could see, and probably beyond. And for the first time in her life, she felt no dread. Sitting there facing them, she shed a little of her darkness, and felt the first faint glimmer of hope that her future, contrary to every expectation she'd ever had, might be better than her past. "Bring them on," she whispered. "Bring them on."

Cat Creek

Lauren woke with the electric feel of magic pulsing through her blood. The mirror called to her, painfully loud and inescapable. Her stomach knotted and her fingers twisted the sheets; she sat up, dreading what was to come but invigorated by it as well. A lifetime of uncertainty lay behind her. Ahead of her, she felt, were the answers she'd been seeking.

She hurried into Jake's room. He was already awake and sitting in the middle of his floor, surrounded by blocks and books. He bounded to his feet when she opened the door and ran to her and hugged her knees. "Mornin', Mama." His smile was so big she got both dimples. She picked him up and hugged him tightly.

"Good morning, monkey-boy."

"Sekimos?"

Sekimos were Eskimo kisses—rubbing noses. Jake was still transposing first consonants on most words that began with vowels, something Lauren knew she was going to miss when he outgrew it. She said, "You bet, Eskimos." She rubbed noses with him, and they gave each other big hugs, too, and kisses on the cheek.

Then, having had enough of the mushy stuff, Jake got down to business. "Diaper. Soggy. B'ocks. Light. Biteys?"

She translated that roughly as, "My diaper is soggy, I played with my blocks, I couldn't turn on the light in my room, and I'm hungry."

She laughed and started putting things right in his very concrete world. An hour later, she and Jake, dressed for winter, with a picnic basket full of food and drinks, stood before the mirror together.

I could back out now, she thought. This isn't the sort of thing a responsible mother does. I have no idea what's on the other side, and going through is just pure craziness.

But she was still two people as she stood there—the sensible one who didn't know what she was getting into, and the other, the one who knew the secrets and would divulge only one: that she had to go through that mirror. Lauren had spent most of her life driven by compulsions she did not understand and could not decipher, wandering in search of things she could not define and could not find. She'd worked so many different jobs she'd lost count: She'd waited tables and mixed drinks, sung in restaurants and taught ballroom dancing and worked at a book bindery and built custom cabinets for new homes, a trade she'd learned from her father. She'd moved restlessly from apartment to apartment, from town to city to village and from state to state, hungry for something she couldn't find anywhere, couldn't name, couldn't even imagine. She wanted so much that she ached with the wanting, but nothing she tried touched that hollow, consuming need.

Then she'd met Brian, and for three years the hollowness had left her. For those three sometimes blissful, sometimes loud years, she had loved and laughed and fought and created a family and happiness, and she had been sure she'd found what she'd been seeking. But Brian's death had left her both grief-stricken and haunted by the return of that burning, nameless ache.

And all she could think was, I have to get home. I have to get home. The insurance money had come at about the same time that the people who owned her old family home were trying to unload it in a very slow market. She'd bought the place without really considering what it would mean to her and Jake to live in tiny Cat Creek; she'd moved back to the place she'd grown up in, driven by blind certainty that she was doing the right thing—knowing only that she had to have the house, that her life would never be complete without it.

Blind instinct.

Like salmon returning to their spawning beds. Or the San Capistrano swallows coming home to roost.

Or lemmings flinging themselves into the sea in suicidal millions.

Blind instinct. Not necessarily good.

This was more of that blind instinct, more of that wordless imperative, more of that *must*. This was, she believed, part of the answer she'd been searching for her whole life. She had to know what lay on the other side of that mirror. She had to go through, even though the sane part of her thought she was crazy for doing it. She had to, because she would not be able to live another day in her home until she did.

She held Jake on her left hip and rested the picnic basket full of food and other useful goodies on her right foot, and pressed her right hand to the mirror, worrying as she did that last night might have been her final chance. If the magic had died—

But it hadn't. Beneath her hand, the mirror thrummed. In the reflection of her eyes, the first flickers of green fire sparked, and following those flickers, the long bright flashes, and in the back of her mind, the low, heavy roll of thunder building in the distance—

—and then the resistance of the glass vanished from beneath the weight of her palm, and Lauren tightened her grip on her son, leaned over and picked up her picnic basket, and stepped through.

A moment in which sound died, in which she and Jake were utterly engulfed in cool, energizing, electrifying green flame, when every cell in her body felt both separate and vibrantly alive. In that moment she felt Brian beside her, and felt his lips brush the nape of her neck, and heard him whisper, "I told you I'd never leave you." And then she and Jake stood in darkness. In her ear, Jake's bright, excited laughter and his voice, suddenly very loud, saying, "Please . . . more?"

And she thought, More for sure, kiddo. That was the best thing since sex.

All she got was that one clear, wondering thought. Then the memories hit her, and with them, shock.

Magic. She was heir to magic, she was a natural gateweaver, she was the child of Sentinels—though she could not at that moment remember what Sentinels did or why they mattered—her abilities had been kept secret from everyone, even her, and in a way she was a secret weapon. Her mother, not merely a schoolteacher; her father, not merely a mailman; her past as she had lived it and remembered it for nearly twenty-five years, a web of carefully constructed lies. Her parents—her own parents—had brought her here when she was ten and used the magic of this place to strip her memories and her understanding of magic from her and planted in the place of those memories—*her* memories, goddammit—two key suggestions. The first, that she would dread the gate-mirror in the foyer while she was a child and believe that she had always dreaded it. The second, that when she was old enough and able, she would find her way through it again. Stepping through to . . . Oria, she thought, suddenly knowing the name of the world on whose surface she stood . . . stepping through to Oria had been the trigger that broke the spell. Or launched the second half of it—the removing half.

And that was why she'd had to go through the mirror. Why she couldn't wait, why she didn't dare question. And *this* was the thing she had been seeking all her life, wandering from place to place and job to job, growing ever more lost and ever more hopeless. This—this place on the other side of the mirror—had been her destination all along.

The odd images that touching the mirror that first time had stirred suddenly fell into focus in her mind. The laughing voices had been friends of hers from this world whom she had liked a great deal once upon a time. The woman in the white, flowered dress was her own mother, whom Lau-

ren had never before recalled having looked so beautiful or
so young. That flickering green lightning . . . magic itself.
Her magic.

And other memories flooded her, too. Her father when he
was actually happy and idealistic and full of hope. And the
way she had seen herself then—as someone with a destiny, a
plan, a place in the world. She'd lived without any of those
things—destiny, plan, or place—for most of the past twenty-
five years. She had been as lost in her life as a rudderless
boat in a typhoon, and her hopeless, confused wandering
had all been for nothing, because she'd been living a lie. A
huge, vile lie that felt like the rape of her own life. Why had
her parents crushed her this way?

The reason why they had done this to her . . .

She couldn't remember, but it had to be in there—in with
all her newly found memories.

The reason why they had done this to her . . .

She fought through everything she could call up from the
dark recesses of her mind, chased down every fleeting newly
released image of her parents, of magic, of Oria. She hunted,
she rummaged, she sought with desperation. It was important, it was something that mattered so much she had given
up who she was and what she loved for it.

The reason why they had done this to her . . .

Was gone.

And that, she discovered, was the most hellish betrayal of
all. There had been a reason. It had been important. Frightening to a ten-year-old girl who knew when her parents told
her what they had to do that she could stop them. Instead,
she had *agreed* to this horror, had agreed to have this awful
thing done to her. She had agreed to let her parents remove
her memories and bar her from her own magic because they
had promised her when it was over, she would get her memories back, and with it, her destiny, her place . . . and the
Plan. The thing her parents had been working on, the thing
that was so important they hid the real Lauren inside a shell
of herself for twenty-five years.

And the Plan wasn't there.

Lauren stood in the center of a boarded-up, freezing

house in the middle of a world that she had once known as
well as she knew Earth, clutching her son in one arm and a
picnic basket in the other, and she wept—tears of rage and
grief and loss and hurt and betrayal. If her parents hadn't
been dead already, she could have killed them for what they
had done to her. She tipped her head back and howled. Her
breath clouded around her, and Jake patted her face, saying,
"Mama . . . okay . . . Mama . . . okay . . ." and then, when he
couldn't comfort her, Jake burst into tears of his own.

That stopped her more effectively than any slap to the
face could have. She caught her breath, brought the tears to
an end with a few hiccups, and put the basket down. Then
she cuddled her son. "Jake, sweetheart . . . oh, baby . . . it's
okay . . . it's okay . . . it's okay . . ." She rocked him back
and forth, and he laid his head against her shoulder and snuf-
fled, and after a moment she felt his little arm slip around the
back of her neck and pat her in rhythm to their rocking.

"Okay . . ." he whispered. ". . . Mama okay."

They stood that way for a long time, holding each other,
comforting each other. Jake, as usual, was the one who decided enough was enough. He lifted his head, looked in her
eyes, and said, "Please . . . down."

She didn't want to let go of him yet, but she didn't want to
cling, either. That she needed more comfort than he could
give was a problem for her. She didn't wish to make it one
for him. She'd need to let him get down and be two for a
while, but she couldn't let him run until she checked the
place out.

"Hang on," she said. "We'll walk through it together, and
I'll see if there's someplace here that I can let you play."

"Hang on," he muttered. "Hang on." One of his least favorite commands—she occasionally heard him telling it to
the big white stuffed bunny just before the bunny ended up
someplace unpleasant. She had no doubt what he was thinking of her at that moment. So she hurried.

The place was dusty and cobwebby, but in remarkably
good shape. If it hadn't been used since her parents had done
whatever they did to her, it was in impossibly good shape.
She did a quick tour; the house included the room that had

served as her parents' bedroom when they had been here—
which, oddly, was the room she had stepped through the
mirror into, and it still held the chair she'd shoved through
the night before—her bedroom, a very primitive indoor
bathroom, and a central room that would serve as kitchen,
living room, dining room, and family room all at once. A
huge black cast-iron woodstove dominated the center of the
main room; a small trestle table and two benches sat to one
side of it near the front door, and a gaggle of rocking chairs
clustered around a rag rug on the other side. She saw a wash-
tub and drying rack hanging on the wall behind the stove, a
hand-cranked clothes wringer bolted to one end of a counter
that ran the length of the room and had been designed as an
all-purpose utility area. The house had indoor running water
of a sort—a hand-pumped well had been brought up through
the counter. When the pipes thawed, Lauren thought, if the
years of disuse hadn't destroyed the pump, she could probably pump a glass of water for herself and Jake. She remembered the water in this house tasting wonderful. She saw
nothing that seemed out of place and nothing that seemed
dangerous.

Jake said, "Please . . . down," again, this time more loudly
and less accommodatingly. He was getting squirmy. She
dusted off one of the rocking chairs with the sleeve of her
coat and put him down on it, and said "Rock, rock."

As she looked for cleaning supplies, she heard the reassuring squeak, squeak of Jake rocking. "Rock . . . rock . . .
the baby," he crooned. "Rock . . . rock . . . the baby . . ."

The windows were boarded shut, which made the place
pretty dark. Light was coming in from somewhere,
though. She looked around. It was diffuse light, really
dim—it seemed to be coming from everywhere and
nowhere. She frowned. If it were just a bit brighter, she'd
be able to locate the source, she thought. She *wanted* it to
be brighter.

And suddenly it was. She yelped and looked around the
room to see if Jake had done something, but Jake was still
rocking happily and singing to himself. The room was as
bright and sunny as if she were standing in a meadow at

midday. And she still couldn't figure out the source of the light.

She frowned, and a bit more memory trickled back.

Wanting was a key.

She wanted the light to be dimmer. And when she wanted it so, it was.

Right. The magic. It ran on desire. Will. Focused intent.

I want it to be nice and warm in here, she thought. Take-off-your-coat-and-stay-a-while warm.

And it was.

Oh, yeah.

She slipped off her coat and dropped it on the trestle table. "Rock . . . rock . . . the baby . . ." Jake sang. The chair squeaked. She thought, I want this place to be clean inside, and she imagined it clean.

The dust and the cobwebs vanished, the floor and the table and the rocking chairs acquired a smooth, hand-rubbed sheen, and the whole place smelled just slightly of furniture wax and dried lavender. Perfect.

Then she thought, I want it *prettier* in here. She imagined the spacious, warm, welcoming interior she'd seen on the front cover of a log-home magazine—broad beams, brilliantly white ceilings, soft, deep, tan carpets, a curving log staircase that had been a miracle of the joiner's art, massive overstuffed furniture that had still fit the interior scale of the place, a beautiful brass-and-glass chandelier, a huge and welcoming fireplace with a merry fire burning behind the spark screen. Fire and all.

And there it was.

Behind her, Jake whispered, "Wo-o-o-o-ow!"

She turned in circles, thrilled and awed and full of admiration for her handiwork. Perfect.

Then she heard a soft thump. And Jake said, "Oh, Jake!" in a voice that was half-mournful and half-chastising, and she thought, Torn? Broken? Or spilled? And turned to see what sort of mess he'd made. And found it was none of the above.

Jake was squatting nose to nose with a pale blue-green

creature with yellow eyes the size of plums. The creature itself couldn't have been much bigger than an average cocker spaniel, but what it lacked in size it made up for in ugliness. Ratty, tangled hair stood up from its low forehead in a crest that ran in a stripe down the back of its otherwise bald skull to the base of its neck. Its skin hung in wrinkles and wattles and tags, its thin shoulders hunched forward and its knobby spine curved in a perpetual stoop. It wore, however, an elegant wool tunic and pants and beautiful beaded boots with thick leather soles; the phrase "shoes on a pig" ran through her mind before she could stop it.

It licked its lips and glanced from Jake to her. "Cute kid, Lauren," it said, and the voice could have belonged to Orson Welles.

She froze, caught between a scream and bewilderment, and stared at the thing in the middle of her floor, trying to place it . . . him . . . Yes. Him.

"Embar?" she whispered.

"Who else?" Into her stunned silence, he gave the magically redecorated room a single wary glance and shook his head. "You want to watch this sort of thing, Lauren. The feedback can be a bitch. Or have you forgotten? And what the hell took you so long to get back here?"

They sat behind closed doors in the converted upstairs of the Daisies and Dahlias Florist—fifteen men and women perched on metal folding chairs in a semicircle, with their gateweaver sitting half in and half out of the gate-mirror that ran from floor to ceiling on the north wall and glowed with green fire. They all held hands as if they were part of some old spiritualist cult in the midst of a séance; they all had their eyes tightly closed. All of them glowed faintly with a green light. They waited and watched with senses other than their eyes—had been waiting and watching for hours. From time to time one of them would get up to go to the bathroom; the choreographed ritual that accompanied this looked like a cross between Musical Chairs and Blind Man's Bluff with, perhaps, a bit of London Bridge is Falling Down thrown in for good measure.

In the room with its walls lined with florist's foam and boxes of vases and plastic-wrapped bundles of silk flowers, with its single flat file and its single old oak worktable shoved beside the mirror, they held their silence, and the air curled thick around them, heavy with weariness and fear and expectation.

Then Eric felt the flick as an unauthorized gate opened and closed again far too quickly. He had only the vaguest impression of direction, but he let go of the hands he held, opened his eyes, and quickly drew an arrow on the floor with chalk. He opened his eyes and noted that others among the waiting Sentinels were also marking their impressions.

"Fairly close," Willie said.

"Not as strong as I'd expected," June Bug Tate said.

Tom's expression grew defensive. "Wasn't anything like that when the last one came through. This one you barely felt. The last one . . . it threw me clean out of the mirror. Knocked me on my ass." He flushed. "Pardon my French," he said in quick apology to the women present.

June "June Bug" Tate, who, now in her late sixties, had been smoking cigars since she was twelve, glanced around the circle at the four other women there and rolled her eyes. "We've all of us heard the word 'ass' before, boy. We all even have one. Do us the favor of *not* apologizing."

Her sister Bethellen, Tom's mother, flushed, and said, "I taught you better than that," and Louisa, the other Tate sister, just snorted and pursed her lips in disapproval. Nancine giggled, but that was Nancine's usual response. Debora Bathingsgate rolled her eyes but said nothing.

Tom sighed.

Eric had a sheet of paper out and was adding up all the angles of his people's directionals and averaging them for an approximate vector. "First we're going to need a reading from a second location so that the next time a blip goes through we can triangulate the position. The second thing we're going to need is ranging. I don't remember offhand;

who else besides me and Willie has successfully ranged a target before?"

To the people who indicated previous success in this area, he said, "Then you're also on the short list for off-site watch until we find out what's going on here." He leaned forward and looked from one grim face to the next. "We don't know what we're dealing with. We don't know if it's tied in with the disappearance of Molly McColl. I'll remind you that you don't prepare for what the enemy might do, but for what he can do. If you don't know who the enemy is, you must prepare for what *any* enemy can do—because the worst one possible might be the one you have to face. With that in mind, remember that more than just your own life is on the line here. Everyone and everything you love lies in your hands, and if you falter, they fall. Until and unless we find proof to the contrary, the enemy has made his opening gambit in a covert operation, and we have been fortunate enough to intercept early signs. But right now the enemy knows everything, and we know nothing. Therefore, we are at war. You will keep that foremost in your minds and conduct yourselves appropriately."

He rose, and the rest of the Sentinels rose with him. "Who has the first watch, then?" Deever Duncan asked.

"You rested?" Eric asked.

Deever yawned and stretched, then straightened his shoulders. His combed-over hair sat across his bald spot like a greased spider, his paunch wobbled, and the bags under his eyes stood out clearly in the light of the room's single naked bulb. He looked weary, ten years older than the early forties that he actually was; he looked like if he slept for a week, that would only be a good start in the right direction. But he nodded. "Good as I'm going to get, I reckon."

"It's all yours."

"I can take it until two—I have to be into work by three." Deever owned Cat Creek's hardware store, and had a problem with getting reliable help. But the boy working for him at the moment looked promising.

Eric filled in the rest of the revised schedule quickly, and said, "Everybody go home. Or to work—whichever. Stay close to your phones. First one who hears anything calls the rest."

Willie waited to be last out so that he could walk with Eric. He was smiling faintly. "There's an upside to this, you know."

Eric arched an eyebrow. "I couldn't find one."

"We were all there when the gate opened and closed this time. So it looks like we don't have any traitors—and that's a relief."

Eric shook his head. "Doesn't clear a one of us, Willie. Not a single soul."

Willie glanced at him from under bushy gray brows, and said, "How not?"

"If the gatecrasher is human, then one of ours had to teach him or her how to open it. The fact that near about anyone can learn to open a gate doesn't mean anyone can *teach* it."

Willie said nothing while he gave that his due consideration. Finally, he said, "I don't see how any of 'em could be traitors—how any of 'em could sell their own race and their own world to the Orians."

"We don't know if the Orians are involved. Could be a traitor has taken up with refugee upworlders or another Sentinel nexus that's getting ready to run, could be we're dealing with outsiders who stumbled on a gate like the Heidelmann group put together back in the thirties. We don't know *anything*," Eric said. He jammed his hands into his pants pockets and walked with his head down, staring at the gravel his work shoes displaced as he crunched across the parking lot. "Except that the temptations could get to anyone after a while. Any one of us could break. Work law enforcement a few years, and you lose a lot of your faith in your fellow humans—and the faith you have in fellow humans who could be gods for nothing more than the price of their honor . . . that becomes real damn thin indeed."

"I do not envy you your cynicism, my friend. You might

be right—but I have to believe in the triumph of good over evil in order to keep doing what I do."

Eric reached his car and opened the door. He braced a foot on the car's door frame and gave Willie a weary smile. "Believe all you want. Just be sure you watch your back."

CHAPTER 4

Copper House, Ballahara

BIRRA ANNOUNCED his presence in the green chamber with a soft clearing of his throat. The Great High Imallin Seolar, master of Copper House, had been sitting at his desk, poring over one of the massive tomes from his library with pen and notepaper in hand; he glanced up, saw that it was Birra, and shoved notes, writing supplies, and book to the side. His smile was tentative. "How goes it?"

"Where the healing is concerned, she is everything you had hoped she would be, Imallin. Her slightest touch is magic; the sick, the dying, the crippled, the mad—all regain their health at her word. Given time enough and access, she could heal everyone this new god-poison touches."

Seolar nodded. "But any human could give us that."

"I have seen no signs yet that she is anything but human." Birra shrugged. "But, then, I don't know what signs to look for."

"Nor do I." Seolar rose, his heavy silk *beya* rustling. "Is she happy here?"

Birra cleared his throat. "She is . . . difficult. Aside from getting free of the manacles the night we brought her here, and her attack on me that, had I not been truly willing to die at that moment, would have succeeded, she . . . ah . . . she eyes each of us as if she were determining the quickest way to break our necks, steal our weapons, and escape. It is most unnerving. All records of past Vodian indicate that they were reasonable people—compassionate, tremendously kind and

patient, and . . . well, *tractable*. Your Gloriousness. She's
rather more like a caged and hungry tiger."

"She has not found her accommodations to her liking?"

"She hasn't found anything to her liking, at least not that
we've been able to tell. She paces the room, measures the
bars and the thickness of the doors, plans traps to capture us
as we enter the room—were it not for the spy-eye you in-
stalled in the ceiling above the door, we would not have seen
the very clever trap that she built from portions of her bed,
the covers, and some of the garment hangers in her
wardrobe. She has a remarkable talent for taking things
apart, Your Gloriousness; we're rather afraid that talent will
extend to us in the near future if you don't, ah, talk to her."

"The instrument? The wools and silks? The paints? She
has not amused herself with any of those?"

"Well, she was testing combinations of paints and other
things to see if she could make an explosion, I think, but she
hasn't used them properly yet. Except for the candies."

"Dove chocolate. Our spies were very specific about that.
Well . . ." Seolar sighed. ". . . put more chocolate in the
room. Have the cooks prepare something that she likes. En-
tertain her. Make her like this place."

"As long as we keep her in the Copper Suite against her
will, I don't believe she'll ever come around. She does not
have a personality that gladly accepts cages."

"Yet once she is no longer in the Copper Suite, nothing I
do can keep her here." He sighed. "Birra . . . lie to her. Tell
her that I am away—that until I return, you have been ordered
on penalty of your life to keep her safe from those who would
destroy her, and the Copper Suite is the only truly safe place
in this house. Remind her of the rrôn. Tell her she is behind
copper because only copper is guaranteed to keep them from
her. It isn't that much of a lie—if the rrôn knew she'd survived and was here, they would be at us day and night. Tell
her that when I return, I will be eager to meet with her, and
that she will surely be given the freedom of the entire *imal*—
from forest to sea—but that she must be patient until then."

Birra nodded. "And when will you return from your . . .
trip?"

Seolar sighed and walked to the window. He stared down at the courtyard and shook his head. "When she can see her future in Oria."

Natta Cottage, Ballahara

"You want to watch this sort of thing, Lauren," Embar said, waving an arm to encompass all the changes she had made. "The feedback can be a bitch. Or have you forgotten? And what the hell took you so long to get back here?"

Jake reached out, grabbed one of Embar's enormous ears, and said, "Ear." He poked a finger toward Embar's face, and the creature flinched backward. "Eye!" He made a grab for the enormous lower lip, unfazed by the protruding canines, and shouted, "Mout'!" To Jake, apparently, Embar looked like the perfect toy. Lauren seemed to remember feeling that way about him once herself.

"I don't remember half of what I'm supposed to," Lauren confessed, walking over and picking up Jake before he damaged the poor creature. *Goroth*, her mind insisted. *Embar is a goroth.* And she couldn't help but be annoyed that she could remember what Embar was but couldn't remember what had been so important that she'd let her parents remove her memories to hide them from whoever might come looking through her mind to find them.

"Oh," she whispered. Because suddenly she'd remembered that. There was someone who could read her mind—someone very bad—and that someone couldn't know that she could create gates.

"Oh, what?"

Lauren sat in one of the rocking chairs with Jake on her lap and began to rock. He'd sit with her for a while before he got impatient. Or maybe he'd take a nap. "I just remembered that my parents were hiding my gateweaving from someone who could read my mind. Someone who wanted to kill me. But I can't remember who it was."

"Your parents never knew," Embar said. "But gateweavers

were dying like flies back then. Cat Creek had two when everything started going wrong. The Cat Creek sister nexus in Hope Mills had three. Now Hope Mills hasn't had a gateweaver in twenty-five years, and Cat Creek's last one is getting old with no replacement in sight. They told me about it when they asked me to look out for you."

Lauren said, "They did what?"

The little creature across from her rested his head in his cupped hands, his expression mournful. "They asked me to look out for you. When they were thrown out of the Sentinels, they worried that something might happen to them and that you would become vulnerable. And it did. And you did, I suppose, though you seem to have survived well enough without me. I did a terrible job of doing what they asked—I lost track of you when you quit your university and moved."

"Right after they died?"

"Right after . . . ? Yes. I tried for years to find you, but every time I'd get close, I'd discover that you'd just moved again. Finally, I came back here to wait. I hoped you would find your way back through the gate; your parents said you would."

Lauren felt completely at sea. "Okay, you're going to have to go through this slowly for me. Start from the beginning and tell me everything— Why are you shaking your head like that?"

"I can't tell you everything. I can't tell you much of anything. Your parents were *Sentinels*. Around here, that's like . . . like *gods*. I was just this little nuisance that they befriended because I hung around them hoping some of their magic would rub off on me; they told me the fact that they treated me and others like me as friends is the reason the Sentinels ousted them and closed down their main gate. Gods aren't supposed to hobnob with the mortals, I suppose. Bad for business."

"They weren't gods."

Embar winked at her. "But if they hadn't hobnobbed with me, I wouldn't have known that, would I? The Sentinels lose some of their mystique when we begin to understand who and what they are."

"Well, fine. Then tell me who and what the Sentinels are."

Embar chuckled. "I don't exactly know that, either. I *began* to understand. That's different, beginning is. I know the Sentinels work to protect your world from the magic of this world. I know they aren't gods or immortals—they're just people. That—all by itself—is more than anyone from my world is supposed to know. As for your parents, I know they were working on something important, but I don't know what. I don't know who was after gateweavers; I don't know why your parents did what they did instead of just moving away; I don't know how to fill in what you don't know."

Lauren leaned her head against the back of the rocker and closed her eyes. "Right. Wonderful. Then how am I supposed to find out what's going on, and what's so important that I gave up most of my life so far for it without even knowing what I was doing?"

"Well, your parents hid their notebooks in your house. All you have to do is find them."

Lauren stared at him in disbelief. "Why didn't you just tell me that?"

"You didn't ask."

Cat Creek & Sentinel Circle, Ballahara

The phone rang, and rang, and rang, and rang, and finally Eric opened his eyes. Five minutes, he thought. I haven't been asleep more than five minutes. He picked up the phone. "What?"

"We have a level five rebound breakthrough. We need you here now."

He hung up the phone without saying another word. He pulled on jeans only because they were lying right by the bed. He didn't bother with a shirt or socks. He managed to kick his shoes on his feet because they were beside the door and he had to slow down anyway to grab his keys from the hook—if the shoes hadn't been there, he would have left the house in bare feet.

The cold slapped him awake, and all he could think was level five . . . level five . . . I couldn't have heard that correctly. He considered putting the flashing lights on as he drove, but this wasn't sheriff's business, and he didn't want bystanders.

Level five.

Holy shit.

The really useful people were already up in the workroom when he got there. Ernest and Nancine Tubbs, June Bug Tate, Willie Locklear, Debora Bathingsgate, Granger Baldwin, and Deever Duncan were prepping the gate and gathering tools.

"Level *five*?" he asked.

June Bug didn't even look up from the handheld mirrorgate she was using to trace the source of the rebound. "Yes. I put the rebound effect at 180 million deaths in the U.S., three billion worldwide. Best guess from the early read."

"Three billion? People?" His words sounded strangled even to his own ears.

"Give or take a few hundred million in either direction."

"God have mercy," he whispered. "Time frame?"

"About three months to full expression. Give or take a few days. The read gets pretty foggy at the outside perimeters— the best information I can give you on this is a kill-rate planetwide of about fifty percent, about two to two and a half months until *half* of everyone who is going to die from the primary effect is dead, mammoth acceleration within the next fifteen days as the other half of those susceptible to the primary cause die, . . . and I get no read at all on what secondary deaths are going to be."

Eric bit his lip. "But this is going to wipe out the planetary infrastructure. If half the people on the planet die of the primary effect, you have to figure fifty percent of the survivors dead within a year from secondary effects. There will be kids who survive their parents' deaths but can't get by on their own, whole industries collapsed because of lack of manpower, people trapped by circumstances who can't get food or water, deaths from violence . . ." He shook his head as if to clear the dark future from his thoughts. "And what-

ever's left is going to be very different from what we have
now."

Now June Bug did look up from her mirror. Her gaze met
his for an instant, and he was shocked by the bleakness he
found there. She said, "I think you're being optimistic."

"Maybe." He didn't have June Bug's statistical back-
ground. He could concede that things might be even worse
than he envisioned them, though he couldn't imagine worse.
He discovered that he couldn't wrap his mind around the
magnitude of what he knew for certain. "Why is this mess
ours?"

"Because the rebound punched through in Rockingham."

He rubbed his forehead. "That's ours, all right."

Willie said, "I've put the call through to the Hope Mills
Sentinels. They don't have a gateweaver yet, so they're limited in the help they can give us, but Richard said they'll
have their people down this way as soon as possible. I talked
to Carolina in Ellerbe, and she says she'll come down herself, and then bring in whoever we need. I had Deever get in
touch with the Vass group."

"So we'll have backup soon."

Willie nodded.

Eric spread his arms, hands turned palm up. "What the
hell happened? Who did this? You locate the trigger?"

June Bug said, "No. But the rest of the bad news is that
this has already had time to start building. I read that we've
missed the initial breakthrough—first effects are already
starting. It might have been that big shake that Tom Watson
didn't get a bead on that started this. Might have been something a whole lot more subtle. The breakthrough itself
doesn't look like it was all that much, but it has an acceleration factor like nothing I've ever seen."

"Do we have any idea how the rebound is going to mani-
fest yet? Terrorists with nuclear weapons? Black Death? Altered cometary trajectory; meteor strike; shift in the Earth's
axis? What?"

"We have no idea," Willie said. His voice was as grim and
flat as Eric had ever heard it. "All we know is, it's big and
fast and ugly."

"And there's going to be hell to pay if we can't get it stopped."

Willie nodded to him, and for the first time in Eric's memory, the old man looked shaken. Willie said, "Gate's ready."

Eric looked at the other Sentinels. "Where's everybody else?"

"We had to leave messages," June Bug said. "Both of my sisters are out of town visiting, Tom's girlfriend said he went fishing . . . things like that."

Things like that. They had to stop a level five disaster and half of his team was missing. "Well, this can't wait. Willie, make sure you leave the gate clear for anyone else who shows up."

Willie nodded. "You better put a coat on," he said. "Colder in Oria than here, and now isn't the time to be playing with heat spells."

Eric shrugged. "Don't have one with me."

"I have an extra coat out in the trunk," Ernest said. "My work coat. Smells like a backed-up septic tank, but . . ."

"I'll take it. Thanks."

They went through in a rush, the way they'd done in a hundred drills, and formed a tight circle with all of them facing outward as soon as they hit the other side. Those who used tools or objects to focus their magic set them up. Ernest jammed a four-inch piece of lead pipe soldered to a tripod into the ground in front of him; June Bug gripped her hand mirror; Granger put the silver chain of a large medallion over his head—the medallion itself was a three-inch brass plate on which he'd had empty flowchart boxes and arrows engraved; Nancine pulled out a scruffy plastic digital watch that on Earth hadn't worked in years. Debora held a bulky old Texas Instruments calculator—the kind that had once had glowing red numbers and had run on batteries. The battery cover was missing and the compartment empty of batteries. Eric clutched his sheriff's star in his left hand. Willie used neither tools nor focus, and Deever, his student, followed his mentor's example.

The Sentinels occupied a clearing ringed around by a wall of massive, ancient trees, and in the center of their clearing stood their gate mirror, a rectangular mirror eight feet tall and six feet wide that earlier Sentinels had built into a stone arch and protected from the weather with a small, slate-roofed pavilion. The clearing ran out about thirty yards in all directions. The Cat Creek Sentinels' primary gate lay in the heart of Mourning Forest. No roads or paths led out of the clearing; no footprints marred the smooth surface of the snow in any direction. Not even wild animals entered the spelled circle.

Eric tightened his fingers around the star and narrowed his thoughts to his single immediate need. He said, "Shield," and a bubble of green fire sprang to life around them. Deever said, "Ward," and the green fire paled and shimmered and suddenly looked more solid. Debora said, "Patrol." Tiny bits of light peeled off from Eric's shield and shot out in all directions, looking for anything that might be trouble. Willie stayed beside the gate. "Gate's steady," he reported.

Nancine stared at the broken watch that lay across her palm. She said, "Clock." A digital display appeared on the curve of the bubble that shielded them, its red glow eerie in the green-tinted light. It split into seven identical displays, and each display dropped in front of a Sentinel, so that no one had to turn to see the amount of time they'd spent in Oria. The clock timer started at 0:00.00, but the tenths of seconds were a blur and the seconds began to add up quickly, too. Ernest said, "Light feet." His spell seemed to do nothing, but was, perhaps, the most important spell of all. While they were in Oria, Ernest would control the Sentinels' magic expenditure—he'd channel all their spells through a very narrow magical pipeline so that they didn't create the same sort of rebound back on Earth that they were trying to reverse.

June Bug, still holding her mirror, said, "Show me our source," and a blaze of white light erupted from her mirror. The rest of the team waited.

"This is muddy as hell," she said after a moment.

No one said anything. They all held their positions and their spells, and kept waiting.

"Find the *fresh* magic," June Bug said. A short pause,

then, "Due east of here—pretty close. A big spellburst, very recent."

"How fresh?"

"A couple of hours at the outside."

"That's too new," Eric said.

Willie glanced over his shoulder at Eric. "It is. But whoever or whatever caused the most recent spellburst is most likely linked to the problem we're trying to correct."

"I know. But we can't be sure."

Deever said, "I say we deal with the spellburst June Bug found first and see if that takes care of the problem. We can come back if we have to."

June Bug agreed. "The clock is running. We've already spent five minutes here."

I can read the damned clock, Eric thought, but he didn't say it. Instead, he said, "Focus east. We're going to drop both shield and ward and limit patrol to our immediate perimeter. Granger, you're doing the primary reset cast. Nancine, June Bug, Deever, and I will buffer feedback. Debora will maintain close perimeter patrol. Willie, you keep the gate steady, and Ernest has the pipe . . . Ernest, don't let this get away from us. Ready?"

Murmurs of assent.

"Then drop our extra baggage at seven minutes, and Granger, you be ready to cast ten seconds later."

"Right," Granger said.

"I wish we had more people here to handle the feedback," June Bug muttered.

No one else said anything. Their eyes were on the glowing red displays that hung in the air in front of them. With ten seconds to go, Eric braced himself and focused on the glow of the shield that surrounded them all, formulating the few words and the many shapes and sensations that comprised its unmaking and that would have to be cast without causing Oria's magical energy to flux.

Five . . . four . . . three . . . two . . . one . . .

Simultaneously, Eric said, "Drop shield," and Deever said, "Drop ward," and Debora said, "Patrol in close." Nancine said, "Clock on auto." Running a spell on automatic was risky, but June Bug had been right—there weren't enough of them to safely buffer a big feedback; they *had* to have Nancine's help.

The comforting, shimmering green sphere vanished, and a handful of tiny green stars appeared from the forest and began racing in a circle around the edge of the clearing.

"Brace for it," Granger said softly.

All eyes on the clock, on the racing numbers.

"Trace east, near and fresh," he said cryptically. "Identify; sequence; set strength; undo; equal return Eric, Nancine, Deever, June Bug, me." The spell he held in his head would be much more complex, but magic had little do to with words and everything to do with clear imagery and clear intent. The words just gave the intent and the imagery focus and set them loose. Eric could guess at the way Granger had structured the spell from those few words, though. Granger's spell would go to the site of the new disturbance and identify the magic that had been used and the things it had been used on. Then it would use the residual echoes from the spell to build a counterspell that would undo the spells that had been cast in the exact reverse order of their casting. At that point, it would measure the precise amount of power the counter-spell would take—it would then pull power from the seven Sentinels to set off the counterspell and send the feedback through Ernest's pipeline back to them, where they would have to deal with it as best they could. It was a complex spell, neatly structured and economical, something Granger excelled at.

Eric felt the first little tendrils of magic curl out to the east. He waited. And waited. The clock in front of him showed that five seconds had passed, then ten, then fifteen. He tried to keep his teeth from rattling—the cold was getting to him, but worse than the cold was the stark terror at what he and the others were about to face; the longer Granger's probe took to build the counterspell, the worse the final news was likely to be when they got it. Abruptly, a massive surge of power poured into Ernest's pipeline—feeling it going out, all Eric could think was, This is going to be a bitch coming back.

He counted ten seconds on the clock—ten full seconds of waiting for the feedback to hit. It felt like ten hours. Then the magic hit; a wall of energy like a tsunami that rippled and stretched Ernest's pipeline and erupted over the five of them who were waiting to receive it. Eric lost his vision in a burst of whiteness and immediately after that lost his hearing as a thunderclap went off inside his skull. Hit by lightning, he thought, but that was the only coherent thought he could manage; in darkness and utter silence he fell to hands and knees as fire exploded inside his body and raged outward, searing and flaying every cell. Dying, he thought. Dying. He pulled himself into a tight ball and screamed silently, while inside his blazing flesh his melting bones waged war on his boiling blood. Dying. Dying. Let me die.

He could breathe again. Still blind, still deaf, he felt the worst of the pain begin to ease. He couldn't move. Couldn't feel any part of his body. And he thought, maybe I *am* dead. That wouldn't be so bad.

And then the unmistakable sudden vibrant electric surge of well-being that came from going through a gate.

Then darkness.

Silence.

Time passed, and he could not move, could not see, could not hear. This is it, he thought. The rest of my life with my mind trapped inside a body that doesn't work.

And then, gradually, he began to notice light. Next, movement. After a long while, he began make out shapes. And then he blinked and Willie and Debora were moving through the upstairs room in the flower shop in front of him, talking animatedly. He could catch little rumbles when Willie talked.

Then he could hear Debora clearly. "You're sure there's no permanent damage?"

"I checked before I brought them through. I *checked*. We couldn't have done anything for them if there was, but I'm positive they're all fine."

"I'm okay, I think," Eric said.

Debora jumped, and Willie turned, an expression of relief on his face.

"Eric, you're back with us."

"What happened?"

"Whoever cast that series of spells was . . . unreal. As far as Debora and I could tell, the main spell was pretty straightforward—it was the add-ons that were so nasty. In the middle of Granger's reversal, we had two ghosts show up—I think they looked familiar, but I only got a glimpse of them before they vanished—and there was this brief parade of images from different parts of the world. Almost like a slide show. And a good-looking fella in Air Force blues, and a little boy. And throughout the entire reversal, a thunderstorm was tearing up the clearing. Absolutely terrifying. Tornadoes touching down everywhere. The storm came first and finished last. Worst thing I've seen in seventy years."

"So the thunder and the lightning—"

"Went straight through you. If it had been real lightning instead of some sort of magical artwork, you would have all been dead."

"Why the hell would anyone attach a thunderstorm to another spell?"

Willie said, "Signature, I reckon. We tracked down a fella once who signed his work with a wolf. Long before your time, Eric, though June Bug will remember it. Damnedest thing. Every spell of his that we reversed, when we got to the end of it, a big white wolf would appear and rush straight for our throats. Made us jumpy, you can imagine."

"Why did he do that?"

"Turns out it was the way he saw himself. The lone wolf, the mighty hunter. He was self-trained—he didn't even know he'd made the wolf part of the spells."

Eric lay back and closed his eyes. His body still felt like it had been run through a cement mixer and poured. "So—did we fix it?"

"We don't know. June Bug hasn't come around yet, and neither Debora nor I have the coordinates she was tracking through the hand-gate. We're going to have to wait until she wakes up and gets her legs under her to find that out."

Natta Cottage, Ballahara

First, without warning, the house reverted to its old configuration. Lauren's grip around Jake tightened. He looked around and said, "Wow," again, softly.

Then the dust and the dirt returned.

Then the room got icy cold.

Then the lights went out.

"That can't be good," Embar said quietly.

"I think it's time to go home." Lauren picked up Jake and ran for the bedroom. Embar chased after her.

"What about finding your parents' records? I can help you."

"We'll talk later," Lauren said. Her hand was already on the gate, the green fire was coming.

"I can come through if you want me to. I'm good at finding things."

Her hand slipped through the glass, and she began to step into the green fire.

"Do that," she said.

"I'll be along in a bit, then," he called after her.

And then she stepped out into her foyer.

CHAPTER 5

Cat Creek, North Carolina

TERRY MAYHEW SHOULDN'T even have been watching the nexus. He was supposed to be out selling a whole-life policy to a woman in Maxton who he'd sincerely hoped would want more than insurance from him, but she'd canceled on him at the last minute—and since he was already out of the office, he went home instead. Got himself a snack. Went into the spare bedroom that held his homegate. Opened the gate just enough that he could sit on the mirror frame, so that the magic that coursed between the two worlds would have to run through him.

He closed his eyes and felt the wonderful buzz that he always got from being in the midst of that energy flow. And then he sat there for a while, letting the green fire course through him, while his mind wandered. Nothing moving through the nexus except the usual noise; he was probably wasting his time. Eric had been adamant about all Sentinels putting in every spare minute they had watching for disturbances, at least until they found out what had happened to Molly McColl. Assuming the girl hadn't just gone out of town for a few days, which Terry figured was a big assumption, what were the odds that he was going to be the one to catch the kidnapper? He figured he'd get better odds playing slots in Vegas.

But the watching was pleasant enough, and better than getting the afternoon sales talk from the manager.

When the gate opened and closed, it did it so quickly and

with such little fuss that Terry almost didn't check the directionals. The movement felt too normal. The gentle click ran through him in three dimensions, though he could only use two of them; they resonated through him like music through a good stereo headset. And just like wearing the headset—where he could visualize where the drummer and the guitarist were standing—he got a feel for the location of the opened gate. But unlike the effect he got while wearing a headset, when he turned his head within the energy flow of the gate, the distant point he was focusing on moved. And it wasn't in the direction of the Sentinels' main gate or any of their homegates, which meant this might be the disturbance Eric was tracking down. Heart pounding, Terry scratched the directional arrow on the wood floor with the tip of a wire hanger that was lying close at hand. Then he closed his homegate, ran for paper and pencil and compass, and spread them out on the floor beside the arrow he'd drawn. When he had the top edge of his paper aimed exactly north, he marked that edge with an "N," then copied the vector exactly, drawing it with a ruler. The line was only an approximation, he knew, but he felt sure it was a good approximation. It might be the final vector Eric needed to triangulate and pinpoint the site of the disturbance.

I might have him, he thought, and his mind tossed him the image of piles of silver coins clattering out of the belly of a one-armed bandit. Jackpot. I might have the kidnapper.

Paper in hand, he ran from the house, jumped in his car, and tore across town to Daisies and Dahlias. He hid the 'Vette back behind the flower shop and got a chill when he saw the number of other Sentinel cars already there. No one could have gotten to the shop from home any faster than he had, which meant that they had to be there for another reason. And when they got together at midday on a workday, the news was never good.

He ran through the back door and past Maycine Meyers, who was putting together a big funeral piece with mums and something purple and hideous; he managed to mutter, "Hey, Maycine," to her flirty greeting, but he was around the corner and up the stairs too fast to hear exactly what she said next. Didn't matter. She would hit him with it on his way down. The woman had a one-track mind, and whenever she saw him that track seemed to run right to his station.

He burst into the Sentinels' watch-room and seven pairs of eyes turned to him. "Where the hell have you been?" Eric snapped, and Debora, who looked like she'd been run through a wringer, snarled, "Figures you'd show up now."

Bewildered by the hostility, he said, "I got the vector." He held up his piece of paper.

Now all seven of them looked lost. "Vector?" Willie asked.

"On the gate that just opened and closed. I was in the loop when it did, and it wasn't one of ours, and I got the vector from my house."

"What about the level five—" June Bug started to say, but Eric cut her off.

"Not now, June Bug. Deever, maps."

Deever ran for the stack of topographical maps of the region that Eric kept in the Sentinels' flat file.

"When did the gate open?" Willie asked.

"Just a couple of minutes ago. Wasn't anyone here watching?"

Willie said, "We've had our hands full with other things. Thought for a moment that we'd lost five Sentinels—bad, bad feedback. Now we're trying to figure out if all that pain did any good. June Bug still hasn't got a read on whether the unspelling worked."

Terry felt that chill in his blood drop about ten more degrees. "*Lost*—" he started to say, but Eric cut him off.

"Not now. Give me your paper." Terry handed it to him without a word. While Eric lined up Terry's arrow from his house and penciled in the line, Terry asked Willie what was going on. He thought he was going to throw up when Willie told him about the level five rebound breakthrough and gave him June Bug's projected death toll.

"I was on my way to see a customer," he said softly. "Man, I had no idea—my cell phone didn't ring and my beeper didn't go off. It's just luck I was home for the gate. Just luck."

"Looks like good luck," Eric said from his table.

Terry glanced over at him, still feeling the sinking dread from Willie's news. "How so?"

"Cross your vector with the one we had from here, and it hits the center of that cluster of old houses on Herndon Street, between Guthrie and 381."

"I know the block," Terry said. "Passed it getting here."

"So do I," June Bug said. "The old Hotchkiss house is at the center of that block."

"Right," Eric said. He waited, an expectant look on his face.

Willie said, "With that gate we sealed off damn near twenty years ago."

"Right."

Deever was nodding, looking excited. "And Tom told us the first time he felt the disturbance, it felt like a gate being blasted open."

Eric scooped up the maps and headed for the flat file. "Any takers on a bet where our trouble is coming from?"

"Nobody's even living there," June Bug said.

"Not true." Eric shoved the maps into the flat file and turned to them all with a grim smile. "Not true. Place has been on the market for ages, but it sold a month or two ago. And I've seen lights on there the past couple nights when I've been patrolling."

Willie said, "Any idea who lives there?"

"Nope. Pete and I have had our hands full the past few days, so I haven't heard and haven't asked. But I'm about to find out."

Lauren, unpacking boxes in the foyer with Jake, felt the soft thrum of energy at her back that warned her that the gate had come to life. She turned, scared, braced for whatever might be going wrong; she grabbed Jake and tried to figure out where she could run if running were called for—and then Embar stepped through. At least, *part* of Embar stepped through. She could make out his form clearly enough, but she could see the mirror and her own reflection through him.

She took a step back. Jake, however, grinned and said,

"Hi, doggie." Then he tugged at her shirt and said, "Please . . . down."

"Anything else going to be coming out of that gate," she asked Embar. "Or the rest of you? Or anything?"

Embar grinned at her obvious discomfiture. "Forgot that too, did you?" His voice sounded faint and breathy and far away.

"Forgot what?"

"That when we go upworld, we *all* get—thin."

"You aren't thin. You're damned-near nonexistent."

"I'm all here. The same thing would happen to you if you ventured into your upworld. Makes it very hard to pick things up, but very easy to look around." To demonstrate, he seeped through her floor. Jake shrieked in terror, and Embar immediately rose out of the floorboards, looking chagrined. "Sorry about that. Didn't realize it would scare him."

Lauren patted and rocked Jake, who wrapped arms around her neck and shoved his head against her shoulder, and he calmed quickly.

"There were things I wanted to tell you," Embar said. "I was trying to find the right way to get around it"—and here he closed his eyes and rubbed the bridge of his squashed nose in an oddly human gesture—"but I hadn't quite found the words when you ran off. I thought about things a little, and then I came on. Might as well get things over with, right?"

Lauren waited. He didn't say anything, and after a moment she said, "Well . . . ?"

"Look." Embar sighed, the sound oddly whispery and fragile, "Let's go looking for your parents' notes. I'll go through the walls and the floors and you can walk through the rooms. Knock on walls and look for hidden doors and panels and secret compartments in built-in shelves and cabinets. And while we're doing that, I'll see if I can figure out how to put all these other things that you need to know."

She felt a chill coming off him, a grim, unhappy dampness of the mind, like a miserable, icy, rainy day carrying itself on entirely within the confines of her skull. "It's bad news, isn't it?"

He nodded. "But *old* bad news," he said, his expression faintly hopeful.

"DOWN!" Jake had tired of waiting patiently; he began kicking vigorously.

Lauren put him down and he ran to Embar and put his hand through the goroth's torso. He shrieked and pulled his hand back, then did it again. This time he laughed.

Embar arched a scraggly eyebrow at him.

Lauren said, "Does that hurt you?"

"No. Tingles a bit." Jake had pulled his hand back again, however, and was staring thoughtfully at the goroth. Without another word, he walked back to Lauren's side and sat at her feet. "Not a problem, really. I simply convinced him he doesn't want to do that anymore."

"To my knowledge, no one has ever successfully convinced Jake to do anything he didn't already want to do."

"Gods' boiled balls, you *have* forgotten a lot." Embar shook his head sadly. "This is basic, basic stuff. Gates, Lauren. The natural gates are constantly opening and closing, and the force that keeps all the universes alive flows through them. Inspiration flows from downworld to upworld; energy flows from upworld to downworld."

Lauren frowned. "I don't get it."

"When you—when anyone—travels through a gate to your downworld, you become a wizard. You can affect almost anything physical and use the energy of the downworld to do magic. Like you did in Oria. But when you travel upworld, you can't affect the physical in any but the weakest of ways. No magical spells, not even much in the way of moving physical objects." To demonstrate, he walked over to a toy truck Jake had left on the foyer floor. He tried to pick it up, and Lauren could see him struggling. After a moment, the truck's rear wheels lifted off the ground. He shoved, and the truck slowly moved forward a few inches. "You see what I mean. But in your upworld, you have other strengths. You can affect the mental and the spiritual. You become a . . . a muse, for lack of a better word in your language. You whisper directly into the souls of those you contact. You can do it while they see you, or if you choose, while they can't." To demonstrate, he faded to invisibility. "This comes in handy from time to time," he said. His voice washed away to the faintest of whispers. "It's also takes less effort."

"But it's unnerving."

He reappeared like washes of watercolor poured into an Embar-shaped jar. "Unnerving, yes. Useful, also yes. I convinced Jake that he didn't want to stick his hand through me anymore, and that sitting on the floor playing quietly would be a lot of fun."

"Well, it's a nice trick." She said, "I wish I could do it. But it's also beside the point. Let's get back to what you wanted to tell me. I don't like to have things sugarcoated. Why don't you give me the old bad news now so that I don't have the dread of it hanging over my head while we search? Then we'll go through the house and find my parents' notes. And if you think of anything else I need to know, tell me as you think of it."

Embar sighed. "You were an impatient child, too." He shrugged. "All right. The bad news, without sugarcoating. Your parents were murdered. My friends and I think one of the Sentinels killed them, or at least that the Sentinels were involved in covering up the cause of their deaths." He stared at her, the stance of his body and the defiance in his eyes telling her that he expected a scene; that he expected her behavior to prove him right in wanting to dance around his news and soften the blow.

Lauren had no intention of falling to pieces. However, she didn't believe him either. "Bullshit. My parents died in a car accident; their brakes failed and an eighteen-wheeler rolled over them."

"Their brake lines were cut. We came in through their secret gate after they didn't return to Oria when they told us they would and found out they were dead; my friends and I investigated everything we could to discover why they had died and who was responsible."

Lauren sat down on the floor beside Jake, who was still uncharacteristically quiet. "Surely someone would have noticed a cut brake line."

"Someone surely did. But if the person who was supposed

to notice was in on the murder, he wouldn't say anything about it. Right?"

"Who, then? Who did this, and why?"

"I don't know that. We couldn't find out anything that pointed us in the direction of who. But I do know that you don't dare trust anyone in this town. Not anyone. Don't let an old friend watch Jake for you, don't tell your next-door neighbor any of your secrets, don't say a word about any suspicions you have about your parents' deaths. Whoever killed your parents might still be around. If he knows you're looking for him, he might come after you. You and Jake."

Lauren shivered.

Embar was suddenly staring past her. "Trouble," he said flatly, and faded out of sight. "I hope to the gods you're a good liar."

Lauren saw the reflection of a man in a tan uniform with a silver six-pointed star pinned to his chest at the same time she heard his heavy footsteps crossing the porch. He looked familiar—solid, powerful, with dark hair and a plain, honest, tired face that she was sure she knew. And then she realized she was looking at Eric MacAvery, who had been two years behind her in school. So he was with the Sheriff's Department. That was the other side of the law from the one she would have expected him to end up on.

She turned as he tapped on the door; she nodded and rose and crossed the foyer to greet him, and on his badge she could read the word "Sheriff." So he wasn't merely with the department; he was in charge. More surprise, that. Last she'd heard, old Paulie Darnell had still been in office.

She opened the door and leaned against the frame. "Eric MacAvery," she said, and gave him a friendly smile. "Didn't have any idea you'd become the sheriff."

He was studying her face with some puzzlement. "Been in office going on three years now," he said, and suddenly surprise replaced the uncertainty. "Lauren Hotchkiss?"

"Lauren Dane now, but yes—that's me."

"*Lord* have mercy. I would never have recognized you."

She smiled. "I spent all those years since I left remaking myself."

"I always thought you were pretty good to start with." In his eyes she saw frank approval, but that clouded quickly, replaced by the worry that had been clear on his face when he walked up to the door. "I didn't know you'd moved back to town, and sure didn't know you folks were the ones who bought your parents' old house. Any case . . . may I speak with you and your husband for a few minutes?"

"My husband's dead," she said, getting those hated words out of her mouth without stumbling over them. "You can talk to me. You want to come in out of the cold?"

He nodded. "I appreciate that."

He stepped across the threshold, and his eyes were moving—quick, intense glances into the living room, the parlor, down the hall to the mirror. He glanced into the parlor again, and she realized at the same moment that Jake had disappeared; in the next instant, Eric was giving a second long, hard look at the mirror. "One of your neighbors thought she saw a man breaking into your house," he said, but his glance kept drifting from her face to that mirror. "I got the call about five minutes ago."

Where was Jake, she thought, and glanced in the parlor, and then in the living room. "Breaking in," she asked in a distracted tone.

"Dark shape at the back door, your neighbor said. Hard to see through the bushes, she said, but she thought I ought to check it out." He smiled a little. "Marcelle may not be the most reliable soul, but we've had a missing person the last two days, so I'm being very serious about any calls I get— even from the ones who are prone to see dancing elephants, if you know what I mean."

Lauren said, "I haven't heard anything." Where was Jake? Where was Jake? She hadn't heard Jake go up the stairs, she hadn't felt the mirror-gate open, he wasn't in the parlor, he wasn't in the living room. That left the kitchen.

In confirmation, she heard Jake say, "Play, doggie! Hi, doggie." Eric jumped just a bit and looked toward the kitchen. At that instant, the kitchen erupted with an incredible racket, as Jake began to pound on pots and pans with a metal spoon while singing at the top of his lungs. "Spi-i-i-i-i-i-der! . . . Spou-ou-ou-out! . . . Rai-ai-ain! . . . *OUT*!"

"My son," she yelled over the racket, and hurried to the kitchen. "Part of the reason I'm afraid I *couldn't* have heard much of anything."

Eric followed her, nodding, a bemused smile on his face. "I reckon you could have had the elephant parade with hundred-piece marching band going through your attic and you wouldn't have noticed," he yelled back, and Lauren pulled the spoon from Jake's hand. Jake shrieked with instant affronted fury and yelled, "Foooon! Foooon!"

"You can't have the spoon right now. I'm talking to someone." Jake gave Sheriff MacAvery a wary look, rose with two-year-old gracelessness, and moved behind her legs. "Say hi, Jake," she told him.

He studied Eric for another moment, then waved his fingers and said, "Hi." He did not move out from behind her legs.

"I thought I ought to look around, with your permission," Eric said.

"Hi," Jake said again, a bit louder.

"Hi," Eric answered. He grinned at Jake and waved, and Jake waved back. "How old is he?"

"He's two. He's *very* two."

"He's really cute."

"Thank you. He's . . . busy." She considered what Eric had asked her, and as she did, more old memories shook loose. Eric's father had been a friend of her parents, back when she was seven or eight. A good friend, she guessed, because he'd come over to this house all the time. And he had been, she realized, a Sentinel. She remembered snatches of conversation between her parents regarding James "Mac" MacAvery. She couldn't recall the content of those conversations, but she could recall them laughing about Mac and talking about gates in the same breath. Those memories and Eric's fascination with the mirror-gate cemented her suspicion of his sudden arrival at her front door. His presence was somehow related to her use of the gate, and maybe to what had happened to her house in Oria.

She'd let him look around the house if he wanted—she didn't have anything to hide. Yet. But she'd be damned if she'd let him look around without her supervision. "Go ahead," she said, managing to sound a little unsure. "I'll bring Jake and come with you."

"I'd rather you stayed put. If I run into someone—"

"You have a gun," she interrupted. "If a man has broken into my house, I don't want him to show up down here with us while you're up in the attic."

He nodded, watching her—and she saw her own suspicion reflected in his eyes. Don't trust anyone, Embar had said. Eric seemed to have taken a similar admonition to heart. "All right, then. But stay well back," he told her. "I don't want either of you in the line of fire."

They went through the house quickly, but Lauren noticed that Eric was tensing at all the wrong spots. His body language told her he was completely at ease going through doors and around corners, but his shoulders drew in and his spine stiffened every time they passed a mirror. And he made sure he moved close to every single mirror in the house—feeling for the thrum, she realized. He wasn't obvious about it. If she hadn't discovered the mirror-gate in her foyer, she would never have suspected his movements.

But she had, and she did. She'd made some sort of mistake, had triggered something, and here he was. Looking.

But evidently not finding. When at last he said, "Everything seems fine. You might want to keep your doors and windows locked for a while—at least until we find out what happened to our missing person," she simply nodded and thanked him and walked him to the door and watched him drive away.

"He didn't miss a thing," Embar said behind her, and Lauren jumped.

"Doggie!" Jake yelled gleefully, and Lauren put him down.

"No?"

"He knows your parents' old gate is unlocked again. That's not good. He can't tell that you did it, which is lucky for you, and he doesn't even know if you're involved in anything going on here, but he knows something is going on here, and he *thinks* you're the one making it happen. And he's scared."

Lauren stared at the ghostly goroth. "How could you possibly know all of that?"

"I read him when he walked through me. He was distracted enough that he didn't notice me, even though he knows what to look for. Something very bad is happening, Lauren, and he thinks you're the person causing it. You and Jake need to be careful."

"What I really need to do right now is understand what's going on."

"Then I suggest we start by locating your parents' notes."

CHAPTER 6

Sentinel Nexus, Cat Creek

"THE OLD HOTCHKISS GATE is open and in perfect order," Eric told the assembled Sentinels. "The Hotchkiss daughter . . . Lauren Dane now . . . has moved in. She and her baby went through the house with me. I get the feeling she's hiding something, but I didn't find anything that I could charge her with. No signs of Molly. No signs of anything unusual." He sighed. "She's still unpacking, though. It might be a different story when she gets her things out of those boxes. If we could take her through to Oria, we could check her for magic residue—see if she's the one who cast that spell we undid today. And speaking of that spell—" He turned to June Bug. "What's the news on the rebound breakthrough? We reverse it?"

June Bug, he realized, was as gray-skinned and dead-eyed as a corpse. Very quietly, she said, "Things are a tangled mess in Oria. I'm still working on it."

He chewed on the corner of his mouth for a moment, then said, "Keep at it; let me know when you get something." He turned to the rest of the Sentinels. "Any rebound from our work in Oria that we didn't completely buffer?"

Granger sighed. "Unfortunately. We managed to rebound an approved subdivision construction project in Laurinburg all the way to oblivion."

George Mercer, who'd arrived while Eric was at Lauren's, said, "One of my clients paged me about ten minutes ago; when I called him back, he was three inches from killing someone. Blue's Farm Estates was ready to roll—permits, money, backing, everything. And right after we got back, the whole damned thing fell through from top to bottom. Loan got canceled, backers dropped out, Billy started getting calls that his permits weren't in order and he was going to have to reapply but that any new application would have a hard time getting approved because he hadn't done things right the first time through. Except he had. He's chewing nails."

"We crashed a *subdivision*?"

"It makes sense," Granger said, "in a stupid sort of way. When I untangled the spells, the majority of them felt like nothing more than home redecorating. Path of the rebound's least resistance after we failed to buffer it all would be through home construction."

"Lord have mercy," Eric whispered. "That lightning storm and the explosions and the kick of that thing were *home redecorating*?"

"Spellcaster was a complete novice," Granger said flatly. "Too much energy, no direction, and everything but the kitchen sink tangled up in the middle of the mess." He managed a weak smile. "Or in this case, everything *including* the kitchen sink."

"So how did a novice's home-redecorating spell precipitate a class-five rebound breakthrough?"

"It didn't," June Bug said from over in her corner, where she still stared into the glowing hand mirror. "It doesn't look like we touched that at all."

The whole world seemed to hang suspended in utter silence for one long, terrible moment. Three billion people, Eric thought, trying to grasp what he and the other Sentinels faced. Three billion lives would cease to exist in the next three months unless they could find the source of the breakthrough and reverse it. Roughly one out of every two people he knew would die—and the roll of Life's dice being what it was, perhaps *everyone* he knew would die. Perhaps *he* would die. And unraveling that nastiness in Oria—that nasti-

ness that had kicked the shit out of five veteran Sentinels—
hadn't helped at all.

"We cleared that source of magic completely?" he asked.

"Yes. Now I'm trying to untangle a mess." June Bug's
voice was cold and hard and angry.

"What sort of a mess? What have you found?"

"We have a source of massive magical expenditure south-
west of us. Absolutely enormous. It's clear, unshielded, and
has the marks of being done by a novice. But I can't find any
sign of breakthrough from it, or even of rebound. On the
other hand, I read very faint, very dark traces of an entirely
different sort of magic with an iffy directional of north and
west. *This* magic feels like the source of our trouble; it's
small and tight and professionally neat. But *it* has also been
very carefully shielded and disguised."

"Northwest would correspond with Rockingham," Eric
interrupted.

"More or less," June Bug agreed, "but we're going to have
a hell of a time tracking down the source. Whoever cast
these spells knows exactly what he's doing, and exactly how
to bypass my tracking."

"Which would mean a turned Sentinel," Willie Locklear
said.

"That's one possibility," Eric agreed, and now he understood the anger in June Bug's voice. It was the most likely
possibility. One of their own was working against them. One
of their own had forsworn himself and cast a spell that
would wipe out much of the world, and he knew it, and had
hidden his tracks because he didn't care whether the world
died or not.

"One of us?" Nancine asked. Eric could hear the anguish
in her voice. "One of us in this room?"

Eric was trying to stay calm. "Not necessarily one of ours.
Maybe someone gone rogue from another nexus and moved
into our territory to keep out of sight a bit longer. Maybe a
civilian who found a gate and went through it and somehow
figured out the finer points of spellcasting." Though that
sounded thin even to him. "Maybe one of the Old Gods set
up shop in the area."

There were groans around the room at the thought of having to deal with the Old Gods—the Sentinels' only-half-joking term for Earth's upworlders, who on Earth wielded the same powers that humans wielded in Oria. Dealing with the Old Gods could be an ordeal under the best of circumstances.

"And maybe," June Bug said softly, "it's one of us in this room. Let's not pretend."

"Let's not," Eric agreed. "Let's simply eliminate ourselves as a possible source of the problem. Then we'll all be able to work together without thinking one of us is a genocidal monster. We'll go back into Oria, do a reveal spell, and see if any of us have been doing magic on the side."

"Guilty until proven innocent," Terry Mayhew muttered.

Everyone looked at him with narrowed eyes, and Eric said, "Mayhem, this isn't the time to ask for your Miranda rights. Our responsibility is to protect the civilians and our world, and our rights are secondary when either civilians or Earth is threatened. You know that. You knew it when you took your oath."

"I was just joking," Terry said.

"No one was laughing," Willie said.

Terry's cheeks went red.

"We all go through, then," Eric said.

"What about the ones who aren't back yet? Bethellen and Louisa and Jimmy and Tom?"

"They go through as soon as they show up," Eric said. "We do reveals on them, too. I'd rather have everyone here at the same time, but this won't wait. We have work to do, and we have to know we can trust each other."

"And who casts the reveal spell?" June Bug wanted to know.

Eric frowned and considered. "Willie Locklear does first cast. Granger does second. I do third. That suit everyone?"

"Three reveals?"

"To prevent a traitor from failing to reveal his own complicity."

"And if all three of you are in on it together?" June Bug asked, and that rage was still in her voice.

"You want to do a reveal, too?"

"Yes."

"Fine. In fact, since you're the one who uncovered the rebound breakthrough, you do first cast. Rest of the cast order remains the same. Ernest, you're in charge of keeping the spells locked down—I don't want us adding to the rebound problem. And Nancine, I want you to keep the clock running. We need to make our impact as small and fast as possible. Those who are casting reveals, make sure you have the whole of the spell in your head before we go through, and don't add any flourishes. Keep it small and tight and precise. Make allowances for the magic Ernest is using to cast his pipeline, and the magic that Nancine is casting to maintain our clock, and that's it—no allowances for anything else. You have five minutes for prep, and a minute apiece to cast when we go through. We're going to run without shields or perimeter guards this time—we'll let the standing protections around the circle suffice. I don't want any extra spells contaminating the read. And I want us back out of there in five minutes." He glanced from June Bug to Willie to Granger. "Got it?"

They nodded. Everyone in the room sat quietly, waiting. Eric, who kept a reveal spell prepared in the back of his mind at all times, just in case, used the prep time to watch his colleagues. He didn't see any clear signs of guilt. They all looked scared, they all looked nervous, they all looked like they wanted to run away, but since he was scared and nervous and wishing he was in another universe, too, he couldn't take any of those things as indications of guilt.

Willie spoke first. "My reveal will show surreptitious trace magic as a red glow."

June Bug was ready next. "My spell will circle traitors with a ring of fire."

"Nonlethal," Eric said.

"If you insist."

"I insist."

June Bug shrugged.

Granger laughed a nervous laugh. "My approach will be self-explanatory if we have a guilty party."

Eric said, "Nothing lethal."

"No."

"That's fine, then." He nodded. "Mine will be self-explanatory, as well. Let's go."

For the second time that day, they moved through the gate into the clearing in Oria. Without shields, the wind cut into them, and the cold shot straight to their bones. This time they stood facing inward, a tight cluster of men and women who shared a single unhappy expression. Willie let the gate shut. Nancine cast the clock, and Ernest created the pipeline through which each reveal spell would be channeled and controlled.

June Bug cast the first reveal. "Seek trace, seek hiding, seek revision. Reveal."

Eric watched for jumpiness, for people staring at their own feet—and everyone checked their own feet first, then looked at everyone else's, and he only barely managed to keep himself from swearing. He knew they weren't all traitors—but human nature being what it was, the guilty would check to see if they'd been found out, and the innocent would check to be sure they had not been wrongly accused.

But no fires sprang up around anyone.

He watched the clock—the spell ran its course, and he said, "Satisfied, June Bug?"

She only said, "One down, three to go."

"My turn," Willie said. He closed his eyes, and Eric could feel the first movements of his spell before he spoke a word. And the only word Willie spoke was, "Reveal."

Eric had no idea what Willie's spell was doing. He had never been able to catch the shape of the gateweaver's magic—and had he been able to, he supposed he would have been able to see the subtle lines of force that ran through the universes, connecting them, and then he would have been a gateweaver too.

Willie's spell took the form of a ghostly man who walked from Sentinel to Sentinel. He stopped in front of each, rested his hand on the forehead, and stared into his subject's eyes. When he reached Eric and that clammy, weightless hand settled on his forehead and those nightmarish dead eyes stared into his, the hair on Eric's arms and the back of his neck stood up, and his mouth went dry. The phantasm looked right into his brain—and then it moved on, taking the terror it had instilled with it.

Good Lord, Eric thought. Willie had a dark side, didn't he? That had been terrifying. But, looking around the ring, no one was glowing red.

Granger was next. "Follow threads northwest, high-speed run, bring back fingerprints. Reveal."

Eric was just able to catch the shape of the spell Granger had cast. It was elegant—a lean and clever greyhound to the lumbering bloodhound he held in reserve. It raced off, raced back, and zipped around the ring of Sentinels with astonishing speed and economy. Eric had been responsible for bringing Granger and Debora in from the main Canadian nexus in Ontario; he'd taken a lot of heat at the time for opening up the ranks of the tightly knit and mostly hereditary Cat Creek Sentinels to strangers and foreigners. But he was learning a hell of a lot about other approaches to magic from the two of them, and the other Sentinels had finally accepted them. He just hoped he hadn't brought traitors into the nexus.

He felt three rushes of warmth from Granger's spell, but he could see no visible change in himself, or in anyone else. When Granger's minute was up, he gave Eric a relieved smile. "All clear."

Three down. Only his reveal remained—but he wasn't going to try to track the magic to its maker. He was looking for something else entirely. He was looking for guilt.

The parameters were clearly defined in his mind—he wanted the spell to check each Sentinel in turn, force from his thoughts any connection with the disaster that was being born in Rockingham, and make the guilty party confess guilt in front of the rest of the Sentinels.

With his star pressed tight against his palm, he focused his intent, cleared his thoughts of everything but the single purpose of his spell, and said, "Guilt, confess, reveal."

A tiny star of the pale green fire that was the magic of Oria flickered to life. It moved to the Sentinel on Eric's immediate right, Nancine Tubbs, and settled above her head. Her eyes went wide, and she looked terrified, and the next instant her mouth opened, and she said, "I'm guilty," and Eric felt his heart lurch.

But her next words had nothing to do with spellcasting, illicit magic, or betraying the Sentinels. Instead, she said, "I slept with Deever Duncan seven years after Ernest and I got married—we had an affair for almost a year. We'd get together when I'd run down to the hardware store to pick up parts for Ernest when he was on a job, or when Deever would come by the shop to pick up flowers for his wife. There's been more than flowers in that cooler."

Deever's face went a dull, beefy red that didn't bode well for his blood pressure, and he was dragging his fingers through the combed-over hair on the top of his head, making it look more than ever like an oily spider perched on his bare scalp. Ernest, on the other hand, clenched his big hands into white-knuckled fists and lowered his head, like a bull ready to charge. His eyes threatened Deever with slow and painful death.

Eric thought, This isn't right. The spell can't possibly be doing this. I focused on the rebound breakthrough, on Rockingham, on deaths that would wipe out half of humanity. The focus was as narrow as I could make it. Nancine's affair has nothing to do with any of that—not even remotely. He forced his mind to calm, and sent the spell a tight, clear redirection.

It lifted from Nancine's head, and she shuddered. "I fixed it," Eric said, and the spell-light moved right again, to Granger. But when it settled over Granger's head, and Granger said, "I'm guilty," Eric's stomach lurched. And Granger's next words confirmed his fears. "Back in college," Granger said, "I had a one-night stand with a girl who later told me that she was pregnant, and that the baby was mine. She wanted me to marry her, but rather than marry her, I gave her money for an abortion. I heard later that she really was pregnant, and that she'd kept the baby, but I've never looked her up to see if it was true, or if the baby really was mine." His face was gray when the light moved away from him.

Eric said, "Something is wrong with the spell. Something

about it has gone haywire. It's only supposed to be looking for guilt related to the rebound breakthrough."

The rest of the Sentinels were glaring at him.

The spell came to rest over Ernest Tubbs's head, and in Ernest's eyes, Eric saw pure panic. What dirty little secret had he been hiding from Nancine that was now going to be dumped in front of all of them? Sweaty sex with someone they all knew?

Eric didn't want to know. He didn't *need* to know.

"Stop," he said, and the spell froze in midair, then rebounded to him. He took the hit alone, buffering the whole thing himself. It slammed into him, and he found himself blurting out, "I'm guilty. When I was in high school, I used marijuana and I inhaled. And I was the one who took Willie Locklear's car for a joyride when I was fourteen and wrecked it in the ditch on Railroad Street. And Janie Thompson and I broke into the high school with a bottle of Jack Daniel's and a blanket when we were both seniors and we had sex on the auditorium stage, and then on top of Mrs. McCormick's desk. And I didn't report all of my cash income on my income taxes two years ago—I got a gift of two thousand dollars from my aunt up in High Point and I didn't say a thing. And I lusted after Mrs. Brandt in the ninth grade, and I put my hand up Shannon Breeley's blouse in seventh grade and . . ."

At that point, the spell finally ran out of energy, and Eric collapsed to the hard ground, with sweat pouring down his face in spite of the freezing temperatures and icy wind in the clearing, and he vomited.

The horrified silence following Eric's outburst was thick enough to cut with a chain saw. Then George Mercer, ever the accountant, cleared his throat and said, "You don't need to feel guilty about not reporting that gift from your aunt. It was within the allowable limits for gifts, so it didn't count as income that year."

"And I knew about you and my car," Willie said, and Eric could hear the faintest hint of humor in his voice. "I've known about that for years."

The rest of the Sentinels, however, were still stunned to

silence. Terry managed to croak, "Thank God it didn't reach me." At that, Eric heard a few nervous chuckles.

"If we'd had to listen to your confession of tawdry sex with married women, we would have been here all day, hey, Mayhem?" June Bug said, but even she, who Eric would have sworn had never thought a corrupt thought in her life, looked desperately relieved that the spell hadn't reached her.

"The spell wasn't supposed to do that," Eric said again. "Something went wrong with it."

June Bug was looking at him with suddenly wary eyes. She dropped her mirror, bent down with old-woman creakiness, and splayed the fingers of one hand on the frozen ground while she picked it up with the other. Eric caught the faintest flicker of light from the mirror; then June Bug was shoving herself to her feet again, grunting softly. "You just screwed up, Eric. Can happen to anyone, even you." She looked straight into his eyes when she said it, though, and suddenly he was sure that she had found something, but that it wasn't something she was willing to admit to finding with the rest of the Sentinels present.

He wiped his mouth on his sleeve, got weakly to his feet, and nodded. "I'm sorry. All of you—I'm truly sorry."

He glanced at Nancine, who was crying, and at Ernest, who had an arm around her round shoulders and was telling her it was okay, these things sometimes happened, but he forgave her if she just promised that she'd never stray again, and he thought, Who *would* have come crawling out of your closet, Ernest?

"None of us, then," Debora said with a shaky smile.

"None of us," Eric agreed. "So let's go home."

They started back through the gate, and somehow Terry managed to wait so that he and Eric and Willie were the last three in Oria. Terry turned to Eric and said, "On Mrs. McCormick's desk. She would have had a heart attack if she knew. She used to wipe off the classroom doorknob with alcohol before she'd even open the door."

"I know," Eric said. "That's why we used her desk. I had her for algebra and geometry, and I couldn't stand her."

Terry said, "*That* was genuinely funny."

Eric looked at him sidelong, and said, "You think so? And what funny stories would you have told?"

Terry's smile looked a little strained. "They don't call me Mayhem for nothing."

June Bug had her mirror out when Eric went through the gate, and was studying something she saw within it. When he stepped through, she waved him over.

"What do you have?"

Her shoulders lifted and dropped. "Just little tracks and traces around Rockingham. Here—look." She held the mirror up for him to see, and at the same time kicked him sharply in the shin.

"Ow," he muttered, and looked into the mirror. The image glowing in the reflection was nowhere near Rockingham. It was, in fact, the circle he and the rest of the Sentinels had just left. He said nothing, simply waiting.

"Note the black areas here . . . and here . . . and here?" she asked him. She set the mirror's image racing along the perimeter of the circle, and he saw precise, geometric, diamond-shaped dead areas in what should have been a smooth, even green glow.

Places where magic had been . . . blanked. Negated. Where the ambient current had been channeled to swallow magic, or subvert it, or . . .

"That's not good," Eric whispered.

June Bug eyed him steadily. "No."

Those diamonds marked the spots—exactly the spots— where each of the Sentinels had stood during the reveals. He'd been standing on a diamond, June Bug had, Debora had, Willie had . . . They all had.

Not good at all.

The utter awfulness of that started sinking in on him. Those black, dead spots couldn't have been placed there prior to the Sentinels' arrival in the clearing—their placement was far too exact, and there was only one for each of the Sentinels who had been there, with none extra for those who were still absent.

And that meant that one of their own had gone through the gate, set a spell with the rest of the Sentinels present—but so quickly and smoothly that none of them had noticed it—and had then taken his or her place in the circle, confident that his ... or her ... treachery would be masked by the misfiring reveal spells.

All of the spells would have misfired. Eric's, however, was the only one that had done so in such a way that it had been obvious—and that childish obviousness he had shown in casting his spell had to have been the one variable that the traitor could not have planned for. He was certain that all of the reveals had failed, tampered with by the traitor—but only his had failed in such a big, sloppy, humiliating way that no one could overlook it or think that it had done what it was supposed to do.

Had he not failed so spectacularly, June Bug would not have suspected the tampering. She might not have checked the circle for spell residue after they left. They would have thought all of their number had been cleared.

Instead, Eric now knew the Sentinels were being betrayed by one of their own.

But who?

The only person he could trust was June Bug. And she had decided the only person she could trust was him. He supposed that made sense. Had he been the one to cast the subversion spell, he certainly wouldn't have also cast a reveal spell that would backfire so spectacularly, or that would leave him the humiliated public confessor of numerous secret sins.

"I think," June Bug said, "that you and I ought to take a ride out to Rockingham. Maybe walk around a bit, see if we can figure out what caused those marks."

"Anything you'll need me for?" Willie asked. He was leaning against the far wall of the room, his eyes half-closed and an expression of utter exhaustion etched into his face.

"Get some rest," Eric said. "You look like you could use it, and we aren't going to need any gates for this reconnaissance. We'll get the lay of the land this time out. I want to see if we can track down some of these energy trails June Bug has found. When we do go in, I'm going to want more than you, me, and June Bug there."

"Good enough." Willie sighed heavily. "I haven't had a good night's sleep in about a week. I think I'm going to go home and take a nap. You need me . . . you call me. Y'hear? Soon as you get anything."

Eric said, "The second we know anything."

"Then I'll see you all later." Willie left, and Debora left behind him. The other Sentinels hung around. Eric put Mayhem on the next watch with Deever Duncan as backup, sent everyone else back to what they'd been doing before with the admonishment that they were to stay close to their phones. Then he and June Bug headed out to his patrol car, ostensibly to drive to Rockingham.

Lauren was tapping on the walls in her mother's old sewing room—still done in the same pale cream wallpaper with the tiny cornflowers that she had helped her mother hang when she was a child—when Embar materialized out of the built-in shelving her father had made so that her mother would have a place for all of her cloth.

"Found it," he said.

"The notebook. Just like that?"

"You'll still have to get it out. It's hidden in a secret compartment in the shelving."

Jake sat on the floor, for the moment content to be crashing a big plastic car into the baseboard. The monotonous clack-clack-clack-thud, clack-clack-clack-thud was going to start getting under Lauren's skin pretty soon, she was sure—but as long as Jake wasn't running around trying to stick coat hangers into electrical outlets or to pull everything from above his head onto his head, she'd take Annoying Noises for $500, Alex, and count her blessings.

"Can you see how to open the compartment?"

"I can show you where it is. You're going to have to figure out how to open it yourself."

He drifted to her left, fading part of the way into one shelf. "The notebook is right here," he said. "I'm standing on it."

Lauren crouched by the shelf he indicated and—once he had moved out of her way—started pressing on the shelf and the backboard, and tapping on the fine old hardwood, listening for anything different that might indicate the manner in which she should get into the shelving. She tugged and thumped and looked for any unusual signs of wear. She could find nothing.

Her father had loved woodworking. He'd spent hours out back in his workshop after he'd done his mail route each day, working with handsaws and planers and chisels and rasps and router bits, creating beautiful wooden rocking horses and bookcases and tables and cabinets. People all over the county owned work by him; each piece carefully signed on the bottom with his carved name and the date he'd finished the job. The little freestanding bookshelves that had been in Lauren's room when she was a child had been his work, as was the jewelry box she still owned.

She tipped her head, thinking of the jewelry box. It was a puzzle box, a beautiful little piece of woodworking made to look like a row of books stacked between a base book and a top book. The trick to getting into it was to slide one of the "page" panels from the bottom out, then to slide the spine of the bottom book to the left as far as it would go, then to move the spines of the third and eighth books in the row down into the space created by the shifted spine. The titles on the two panels were *The Black Stallion* and *Misty of Chincoteague*—her two favorite books at the time he'd made the box for her. Moved, the little panels revealed a hidden key and a tiny keyhole.

Nothing on the jewelry box wiggled or rattled, and it had been designed so that each sliding part would show no wear; after years of use, it was still impossible to tell when the box was closed that it was anything other than a charming wood carving of a stack of books.

She studied the shelves, the design of that little box in her mind. The shelves ended at the window, and resumed on the other side. Her mother had kept a fern on a brass stand in the space between the shelves, and Lauren suddenly remembered that it was frequently out of place in the room. "It was getting too much light," her mother had said when Lauren asked about it once—but the window faced north.

Her father had done decorative routing along the edge of each panel—a little groove half an inch from the edge than ran from ceiling to floor—and had given each shelf and side panel a thick bullnose. When she looked carefully at the design, she realized that those two elements—groove and bullnose—would give someone moving pieces a handhold while hiding any wear from sliding pieces, in the same fashion that the spines of her books had been designed to overlap and conceal their hidden workings.

She slid her fingers along the groove of the vertical panel beside the window, gently tugging toward herself. Embar stood beside her, watching.

"The books are in the middle section," he said.

"I know. You showed me." Lauren kept sliding her fingers downward, kept applying pressure.

Embar sighed.

Her fingers crossed the line where the vertical panel joined the baseboard—and the baseboard moved. She pulled harder, and it slid smoothly toward her and pulled completely out.

She nodded. Behind the removed baseboard was a solid panel of wood—but she'd expected that. She pressed her hands against the front baseboard, which had no grooves or other features to make it stand out, and tried to slide it to the left. After initial resistance, it moved smoothly about four feet to the left, then stopped. She nodded. The middle shelves now showed a gap in the baseboard. The carefully crafted bullnose shelving proved to have a lip; when she used the lip as a drawer pull, the entire shelf moved smoothly out.

In the space beneath it lay a notebook—a simple leather-bound three-ring binder. It was stuffed full, its uneven, yellowed pages looked like they were ready to burst out of the binder and spill across the room like a snowdrift.

"Good God," she murmured. "What a mess." She lifted the notebook from its hiding place and opened it at random.

The page was a diagram of some sort of mechanical device—drawn in blue ballpoint pen by her mother, with her mother's neat, sharply angled script running out from arrows that indicated the names and purposes of various parts. The diagram was titled Universal Speller, Version 4. Lauren started reading some of the notations.

> *psychic equalizer*—.999 silver, minimum three ounces for best damping, make sure the copper wiring harness is firmly attached to both the Quatting coupler and the blackbox
> *thram*—(4) connect in series—silver wire with rubber cladding. DON'T let the thrams touch the babbler
> *Quatting coupler*— . . .

Lauren frowned and thumbed through other pages. More diagrams. More notes that made no sense, using words from a vocabulary drawn out of a discipline she knew nothing about. She couldn't figure out what the equipment was supposed to do, she couldn't figure out how any of it might be made to work, and she had the momentary, almost hysterical suspicion that someone was having a huge laugh at her expense. What sort of nonsense was all of this?

There were pages upon pages of dated journal entries, too—these were less bizarre than the diagrams, and written both by her mother and her father, but they frequently referred to the Project, without defining, even in context, what the Project was.

"This is supposed to mean something," she said to Embar.

He nodded. "You can't make out what they were doing?"

"They seem to have written the thing with the assumption that the people who would read it would already know what they were doing, and that anyone else didn't need to know and wouldn't find out by reading their notes."

"Well . . . the Sentinels . . . I'm sure they didn't want to take the chance of their work falling into Sentinel hands after all the unpleasantness. It would explain why they were cryptic in their notes." Embar murmured. "You don't remember what their plan was?"

"No. And even if I did, I don't know that any of this would make sense. Were they crazy, Embar? I'm beginning to realize that I never knew them—is it possible that they were both just completely out of their minds?"

Embar sighed. "Anything is possible, I suppose. But I don't think it's likely. They seemed perfectly rational to me. What they did, worked. And . . . people rarely take the trouble to murder the harmlessly eccentric or the purely crazy. They only murder people who are a threat to them."

Lauren bit her lip and nodded slowly. "There's always the possibility that I'm simply not bright enough to get this."

Embar's forehead creased, and he gave her a nervous smile. "I'm sure you'll do just fine," he said, his whispery voice making it clear to her that he wasn't sure at all. "Just read through the notes. They're bound to stir memories of some sort. Your parents wouldn't have left you without some sort of key for unlocking what they worked on all those years." He turned away, and she heard him mutter, in a voice she was certainly not intended to hear, "They *couldn't* have."

"Ma-aaa-ma-aaa," Jake said plaintively. "Biteys. Pleeeease, biteys?"

Lauren looked at her son, now clearly done with cars and being patient. "Biteys in a minute," she said. She kept the notebook out, but put the shelf back together. "I'll look over this later," she told Embar.

He nodded. "Take your time. Just start from the front and work your way through. I have to believe that at some point, you'll start recognizing things." He stood. "I'm going to go back home. The . . . the weight of this place gets to me after a while."

"The house?"

"The whole universe." Embar shrugged. "I'll hang around your parents' old place in Oria. When you're ready, just come through and call me. I'll hear you."

Lauren rose, tucking the notebook under one arm. With the other, she lifted Jake and swung him onto her hip. "I'll do that. Give me a few days to see if I have any hope of figuring this stuff out."

"I'll see you soon, then," Embar said. He faded into the floor and dropped out of sight.

"Bye, doggie," Jake called.

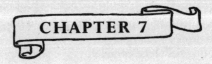

CHAPTER 7

Copper House, Ballahara

MOLLY YAWNED and stretched and burrowed out from beneath thick silk sheets. Morning sunlight streamed into the room, filling it from floor to ceiling with glorious warmth.

It would be so easy to give in, to let herself think of all this luxury as hers. She had always been able to imagine something better for herself than the single-wide, which, though clean and adequate, could never have been mistaken for luxurious.

She kicked her feet into a pair of beaded, cashmere-lined slippers and wrapped a robe around herself. She felt wonderful, and she had to think about the reasons for that; she hadn't had to suffer through anyone else's pain for days, and it became easy to forget that, when she got back home, the pain would be waiting. She didn't want to think about that, because for the first time in as long as she could remember, she felt as good around people as she felt alone.

She started filling the ornate tub, and wondered as she did what such a thing would cost back home. More than she could afford, certainly. While the water thundered gently behind her, she walked to the window and stared down at this world that she could not yet believe. Not a fairy-tale world at all; from her vantage point, she could see both well-kept houses and run-down hovels in the village contained within high stone walls. But she found it pictur-esque; the cobblestone streets, the oddly rounded architecture that looked almost like mushroom houses carved of wood and sprung from ungiving ground. The people in the streets weren't human, but they were people. They loved their kids, they loved each other, they hoped and dreamed and worked hard, and eventually they ran to the end of their time and died.

Palms flat on the cool copper sill, staring down through the thick copper grille, Molly tried to imagine fitting in this place where nothing hurt. She tried to imagine finding a reason to stay.

Birra, the blue creature, had come to talk to her the night before. He told her that the veyâr, his people, were dying— that they had been cursed by the rrôn, and that all the sick she had cured were victims of the rrôn magic.

She didn't know if she believed him, even though she had seen magic pouring through her own fingertips. The idea of a curse on an entire people seemed so terribly archaic and ludicrously paranoid. But the idea of touching a woman and sending green fire through her body that devoured her cancer seemed, on the surface, impossible as well.

This was not Cat Creek. She could not judge the world of Oria based on what she knew.

"You are very far away this morning."

Birra again. Molly didn't jump at the sound of the veyâr's voice, though she hadn't heard him enter the suite. She needed to have *something* at the front door to tell her when anyone entered, however. Perhaps not the tiger trap she'd fashioned, though she would hold that in reserve. But something. "I'm here," she said. "Just wondering how long I'll be here."

She turned away from the window. Birra came most often, though the seafoam-green one—Laath—stopped by almost every evening, just to see if she needed any more chocolate. She always offered him one piece; he always accepted. The rest varied from day to day, and none of them wore robes of the richness that Birra or Laath wore, and none of them sported facial tattoos as intricate or as beautiful.

"Ah. A reasonable question. We had word from His Gloriousness after I spoke with you last night; his negotiations have taken an unexpected turn, and he will be yet another several days. He wishes you comfort and happiness, and says that on his return he will feast you and honor you." He moved to her side and looked out the window with her. And he asked her an odd question. "Have you felt anything calling to you? Urging you to come to the window?"

She turned, crossed her arms over her chest, and stared up at him until he met her gaze. "I'm easily sixty feet above the ground in a smooth-sided tower. What *exactly* would call me to the window?"

She couldn't read his face. His expression didn't change the tiniest bit. He said, "Well, Oria has a number of intelligent species that can fly."

"Like the rrôn."

Now he cringed. "Even here, you shouldn't say that name too loudly. We believe they come when summoned by the speaking of their name; you understand why that would be a bad thing."

She nodded. "Is it them flapping around my window that you're worried about?"

"Not so much as"—he closed his eyes and took a deep breath—"as others. I dare not even whisper about them— they never speak out loud, but they can speak straight to the soul. They are beautiful; they are evil; they can make all mortal creatures do as they bid, think what they would have us think. And they would want to own a Vodi, if they found out one was here."

Molly turned back to the window. "Copper keeps them away?"

"They cannot exercise their magic through copper. But their soul-speech is not hampered by physical barriers. Should they call to you, you would do anything within your power to obey. Well, perhaps you would not, because you are a Vodi. But be careful. Do not trust impulses that would lead you away from safety."

"Right. I'll keep that in mind." Molly turned, stared pointedly at her tub, which had filled, and said, "I need to get my bath now."

Birra bowed. "Yes, Vodi. I will be on my way. Please pull the bell-cord when you are dressed; a lovely breakfast awaits you in the solar, along with allies of the veyâr who came to meet you. You need do no healing today—this is the Sixteenday, and all of Ballahara rests."

She bathed, she dressed, and all the while she tried to decide if Birra's story about the creatures that spoke to the soul was a genuine warning or a tale he'd made up to scare her out of any more escape attempts. It had a real beware-the-bogeyman feel to it. But then, she wouldn't have believed in the rrôn had she not seen their aftermath.

She sucked on a piece of chocolate while she picked out clothes. Clothes in this place were complicated enough that she almost wished she had an assistant to help her get into them. She felt pretty sure she put everything on right, but since she could only see everyone's outer garments, she was reduced to guessing about the purposes of some of the odder underthings. When in doubt, she skipped pieces entirely.

She tugged on soft brushed-cotton bloomers and breast-binder, took another stab at a corsetlike contraption that held everything else together, and noticed that all the lacings on it were way too loose—so someone had been in her clothing while she slept.

Tiger trap, goddammit. They weren't going to be sneaking into her room while she was asleep. She would not have that.

She tightened the laces and began attaching skirts to the rows of hooks that went from hips to just below the waist, one skirt per layer. All the skirts were silk, all diaphanous and very light, but when she'd added the seventh layer, she could feel the weight of them. Then two light silk blousons, a black underblouse, and on top of that a sheer white one. Each of these had a ruffed collar that had to be layered correctly. Then the outer robe—for this meeting, she chose one as copper as the room, with a rich mahogany undersheen, covered with embroidered emerald-green vines. At the end of each vining curlicue was a gemstone bud—she would guess rubies from the deep redness of the stones and their astonishing depth, but she supposed they might have been garnets, too.

The sleeves seemed a bit short—her wrists came out the ends. She sighed, not willing to go through the ordeal of another outfit, and rolled up the sleeves.

She added knitted-cotton hose and a pair of woven flats, and when she'd finished tying all the ties in the right places and pulling her hair into a single braid down her back, she checked the floor-length mirror. And frowned.

Her hair, always a rich brown, in the mirror now looked almost copper. Her eyes, always hazel, now looked pure amber, and her once-pale skin had an amber cast to it, too. She would have blamed this on the color that light reflected in a copper room, except that she could see that the bone structure of her face had changed, too. Her eyes tilted upward at the outer corners, her cheekbones were more pronounced, and her neck looked both longer and more slender. For that matter, she was too tall for the mirror. It had been angled correctly the night before, but until she moved it to get a better look at herself, it cut off a good six inches of her head. And she could see her ankles at the bottom of the bottommost skirt, whereas previously the skirts had hung no more than a half inch above the ground.

She stared at the mirror, and something that had been niggling in the back of her mind while she was talking to Birra suddenly resolved with crystal clarity. When she talked to him, she had looked him in the eye, but she hadn't had too look up in the neck-straining manner that she had previously.

"I quit growing when I was sixteen," she muttered, but she could tell just by looking at her reflection that she had grown. A lot. She'd gotten taller and thinner, and she'd done it overnight.

What the hell?

She rang the bell for Birra. She hoped he had an explanation for this, because she was goddamned tired of weirdness and surprises.

Cat Creek

Lauren, making Jake a snack, saw Eric drive by with one of the Weird Sisters in his squad car. Lauren squinted through the glass. June Bug. The old one. She wondered what they were up to.

June Bug was a Sentinel, so the two of them were doing something that she could expect wouldn't be good for her. Still, she found that she had a hard time thinking of Eric as the enemy. They'd never been friends in high school—he'd been the Designated Bad Boy, and she'd been the Designated Good Girl—but they had walked home from classes together sometimes, in those on-again, off-again times when Eric had been suspended from driving the family car. They'd talked, and the talks had never been about the people they went to school with, or the miserable performance of the football team. They'd *really* talked.

Funny. She spread peanut butter and jelly on the whole wheat bread and cut the sandwiches into triangles—Jake called them "tragadals," and insisted on them. She could still remember what she and Eric had talked about, some of those days. About his dreams of going to West Point, of becoming the reincarnation of some of his heroes; Robert E. Lee, George Patton, Douglas MacArthur, Dwight D. Eisenhower, and of course Lieutenant Alexander R. Nininger, good Georgia boy, whose one-man stand in the Philippines had seemed to Eric the perfect military career. He'd been an avid reader of military histories, something that amazed Lauren since Eric never read anything assigned for class and never, ever did homework. Which had probably been what had kept him out of West Point. Or had it been the fact that he was slated to become a Sentinel—that his father wouldn't let him even consider making the military his career? She did remember them fighting a lot about Eric *not* becoming an officer in the Army.

And she and Eric had talked about her uncertainty over her own future; her absolute dedication to not learning to type because she'd made up her mind that she was never going to be part of someone's typing pool somewhere, her hunger to see other places, her restless feeling that she was missing something—that she was supposed to be doing something important with her life but that she couldn't even imagine what that something might be.

Eric had smiled sadly when she discussed that hunger, and had seemed to understand her. She'd liked him for that. A lot. They couldn't date, of course—because in a town as small as Cat Creek, people kept to their roles. Her role was to be the Good Girl, virginal and studious, and his was to be the Bad Boy, driving too fast, drinking, smoking in the rest rooms, keeping company with the girls whose names parents only whispered. Even when they were very young, they had understood the importance of roles.

But they'd kissed once, when they were standing by her father's workshop in back of the house. Just talking, and they hit a lull in the conversation and made the mistake of looking into each other's eyes. And then he was holding her, and she was holding him—tentatively, cautiously, like people who might be looking at something they could keep—and standing in the kitchen all those years later, when she closed her eyes she could still remember that kiss.

Then they'd backed away, because she wouldn't have been good for his reputation, and he wouldn't have been good for hers. And not long after that, he got permission to drive to school again, and not long after that she graduated and moved on.

She'd never talked about Eric with Brian. There had just been the one kiss, and it hadn't meant anything to either of them.

Except, standing in the kitchen right then, knowing what she knew about the Sentinels, about Eric, about her parents, she could still catch a glimpse of Eric driving by and remember the boy with the dreams of greatness, and the feel of the sun on her cheeks when he kissed her.

Copper House, Ballahara

Birra could offer Molly no explanations. "You do perhaps seem taller, but perhaps it is just your shoes."

She showed him the flats.

"Well, perhaps not the shoes, then."

"I'm *taller*," she said. "My face has changed, my hair is a different color, my eyes are a different color. I want to know what is going on!"

Birra held one long-fingered hand to his forehead and closed his eyes. "The Imallin will be returning soon. Soon. Perhaps he will have the answers you require. But I, Vodi, I do not have them. I am a humble servant of the house—"

"Bullshit. You're neither a servant, nor are you humble. I put you second-in-command here, if not in charge of the armed forces, then at least high enough in rank that everyone present bows to you and you bow to no one. Except me. I know bureaucracies, I know military hierarchies. And I know bullshit when I'm being fed it."

Birra's demeanor changed. He stood straighter, took a deep breath, and nodded somberly. "Very well. You are quite correct; in your position, I would wish the same honesty you demand. Here, then, the truth. My orders are that I not discuss the nature of the changes you are experiencing; this is the duty and privilege of the Imallin. You understand orders?"

Molly nodded. "Orders, I understand."

"Then please—come with me, enjoy meeting our guests, enjoy the feast that has been prepared for you, and I will do what I can to hurry the Imallin back from his post. I will give him to understand that the situation is urgent, requiring his soonest attention."

"Your word on it?"

"My word of honor."

"I'll accept that."

Molly had expected the guests to be more veyâr. That wasn't who, or what, she got. Three short, rotund, beautifully furred creatures in elegant tabards and belts sat at one end of a long table, sipping daintily from cups and conversing with a half dozen wrinkled, gray-skinned knuckle-draggers whose speech sounded to Molly like they were trying to gargle and sing at the same time. As she and Birra stepped into the room, the conversation died and everyone stood up.

The knuckle-draggers bowed so deeply their pointed chins touched their bare, knobby knees. They whispered, "Welcome, welcome, Vodi," and kept their eyes on the floor, as if they dared not even look at her. The furry little creatures were less shy—they, too, bowed low to the ground, but when they straightened up, they lifted their heads and met her gaze directly. "You don't look like the Vodi," one of them said, and was quickly hushed by the veyâr and the gray-skinned creatures.

He gestured to the three furry creatures. "I give you The Dark, The Bright, and The Deep, of the Tradona People." With a nod to the still-bowed-over gray people, he said, "And Neighbor-Winter Son of River-Winter, and Down-The-Long-Path Daughter of Hollow-Fire, of the Faolshe."

She returned the bows of the creatures who greeted her.

Then she turned to Birra, and whispered to him, "Are those names—The Dark, The Bright, The Deep?"

"The low Tradona have names," Birra told her, "but these are the highest of the high Tradona. They have places—The Dark presides over the Tradona colony in Mourning Forest; The Bright over the colony in White Hold, in far Ayem; and The Deep over the grand Tradona city of Grimarr in the Silver Chain. They are the three greatest of the Tradona, as demonstrated by the simple form by which they are known."

She nodded and moved to take the seat offered her at the head of the table.

The Faolshe were a mystery of another sort—she wondered why they were so frightened of her. Who was she to them? What was their story of the Vodi about, and how was she supposed to fit into it?

That, really, was the question she had to ask about all of Oria. Who did these people think she was, and what, exactly, did they expect her to do?

Servants appeared as soon as she sat, carrying platters of steaming vegetables and a large cup of tea, which they set before her. The two Faolshe stared at their plates as if salvation lay within the food. The Tradona, on the other hand, studied her with unblinking, unnerving stares.

"You're sure she's the one," The Dark asked Birra.

Birra bowed his head. "Great Dark, we are as sure as we are that the sun rises in the east, that the sea is deep and cold, that the Forest is vast and deadly." Molly would have sworn that his last statement held some sort of barb in it, so sharp was his tone, but his face remained neutral and his position remained relaxed.

"Indeed," The Dark said. "Such dangers as we all face do not lie within the sole domain of the Forest," and his tone was even more clearly strained than Birra's.

There *had* been a barb, then—but one she couldn't begin to guess at.

What she did guess was that she wasn't what any of them had come hoping to see; the Tradona clearly didn't care for her, and she frightened the Faolshe.

"What is the Vodi supposed to be?" she asked them. She saw Birra wince, and the Faolshe cringe. The Tradona, however, burst into laughter.

"Sure as the sea is wet, eh?" The Bright asked. "You would have us believe she will clear our world of unnatural death, return the True Folk to power and send rrôn and keth back to the hells that spawned them?"

The two Faolshe buried their faces in their hands and uttered frightened cries at that, and the other two Tradona turned to stare at their compatriot. Even Birra blanched and said, "Such words are not to be spoken in this house. What you call down upon your own homes, only you decide. But They will not be mentioned here again.

The Dark shrugged. "What I have to say remains the same, whether I mention . . . *Them*"—he gave Birra a condescending nod of acknowledgment—"by name or not. You would have us believe she is the Vodi. As easy to believe she could reseat fallen stars in their sockets, or turn out the light of the moon with a wave of her hand. She doesn't even know who the Vodi is."

"She has passed every test we have so far given her."

"She isn't one of us. She's an outsider."

"You don't know her. You have not seen her. You cannot understand. She *is* one of us."

"The proof lies in the future. If she is who you claim she is, it will become plain soon enough, won't it?"

Birra rubbed his temples in a gesture that reminded Molly oddly of her adoptive father, back when she was little and he spent a great deal of time worrying about how he was going to pay the bills. Oddly, the reminder didn't upset her the way she would have expected—instead, for just a moment, she felt pity for the man who had, at least in the early years, tried so hard to raise her, even though she was not an easy child to raise or even to love.

She patted Birra's arm gently, and he turned to her with amazement on his face, as if . . .

. . . as if she had healed him. It was the same expression she saw on the faces of the supplicants who came to her every day.

. . . as if he had been touched by God.

That's part of who I am to him, she realized. She hadn't really considered how her captors thought of her before. They were too alien to her, and in ways both too intimately connected to the circumstances of her abduction and too much in control of her present and future fate for her to have allowed herself to wonder about their "human" side.

Yet suddenly she was looking at Birra and wondering whether he had a wife and kids at home, and what it was that he hoped she was going to do for him and his world that he couldn't do for himself.

Suddenly she was annoyed at those smug little Tradona bastards for having the temerity to doubt her—and she didn't even know why she was in Oria.

She'd heard of people identifying with their captors. She'd taken survival-school training on how to handle interrogation and torture and more and how to come out the other side of it not too scrambled—assuming survival, of course.

She recognized signs in herself that she didn't like—signs that she was identifying with her captors.

She needed to get away, fast.

But she wasn't entirely certain anymore that she wanted to.

Cat Creek

Eric and June Bug sat in the squad car about two miles outside of Cat Creek, on a dirt access road that paralleled both Hepner's Road and the old MaCready cotton fields.

"Not going any closer to Rockingham?" June Bug asked him.

"Not yet. Not sure what we have going on here, and I don't want my enemies at my back when I deal with that."

June Bug nodded. "I know it wasn't you who cast that spell, and I know it wasn't me. You get any read on who it was?"

Eric shook his head slowly and studied his hands, gripping the steering wheel so hard the knuckles were blanched white as steamed almonds. "Son of a bitch has us, whoever it is. He can go where he wants, do what he wants—"

"—Could be a she," June Bug interjected.

"I'm using *he* in the universal sense."

"That's fine, then. Just don't let it blind you to the possibilities."

"I was saying." He looked over at her to make sure she was going to let him finish this time. She met his gaze with calm, unwavering eyes and said nothing. He cleared his throat. "I was saying . . . whoever has done this can go where he wants, do what he wants, and because he . . . *or* she . . . knows who we are and where we are and how we work, he can walk around us like we weren't even there. We're blind, and he has twenty-twenty vision and goddamned radar, sonar, and night vision."

"Right now we know one thing he doesn't know," June Bug said.

"And that would be?"

"That he's one of us."

Eric leaned back against the upholstery and closed his eyes and rubbed his temples. A headache was forming behind his eyeballs, the pressure building and squeezing like storm clouds growing inside his skull. He wasn't getting enough sleep. The sleep he was getting wasn't restful. The nightmares that plagued his dreams had moved out into the real world, and if he didn't figure out what was going on fast—and how to fix it at the same time—the world as he knew it was going to end.

And it was going to be his fault.

"One of them is one of us," Eric agreed. "If we can keep the one who is from finding out that we know that, we might be able to discover what he's done and undo it."

"Wait a minute." June Bug looked genuinely bewildered. "*One of them* is one of us? What makes you think there's more than one?"

"Couple of things. Lauren Dane has suddenly appeared in town; a gate is open in her house that was closed until she arrived; her parents betrayed the Sentinels; and no sooner did she get here than Molly McColl disappeared and the problem up in Rockingham started."

"Lauren never had a touch of ability with magic. I'm one of the ones who tested her, way back when. She was a magnet for trouble, even when she was little, but she couldn't do what either of her parents could. It was one of their biggest disappointments."

"What if she could?"

"I'm telling you, she couldn't. Children can't hide things like that."

"No. They can't. But if their parents are traitors, maybe they could."

June Bug said, "Her parents were in the good graces of the Sentinels back when I tested Lauren. It was right after we had all those gateweaver deaths, and we were looking for anyone to fill in the holes; we were ready to start training even small children if we could just find someone to back up Willie."

Eric gave her a meaningful look.

She frowned at him. "What?"

"You aren't a mother. Pretend you are. Pretend that gateweavers have started dying like fish in a poisoned stream, and you have a child with gateweaver potential—someone who, when she got older, would be able to blast open a gate that had been shut and sealed by one of the finest and most proficient gateweavers the Sentinels have ever had. You love your kid. You don't want anything to happen to her—and as long as no one knows she could become a gateweaver, nothing is likely to. What would you do?"

June Bug considered. "I'd find some way of hiding her potential. But you don't understand—adults can hide things from other adults, but children are lousy liars. She hadn't been tampered with. I would have known."

"From everything I have heard, her parents were brilliant. They could have been on the Northern Council; they could have been representatives to the European Council . . . they were way too good to have stayed here. But they stayed. Even after they were thrown out of the Sentinels they stayed."

"You're saying they tampered with her, that they did such a brilliant job of hiding it that I never saw a clue, that even back then they had ulterior motives for her, that she is here now to carry out some vast conspiratorial plan which they concocted a quarter century ago, and that she is in cahoots with one of our people . . . which would mean that we've had a traitor in our midst for at least twenty-five years."

"No. I'm saying that she's here, her gate is open, and as far as I can tell no one else had been in her house. _And_ that since she's come back to town, things have been going wrong in a very big, very bad way." Eric's head felt like it truly might explode. He cupped his palms over his eyes and pressed inward, hoping to deaden the pain, but it didn't work. "I can't say anything more than that without talking to her. But I think I need to talk to her."

"And if she doesn't know anything about the Sentinels, or

the gates, or the flow of magic between the worlds . . . ?"

"Then she's going to think I've been doing drugs. Which is what I suspect she thought of me when she knew me before."

"Some truth in it back then."

Eric opened his eyes and turned the key in the ignition. "Some. I wasn't a perfect kid. I like to think I grew up to be a decent man, though."

June Bug laughed softly and patted his hand. "You've done all right." She said, "You know, I've been thinking about that spell of yours that went wrong in the circle today."

"Christ."

"It was bad. But I found myself almost wishing it would come to me."

Eric had been ready to put the car in gear, but he took his hand away from the shifter and looked at her. "You have something you want to tell someone, June Bug?"

"Not everyone. But someone, I reckon. Secrets you keep too long get pretty heavy to carry."

"You want to tell me, I'll treat it as privileged information. Won't tell anyone unless you ask me to."

He watched her turn and stare out the window, and watched her start fidgeting with the zipper of her jacket, running it up and down the little metal teeth. "I know. I want somebody to know. Dammit all, how long have you known me?"

"All my life."

"Ever wonder why I didn't get married?"

"Not really. Heard some young traveling salesman back in the Depression came calling on you, then disappeared back the way he'd come, and that you and your broken heart just never went looking for love again."

"That was one of my better stories."

Eric turned to find her looking straight at him, an odd defiance in her expression.

"If it's a story, it's a good one. Heard descriptions of the fella from some of the good ol' boys around town, heard about how your father went looking for him with a shotgun—heard all sorts of things."

"You tell a lie long enough and people become so convinced it's true that they start adding their own embellishments to it. There wasn't any salesman. Wasn't anyone. Not ever."

"That's sad."

June Bug pursed her lips and looked away. "Yes. Well. I've been in love a couple of times in my life. Just couldn't have the someone I wanted—not and live in Cat Creek and do my duty as a Sentinel."

Eric, as much in love with gossip as anyone, found himself fascinated by this confession. "Who?" he asked her, expecting the name of a Catholic priest from up in Laurinburg or some married man who had never given her the time of day.

She said, "Back when she was still alive, Marian Hotchkiss. The last few years, Charlise Tubbs."

She said it so softly he wasn't sure at first whether she'd actually said what he thought he heard, or whether his mind had just thrown those outrageous suggestions into the wind. "Lauren's mother and Nancine's older sister?"

"The same."

He considered that for a good long time, and all the implications of it. "Well," he said at last, and then couldn't think of anything else to say.

June Bug's sidelong glance sized him up. "Going to avoid me on the streets from now on?"

Eric smiled a little. "Not at all. Just a little funny thinking you and I might be looking at the same person and thinking the same sort of thoughts."

"Never acted on the way I felt," June Bug said after a bit. She stared out at the brown stubble that was all that remained of the summer's cotton crop. "Wasn't brought up that way—never thought it was right. Now . . . I sort of wish I had. If the world's going to end anyway, it would have been nice to . . . know. Just once."

Jake finally fell asleep for the night, and Lauren, with a sigh of relief, stretched out on her bed with her parents' notebook and a pen and tablet of her own. She was determined to make sense of the legacy they had left her—determined to unravel the tangled mess of her past and find the truth at the end of all those skeins of lies.

The notebook, when read front to back, made a bit more sense than it had when she'd started in the middle, and that at least reassured her. Her parents laid out their objective— to develop a method of running the magical energy from the world of Oria through Earth and into the world they referred to as Kerras without any loss or transmutation. She could make some sense of that—she knew where Earth was and she knew where Oria was, and she had some personal experience now with magic. Kerras remained a blank to her, but it was a funny sort of blank. She could feel the tampered places inside of her mind every time she thought of it, and she realized that her memories regarding Kerras were intact behind the barrier that her parents had created. To reach those memories, she only had to find the tool that would remove the wall.

She kept reading, while the hour grew later and the quiet around her became so thick it had a darkness all its own. Beyond the yellow light that puddled around the lamp on her bedside table, outside with the cold, pale stars and the faint sheen of frost on moon-spun grass, she could feel the weight of movement, the unblinking intensity of watching eyes, the patient breath of someone or something that waited for her to fall into a trap; and she sought through the yellowed pages for the shape and the texture and the mechanism of the trap that had been set for her.

When she closed her eyes for a moment, she could feel the magic again—the rumbling storm in the distance, the ecstatic green lightning that she could ride from one world to the next. She could see Brian smiling at her from within the heart of the storm. He seemed so close that she could reach out and touch him—so close that she could walk across the chasm of death and bring him back with her. So close she could almost lose herself in his embrace.

She drifted in the comfort of that nearness, in the sense of safety it spun around her, until she could almost see his face . . . could almost hear his voice.

He stood close to her. Another step, a few more inches, just lean a little more, reach out her hand, hold her breath and *try*. She pushed, fought for that extra something that would take her to him, and as if she were in a dream, she stumbled. And caught herself.

And the illusion that he was with her shattered like sugar glass. She lurched upright, her eyes flying open, tears streaming down her cheeks. She was sobbing as she had the night she received the news of his death; in that moment, her loss was as fresh as it had been that very first day, and she almost couldn't breathe with the agony. He'd been pulled away from her a second time.

When she could catch her breath and dry her eyes without them immediately refilling with tears, she looked at his picture, which smiled at her from the nightstand. She had never spent a night where she could not see that picture. Not before his death. Not after it. She looked at him now, and he seemed farther away than he had ever been, as if she had somehow failed a test, and because of her failure even her memory of him was being stretched thin and pale and hollow.

His dress blues bore ribbons from tours in Germany and Italy and Saudi Arabia—testament to his love for his country; the jaunty angle of his flight cap told of his eternal optimism; and the warm reassurance in his eyes spoke of his love for her. He'd told her he'd been thinking of her when the picture was taken; that he'd wanted her to know that he loved her and that he would always be with her.

That smile and those eyes had seemed like a betrayal the night she received the news that he was dead.

It had been a stupid, pointless accident. He was on his way home, taking a bus from the base, and the bus skidded on a patch of black ice and rolled. It was a bad accident; the bus looked like a tin can run over by a truck. But everyone walked—or at least crawled—away from it, except for Brian. It could have been anyone else. It *should* have been anyone else. But it wasn't.

The doctor told her Brian had been killed instantly, that he'd experienced no pain; the base chaplain offered her what little comfort he could; Brian's friends cried and told her what a great guy he had been; the other Air Force wives came around with baked goods and hugs and tears.

The funeral was closed-casket, but she knew Brian was really in there. Really gone. She could feel it in the emptiness of the planet, in the hollowness of her heart, the way the world no longer had enough air in it. He was gone, his promise broken, and the dream that had hung so tantalizingly before her was a lie.

Then here, lying in her bed feeling something of him hanging close to her, feeling the magic that was her birthright flowing through her veins, she had thought perhaps his promise had meant something more than the words lovers tell each other to hold the darkness at bay—that perhaps she might have him back again, might cheat death, might truly win him from Death's grasp.

Death laughed instead. It was the ultimate reality, and Brian was gone forever, and she had been foolish to think that even magic might let her see him again, touch him again, make her even for one more moment the complete human being she had been only when he was in her life. The echoes she felt of him when she moved between the worlds were just that, weren't they? Echoes.

She wanted to scream and throw her parents' book across the room. She wanted, for just an instant, to die. She wanted to believe that Brian would be waiting for her on the other side of Death. She wanted to hate him for leaving her behind, alone, when after a lifetime of emptiness and loneliness she had finally found the love she had hungered for. If magic couldn't give him back to her, what good was it?

She got out of bed, shivering in the cold room, and walked to the window. The bare trees in front of her clawed at the moon; nothing soft or friendly about them now. The harsh white moon glared down at her. No sound echoed into the well of silence in which she stood.

She studied the darkness outside, the icy, fierce world beyond her little puddle of warmth and light. She glared up at the stars, spattered through the infinite velvet black of space, promising worlds and wonders beyond her reach. She thought, I never wanted much. My little bit of time and space, my small corner of order and love and direction, my few people to give my universe boundaries and borders and a reason for existing. Brian . . . Jake . . . me. I accepted the loss of my parents. I accepted that we three were all we had.

But I want him back, and I can feel him out there, and I won't just stand idly by and concede defeat if there is any way, *any* way, that I can undo the awful injustice that stole him from me.

She understood the Greek hero who strode into Hell to win back his love. She would have gladly faced the rigors of a quest that had a clear objective and clear rules. Go into Hell, take what you want, fight your way out, don't look back.

She could have done it. She would have.

Just tell me what to do.

That wouldn't happen—her parents' book mentioned nothing about raising the dead, summoning lost loves, giving flesh to ghosts. No simple quest, no clear-cut rules, nothing but a slippery feeling that she might be able to do . . . something.

She lifted her chin and pulled back her shoulders. "Might be able to do something." How many widows ever got even that much?

She kicked her feet into terry slippers and pulled on a thick robe and strode down the front stairs. She walked to the mirror in the foyer and stood there, glaring into it, willing the green fire to come to her. At first the mirror stayed dark; perhaps she was not hungry enough for the touch of the other world, or perhaps she was still too shaken by her dream of Brian. She touched the dark mirror, pressing her face close so that she could look into the black pools of her reflection's eyes. What knowledge had her parents hidden inside of her? What secrets lay buried within her scarred memory? And of what importance was her information to anyone else? According to Embar, her parents had died for it. Again according to him, there were people who would be willing to kill her for it.

She had to find out what it was.

She thought of Jake, wondering what would happen to him if someone came after her. Fear warred with anger—and in her reflection's eyes, the green fire crackled and faraway thunder rumbled.

She kept the fire at a distance this time—she did not summon it all the way to her. The gate remained closed, but when she held her palms in front of the mirror, she could feel the energy crackling through them, willing her to pull it closer, willing her to join with it. She wanted only to feel the magic, to listen to the storm running through her veins.

With the cold green fire thrumming against her fingertips, she closed her eyes and let herself simply feel the movement of the magic. At first she could feel nothing but the surge and crackle of the bit that brushed her palms—but with her eyes closed and her senses open, that began to change.

Almost as if while entranced by the touch of a single wave she slowly allowed herself to hear the crashing of the surf, she discovered that once she let herself experience the flow of the magical energy, she could see it as a web that spun all around her, lines of brighter energy spinning out in all directions. She might have been the tiny spider in the heart of a vast web, but the spiderwebs she knew had a delicate order, a coherent shape, a sense of direction and purpose. The web of magic that surrounded her had none of those things. The brighter areas all connected to each other, crossing from her world down into Oria without any apparent barrier, then stretching deeper than that. The web flowed upward, too—but the upward-reaching tendrils seemed stunted and shriveled and terrifying in a way she could neither define nor comprehend.

She concentrated on the one thing she wanted within the energy flow: She called to Brian.

The power coursed beneath her fingertips, surging, swelling, humming. She communed with it, offering it everything she knew of Brian, everything she remembered and had ever loved. She asked the void and the vastness only one thing—If he is in there, if he still exists, if he still knows me and loves me as I know and love him . . . bring him to me.

She was certain that if she stepped into the gate, she would be able to feel the answer more clearly; she had no doubt that, pouring directly through her flesh and nerves and sinews and blood, the magic would speak to her clearly. But while Jake slept upstairs in his bed, helpless and tiny, she would not separate herself from him even to that extent. She would read the answer of the magic only with her fingertips, only at a distance. And if the void returned no answer to her, in the morning she would take Jake and ask the question again.

She waited, watching the magical storm in the mirror, feeling and somehow hearing in the silent creaking of the house the thunder of a tempest a world and a time away. She shivered from the cold, and perhaps from more than that.

And suddenly in the glass, eyes that were not hers but were as familiar to her as her own looked out at her. No sound, no warning; one instant she saw only herself, and in the next, she saw Brian. She almost screamed.

He rested his hands against the other side of the mirror as if he were looking at her through a regular window. He looked just as she remembered him; tall and lean and handsome, dressed in the black T-shirt and BDUs he'd worn the last time she saw him alive. He smiled at her, and she started to cry.

"Brian."

His lips moved, but she couldn't hear him.

"I can't hear you," she said, and then she managed to read his lips. He was saying, "I can't hear you."

The wall of a universe stood between them, but if she could pass through it, could he? The gate could work both ways. Left open, it would not close again until something went through in one direction or the other. If the something that came through was Brian . . .

She pressed her hands into the surface of the mirror and recklessly willed the gate open.

The storm was, for just an instant, upon her. The green fire flashed across the surface of the mirror and illuminated the room, the seductive thrum of magic begged her to immerse herself in its embrace. But this time she stepped back, beckoned Brian to come to her.

The mirror bowed outward beneath his pressing hands, then poured away from him as he stepped through, almost as if he were rising out of a glass-smooth lake face first. The green fire died, and he was standing before her so close that she could feel the warmth of his skin, that she could smell his aftershave, so close that she could reach out and touch him. With a trembling hand, she did, and her fingers touched the warm, solid flesh of his forearm—the soft furring of golden hairs, the hard muscles, the smooth, perfect skin.

Suddenly she couldn't breathe and couldn't see, her throat was so tight and her eyes so full of tears. "Oh, Brian," she whispered, and fell into his embrace, wrapping her arms around his neck and sobbing into his shirt. "Oh, God, Brian, you're really here." She felt the strength of the arms that wrapped around her, the hands that held her, the chest against which she pressed herself, and she tipped her head back to kiss him, as she had dreamed of kissing him, as she had yearned to kiss him. And he pulled away, slowly shaking his head no.

"Brian," she whispered, stunned, aching.

"I'm not your Brian," he told her in the voice that she would never forget, that she would never stop loving.

"You are. You *are*. You're back with me now, and everything is going to be okay." But he was shaking his head. No. No.

She wanted to scream. "Yes!" she said. "I got you back. You're mine now. Death loses. I don't have to let you go."

And he said, "I wasn't dead. I've never been dead." He frowned, and she could see hurt in his eyes as he told her, "You're a Lauren, but you're not *my* Lauren. My Lauren is six months pregnant with our second child. I'm separating from the Air Force in three weeks, and we're moving back to Charlotte so I can start the security business."

Brian's security business. His dream, the thing he wanted to do when he got out. He'd talked about it endlessly. And now he said he was going to make it happen. Except not with her. With some other Lauren. Some pregnant Lauren.

"How can this be?" she whispered. "Where have you been, and what do you mean you aren't my Brian, that you have some other Lauren. Look at me." She spread her arms wide. "Look at me."

He said, "My Lauren is a gateweaver. You are, too, or I wouldn't be here. I've been through the gates with her a lot of times." He smiled. "She's giving it up for a while—give us time to spend with the kids, her parents, my parents—"

"Her *parents*?"

"Sure."

"My parents are dead."

"I'm sorry. Different universe, different rules."

She was shaking. "Tell me. Tell me what you know."

He nodded. "I don't have long. The more time I spend here, the closer my presence pulls your world and mine— I'm an anomaly. You know about the upworld, the downworld, fronttime, backtime, sideways?"

"Upworld and downworld. I've only been downworld that I can remember, though when I was a kid. The rest . . ." She shrugged.

He frowned. "You should know this. You should already know the danger you face in calling me."

"There have been some problems," she said, but didn't elaborate.

"Quickly, then. Fronttime is the world that runs ahead of yours timewise, but on the same track. You can only reach the parts of it that exist after you die—but those parts change from day to day. If you take up smoking one day, you may find that you can reach a spot twenty years closer to you than you could reach the day before—the result of your decision will, if things remain as they are, cut your life shorter by twenty years. If you give up smoking the next day, you may find those same twenty years inaccessible again. Fronttime is dangerous to enter—you arrive solid, and you can interact and make changes . . . but if you do, you're barred from going back. All of the time behind the moment when you changed things becomes your past. Backtime is the same. You can only go to the times when you didn't exist. You're barred from the moment of your conception on. And you don't arrive in solid form—

you're almost a spirit, same as you would be going upworld."

"I know about upworld."

"Okay. You can't make physical changes in backtime, but you can sometimes influence decisions, make suggestions. No magic—you can't do any more in either fronttime or backtime than you can do here."

"Sideways?"

"Sideways is where you called me from. Worlds that exist in parallel with yours. The ones close to yours are pretty much the same. The ones farther out become increasingly different. You cannot go into a sideways world in which you are already alive."

"Which is why you're here, but you aren't my Brian."

He nodded. "I'm sorry. And you can't stay in any of your sideways worlds. The link between the two starts tearing at reality."

"So even if I could find a Brian who had lost his Lauren, and who wanted to be with me . . ."

"It wouldn't work out. At most you would have a couple of hours together before things started to break through. You could only dare to see each other rarely."

"How rarely?"

"A few times a year, I would guess. Repeated crossings start thinning the fabric of reality between the two worlds, and breakthroughs become more and more common even as the duration of your safe visits becomes shorter and shorter."

"Is there any way I can get him back?"

Brian bit his lip. "Not in any form that you would want him."

"But I can feel his presence sometimes. I can feel him when I cross between the worlds, watching over me. I can hear his voice. I can feel his touch."

"I can't explain that. I don't know any more about what happens to us when we die than you do. But from Lauren— *my* Lauren—I know this: Death is the door you dare not open."

"He's right there and I can feel him and I can't have him back? I can't do some sort of magic to bring him all the way back?"

"No."

"There are an infinite number of worlds in which he lives—"

"And an infinite number of worlds in which he has died. That truth is the same for each of us."

"Infinite."

"Yes."

"And I *can't* have him back?"

"That's right."

"I would move Heaven and Hell to be with him again."

Brian—the Brian who was not her Brian, who studied her with compassionate eyes but without the love that she had felt from *her* Brian—said, "And on the far side of Heaven and Hell, perhaps he waits for you. But you cannot bring him back from there. You can only go to meet him."

"I can die."

"Someday. Not right now."

"I can die."

"That's all."

"I can create with a breath, with a thought—I can build and destroy with just a wish and the blink of my eye. I can walk between the worlds, I can summon storms and level mountains. And you're telling me that I cannot have *my* Brian back?"

"You and your world and your universe pay a price for every action you take. You can walk between the worlds and you can summon storms and you can level mountains, Lauren, but you . . . are . . . not . . . a . . . god." His voice grew soft. He rested his hands on her shoulders and they were the hands she had known and loved and lost, and her knees went weak and her eyes blurred with tears. They were the hands she wanted to have back, and in the voice she wanted to hear whispering to her from the other side of the bed every morning for the rest of her life, the man who was not hers told her, "You are only human, but because you can reach beyond your own world, you can screw things up for yourself and everyone in it so completely that the entire planet might not survive. Your action could destroy it."

"The whole planet?"

He nodded.

She wanted to scream, It isn't fair! She wanted to point a finger at him and say, You will be *my* Brian from now on. She wanted to unmake the world she lived in and remake it as a world in which her Brian still lived.

But she was not a god. And somewhere in her core, somewhere deep inside where the buried memories had not all resurfaced, an absolute conviction that this man was telling her the truth surfaced. She could not raise the dead—or perhaps she could, but what she raised would not be what she wanted. Her Brian was gone, gone somewhere beyond her farthest reach. Nothing she could do would restore him to her as he had been, as she wanted him to be again. He had been mortal and he had died, and she was mortal and she would have to live with that truth, and the pain, until she too died and found out whether anything waited for her beyond the dark void of Death.

She hung her head and fought to control her breathing; clenched her fists tight to her sides and gritted her teeth and squeezed her eyes tightly shut until the tears stopped forming. "Why did you come when I called?" she asked when at last she had control of her voice.

"Because I love your . . . twin, for lack of better words . . . with all my heart and soul. Because she heard you and begged me to respond before someone—or something—else came in my place."

At his words, Lauren's flesh crawled, and her blood chilled. "What do you mean?"

"Any Brian from any of an infinite number of worlds could have responded to your call, depending on how loudly you called and how hard you pushed. But not every Brian loves you. Not everyone who would come to your summons would wish you well. For every Brian who would move the world to love you if he could, there is a Brian who would move the world to hurt you. And you cannot know when you call who will come."

She thought of Jake, lying innocent and trusting in his bed upstairs, and of how quick she had been to let the man who looked like Brian step into her home. How ready she had been to trust him, to want him. He could have been anyone, anything . . . but because she wanted so much to have Brian back, she would not have questioned him until it was too late. Had he wanted to hurt her, this Brian could have stepped through the mirror, destroyed her and Jake, and vanished without a trace. She shivered, and Brian nodded.

"You see the danger."

"Yes," she whispered, wrapping her arms around herself, staring at him.

"Good." He turned. "I don't dare stay any longer. Things begin to fall apart quickly in both worlds when we step sideways—I won't jeopardize *my* Lauren and *my* Jake. I need to get back."

She nodded, not speaking. She stared at the back of his neck, at the vulnerability of it—the curve down to his shoulders, the close-cropped line of his hair. She could have drawn that gentle slope in her sleep; she could close her eyes and know what it would feel like to lie in bed, her arm thrown over him, her face pressed to that spot at the back of his neck, breathing his scent. So close. So close she could reach out and touch him, but he was not hers and could never be hers again. "Do I need to send you home?"

"If you'll open the gate for me, I can find my own way home."

She moved past him, being careful not to brush against him; at that moment she could not bear the thought of his touch, of knowing it would be the last touch. She pressed her palms to the mirror and willed the fire and the storm to her, and when the glass blazed with the otherworldly flames, she stepped back.

"Thank you," she managed to tell him. Her voice was in control, her shoulders were back, her head held high. She did not try to smile—that would have been too much for her to carry off.

He rested a hand lightly on her shoulder, and said, "For every door that closes, a window opens somewhere else."

Brian's saying. *Her* Brian's saying. Her fists clenched again, and she nodded, unable to speak around the lump that had returned to her throat.

Then he was gone.

CHAPTER 8

Cat Creek, North Carolina

ERIC, HEADING INTO the tiny renovated storefront that served as headquarters for Cat Creek's Sheriff's Department, caught a glimpse through the front window of Pete Stark, with his feet up on the desk and his nose buried in a book. By the time the door slammed shut and he got around the corner, though, Pete's feet were on the floor and he had paperwork spread out in front of him.

"I don't care if you read."

Pete blushed. "I know."

"Not too crazy about you having your feet up on the desk, though—doesn't look too good to the people who see you when they drive by. And since they're the ones who pay your salary—and mine . . ."

Pete sighed. "I got in early. Hoped you'd heard something about the Molly McColl case."

"I'm still not even sure we have a case. Girl hasn't been back home, but there's nothing to say she didn't just go out of town for a week to visit family and think that she shut her door behind her when she didn't."

"I know. Doesn't feel like that to me, though."

Eric nodded. "Doesn't feel like that to me, either. I have some errands I have to run today—you're going to have the place to yourself for a while."

"Anything big?"

Eric shrugged. "Mostly, no. I have one possible lead on what might be the Molly McColl case if we do have a case, and I'm going to check that out in a while, but mostly I just have some housekeeping to do."

"I'll give you a call if things get interesting."

Eric raised an eyebrow. "And interesting would be . . . ?"

"Riots in the streets, vagrants on the benches, naked women on the green." Pete grinned just a little and said, "Though if we had naked women on the green, I could probably handle that myself."

Like Eric, Pete was single, though unlike Eric, he had never been married. He was a good-looking kid, burly and easygoing, and Eric gave him another two years in Cat Creek before the boredom of the place and the lack of young, single women drove him to a bigger town.

"I'm certain you could." He yawned and shook his head. "For anything but naked women, then, you give me a call, all right?"

Pete tipped his head and studied Eric through narrowed eyes. "*You* all right, boss?"

"Not sleeping too well lately."

"Had company?"

"I wish."

"You want to go home and get some rest, I'll hold down the fort."

"Appreciate it—but today is not the day."

By the time Eric was back in the cruiser, Pete's nose was back in the book. At least this time his feet weren't on the desk.

Granger had the watch when Eric went into the upper room of the flower shop.

"Quiet?"

"Not on my shift. I took over from Willie at one—he said he didn't have a blip. But a rogue gate opened twice on my watch, and there was a power surge. Vectors point to the same house."

"Lauren Dane."

"Sure looks like it."

Eric grimaced. A traitor, from a family of traitors. It figured. He didn't like thinking of her that way, but what the hell. People were what they were, and teenage crushes never changed basic truth.

"I'll take the next watch. You go on to whatever you had to do."

He had a plan, but because he didn't know which of the Sentinels was working with Lauren, he didn't want anyone around to find out what he was up to. He had a hard time thinking that Granger might be the traitor on the inside, or that he might have been the person responsible for bringing such potential devastation to Cat Creek, but he had to face facts. *He* wasn't the traitor, and *June Bug* wasn't the traitor. But any of the others might be.

"I'll be at home asleep," Granger told him. "Probably with the help of a couple of Seconal. I haven't had a real minute's rest since . . ."

His voice trailed off, and Eric nodded. "Me, either. Hope your sleep goes better than mine."

When Granger was gone, Eric opened the gate in the mirror and settled himself inside of it, a pad of paper, a straight edge, a protractor, a compass, and a pencil on his lap. He was determined to get the vectors right; he wouldn't accuse Lauren Dane without being as certain as possible that she was the one responsible for Molly's disappearance, and that meant making sure to within a fraction of a degree that her house was the source of the rogue disturbances—and that she was the one causing them. It might take some fast footwork on his part, but he had the plan, he had the tools, and, thanks to Pete, he had the time.

Sitting bathed in the energy of the gate, he began to revive. He let himself absorb some of the power that flowed between the worlds; usually the Sentinels tried to take nothing and leave nothing behind, but he would be useless if he couldn't stay awake.

By the time he felt the gate open, he was alert, well rested, and ready for anything. He quickly plotted out the vector, and his heart sank. The gate was Lauren's. If he hurried, he could get over to her house, and if she had gone through, he could make sure he was waiting for her when she came back out. He'd considered tracking her through to Oria, but memories of the storm that had come attached to her spell made him think that when he confronted her, he didn't want to have to deal with any magic she might throw at him.

He took off down the back stairs, gave a cursory wave to Nancine, told her not to worry about watch—that he was on it—and took off for Lauren's house.

He left the cruiser running and knocked on the front door first—after all, the gate might have opened because Lauren was returning, not leaving. But she didn't answer, even though her car was parked beneath the portico. He got back in the cruiser, drove it around back of the house, and parked it out of sight of the street, behind the dilapidated old workshop.

Then he broke into her house through the back. He felt bad about it, but he had to catch her stepping out of the mirror. He had to. He had to know for himself that she was the one using the gate, that there was no mistake—because he wasn't going to be either kind or understanding to the traitor who had threatened the survival of his world, and he didn't want to accuse the wrong person.

Once inside, he locked the back door again, found a comfortable chair that gave him a good view of the mirror in the hallway without making his presence immediately obvious to anyone stepping out of the mirror, and settled down for what might turn out to be a long wait.

Natta Cottage, Ballahara

With Jake on her hip and her parents' notebook tucked under her arm, Lauren went through the gate to find Embar. She had to talk to someone about Brian, and Embar was the only living creature she knew that she dared confront.

But something was wrong at her parents' old cottage in Oria. She should have stepped through the mirror into the inside of the house, but instead she stepped through the other side of the mirror into a snowdrift behind the house, facing the boarded-shut back door. From where she stepped out, she could see that the once-pristine snow had been trampled all around the outside of the house, and frozen spatters of pink dotted the snowdrifts beneath some of the boarded-over windows, reminding her uncomfortably of blood.

Her grip tightened around Jake. She held still, listening for any sound of intruders, but the only sounds in the clearing were the whistling of the wind over the top of the chimney and the irregular creaking of the front door. The intruders must have left it open.

She debated going straight back through the gate, but in Oria, she commanded considerable magic. If anyone were hanging around her house, she would be able to take care of them with a word. She did put some thought into what that word would be if anyone came bounding out of the shadows at her; she readied a spell that would freeze any intruders as solid as the icicles that hung from the gables and hold them frozen long enough for her to dispose of them appropriately.

With the word that would summon her prepared spell at the ready, she marched through the beaten-down snow around the house to the front door, and, with her heart thumping erratically, cautiously stepped inside. Destruction greeted her. Someone had smashed the old furniture—the rocking chair, the table, the other chairs. Someone had shredded the old quilts that had been folded in the bedroom and flung the shreds and the stuffing all around in a frenzy. Someone had smashed every one of the heavy brown stoneware plates to the floor, had shattered the stoneware mugs, had taken a hammer and destroyed the little hand pump that had brought water into the kitchen. The stream of water had eventually frozen, but not before it had created a glassy pool over much of the floor.

The destruction had been very thorough. It had also been very . . . showy. She frowned. Whoever had broken into the old house had gone methodically from cabinet to cabinet, from drawer to drawer, and had pulled out and destroyed each item in turn. Nothing had been spared, nothing had been overlooked. But nothing was missing, either. Whoever had done this had wanted to leave the largest possible mess—he hadn't been looking for something specific or even for anything worth stealing.

The destruction had been the point. In which case, why not just set the place on fire and be done with it?

She walked deeper into the house, skirting the icy spots on the floor, braced for any movement, for any attack. The bedroom door was closed. She didn't like that. It seemed out of character—closed doors left an appearance of neatness, hiding what was certainly more devastation, when an open door would have permitted her to see the scope of the wreckage all at once.

Carefully, with the word that would summon her spell on her tongue, she opened the door.

And quickly shielded Jake's eyes from the sight that greeted them.

Embar was in the room—or what was left of him. He'd been stabbed in a dozen places, mutilated, and nailed to the far wall. Written on the wall in blood were the words, "Think you're ready to play in our league?" Embar was dead, frozen, the frost whiting out his open eyes.

She could not help him. Dead was dead, as Brian had told her only hours before—the one unfixable thing in the universe, even for those with the powers of gods. She could not save him, but she could endanger her son by staying around. And that she would not do.

Later, she promised Embar, backing out of the room. Later, she would find a way to return, to take him down from the wall and give him decent burial and say a few words that expressed her grief and her loss—the loss of her only link to her true childhood, and the loss of a friend she had only just rediscovered.

Later.

First she had to save her son, and herself.

Cat Creek

Lauren came through the mirror clutching her little boy and a thick black notebook, her eyes wild and her hair in disarray, and from his secluded chair in the corner of the sitting room Eric could feel her fear. She dropped the notebook, which skidded across the smooth wooden floor toward him, and she turned on the mirror she had just stepped out of as if it were her enemy and shoved a hand against it hard, and slammed the gate tight behind her. As if, he thought, something was after her.

He waited, making no sound, but he rested his hand on the butt of his handgun and soundlessly clicked the safety off. The possibilities of what might come bursting through the mirror in pursuit ticked through his mind. Her coconspirator; one of Oria's many troublesome creatures; or something genuinely evil. Like renegades from among the ranks of the Old Gods. Sideslippers. Or perhaps the thing behind the spell-gone-wrong that was causing the spreading flu epidemic on Earth.

He watched her shift her little boy to the other hip and jog right past him and hit the steps at a run; she was saying, "We're going to pack, sweetie, and we're going to get out of here right now. Right now. We can rent a hotel room for a little while—just a little while, and then maybe we'll be able to rent someplace else to live. We'll manage." He heard her choking up as she headed up the stairs, and he realized that she was crying. "There are other places in the world. I promise. Better places than this."

Eric heard her running through the upstairs, heard doors opened hard and shoved against walls, heard her dragging open drawers and flinging their contents on the floor.

With one eye on the mirror, he edged over to the notebook lying on the floor. He flipped it open and skimmed it, paused over carefully rendered diagrams and neatly penned instructions, and as he realized what he held in his hands, his heart beat faster and his mouth went dry. The Sentinels had suspected the Hotchkisses of unauthorized experimentation with magic, but that charge, unlike the others, had never been proven. Now, though, he had proof. What he held in his hand was a complete record of their transgressions. Years worth of experiments, of gambles taken when every roll of the dice might mean the end of Earth, or just their part of it.

He didn't have enough—yet—to charge Lauren with the

abduction of Molly McColl, but he certainly had enough to take her in for questioning. Quietly, though. No fuss, nothing called in over the scanner. He didn't want to alert her partner inside the Sentinels.

He considered her state of anxiety, and thought he had a good plan for moving her with the least amount of fuss.

He was standing just inside the door, facing the foot of the staircase, when she appeared at the top landing. She'd changed into lighter clothing and she held the boy on one hip and a duffel bag with the name Dane stenciled on its side in the other hand. He recognized the bag as military issue. The dead husband's. She started down the stairs, watching her feet as she came down them dragging the heavy bag; she still had not seen him. Her cheeks were streaked with tears, but she was no longer crying.

He said, "Lauren, we need to talk."

Her head snapped up and she stared at him and he could see her starting to scream—but then she didn't. Her eyes went hard and cold and dangerous, and she said, "If you're the one behind that mess"—and she nodded toward the mirror—"just get out of my way. You've won. We're leaving. But if you try to touch my son, so help me God, I'll dig your eyes out with my thumbs and rip your head off with my bare hands."

She sounded serious. More, she looked almost convincing. He wouldn't test her, he thought, unless he absolutely had to. Women could be vicious fighters.

Instead, he said, "I know what you are."

And she snarled, "That goes both ways, honey. I know what you are, too. And your parents, and some of the other freaks in this evil, awful town. I should never have come back. Never."

She reached the bottom of the stairs, and he found himself looking her straight in the eye. She was taller than he'd realized; her height always took him a little bit by surprise, because she had always struck him as being rather delicate, a state he didn't equate with height.

"Well, you probably shouldn't have, but you did. And now I need you to come down to the station with me for a while; we have to talk."

"And I'll get into your car with my son and that will be the last anyone ever sees of either of us." She saw that he was holding her book. "Give me that. It doesn't belong to you."

"For the time being, it does. And nothing is going to happen to you if you come with me. I swear it. I don't know what you're running from, though I can imagine some of the possibilities. I do know that I won't hurt you or your son, and I won't let anyone else hurt the two of you." She was a traitor, he thought. A traitor to her species, to her world, to her universe—just as her parents had been traitors. But when he looked at her, he didn't see a traitor. He saw a seventeen-year-old girl with dreams of faraway places, with a hunger to see the world; and he saw a spring afternoon when he got up the nerve, just once, to steal a kiss, and to find that kiss returned.

"Am I under arrest?"

"Not yet. But if you don't come with me voluntarily, you will be. Voluntary is better."

And she studied him with those haunted, fear-filled eyes, and she looked at her son, who clung to her shoulder. "Let's go."

Pete jumped and dropped his book, and his boots clattered off the desktop to the floor. "Didn't hear you come in," he said, and had the grace to looked embarrassed.

"Came in through the back." Eric hung the cruiser's keys on the pegboard next to his coffee cup, and said, "We're going to be in the back talking for a bit. You have everything unless there's an emergency."

Pete arched an eyebrow, nodded toward the woman and her son, but said nothing.

"Molly McColl case."

Now Pete's eyebrows nearly slid off his face. "Her?"

"Don't know. That's why I'm questioning her."

"Good Lord." Pete shook his head. "Let you know if anything comes up, then . . ." Eric could see that the deputy was just dying to ask him why he was questioning a young mama with her baby on her hip. Eric couldn't tell him. Not in any way that wouldn't make him sound insane, anyway. He just gave Pete a "shut up" look and pointed Lauren down the hall to the break room, which sometimes had to double for an interrogation room. He could have talked to her in one of the two cells, he supposed, but he wanted her to feel comfortable. If she thought he trusted her, she would be more willing to tell him what he needed to know—and he needed to know a lot, and fast.

When Lauren was seated in the break room with a cup of coffee for her and a cup of juice for Jake, Eric excused himself for a moment and went back to the front desk.

"We're not here," he told Pete. "If anyone—and I mean *anyone*—asks where I am or what I'm doing, I'm following up leads to the Molly McColl case up in Rockingham. You've never seen her, she's never been here, and you don't know anything. Got it?"

He nodded. "Who is she?"

"Lauren Dane. Right now she's the chief suspect in the abduction."

"Her? You've got to be joking."

"Not a word."

"That little darlin' would never hurt a fly."

Eric considered the fury he'd seen in her when she threatened to gouge his eyes out, and gave Pete a knowing smile. "You just keep thinking that. People need their illusions."

"How are you doing?" he asked Lauren when he walked back into the break room.

"I'd be better if I knew what was going on."

"Well, why don't we start by you just telling me what you were doing in Oria that had you coming back so scared you were going to run away from home."

"I think I should have a lawyer."

Eric shook his head slowly. "Not for this, Lauren. Lawyers are for the little things—but the secrets of the Sentinels and the gates stay between us. Always. When you start walking across universes, the laws of North Carolina stop applying to you. And you're here on something that didn't start in this world. So. What scared you over there?"

"You have to let me go if you don't arrest me."

Eric frowned at her. "I can hold you for twenty-four hours

on suspicion, and during that time I don't have to let you let anyone know you're here. Because I don't trust your cronies, that's what I'll have to do if you don't start giving me some answers to my questions. I'm being friendly, Lauren. I'm being friendly in spite of the trouble you've caused, and that's mostly because I remember who you used to be. I don't know who the hell you are now."

She didn't react the way he expected her to. He didn't see any flash of guilt cross her face, she didn't stammer, she didn't look angry. For a moment she just looked lost. "My *cohorts*?" She shook her head. "Look here, Eric MacAvery—you're the one with *cohorts*. Your blessed Sentinels are the people who murdered my parents, who killed my friend in Oria, and who are coming after me and Jake now. So don't you give me any of your nonsense about cohorts. Jake and I are all we have in the world."

It was Eric's turn to feel baffled. "Your parents weren't murdered. They were killed in a car accident."

"Their brake lines were cut, and their steering was tampered with."

"That's ridiculous. Their deaths were investigated."

"By Sentinels."

"By . . ." He was going to say "by the Sheriff's Department"—but the previous sheriff had been a Sentinel, too. In Cat Creek, the Sentinels made sure they kept their own in power. They couldn't afford to have anyone in authority looking into their activities. That meant they had to *be* the authorities. From time to time the system led to abuses.

"Do you have proof?" he asked her instead.

"I did. Until this morning. I found my witness nailed to the wall in my parents' house in Oria."

Eric stared at her in disbelief. "Someone is nailed to the wall in your parents' house and we're sitting here *chatting*? Just when did you intend to mention this?"

"I didn't," she said. "If you already knew about it, I didn't need to. If you didn't know about it, there isn't anything you could do."

"Who's dead? Who was your witness?"

"Embar. A friend from my childhood."

"Embar what? I don't recognize the name."

"Just Embar. He was a goroth."

Eric rubbed his index finger up and down the bridge of his nose, trying to rub away the headache that was building. "Right . . . and what's a goroth."

"You're a Sentinel. You've been to Oria, right?"

"That's classified information. And we aren't talking about me, anyway."

"Don't play word games, Eric. Have you been to Oria?"

He looked at her levelly. Something had happened to her. She knew something important. He could afford to give her a little information of his own to gain some reciprocity. "Yes. Of course."

"Then you know the goroths, though maybe that isn't what you call them. Little guys with big ears, ugly as hell, wrinkled and kind of gray . . ."

He held up a hand to stop her. "You're talking about a member of one of the indigenous Orian species."

"I am."

"Sentinels keep their presence hidden from the indigenous population. At least they're supposed to. You start tampering with the people from there, you can buy exactly the sort of trouble . . ." He stared at her, comprehension dawning. "Exactly the sort of trouble we have now. You've had contact with them."

"Just one. And now he's dead. Nailed to the wall of my parents' old house there, with a warning to me written in his blood."

Eric paled. "What did it say?"

" 'So you think you're ready to play in the big leagues' . . . something like that."

"Signed?"

"No."

"Written in what language?"

"English. Only one I speak."

Eric nodded, hiding his confusion and his sense that he'd hit a major snag in his theory somewhere with the professional persona of the cop asking questions. "And you have known this . . . goroth . . . for how long?"

"Since I was old enough to walk. Maybe longer than that. But I hadn't seen him since I . . ." She faltered, and he saw evasion in her eyes. "Since I was a kid. Until I came back here, that is, and discovered the mirror."

"And he was dead when you got there?"

"Had been for a while. His eyes were frosted over from the cold."

"Anything else?"

"The house had been trashed. Nothing taken that I could see, but everything in the house was destroyed in such a way that it made the biggest visible mess possible."

"Someone trying to scare you off."

"Obviously."

"Off from what, Lauren?"

She stared into his eyes and said, "I don't know."

Though he couldn't explain why, he believed her.

"So someone is threatening you. Maybe coming after you."

"It looks that way."

"Tell me who you're working with. Tell me who your insider is—chances are that's the person who wants to hurt you."

"My insider?" Lauren leaned back in her chair, tipped her head to one side, and frowned at him. "*My* insider. Inside *what?*"

"Please don't play games here, Lauren. Your life and your child's life could be in danger. You need to tell me what you know."

"I am. But you're going to have to explain a few things. I just moved back here after being gone for years. The entire time I was gone, I had no contact with anyone in the town at all. The only reason I came back here was because I found my parents' house listed for sale on the Internet at about the same time that I got Brian's death benefit. I felt like I had a home with Brian, but once he was gone . . ." She shrugged and looked away. "At the time, moving back here seemed like a good idea."

"So you're saying that moving back to a Sentinel town where your parents were branded as traitors never seemed to you like an . . . *odd* . . . decision?"

She sighed, looked at him again, and said, "I didn't know about that."

"But you know about it now."

"I do."

"What changed?"

She was quiet for a long time, searching his face for only she knew what, and from her expression, not finding whatever it was she was looking for. Voice heavy with frustration, she said, "I don't know you, Eric. I thought I knew the person you were when we were both in school, but that was a long time ago, and things change. My parents were murdered in this town, and the fact that their deaths were covered up makes it pretty clear the Sheriff's Department was involved. And that means the Sentinels. You weren't in office then, but you are in office now—so I can count on the fact that you represent Authority—capital 'A.' Which means you're pals with whoever killed my parents, even if you weren't in on it yourself."

She looked away from him.

"You're saying you don't trust me?"

"I'm saying I *can't*. There's a difference."

"You can."

She was watching her son, who had climbed down from her lap and was eyeing a doughnut box sitting next to the coffeemaker. "Don't touch, Jake."

Jake turned to face her, and his bottom lip popped out, and he said, "No." And then he reached for the box.

She was fast. She'd jumped from her chair and grabbed him away from doughnuts and coffee machine before Eric had done more than start to move from his seat.

The kid screamed—a furious, cat-caught-in-a-clothes-dryer banshee howl that stopped Eric dead.

Lauren was telling him, "I said don't touch," but it was like listening to someone talking to an air-raid siren. Eric had never heard so much noise from such a tiny source in his life.

Then she was back in her seat with the screaming, kicking two-year-old pinned firmly to her lap. Eric tried to think of what to say, but the noise shut down all thought as effec-

tively as any Chinese water torture. All he could think was,
Make it stop.

"He can have one of the damned doughnuts," he shouted.

"Not until he stops screaming and asks nicely, he can't,"
Lauren yelled back.

Like that was going to happen. Give him the goddamned
doughnut, Eric thought, watching the tears pouring down the
kid's face.

"Stop crying and ask nicely," Lauren was telling Jake in
normal tones, just as if she'd been talking to a sane person.
"Say, 'Please, biteys.' "

Miraculously, the kid turned off the tears. Shut down the
air-raid siren. Eric felt like someone had removed his head
from a vise. Snuffling heavily, and with his lower lip trembling, Jake said, "Please . . . biteys?"

"Now he may have a doughnut."

Eric pulled one out of the box—a plain one—and put it on
a Styrofoam plate and grabbed a handful of paper napkins
and handed the treat to Jake.

"Say thank you," Lauren said.

Jake eyed Eric with all the suspicion a jackal would have
for a lion who was hovering too close to his dinner. He
mulled over the whole deal, and only when Eric sat down,
and he was sure the doughnut wasn't going to be taken away,
did he say, "Fank you."

"You're welcome."

Jake picked up the doughnut and took a bite, and smiled
through a mouth full of crumbs.

Pity it wasn't going to be so easy to make the mother
happy. If he could just convince her that he was on her side,
he could find out what she knew. He didn't have time to play
around—whatever had started in Rockingham might already
be killing people. Every life that hung in the balance
weighed heavily on him; if he could save most of them, he
still would fail to save them all, and every single person mattered to someone, somewhere.

"And now that I can hear myself think again," he said,
grinning to show that he was a nice guy who could appreciate the humor of dealing with little kids, "let's talk."

She said, "Give me back my notebook, let me get my son someplace safe, and I'll tell you what I can."

"I can't do that, Lauren. There's too much at stake. You know what's at stake, don't you? I'm sure your partner has told you."

She tucked Jake to one side and leaned forward. "Look. I . . . don't . . . have . . . a partner. I don't know what you think I'm involved in, but I'm not. I'm a widowed mom with a little kid who has ended up in a dangerous place, and I don't know what's going on, and I don't have any answers for you, but whoever you think I am, *Sheriff*, you have the wrong person."

"I wish I could believe you, Lauren. I really do. I always kind of liked you when we were kids . . . but I have all sorts of evidence that points to you. Right now, I can link you to a kidnapping, to violations of the Sentinels' Code, and to a pending disaster so huge I still haven't completely wrapped my mind around it."

"I'm not a Sentinel, so the Sentinels' Code, whatever that might be, doesn't apply to me."

"It applies to any human who travels through the gates, because any human can make the sort of devastating changes you have made."

Her face closed down; she crossed her arms over her chest, pulling Jake in tight, and glared at him.

"If you've already made up your mind, I guess you'd better charge me, or whatever the hell it is you intend to do."

She wasn't going to tell him anything.

"I'm going to keep you in here as long as I legally can and let you think about all the people who are going to die if you don't tell me what is going on and who is behind it. You think about it hard, Lauren, because no matter what you think you have going, one of those people might be him." He nodded toward Jake. "One of them might be you. I'm going to have to go out, but Pete will let me know if you decide to remember that your first loyalty is to the rest of the human beings you share the planet with, and not to whoever has turned you to this . . . twisted power game you're playing."

"Fuck you," Lauren said softly. Jake turned and looked at her with interest.

Eric called down the hall to Pete. "She and the boy are going to spend the night in Two. Make sure nobody knows they're here—she doesn't get a phone call, she doesn't have visitors, and if anyone comes asking for her, you've never seen her and don't know where she might be. Got it?"

"Holding her for questioning?"

"The full twenty-four hours if necessary."

"Will do," Pete called back, and Lauren heard the jangling of keys and heavy footsteps in the hall.

"Time to go," Eric said.

"You're going to put Jake and me in a cell."

"Have to. As long as you're under observation, I know you won't be able to tip off your cohort."

"I don't *have* a cohort!"

"I wish that were true." He pointed her out into the hallway, down toward the cells. "Give them anything they need," he told Pete. "But no mirrors. And if anyone comes asking about them, you don't know *anything*, and you call me immediately to let me know who was asking. I'll be in to spell you at midnight."

Lauren watched Pete watching her. He looked like a typical Southern good old boy who'd grown up on deep-fried chicken and chicken-fried steak; a little round on the corners and a little slow to move. But the occasional glance he sent her way was cool, assessing, and intelligent. He wasn't impressed by the fact that she was female and attractive, and wouldn't be taken in by coy little pleas for a private trip to a rest room or a teary act about how wrong the sheriff was about her. Eric *was* wrong, but the deputy would, she thought, go exactly by the book.

Jake was curled contentedly against her stomach on the narrow mattress, sound asleep. It had to be close to midnight—time for the deputy to trade places with the sheriff. And it was quiet. The deputy had been reading in his chair in the hall the whole time, occasionally glancing over her way.

Metamagical Themas. Douglas Hofstadter. Lauren had read that one once—it had been fascinating: all about fractals and repeating patterns that complicated themselves by adding a tiny change with each repetition, and about strange mathematics.

Not an easy book. So he wasn't Deputy Dawg, even if he looked like Deputy Dawg. Probably didn't have to keep his bullet in his shirt pocket. Young and smart and cautious.

She started to drift off to sleep. No way she was going to be out of his sight, even for a minute.

Too bad, that. An unsupervised trip to the bathroom with Jake and she could be through a mirror and into Oria before the toilet finished flushing.

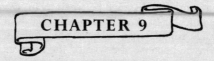

CHAPTER 9

Copper House, Ballahara

THE MOST PLAINLY attired veyâr Molly had yet seen stood framed in the arched doorway to her apartment. He was no taller than any of the other veyâr, but he carried about him an unmistakable aura of power. His skin was a soft gold, his hair darker gold, and his eyes rich, impenetrable jet-black from edge to edge. He was inordinately beautiful, almost angelic-looking. An angel with muddy boots.

"Fair Molly," he said, "I beg your indulgence and forgiveness. I have been too long away from home, and have only now returned; I came at once to greet you personally and welcome you to my home and my domain."

Molly, who had been sitting on the bed playing the guitar, working out a piece of music with fingers which had grown nimbler and stronger in the past few days, put the instrument aside and stood up. "You're the owner of this place then?"

"Seolar, Great High Imallin of Copper House and the Sheren River Domain." He bowed. "Owner of this house is but the smallest part of who I am. You may call me Seolar. Pehaps, if we become friends, you will call me Seo. And you are Molly McColl. The Vodi."

"So I've been told. Mind telling me what the Vodi *is?*"

"We'll discuss it tonight at the feast I'm having prepared for you. No crowds, no noise, no confusion—just you and me and some very good food and a chance for you to ask questions and for me to answer them. We'll have a formal banquet in your honor in the next few days, of course, but I thought you might like to have tonight just to . . . find things out."

He smiled. Molly did not return his smile. She watched him, measuring the distance between them, wondering how hard it would be to cross that space, take him down, hold him hostage for her own release. She could do it. But she didn't. Maybe because she wanted the answers. Maybe because she wanted to pick the arena for her fight, and didn't want it to be in her copper-walled cell. Maybe because she could no longer be sure that going back to the trailer in Cat Creek, and the pain of proximity to the sick and dying, and the loneliness, was the best choice she could make anymore.

"I could use a few answers."

Seolar's smile faded. He nodded after a moment, and edged back toward the door, keeping his eyes on her. He said, "Birra will bring your clothing. Meanwhile, I have a gift for you." He held out a hand. Something gold and gleaming and sparkling lay in it.

Molly stepped forward, and caught a glimpse of the guards who stood just the other side of the door, watching the Imallin. So he hadn't been entirely trusting. She took his offering, and felt the cool weight of solid gold against her palm. She looked at the gift. A necklace, a breathtaking piece of sleek metalwork, each piece of the chain so perfectly fitted and so smoothly interlocked that it seemed a seamless, liquid, living thing and not the creation of a jeweler. In the center, a cluster of inlaid, faceted sapphires rimmed a gold medallion—in the center of the medallion, a winged woman rose from a storm-tossed sea, her arms spread wide, her face calm and reassuring.

"Good God," she murmured. "This thing is worth more than my house back home."

Seolar laughed softly. "It is, in its own way, more valuable than *my* home. And it is yours. Please wear it, and let me see it on you."

But Molly wasn't going to be won over by jewelry. Hadn't worked for the guys in the Air Force, wasn't going to work now.

"Maybe later." She studied it, and thought it was the most

gorgeous piece of jewelry she had ever seen. It had an understated simplicity that appealed to her—though how any piece of jewelry made of three pounds of gold could seem understated was beyond her.

"Will you wear it to dinner?"

"I'll consider it."

Seolar wore his disappointment overtly. Well, he could live with it. She'd check the piece first, make sure that it didn't contain a little compartment that would inject her with drugs at an appropriate time, or anything else some sick but talented jeweler might devise. It seemed to warm too quickly in her hand, and she thought she could feel it humming just the tiniest bit, which seemed like a bad sign. She didn't like being paranoid, but she figured she'd earned the right.

"Well. Birra will arrive before twilight to help you ready yourself. And I will take my leave until this evening. I have many duties to which I must yet attend."

He turned and vanished down the hallway, walking too quickly.

Molly stared after him. The guard who had the duty at her door watched him leave, too, then turned to Molly and slowly, slowly, bowed his head until it nearly touched the floor. Then, without a word, he closed the door between the two of them and bolted it shut again.

Molly didn't begin to know what to think.

Cat Creek

Eric was feeling the weight of the all-nighter watching Lauren when the phone rang. He glanced at the clock that hung across from his desk—5 A.M.

"There's a dead body in the swamp . . . floating! I was going out to fish, and . . . oh, my God, the boat bumped into her, and I didn't know what I hit and I looked with my flashlight to see and she was under the water, looking right up at me!"

Eric was suddenly awake. "This . . . Tom? You sound like Tom Watson."

"It's me, Sheriff. Oh, God, she was just floating there with her eyes all wide and her hair tangled in a tree branch that was hanging into the water, and she looked like she was reaching out to me, only she was dead."

"Breathe, Tom. Calm down."

A moment in which he could hear only sobbing and panting on the other end of the phone. Then, "I'm sorry, Sheriff. I'll be all right."

"Good. Did you recognize the body?"

"It's Debora. Debora Bathingsgate."

The news hit him like a gut punch. His skin was crawling and covered with goose bumps and he had the awful feeling that someone had just walked over his grave. His ear clamped to the phone, he started scrambling through the drawers of his desk for papers, his evidence-collection kit, and film for the camera. "Goddamn, goddamn, goddamn, godDAMN . . . Give me the coordinates."

"A mile east of town on 79, turn right on Sally Brown Road, right again on the second dirt road, straight back to the swamp." Tom hiccuped.

"What in the Sam Hill was she doing out in the goddamned swamp?"

"I don't know."

"What were *you* doing out in the swamp so early in the morning?" He tugged on a shirt, started buttoning it. "Shit, we're out of film. I'm going to have to call Pete in here to mind the store. You . . . where are you right now?"

"At the pay phone at Sweeney's Used Car Parts on 79."

"Get your ass back to the swamp and wait for me there. Stay in your car, don't touch anything, don't move anything, and keep your car doors locked and your head down. If this is an accident, fine. If it isn't . . . well, I don't want you being somebody's next target."

"Yessir," Tom said. "I'll be there."

He called Pete next.

"Get up, get in here. We've got a floater in the swamp, and you're going to have to baby-sit our guests."

"Son of a bitch."

"Pretty much my thoughts, too."

"Who is it? Any idea?"

"Debora Bathingsgate."

"The Yankee."

"She's Canadian. Or was. But, yeah. Her."

"What the hell was she doing out in the swamp?"

"That's what we get to find out."

"Give me ten."

"Anything past five and I'll kick your ass when you get in here. And bring me some film for the camera."

Pete made it to the station in just under four minutes.

"Anything I need to know about them?" he asked, nodding down the hallway.

"They slept all night. Still asleep, actually. I did paperwork half the night and read that damned book of yours the other half. You got to bring in some better books. I wouldn't mind a little Zane Grey."

Pete laughed softly. "Me either. Kind of liked him."

"I've already called the coroner. All you have to do is keep everyone out of the back." Eric sighed. "Keep our, ah, *packages* safe. Don't say anything about what has happened to anyone you see. And as far as you know, you're all alone in the station. If that means you have to shoo people out to keep 'em from hearing the kid, then you do it. You got me?"

Pete was quiet for a minute. "Seems a bit odd, but, yeah, I can manage that."

"I'll be back as soon as I can."

She didn't look too bad when they pulled her out. Carlin Breedy, the coroner, said she'd only been dead for two hours, three tops. She looked pale. Blue. No swelling, no signs that fish or anything else had been at her. Carlin had a thermometer sticking where thermometers had no business being.

"Real fresh," Carlin said to Eric. Eric was pegging off the site, in spite of the fact that Tom and Willie and even June Bug were milling around and had already tromped all over it. There might be some evidence he could salvage. "I'd say young Tom didn't miss her going under by much. Wonder how she got out here."

Eric nodded, and looked over at Tom, deep in animated conversation with Willie and June. Headlights flashed and bumped down the dirt road that led in, and Mayhem's car skidded into the tall grass. The rest would be along soon enough, he figured.

"Cause of death drowning?"

"Looks like . . . from first glance here." Carlin was shining his flashlight on the girl's body. "But I don't much like those." He pointed to several darkly mottled spots on either side of the throat. "Those look like finger marks to me. Unless I miss my guess, boy, somebody had a big hand in helping her drown. Be real interesting to get a look at her lungs."

"Why?"

"See if it's good brown swamp tea in 'em, or clear town tap."

"She was murdered."

"Sure as the sun will rise this morning."

Carlin was on one knee, probing the back of Debora's head. "Funny," he said. "Back of her skull's all spongy. Somebody gave her a good lick." He stared up at Eric. Under his breath, he said, "But if they dented her head, she wouldn't have much fight in her when they dumped her in the water. So why the bruises on her throat?"

Eric's response was as quiet as Carlin's comment. "You get an autopsy for me from Laurinburg, you hear? Put a rush on it."

"I'll do it. You're going to get some funny findings."

"You think?"

"Bet on it. I'm guessing those bruises on the throat weren't supposed to show up."

"Don't mention them. Not to anyone."

"Never saw a thing."

"Good. And neither did I."

Tom, June Bug, Willie, and Mayhem were walking through the grass toward Eric. He waved them back, told Carlin, "Cover her up and get her out of here," and headed over to talk to his colleagues.

"What happened?" Willie wanted to know.

"Hard to say until we get an autopsy. She might have drowned, she might not have."

"What was she doing out here?"

Eric shook his head. "Can't say."

"Can't, or won't?" June Bug wanted to know.

Eric frowned. "Right now, can't. When I know something, then it's won't. This is sheriff business, and it isn't Sentinel business unless it is. You know what I mean?"

He looked from one bleak, haunted face to the next, and said, "Everybody but Tom go on home. We've got problems here, but we've got bigger problems through the gates." He rubbed his temples. He felt sick inside. "How many people you call, Tom?"

"All of us I could get. Granger didn't answer. Neither did Jimmy Norris. But I think Norris said something about having a date last night, so he might have still been out tomcatting around."

"Shit. Why the *hell* did you call everybody? Now I got footprints covering my tracks, and bent grass all over the place, and Willie's goddamned cigarette butts on the ground where they have no business being, and I'm going to have a time sorting out what's evidence and what isn't."

"She's one of ours. I figured they ought to know."

"You figure one of them might have been the one who killed her? Your little party out here just made it easier for the killer to keep on hiding."

"Maybe she just drowned."

"Not with the back of her head bashed in she didn't."

Tom's already-gray face went sheet white. "Oh, Lord."

Eric was still furious. "So I can figure on damn near everybody else showing up out here before I leave?"

"Don't reckon so," Tom said. "Most everybody had to go in to work—they said they'd hear what they needed to know from you."

"Somebody with a little sense. Go wait by your car. I'm going to talk to the coroner for a minute, and get everyone else out of here. Then you and I need to have a talk."

When the other three Sentinels were gone, the ambulance arrived. Eric walked over to Carlin to watch the attendant load the body into the back. "Keep an eye open for anything strange, will you?"

"Already found something." Carlin turned his body so that neither the ambulance attendants nor Tom could see what he was doing, and passed Eric a piece of paper. "Found that in her pocket."

Eric looked at it. Carlin had unfolded the soggy sheet. The writing was still perfectly legible.

Meet me at my house at midnight. I know who the traitor is, and have proof.—Lauren Dane.

"Holy shit," Eric whispered.

"That's what I thought, too."

"If anyone asks, you didn't see this, either, all right? Put it in your report as an effect found on the body, but until I can release information, this is between the two of us. It's . . . dynamite." Eric slipped the note into an evidence bag, quickly labeled it, and slid it into the pocket of his coat. "And you tell me why the hell some fool would be out fishing in the swamp on a morning this goddamned cold, anyway," he muttered.

Carlin said, "You got a mess here, son. I'll get you your information as fast as I can. Meantime . . . well, you watch your back, you hear. This has the feel of something mighty nasty to me."

Eric nodded. "I'll do that."

When the ambulance, Debora, and Carlin pulled out onto the dirt road, Eric strolled back to Tom. "All right. What happened?"

"Brought my boat out here early. I wanted to get in a few hours of fishing before I had to be at work."

"Why would you want to go fishing in this cold?"

"I had the taste for some pan-fry. I don't mind a little cold—my daddy and I used to fish the swamp in cold weather all the time. Fish you get taste better than the ones you catch in warm weather."

"And you were due in to work when?"

"Three this afternoon. I figured I could get a nice mess of

cats and clean 'em and freeze 'em and fry up a plate of them for lunch and still have time to shower and shave and not smell like dead whale by the time I went in."

"So you came out here with your boat and . . . what?"

"Put it in right over there." He pointed to a well-worn low spot in the tall grass—the spot was a popular put-in point for any number of swamp fishermen.

Eric nodded. "And?"

"Started to row out toward the cypress knobs—fish like to collect around the base of those, and you can do pretty good with a jar of worms and maybe a couple of poppers."

"And . . . ?"

Tom looked queasy again. "Boat sort of thumped and skidded along something. You know how when you hit something solid you can feel it jar all the way through your bones, and when something hits you that isn't fixed in place, it sort of . . . slides along the boat. Nasty feeling."

"I know," Eric agreed.

"I got bumped by something big. Figure it wasn't a catfish—Lord knows I was hoping it wasn't a gator lost up our way, but in this weather I don't worry so much about gators. I flashed my light into the water and saw her staring up at me, her face under the water and her hair all fanned out. I pissed myself right then and there. Scared me so bad I damn near fell out of the boat."

Eric glanced at Tom's pants, flicked the flashlight on them for a better view, and looked up into Tom's eyes. "You go home to change before you call me?"

"No. After."

Eric considered the times involved, and nodded. Might have been possible, if only barely. Tom was known to stand on the gas pedal when he drove. "You knew who she was?"

"After a minute. She didn't look like herself, but after a minute, I could make out who she was."

"You try to pull her out?"

"Yes."

"Didn't make it."

"It took you and Carlin and me and that grappling hook you have to work her loose and fish her out of there into your boat. Don't know how you think I could have done that by myself. But I surely did try."

"I'm going to have to confiscate your boat," Eric said. "For evidence."

"What?"

"You're my best suspect right at the moment."

"The *hell* you say!"

"Didn't say I thought you did it—just that you were my best suspect. I'm sorry. You were sure in the wrong place at the wrong time—but until I have better evidence, I'm going to have to impound your boat."

Tom studied him, surprisingly calm for a man standing there under suspicion of murder. "Well . . . that's all right. You'll find some real evidence, I reckon. The innocent don't need to worry. But I have to tell you, I think it's pretty bad that I try to do the right damn thing, and now I'm going to be accused of killing her."

"You aren't accused of anything yet, Tom. I don't have an autopsy. I don't have any evidence. I haven't searched her body or her house or her car or listened to her answering machine or anything else. All I have is a corpse in a bag on its way to autopsy and the boy who found it way too soon after somebody dumped it in a swamp to hide it."

Tom stared at him. "You're not going to railroad me with this, are you, Eric? I know you got a lot on your mind— don't just decide I'm the easy answer to the smallest problem you got because I was in the wrong place at the wrong time, you hear?"

"Never railroaded anyone yet," Eric said stiffly. "Sure nice to know how much you think of my work ethics." He shooed Tom toward his car. "Go home. I'll be in touch if I need you. Just don't leave town."

Eric spent his morning taking plaster castings of tire prints and footprints and everything else he could find from around the swamp, looking for any little thing that might be evidence. Then he drove over to Debora's apartment and let himself in. The place was lived-in messy—a few books piled in front of the worn sofa, one opened to a page and left facedown on the coffee table, a cup of coffee sitting half-finished beside it. But there were no signs of violence, no signs that anyone had been in the place who had no business being there. Eric lifted fingerprints from every questionable surface, but doubted that he'd get anything useful that way. When he was finished, he checked the answering machine. No messages. He looked through her closets, rummaged through her drawers, took both her diary and a stack of notebooks as evidence. He thought about the note that the coroner had found on her body.

That note made him sick to his stomach.

He went into her bedroom, found the full-length mirror bolted to her wall, and ran his fingertips across its surface lightly. The gate hummed softly.

But as he stood there, he had the gut-twisting certainty that he was being watched. The hairs on the back of his neck stood straight up, and the metallic taste of fear filled his mouth. Wanting to flee at a dead run, he instead turned around nonchalantly and walked back to the kitchen, and dialed Willie's number. "Hey. Need you to come over to Debora's and shut down the gate here for me." He listened to Willie's weary grumbling for a moment, then said, "Really need to have it done right now. Things being the way they are, I don't want to leave one untended. If we get someone to take her place, you'll have to build a new one—but that just can't be helped. I don't know that we'll get someone else to fill her place. . . . Yeah. I'll be right here."

When he'd finished at Debora's he drove to the sheriff's station, filled Pete in on what they had to do, then worked out all the devious details. It took some orchestrating, but Eric made sure his ruse looked good. Pete, in one squad car, drove around to the back of Lauren's house while he pulled up in front driving the other. They both had their lights flashing. They had to make it a show—had to make it look good. Because someone was watching.

When Pete was in position, Eric waited a minute longer, then walked slowly up the stairs to the front porch, loosened his gun in its holster, and rang the bell. He made sure anyone watching from the street could see the piece of paper he held in his left hand.

He rang the bell, and after a minute, Lauren came to the front door, holding her son in her arms. He showed her the paper, took her son away from her, and Pete came through the back of the house, carrying a box of stuff. That was, Eric thought, a nice touch. Pete put down the box, cuffed Lauren's hands in front of her. Jake started to cry and reach for his mama.

Make it look good. Make it look really good. Because somewhere a killer is watching us.

Eric carried the child to the car; Pete marched Lauren to it, opened the back door, ushered her in. Eric handed her son to her. Pete slammed the door shut, went back to the house, locked it up, brought the box of stuff to the other car.

Both cars, lights still flashing, paraded back to the station.

Only when they were safely back in the station and away from anything that anyone might see did Eric take Lauren's handcuffs off.

"You mind telling me what that was all about?" Lauren asked. She stroked Jake's hair. He clung to her, his head pressed against her shoulder, staring daggers at Eric.

"You just got an unshakable alibi," Eric told her. "I now know that you aren't working with the Sentinels, and that you don't have a partner on the inside who is feeding you information."

"Thanks for the show of faith. I told you that before you decided to throw a parade. What changed your mind?"

"Someone killed one of the Sentinels—a friend of mine— and signed your name to the crime. The fact that you spent the night in jail with me watching you saved you from a whole lot of mess."

"Then why make the pretense of arresting me, if you know I'm the one person in the world who didn't commit the crime?"

Eric watched her face as he said, "You'll be a lot easier to keep alive if whoever it was that killed Debora thinks I bought the setup. Your story about your parents might have

some merit—they might have been murdered, though I'm
damned if I can figure out how to prove it at this late date.
But say it's true. Say your parents were murdered. Debora
was murdered, too, by someone who wants me to blame you
for her death—to get you out of the way. Now, I don't like
coincidences. Cat Creek is a mighty small town, and if
someone is killing Sentinels, I'm inclined to think it could
be the same person who was killing them before." He leaned
back against the wall and hooked his thumbs into his uniform pants.

"Imagine that the killer or killers are watching me to see
what I do. If you're supposedly arrested for the crime, they
may relax. I took their bait, I'm looking in the wrong direction, they know that you can't tell me anything that will give
them away and for whatever reason, you're safely out of
their way, too, and they can keep doing whatever the hell it
is that they're doing, free from interference for a little
longer."

Lauren had gone pale at his words. She held Jake tight
against her chest, her eyes squeezed shut, tears rolling slowly
down both her cheeks. She didn't so much as whimper.

Eric wanted to hug her.

Instead, from up front, Pete called, "We're about to get
company, boss."

Lauren's eyes opened and stared directly into his. "Hide
us," she said.

He nodded. "Jail cell. It's out of sight of the front. Don't
mention Sentinels to Pete, by the way. He doesn't know."

Lauren nodded, followed him back to the cell, and took a
seat with Jake on the narrow cot.

The bell on the front door jangled, and Eric heard Pete
say, "No sir, he's not making a statement to the press right
now."

Good Lord. That would be either Jim Mulrooney from the
three-times-a-week *Laurinburg Exchange* or Baird McAm-
mond from up in Rockingham. Either way, damned fast.
Like someone had tipped him off way in advance.

"Heard you've already made an arrest on your murder."

Eric headed out front and found Jim, hat pushed back and winter coat unzipped, leaning on the front counter, a cigarette dangling from the corner of his mouth. "Can't smoke in here, Jim," he said. "City property—you know the rules. And I'd love to know where you got your information, since we haven't officially announced the murder yet, pending notification of the next of kin, and we sure as shit haven't announced the arrest."

"Anonymous tip."

"There's a surprise."

"Come on, Eric. You have a murder, you make an arrest just a few hours later . . . you're good, you've been suggested more than once as a replacement for Laurinburg's police chief, who's getting ready to retire. Work with me here. I'll make you look great. PR like this could make your career around here."

Eric said, "And sell a whole lot of papers for you, right?" He smiled thinly. "I have the suspect, I have evidence, and I can't say any more than that right now. You know about due process, you know about admissibility. And before the lawyers get here, I'm not even going to give you a name."

"I have a name. All you have to do is nod and tell me yes or no. I can speculate to my heart's content . . ."

"And get yourself and your paper sued if you're not careful, Jim. Leave this one alone for a few hours."

Jim grinned. "I've got time. We missed today's issue, and we don't go to press again until day after tomorrow."

"Then come back late tomorrow. Maybe we'll have a bit more for you by then."

Lauren felt as scared as she had at any time in the last few days. As scared as when she'd gone through the mirror for the first time, as scared as when she'd found Embar nailed to the wall of her parents' house in Oria. Jake had fallen asleep in her arms, and she stared at his beautiful sleeping face and thought, There is someone out there who would willingly kill him.

Her blood felt like ice in her veins.

Eric came down the hall to her cell, shaking his head. "Pete is going to hold down the door with a steady stream of 'No comments.' Meanwhile, you and I are going to go through this notebook of your parents' and you're going to tell me what it was that they were working on."

"I can't."

Eric came into the cell carrying a folding chair, which he unfolded quietly and set on the floor beside her. She noticed that he was careful not to wake Jake, and that when he spoke, he did so in a soft, measured voice. "Lauren, you and I are all each other has right now. You're innocent—I know that. And I'm what stands between you and whoever killed Debora and tried to frame you for it."

"I know that. I was here and you were here, so whoever killed her, it wasn't us. I'm not telling you that I won't help you, Eric. I'm telling you that I can't. I've been through the notebooks. I don't know what they mean."

"How can you not know? Your parents had to have told you something . . ."

"They told me all sorts of things. Then they took me into Oria and blanked my memory when I was ten so that I couldn't give away the fact that I'm a . . . that I could use the gates, because . . ." It was right there. She could feel it. The reason that they had blanked her memory was because her life would be in danger. Because. Because. Because she was a gateweaver, but why was that such a bad thing? Because someone had been killing the gateweavers, and would be only to happy to get rid of a little kid before she got big enough to be a real problem. Lauren looked at him, and said, "I just got another little fragment of the memories back. When I was ten, Cat Creek and the other Sentinel nexuses in the area started losing their gateweavers. They were dying in a lot of different ways, and a lot of different places, but everyone was pretty sure they were being killed. My parents already knew I could gateweave, but nobody else did. I wasn't supposed to be taught anything about the Sentinels until I was a teenager, but I'd already figured out the gates on

my own, so my parents taught me how to use them the right
way so I wouldn't get me and them and everyone else killed.
When the trouble started, to save my life, they hid my
gateweaving abilities from everyone, even me."

"You're a gateweaver?" Eric shuddered.

Lauren nodded.

"When did you remember?"

Lauren described her first encounter with her parents'
mirror to him, and gave him a quick history of her first trip
across.

When she was finished, he just sat there shaking his head
for a moment. "And you still don't know what they were
working on?"

"Not yet. And the notes make no sense at all to me."

"They make some sense to me, but I can't get any feel for
the big goal they were trying to accomplish yet. I spent most
of last night reading through the first part, making notes and
trying to put pieces together. You think they told you what
this big Plan of theirs was?"

"I'm sure of it. But the memory is gone."

Eric sighed. "Maybe it's only gone the way the other memories were. Maybe you just need something to jar it loose."

She nodded without much hope. "Maybe. It would be
nice to think that I'd get back everything I lost. But I'm not
counting on it."

"Me, either," he agreed. "We'll figure the whole thing out.
And we'll watch each other's back, you and me, because I
have the awful feeling that we're both in a world of trouble
right now. It could be linked to whatever your parents were
on to. It's surely tied up with the Sentinels and what started
up in Rockingham."

"What started up in Rockingham?" Lauren wanted to
know.

He hesitated. Then he told her.

She shivered at the thought of the world ending, at the
thought of her and Jake dead in a few days or weeks of
something that would roll over them like the Four Horsemen
of the Apocalypse. She wished fervently that she hadn't

asked. But she said, "I've got your back, Sheriff, so long as you've got mine."

Eric held out a hand to her, and Lauren carefully shifted Jake in her arms so as not to wake him, and shook hands to seal the pact.

CHAPTER 10

16 NEW VICTIMS BRING FLU
DEATH TOLL TO 35
By Lisa Bannister, Staff Writer
(Richmond County Daily Journal, Rockingham, NC)

Richmond Memorial Hospital announced sixteen new
deaths from the as-yet-unidentified flu that has hit
Richmond County. Occurring within the last 24
hours, these deaths make this flu the deadliest to hit
the county in the last 30 years, and the fact that almost all victims were in their twenties and thirties
makes it the more unexpected. . . .

SCOTLAND DOCTORS INUNDATED
BY NEW FLU
By Jim Mulrooney
(Laurinburg Exchange, Laurinburg, NC)

Scotland County residents are under siege by a new
bout of that winter staple, the flu, report ER physi-
cians Mark Rogers and David Moore. "The ER is
swamped with influenza cases, many of them requiring hospitalization," says Moore. "I've never seen our
traffic jump so fast." Other county doctors, their waiting rooms jam-packed with flu victims, concur. "This
is the worst flu season I've ever been through," says
one doctor who requests not to be named. "And it's
just getting started . . ."

Copper House, Ballahara

MOLLY WENT TO DINNER in the center of a column of elaborately dressed soldiers—all of them still pretending to be servants of the house. She wore the necklace that the Imallin had given her, but in spite of the careful inspection she'd given it, which had revealed nothing but an exquisite piece of jewelry, she had serious misgivings. The necklace had a weight to it beyond the solid heft of its gold. In it, Molly felt memories—other people's memories, and not happy memories, either. Wearing it, she seemed to catch ghosts at the corners of her eyes, walking beside her in the places inhabited by soldiers; wearing it, she caught herself imagining conflagrations and battlefields, grief and destruction, and death in endless lines and endless permutations. For all that it was a pretty piece of jewelry, Molly discovered that she didn't like it much. But when she thought about taking it off, she discovered that she didn't want to do that either. In ways she could not describe, its weight around her neck felt like a shield. Like security.

Her life had been a little thin in the security department lately.

She hadn't known what to expect in her dinner with the Imallin; she'd half anticipated a banquet table laden with food of every sort, with kitchen servants racing back and forth, maybe a roaring fire at one end of a great hall and musicians at the other. She figured the Imallin would be planning on pulling out all the stops, impressing the hell out of her. Convincing her with a great show of power and wealth that she should stay.

But the grand arched doorway through which her escort at last ushered her led not to some magnificent hall, but to a pretty little atrium, filled even in the heart of winter with sweet-smelling flowers that she could not name, a tiny waterfall, and a pond with brightly colored fishes she could not identify, and a charming round table for two in the very center, lit by footlights and lanterns scattered throughout the garden, and, above her, by nothing but the stars.

Seolar, still plainly dressed, but now wearing clean shoes, bowed deeply in greeting. "Vodi," he said, "you honor my world with your presence."

Molly met his eyes and returned his bow with one carefully calculated to be equal to his. "Imallin. My thanks for the dinner—but I haven't forgotten yet how your world came to have the honor of my presence."

He chuckled softly. "No. I don't suppose you would." He offered her a chair at the table, but did not pull it back for her; different customs from different cultures, she supposed. She took a seat, and he sat, and then he said, "Javichi, please. And the first course."

A servant appeared on the path carrying a bucket of ice that held a large bottle in one hand, and in the other hand a little golden tray with two golden goblets and a tiny taster cup.

The servant poured the drink, pale green and slightly bubbly, into the taster cup first, and drank it. Then he handed the goblets to the Imallin, who produced a little black rag with which he wiped out the insides of each glass. The Imallin studied the rag for a moment, nodded, looked at the servant, and nodded again. The servant poured the drink.

Little chills skittered along the back of Molly's neck and between her shoulder blades, and the hair stood up on her arms. Welcome to the cozy life of power.

The Imallin sipped from each glass, wiped the edge of hers, and presented it to her solemnly.

"Is the fear of being poisoned always such an issue for you, or are these precautions especially for my benefit?"

The Imallin sighed. "You are the Ninth Vodi." Molly could hear the emphasis in those last two words, and when he said them, the necklace she wore seemed to vibrate for just an instant. "The veyâr—and indeed all the True Peoples of Oria—embrace your arrival with great joy. But the True Peoples are not Oria's only inhabitants: there are in this world those who would do anything to put an end to you, and with you, to the prophecies that surround you."

"Oh, Christ. Prophecies?" Molly pushed her seat back

from the table. "No. Those little guys mentioned prophecies, too. The Dark, The Deep, and The Bright."

"The Tradona."

"Yes. Them. Look—I don't know who you people think I am, but I'm not. I have a talent, I admit. I'm an odd sort of healer—but that doesn't make me anybody's savior. If I were a doctor, no one would get all strange about me, so just think of me as a doctor with a better-than-average patient survival rate."

But the Imallin said, "You must know better than that. Surely your mother told you *something* of your role in Oria—of what the Ninth Vodi would be, and do."

She took a sip of her drink, and discovered to her surprise that it wasn't alcoholic, and that it was delicious.

"I never met my mother. My father, either, for that matter. They gave me to strangers the instant I was born, and died when I was still a kid, long before I could have hoped to find out who they were or to track them down." She smiled sadly. "When I finally found them, I got to visit their graves."

Seolar's eyes grew wider—something she would have thought impossible. "She'd dead?" he whispered.

"My mother? For a long time now."

"And you never met her. She never told you anything."

"No."

"That explains much. Very much. By the true gods, what a disaster. We're lucky we ever found you. You could have gone anywhere."

"That would have been bad?"

"That would have been the end of the veyâr." While Molly sipped her drink, Seolar leaned forward and said, "The Prophecies of Chu Hua have guided the veyâr for more than seven thousand years. Before that time, when the Old Gods came we mistook them for true gods, and worshiped them—and this, of course, was what they wanted. During the rise of the great veyâr empire of Tasaayan Seeli, though, a woman from your world and a man from my world gave birth to the first Vodi, and that Vodi—Chu Hua—who could summon visions of the future, told the

True Peoples of Oria the nature of the Old Gods, and fore-told a time, far in the future, when the Old Gods would be scattered from the face of our world and sent back to the hells that spawned them. And that that time would begin with the arrival of the Ninth Vodi. You."

Molly sighed. "How did you decide I, out of all the people on not just one, but *two* worlds, was going to be your Ninth Vodi?"

"We did not decide. You were born the Ninth Vodi."

"Yeah. You said that before, but I remain unconvinced."

"Then I shall convince you. Nine women have been born of the union of human woman and veyâr man in all of known history. If there were others, and there may have been, they either did not survive childhood, or did not come to Oria when the time was right—or if they did come, they remained hidden. The Vodi are always women—the union of human woman and veyâr man, when it produces a living off-spring, produces a girl. Why this is, I do not know."

"Sounds like a genetic thing, except that I'm not buying your story. First, I know who my parents were, and they were both human. So I couldn't be a Vodi. Second, what you propose is impossible anyway, because a human woman and a veyâr man come from completely different evolutionary chains on different worlds, in what could very well be different universes. They could not possibly share chromosomes similar enough to produce any offspring. The odds of un-countable billions of evolutionary changes proceeding in lockstep on two worlds, to create two species that are completely different but that can produce viable offspring? Jesus Christ! I only took high-school biology, but even I know that's impossible. And third, I've seen the handiwork of some of your Old Gods, and I'm not leading anybody's army against them. I served my country, and I got my honor-able discharge, and I worked out all my ambitions to save the world in the interim. Sorry."

Servants brought trays in the silence and placed them be-fore Molly and the Imallin, and a taster stepped forward and took a bite of each dish from each plate, and covered the food again, then stood there. Molly realized they were waiting to see if he would die—wouldn't that be an exciting job? Minimal chance of advancement, the only benefit the fact that you got to eat some pretty tasty food—and she had to hope his family would get a good pension if he kicked off in the line of duty.

But he didn't—this time, anyway. Finally satisfied that the food was safe, the Imallin, still silent, picked up his two-pronged fork and took a bite. Molly did as he did.

Good food. Awkward silence.

Finally, when they'd nearly finished the meal, the Imallin said, "When you looked in the mirror today, you noticed a change in your appearance, correct? Birra mentioned to me that you were quite upset."

"That would be putting it mildly."

"And the changes that have taken place in your appearance—they do not suggest anything to you?"

"Suggest what? I figured that you people did some sort of magic on me."

The Imallin shook his head slowly. "We are of this world. We cannot do magic. Only the Old Gods, who come from other worlds, can do magic. And you, of course, but you are the Ninth Vodi."

"Right. I'm the Vodi, who is prophesied to rid your world of the Old Gods. And I can do magic. And I get dragged here against my will, and suddenly I start getting taller and thinner, and my hair turns a funny color, and my eyes turn a funny color, and . . ." She paused, and thought about that for a moment. Her eyes had become as green as veyâr eyes. If she was not as tall as a veyâr, she split the difference between human and veyâr height pretty neatly. Her hands still had the right number of fingers and the right number of joints for a human, but her hair was a color much more akin to veyâr colors than human colors.

Could there be some truth to Seolar's story? Could she have been born of both worlds?

He was watching her eyes, and in them he apparently saw something he liked, for he smiled a satisfied smile. "You begin to grasp the truth."

Molly ran her hands back through her hair in frustration.

"I don't see how what you suggest could be true. Science simply doesn't work that way."

"Ah. Science." The Imallin nodded sagely. "We know of science. It is the simplicity of mass and weight, of action and reaction. It is logic, and things that can be measured, and things that can be seen, and it gives results that anyone who follows directions well can repeat."

"Yes."

"You weren't born of science. Your mother summoned you into her womb through magic. She and your father— your true father—spent three years trying to conceive you, because this world needed you so desperately. There was nothing simple in your conception, and nothing simple in the sacrifices that your mother made to give you life."

"Hard to imagine that I meant so much if she just pawned me off on strangers."

"The only reason I could imagine her doing that was if something threatened your life, and she thought you would be safer hidden away."

Molly took another sip of her drink, then emptied the glass and shoved it across to him so that he could refill it. She was starting to believe him, but believing him wasn't the same as understanding him. She shrugged. "Maybe. I could think better of her if that were the case."

"Your father might know. I will ask him."

Finally, that little bit of data hit Molly. "Wait a minute. You know my father? He's alive?"

"Very much so. He's the Imallin of a domain some way off from this one. He is growing older, and his son is training to take his place."

Molly held up a hand. "His son. My—brother?"

"Half brother. But, yes."

"So I not only have a father and a half sister I've never met, but a half brother, too."

Seolar was studying her with an expression she read as concern. "You're upset by this?"

"I've spent a lot of time being lonely. A lot of time yearning for family I never had. This is—um, it's fairly tough."

He rested a hand lightly on hers. "I'm sorry for your suffering, and for your loneliness. Had we been able to find you, we would have brought you here sooner. As soon, in fact, as you didn't show up when you were expected. I wish we could have done more."

She laughed a little. "Yeah, me too. But I still get a chance—at least with my father and my brother. That's more than I ever thought I'd have." She took a long last gulp of her javichi, and sighed. "I don't know where I fit into this world, but I'm starting to believe that I do. It scares me, but I can deal with being scared. I've been scared a lot of times. I just—don't know what I'm supposed to do."

He refilled her glass and handed it back to her. "You belong here. I'll do everything I can to make sure you find your home here. We want you here, Molly. *I* want you here. I'll help you find your place in Oria."

She studied him as he sat across the table; she found herself liking him. The ornate facial tattoos seemed very subtle in the flickering lamplight. He didn't seem human to her, but in a way she didn't quite understand, he seemed *right*.

Cat Creek

Eric joined Lauren in the jail cell, put down a folding chair for himself and one extra, and sat for a moment watching Jake push a ball across the floor; Jake giggled wildly every time it bounced off the bars and rolled back at him.

Lauren glanced from him to the extra chair, then back to him.

"Pete's coming in any second now. He needed to secure the front door to make sure we wouldn't be disturbed. It would blow hell out of our cover if Pete and I were seen fraternizing with the enemy." He gave her a little smile.

"You explained things to Pete?"

"Not yet. We'll go over that. I got the autopsy reports back—they put a hell of a rush on them, and I figured both of you needed to hear what the pathologist found."

Pete came in, nodded rather stiffly to Lauren, and took the empty seat. "Doors all locked, answering machine on, sign on the door says 'Back in fifteen minutes.' If we take longer than that, I don't see it will be a problem."

Eric nodded. "Fifteen should do us. I'll be quick. First, Lauren, you recognize this?" He handed her an envelope. She turned it over, nodded, and said, "It's one of about a thousand letters I wrote to Brian while he was TDY overseas." She glanced at Pete. "TDY—that's temporary duty. Sorry; I still think in military acronyms. They were a part of Brian's and my life the whole time we *had* a life." She turned back to Eric. "I'm not going to ask how you got it."

"I had to search your house. I'll show you why in a moment, and I do apologize, but it was . . . it was life or death. I'm going to show it to Pete now. Pete, don't read the letter. Just look at the handwriting, okay?"

Pete took the letter, unfolded it carefully, looked at it for a moment, then refolded it and handed it back to Eric. Lauren tried not to be annoyed that he didn't hand it to her. It was, after all, her letter, and if it wasn't as important to her as the stack of letters that Brian had written to her in return, still it was part of what she had left from that time when he had been in her life.

Eric put the letter in an evidence bag, then removed an already-sealed evidence bag, and said, "I can't take this out of the plastic. But Lauren, please look at it and tell me what it is."

Lauren took the plastic from him, looked at the unfolded paper on which was written, "Meet me at my house at midnight. I know who the traitor is, and have proof." The signature read, "Lauren Dane." But she had never seen the paper before, had never seen the handwriting, and couldn't imagine what she was looking at. She looked up at Eric. "A bad joke?"

Eric took the bag from her and handed it to Pete. "What do you think, Pete?"

Pete read it, looked at it carefully, and said, "She didn't write it."

"I agree. It was in Debora's pocket when we fished her out of the swamp—the coroner noticed it and gave it to me. This is the piece of evidence that made me decide that pretending to arrest you would probably be safest for all of us for the time being."

Pete was frowning. "Either you or I was with her all evening and all night the day Debora was murdered."

"Right. But the killer didn't know that. Nobody but you and I knew that Lauren was locked up in the sheriff's station that night. I can't be sure yet, but I think the killer did know Lauren was my prime suspect in Molly McColl's disappearance, and thought it would be pretty easy to pin a second crime on her."

Pete nodded. "You find any other similarities between McColl's disappearance and Bathingsgate's death?"

"At this point, only that there was no sign of struggle at either victim's home. If we find Molly's body, we'll possibly be able to establish some other correlations. In the meantime, let me tell both of you what the pathologist discovered about Debora Bathingsgate. Time of death was roughly 4 A.M. The body was discovered at approximately 5 A.M.—which means whoever dumped her out there didn't waste any time doing it, and when Tom found her, she hadn't been there long."

"If he didn't put her there."

"Which has crossed my mind, but Laurinburg's forensics expert says his boat came up clean—no human blood, no matching fibers, no stray hairs—things that would have been very likely to show up, considering the condition of her body."

Pete said, "All right. Just wanted to make sure we weren't missing anything."

"The water in Debora's lungs was tap water, and the finger marks on her throat, plus ligature marks at her wrists, make it look like she was held under the water in someone's bathtub, or something similar, and that she fought like hell. After death, her killer hit her on the back of the head with something large and heavy. Most likely a cast-iron frying pan from the shape of the skull fracture, and very possibly a frying pan that we're going to discover the killer has planted in Lauren's kitchen for us to find when we search her house."

Lauren felt sick. She glanced at Pete, and saw that he was watching her. In his eyes, for the first time, she saw sympathy.

"Someone wants you in trouble bad, girl," he said softly.

She nodded. "But who? I didn't know I'd managed to piss anyone off that badly."

"We'll get to that. I have some ideas," Eric said. "Back to Debora. After her killer bashed her head in, the body was taken to the swamp and dumped."

Pete said, "Did the killer want it to look like she'd been drowned by accident, or murdered with a pan and then drowned, or *what*?"

"I'm not sure." Eric was pulling out autopsy photos. "The killer obviously wanted it to be clear that Debora was murdered. He also obviously wanted to pin the crime on Lauren. But exactly what he wanted us to think were the sequence of events that got her into the swamp, I have not a clue. I'm guessing that he wanted us to think that Lauren was trying to cover up her crime by making it look like a drowning, or perhaps he wanted us to think that she was still alive when she went into the swamp and she drowned there . . ." He shrugged. "I'm certain he didn't realize those finger marks on the throat would show."

"Why is that?" Lauren asked.

"Because they're a dead giveaway that you didn't kill her. The hand that made them has a reach about a third bigger than mine." He held a hand out, palm forward, to Lauren. After a tiny hesitation, she raised her own hand and pressed her palm to his. His hand dwarfed hers.

She winced at the contact, cringing inside for appreciating the warmth and the pleasure of human touch; she pulled her hand back quickly.

"Not her for sure, then," Pete said. "But we already knew that."

"So we're going to be watching Lauren's house to see if anyone drops off a frying pan. We're going to be watching

people we know, and listening for questions about the arrest
we made. We're going to be waiting to see who wants to
hang around here the most—at this point, I'm going to be
real suspicious of anyone who takes a sudden interest in police work."

Lauren said, "Why me, though?"

Eric's glance flicked left, to Pete, then focused on Lauren's
face. "Your parents had a few enemies." His tone was careful.
"I can only speculate, but this might go back to them."

"Then the . . ." she almost said notebook, but stopped herself in time. ". . . the story I heard about them being murdered might be true, too."

Eric nodded. "Could be. We could really use a lead right
about now."

The phone rang. All three of them jumped. "Want to let
the machine get it?" Pete asked.

"No." Eric jumped to his feet and took off down the hallway.

Lauren heard him answer, heard a couple of cryptic responses, and heard the skritch of a pencil on paper. A few
moments later he came back down the hall, and his expression made it clear he'd had bad news.

"That was Ernest Tubbs," he said slowly. "He was out
hunting and flushed up a few buzzards. He thinks he's found
Molly McColl's body out back of Tucker Farm."

"Oh, hell," Pete said softly. "Want me to take it?"

"No. I have an idea of what I'm looking for, and I saw the
last crime scene. I'll go. You stay here with Lauren and Jake,
and don't let anyone—anyone—near them for any reason."

Pete nodded. "They'll go through me to get to them,
boss." He drawled the "boss" with an irreverent little grin,
and Lauren realized the two were much more colleagues
than boss and employee.

"I'm on my way, then." He stopped, turned to Pete. "You
have any extra film? I used the whole last roll at the swamp,
and I haven't even taken it out of the camera yet."

"Don't have any. Leave the roll with me and I'll drop it
off—that way it won't be rolling around under the seat of

your car for a week. You can pick some up on the way out to the scene. There's two, three places between here and there that stock film."

Eric turned and headed down the hall again.

"Keep us up with what's going on," Pete called after him. "We're going to be stuck in here with nothing to do but stare at our belly buttons and sing campfire songs."

Lauren heard Eric, already at the front door, laugh, though it sounded more like a bark. "I'm almost ready to trade places with you, Pete. Almost."

Then the bell on the door clattered, and the door slammed shut, and Pete and Lauren gave each other appraising looks.

Copper House, Ballahara

Molly enjoyed the sunlight that streamed through the windows of her new apartment. No visible copper in this place, though she suspected hidden copper, just because she assumed the builders would be paranoid enough to want it everywhere, to keep the rrôn away. The bigger rooms, all panel and stone, with pale wood floors and gorgeous silk and tapestry-work everywhere, were actually an improvement over the Copper Suite, hard as that was to imagine. No grilles on the windows, and she wasn't in a tower anymore, but only about one story above the ground. Elegant carved wooden doors this time, and a feeling of warmth to the place that simply hadn't existed with metal walls and a metal floor.

Seolar had been as good as his word. She could open the doors and go out. She simply had no idea where to go, or how to find her way around the place, so after a short trip down the hall to distinguish a few landmarks, she'd returned to the apartment and sat down to play the guitar for a while.

Deep into mangling Beethoven's *Für Elise*, she almost didn't notice the knock at her door. She turned, expecting to

see Birra or one of her other guards, but instead she found
Seolar standing in the doorway, dressed for the outdoors and
with clothing draped over one arm.

"I'd like to take you riding," he said. "The weather is
somewhat less cold than it has been, the beasts are restless
and need to stretch their legs, and I would have you see some
of this world that is to be yours. Will you come with me?"

Outside the walls. Out of confinement. Out into fresh air,
and freedom. "Absolutely," Molly said. "When?"

"As soon as you put on riding gear. We have coats waiting
for us in the front hall, but I did not wish us to have to wear
them all the way from here. It would be too warm." He
smiled and handed her the clothes.

Quilted pants with partial covers of split leather on the
insides of the thighs and calves; tall, lined boots with
blocky heels, a thick cotton shirt and a quilted vest and
fur-lined leather gloves. She put them on when he stepped
out of the room, and was admiring her reflection when he
came back in. She looked—very upper-crust outdoorsy.
She'd always admired the look on women who could carry
it off, and now, to her delight, she discovered that she was
one of those women. Taller and thinner never hurt the
hang of clothes, even if she had lost about a cup size in the
bust.

"Ready?"

"You would not believe how ready. Let's go."

Outside, he gave her a leg up on a huge bay horse and had
her ride the beast in a slow circle around him. She'd done
some riding in her off time when she'd been in the Air Force
and had loved it; the cost of getting and maintaining a good
horse and the amount of time necessary for upkeep, however, had kept her from getting her own once she got out.
She hadn't forgotten how to stay on a horse's back, but she
was definitely only a weekend rider.

"You sit well," Seolar commented.

"Just don't go too fast. I've never really gotten good at
galloping and jumps."

He nodded. "We shall have a pleasant tour of the countryside at a comfortable pace. There are hampers on the pack-horses; we shall have a lovely lunch, and you'll discover what a wondrous place this can be."

"I hate to ask, but what about the . . . ah, the problems you mentioned last night. And the ones I've already seen in action."

"They won't notice me. And with you wearing the necklace, they won't notice you. According to all the historical information we have about it, it will protect you from all attacks, both magical and physical, so long as you wear it."

"Neat—but I'm surprised someone else hadn't confiscated it long before now. That seems like a handy thing to have."

Seolar shrugged. "None but a Vodi can wear it."

That she found terribly interesting. "Anyone try?"

"Yes. There was a reason why we took so long giving it to you. We had to make sure you really were the Vodi first." He didn't elaborate, but from the expression on his face, she decided she didn't want to press for details.

She was studying the huge wicker panniers strapped on the packhorses with amazement. They were taking along enough food to feed a good-size regiment. And she bet it wasn't MREs, or the Orian equivalent. She glanced at Seolar, thinking, Here is a man who has never met a peanut-butter-and-jelly sandwich. She decided she could like that about him.

The two of them and their six horses crossed a huge timbered drawbridge, rode out of the walled enclosure and down a cleared path in the forest. They rode side by side, frequently in companionable silence unless he decided to point out a landmark or interesting wildlife, or unless she had a question about something she saw. She found the trip very pleasant; they saw a gorgeous waterfall and the incredible forest and beautiful snow-covered farms that sat in the center of little swatches of cleared land. From time to time they saw people out, but though the people waved, none ever approached.

As the sun rose in the sky, Molly found herself wondering about her companion. "Tell me about yourself," she said at last. "Up to now, you've told me plenty about me, and plenty about your world, but almost nothing about you."

He shrugged casually. "There is little enough to tell. I am my parents' only surviving child—my father was Imallin of this domain until his death, my mother survived him by half a dozen unhappy years, longing every day to rejoin him beyond the Veil. When my father died, I became Imallin—I have watched helplessly as my people died off and I sought with every means at my disposal for you. That has been the whole and consuming feature of my life—the governing of my people, the saving of my world, and finding you. It makes me quite boring to talk about."

"What about children of your own? A wife, a lover? Hobbies and interests?"

He sighed. "I have been too busy to meet a woman I could love, and in any case, I dreaded having children that I could watch die the way I watched my brothers and sisters die. I lost an even dozen," he said quietly, and Molly glanced over, expecting to see in his eyes the same emotion she heard in his words. His face, however, hid his feelings far better than his voice; she saw nothing in his expression but the same serenity she had seen there all day.

"I'm sorry."

"Thank you," he said. "It did not leave me eager to try my luck with a family until I had found you."

"Because I could stop the diseases."

He glanced at her sidelong. "That, too."

She smiled at him uncertainly. "That, *too?*"

He shrugged. "All along we have believed that you would do more here than simply cure our ills—that you would become one of us, and bring magic to our world. I intended to see what that magic would be before I made any decisions."

"What if you had never found me?" Molly asked, thinking that he had left his life on hold for an awfully big uncertainty.

"Then the veyâr would have ceased to exist in my generation, as would some of our cousin races—and what would my happiness have mattered in the face of that?"

What, indeed.

"Have you ever had the chance to have a little fun?" she asked him after a while.

"I like to dance," he told her. "I like to ride—fortunate for me, since I do so much of it. I raise *petai*—very pretty decorative fish—in indoor ponds. You saw some of them last night. I garden a bit in the summer when I have the chance." He shrugged. "I enjoy reading a great deal."

"I like the gardening. And the reading. I've never tried dancing."

"There are things you've never told me about yourself, either," Seolar said, "and they aren't things I could find out about you from other means. Do you have a husband somewhere? Children? I know about some of your interests, of course—the painting and the musical instrument, anyway. I know you like chocolate, and I must admit that, having tried a few pieces, I very much like it, too. But I have often wondered what your personal life has been like."

Molly sighed. "I spent years in the military, which I liked, and years alone, which I've also liked. I haven't had much of a personal life. A few short-term boyfriends, but men find my reaction to people in public places disconcerting."

"How so?"

"Well, *here* nothing happens to me when I'm near someone who is terribly ill. But back ho— back on *Earth*," she corrected herself, "I'd get deathly ill. Clutch my gut, start vomiting, roll up in a little ball and turn all gray . . ." She laughed a little. "It made dates an adventure, because I would never know when I was about to get too close to someone really sick. Pretty soon, I just stopped trying."

"But that doesn't happen to you here. So here you can have a normal life."

Molly looked at the horses, at the packed panniers, at her

rich clothing, and thought of her beautiful apartments in the fine castle behind her, and she laughed softly. "Somewhat better than normal, I think."

"Good." He looked extremely pleased, but he didn't say anything else.

CHAPTER 11

CAROLINA FLU REACHES WEST COAST
LOS ANGELES, California (AP)

The influenza strain currently devastating the East Coast has arrived on the West Coast with sudden, shocking force. Within six hours after the first positive diagnosis of Carolina flu in Good Samaritan Hospital, doctors diagnosed 56 more cases, and reported 29 fatalities. Case numbers are expected to rise dramatically over the next few days.

Plans for both the declaration of a state of emergency and for a regional quarantine are under discussion . . .

Ballahara

THE PICNIC LUNCH, if such a repast could be called anything so mundane, took place in a sheltered glade where the sun had melted away most of the snow and a ring of trees kept the air as still as indoors. The food was wonderful—the hot foods kept hot by clever insulated warming dishes, the drink—another nonalcoholic beverage—chilled, sparkling, and hinting of apples, the desserts rich and varied.

Molly and Seolar chatted about matters of no importance, told stories about their lives, and simply relaxed, and somewhere in the middle of the conversation, they ceased to be the Imallin and the Vodi, and began calling each other Seolar and Molly. The picnic went from delicious to delightful, and as a result, neither of them paid any attention to the weather. They should have.

The first fat flakes caught Molly on the cheeks. She looked up and realized that the sun was gone and the sky had turned an ominous gunmetal gray. "Oh, no," she said.

Seolar glanced around him. "We need to pack everything quickly and get back." He whistled, and abruptly there were veyâr on horseback pouring into the secluded glen.

Molly gasped.

Seolar said, "I dare not travel alone, ever—and I would be doubly foolish to travel with my world's sole hope unguarded. For all that your necklace will protect you, my world still needs me to make sure that you meet the people you have to meet, and have access to the things you'll need in order to carry out your mission as the Ninth Vodi. My men have kept their distance, but they have been watching over us."

Seolar's guards had the lunch repacked, the horses saddled, and everyone on the trail and moving quickly in a new direction before Molly could really grasp the significance of spending the rest of her life watched, if even from a discreet distance, by armed guards.

No more real privacy, ever. No more taking off on a whim and going wherever she wanted alone. The spontaneity gone from her life.

But she had to balance the importance of spontaneity against the fact that here she did not have to hide from crowds. Neither did she have to dread sudden, agonizing encounters with terminally ill strangers. No more futilely trying to drain the ocean with a thimble—what she did here mattered to the individuals she helped, but also mattered to the world. And what was that worth: knowing that her life was not pointless?

A lot.

She'd never really been all that big on taking off at a moment's notice anyway, she told herself as the group trotted along a well-cleared path. Her moments of spontaneity had pretty much been limited to late-night searches for fast-food french fries, for which she sometimes developed an unbearable craving. No worry about that here—she was a world and possibly a universe away from the nearest greasy fry.

The snow was coming down harder. She remained warm and comfortable . . . but she could barely see. Seolar, riding beside her in the center of the group of scouts and outriders, said, "We're going to have to go faster, Molly. This is getting worse. We have safe shelter ahead, but it will do us little good if we lose our path."

She dreaded trying to hang on to her seat if her horse moved at any gait faster than his easy, boneless trot. "I don't know that I can go faster."

"Then you'll have to ride behind me," Seolar told her. "We can't get trapped away from shelter—blizzards here can last for days."

She thought about trying to hang on to him at a canter, with no stirrups to balance in and no saddle to grip. "I'll manage," she said grimly, and urged her horse to a faster gait.

The ride terrified her. It became a reckless, nightmarish blur of snow that stung her eyes, the muffled thunder of a dozen sets of hooves over packed snow, the panting of the horses, the occasional smack of an untrimmed branch across her face, the terror of falling from her horse and being trampled by it and the packhorses and the riders who followed, none of whom would be able to slow down in time to miss her. Chilled, frightened, hanging on for her life, she thought she felt the heavy necklace she wore vibrate—and immediately after, she experienced a fugue state—or perhaps it was a vision, or a hallucination—in which she became a woman lost in those same woods on foot, caught in a blizzard, freezing alone in the dark and finally dying. The fugue didn't release her until the woman took her last breath. The vision added a surreal hellishness to an already-nightmarish ride.

When at last the lead rider called "Halt," and everyone reined in, she had to fight back tears of relief.

But they had not arrived back at Copper House. Instead, they had reached an unlighted, log-built construction surrounded by a pike fence fifteen feet high. A more unwelcoming place Molly had never seen.

"This is Graywinds," Seolar said. He dismounted quickly and handed the reins of his horse to one of his men, then caught Molly as she swung off her mount. "Inside," he said. "My men will tend to the animals; you and I must open up the house and start the fires."

He moved to a place on the wall that looked no different to Molly than any other, pressed his hands against the logs in a quick pattern, and a hidden door opened. He ushered her in first; his men followed behind.

"Graywinds?" She shivered, partly from the cold but more, she suspected, from the residual terror that the wild, half-blind ride had birthed in her.

He led her through the ever-denser snowfall to a massive, weathered wooden door, unlocked it with a huge key, and led her inside. "One of a number of houses I maintain so that, no matter where I am in my domain, I can reach defensible shelter in a hurry if necessary. Graywinds is perhaps my favorite of all the houses; I like it even better than Copper House, but it lacks the . . . well, *presence* to be an official dwelling for an Imallin. I must, after all, maintain a certain appearance of power in order to maintain the fact of power." He snapped a flint firestarter into a little hillock of tinder, and in the tiny blaze that resulted, Molly could see that kindling, small logs, and larger logs were already set to catch. That single spark had a lovely fire blazing in the hearth within minutes. And by the flickering light of the flames, she got her first clear look at Graywinds.

She could have called it a log cabin, but it was built on a grand scale, with timber framing, a vaulted ceiling, and big fireplaces at either end of the long, narrow main room. From where she stood, she could see a circular staircase that led up to an open second floor, a sort of loft clearly set up as a bunkhouse. To her right and her left lay closed doors. Seolar noticed the direction of her gaze and said, "We have a good kitchen and storerooms through that door, and a bathing room and toilet through there"—he pointed left—"and bedrooms and dressing rooms over that way," as he pointed to the doors on their right. "Most of the men will sleep upstairs. Two will sleep in the barn to guard the horses." He glanced at her. "It's quite safe. Not, of course, the impregnable fortress that Copper House is, but the roof here is copper, and so are all the stabilizing rods in the walls and all the pins. And I made sure copper was mixed into the chinking. Of course we have a copper-free workroom here, too."

Molly frowned. "Copper-free? Why would you want that? Can't the . . ." She dropped her voice to a whisper. ". . . Can't the rrôn get into places that have no copper?"

He looked at her with clear surprise. "The rrôn? You haven't worked out the connection between copper and magic—but no. You have made no forays into magic, other than the healing that you do in the Great Hall, and there, of course, there is no copper." He shook his head. "Copper is not just an impenetrable barrier to the rrôn. And to the keth." His voice dropped on that last word. So the keth must be the creatures who were worse than the rrôn. *Wonderful*. "Copper is an impenetrable barrier to magic. You were completely safe from any attacks by our enemies while you stayed within the Copper Suite, but had you tried to work your own magic in there, you would have found yourself unable to cast the simplest of spells. Here, our protection is less complete; nevertheless, I have found it sufficient, and it has been twice tested within my lifetime."

"So I could not work magic within these walls?"

"No. You could not heal anyone unless you took him into the workroom, or went outside and moved a bit away from the walls. I could not tell you the effective radius of copper, but I know that even the most powerful of the Old Gods must be some ways away from it."

Molly looked thoughtfully at her wrists. She had been wearing copper-threaded rope on her feet when she healed that first child. The Old Gods couldn't do magic while close to copper, but she could do magic while wearing it? Not on the actual hand in question, but still—interesting.

One by one the men came in, shaking off snow at the door, hanging coats and boots on the wall of pegs, talking with animation about the sudden storm, about the horses, about the ride. They sounded happy to be safely in shelter, and a bit amazed by the sudden awfulness of the weather. They gathered around the fire, pulling up chairs, and then three pulled out instruments—one a wooden flute; one a deep-voiced dark-wood cousin of the recorders Molly knew; and one a small, fat-necked, many-stringed cross between a lute and a guitar. They started playing a song all of them seemed to know well, and several began to sing and clap, and the next thing she knew, Seolar was asking her, "Would you like to dance?"

"I've never been much of a dancer."

"So you told me. Now would be a perfect time to learn."

She shrugged. Giddy from the wine and a wonderful supper of leftovers from the picnic, relieved to be out of the weather and off the back of the horse, she decided to be daring. She laughed. "Why not? If I step on your toes, just yell."

Seolar took her hand and began to teach her the steps of a jig. A jump to the left, a jump to the right, kick in front, kick in back, clap hands and spin . . .

She surprised herself by enjoying it. The three musicians were versatile, and they alternated their fast, blood-stirring jigs with slower dances that let her and Seolar catch their breath.

At last, though, she felt the world beginning to fall out from under her feet. "That has to be all for me for tonight," she told Seolar.

"Then let me show you to your room." He took her hand and held a small, glass-shielded oil lamp in his other hand and led her through one of the doors on the right side of the house. It opened into a hallway instead of into the room she'd been expecting. He chose the last of four doors on the left, saying, "If there is sunlight tomorrow morning, this room will get the best of it." A fire was already crackling in the hearth, the room was cozy and otherwise unlit, and someone had turned down the covers on the narrow bed and put out heavy white-cotton pajamas and thick white slippers.

"Where'd the clothes come from?" she asked.

"We keep spares in store," Seolar told her. He stood in the doorway, watching her. "We probably have almost anything you need here. Or anything you want."

His voice changed on that last line, and she turned from admiring the little room to look at him.

He stood studying her, and the intensity of his gaze and the way his eyes met hers sent a not-unpleasant shiver down her spine.

She managed to smile, and hoped he would not notice how her lips trembled when she did, and said, "That's good to know."

"If you need . . . anything . . . my room is just across the hallway from yours."   •

She nodded, unable to find any words.

He looked at her a moment longer, then seemed to come to a decision. "Good night, Molly," he said.

"Good night, Seolar."

He left, closing the door quietly behind him. She stared at it stupidly, trying to sort out her feelings and come to some sort of accommodation with herself over what had just happened.

What *had* happened? Had he implied the possibility of a relationship between the two of them? Had he, possibly, made a pass at her? Had his mention of the fact that his room lay just across the hall been simply for information? Or had it been an invitation?

Would she . . . could she . . . ever be interested in such a proposition, if he truly had made it?

He's not human, she told herself.

But the answer to that was plain enough. Neither was she. And maybe each of her short-lived and ill-fated relationships with human men had failed not because the men were lacking, or because there was something wrong with her, but because she had been looking in the wrong place all along. Maybe . . . maybe in Seolar she could find the chance at happiness that had so far eluded her.

"Maybe. But not tonight," she whispered, and pulled on the too-big pajamas left for her, and climbed into the narrow bed, and, to the sound of the crackling fire and the sweet smell of burning wood, fell asleep.

Cat Creek

"I didn't tell you I was good at chess," Lauren said. "I just told you I knew how to move the pieces."

Pete laughed. "Well . . . you didn't do too badly." He set up the board again.

"How about checkers? I might have a chance at that?"

At her feet, Jake looked up and said, "How 'bout checkers? How 'bout checkers? How 'bout checkers? How *'BOUT* checkers? *How* 'bout checkers?"

"Or maybe not," Lauren said.

Pete grinned down at Jake, who was sliding a roll of duct tape across the floor with a ruler. "That'll drive you nuts in short order."

"That's having kids," she agreed. "You have any?"

"Figure I'd need a wife first, and I'm not likely to find one of those around here. At least, I haven't met a girl yet who can keep my attention."

"Looking for a beauty queen, or one who can cook? Or both?"

"Neither." Pete grinned at her. "Looking for a girl who's read more than three whole books without pictures in them in the last year, and who knows the difference between a black hole and a red dwarf, and who doesn't start every sentence with the word 'like.' "

"You're picky."

"Yep. I'd like to have kids. But I have a long way to go before I can even think about that."

"At least you know what you want."

He chuckled. "What I want right now is for the boss to call in and tell me he's at the scene, and everything is all right."

"That would be nice. I wonder what's taking him so long?"

"I don't know, but if we haven't heard from him in another fifteen minutes, I think I ought to hide you and Jake in the back of the cruiser and head out there to see what's going on."

Lauren glanced at the clock. "You don't want to call him?"

Pete shook his head. "If he's out of the car with his walkie-talkie on and in a position where he needs quiet, and I break radio silence, I could get him killed."

"In that case, he'd turn his radio off, wouldn't he?"

"Depends. Fifteen minutes, anyway."

Eric pulled into the dirt road that led back to Tucker Farm, which until twenty years earlier had been producing cotton and tobacco. It had gone under, though, when the last of the Tuckers died, and had fallen into disrepair while the crew of heirs had squabbled over the will. In the end, the winning heirs had sold off most of the land, but there'd been no takers on the house, an antebellum monstrosity that would have cost two fortunes to return to livable shape.

What remained of the house sat well back from the road in a stand of pecan trees. Kudzu had now covered both trees and the ruins of the old place, almost giving it an air of ivy-covered respectability it didn't deserve.

There were two ways in—the front way, where his approach would be visible from the house, and the back way, which approached through heavy woods that ran for a ways along a soybean field. Logically, he should have just taken the short, open approach, but he sat there for a second, studying the roof of the house and the shield of pecan trees, and his gut twinged. With a shrug, he turned down the hidden approach.

Every sheriff who survives for long learns that there are times when you trust that quiet little voice at the back of your mind. Right then, Eric's was screaming that something about the call from Ernest Tubbs that had rung false. His nerves were so tight he could have played violin on them as he replayed the call. Ernest had been frantic. He'd sounded

scared—his voice had the tightness that came from being
about an inch away from screaming.

Eric considered phlegmatic Ernest, a man who'd spent
much of his life tromping through the swamps and sandhills
of the region hunting its deer, doves, and other game. In all
the years Eric had known him, he had never heard him
sound genuinely frightened of anything except the things
that could go wrong on the Sentinel end of the universe. Until this one call. Ernest found a body. He fell apart like a
fifteen-year-old girl. Now that he had the chance to think,
Eric didn't buy it.

The overhanging canopy of scrub oak and dogwood and
pine, choked by kudzu and dying, matched the ruined house
for mood and appearance. The gray claws of the denuded
trees reached heavenward and scrabbled toward the earth at
the same time.

He wished he had a dozen guys he could call for backup.

He started to call in to Pete, to at least let him know where
he was and what he was doing, but decided to hold off for a
few minutes. He'd wait until he knew something—as soon
as he announced where he was over the air, the busybodies
throughout Cat Creek who lived with one ear glued to their
police scanners would be on their way to Tucker Farm to
revel in the latest disaster and gossip.

So he headed down the drive, hearing the tall grass dragging along the undercarriage, and brambles and branches
scratching both sides of the car. He was musing on hunters,
and what a strange lot they were to voluntarily drive into
places like this, when a brilliant flash of light hit his eye
from out at the point where the woods met the field—where
no such flash should be.

He stopped the car, pulled out his binoculars, and took a
look. It took him a minute to make out what it was that had
caught his attention, and when he did, his stomach twisted
again. Someone had hidden a truck beneath weeds and
branches and bits of netting and other crap. Whoever had put
it there had done an expert job of hiding it—he'd done similar things during his stint in the National Guard. He

wouldn't have seen it except for the reflection of sunlight off a tiny uncamouflaged patch of windshield glass.

He debated going on, then coming back to the truck after he'd talked to Ernest and taken a look at the body. Then he decided that he was a lot closer to the truck. The body wasn't going anywhere; whereas, unlikely though it seemed right then, the truck might. Ernest would just have to understand.

He put the cruiser into park, took the keys out of the ignition, and clambered through the underbrush to the truck—and nearly fell over half a dozen other vehicles, all equally well disguised. Up close he could tell what he was looking at—whoever had done the camouflage was good. Whoever was responsible had broken up every straight line from every possible angle, covered all the shiny places, given the whole project as natural a look as possible. And that made Eric pause. Maybe he was dealing with hunters, maybe with men with Special Forces or survivalist backgrounds, but whoever had hidden the cars felt dangerous. There was nothing of play about this scene, no polite acceptable explanation, no normal scenario that was going to make this all mean nothing important. This was trouble—big, ugly, and frightening.

He looked up the road, toward the house. Ernest, waiting up there, could be right in the middle of whatever was going on. He could be a victim, he could be a participant—or he could be the traitor who had killed Debora and Molly and tried to set up Lauren. Eric might be walking into something way too big for him to walk back out of.

He put his hand on the radio at his hip. He wanted to call Pete—but he didn't want to break radio silence. Pete knew where he was. If he didn't call in soon, Pete would pack Lauren and Jake into the back of the other squad car and come out to see what was going on—and when he came, he'd come with cannons. Pete believed deeply in staying alive.

Eric caught a glimpse of a license plate—and got his second bad shock. The car belonged to Mayhem—no mistaking that personalized CHAOS 1 tag. Eric quickly moved from vehicle to vehicle. All of the cars and trucks belonged to

Sentinels. Besides Mayhem's red 'Vette, Eric found Willie's old white Chevy pickup, the Tubbses' brown Chrysler sedan, and even June Bug's little blue Sunbird. Every Sentinel car except for Granger's, Debora's . . . and his.

He swallowed hard. Then he went back to the cruiser, opened the trunk, and got out the twenty-gauge shotgun, his riot gear, and his tear-gas grenades and grenade launcher, and moved the weapons to the front seat and put on the riot gear.

He tried to remember approaches that would get him all the way up to the house without being seen. If they weren't in the house, he could use the old Victorian tower on the house's front right corner as a lookout point. If they were in the house, he could scope it out and try to figure out what the hell was going on. But either way, he was going to have to cross through broken cover, and he had to assume that there were at least a few hostages along with the traitors—he couldn't just kick down the door and start shooting.

And he couldn't wait. The traitor had already demonstrated a willingness to kill people. Eric had to assume that more were going to die—that this was the final step in whatever the traitor had been planning, and that getting the Sentinels who might stand against him out of the way was part of that plan.

With dry mouth and clammy hands, he drove as close to the house as he dared. He left the car under cover of a stand of pines and started working his way toward the house. The scrub oaks still held on to their brown leaves—they and the pines made useful cover. The blackberry brambles and the dogwoods were worthless, though. Bare and stark, they gave him nothing to work with. For long sections, he crawled through the tall grass on his belly, keeping head and butt down and weapons up.

As he neared the house, he heard voices. Tom Watson was shouting at someone, "He should have been here by now. Something's wrong, dammit. He's on to us."

"Balls, Tom, he's sure that girl in the jail is the killer. He's not on to us. He's just taking his time. What's he got to hurry for? He's coming to see a dead body, right? That ain't going anywhere." Deever Duncan's voice. Eric couldn't believe his ears. Tom, the most gung ho of the Sentinels, and Deever, who'd been a Sentinel since Eric was a kid, and who was as loyal as a summer day was long. These were the people who were destroying the world and everyone in it?

How could that be?

He got up to the house, and with his heart hammering in his chest, he raised up and peeked through a gap in one of the boarded-over windows. Sentinels were all over the floor—bound, gagged, and by the looks of them, unconscious. Nobody looked dead yet; he saw chests moving. Deever stood by the front window, looking out. Tom crouched near a glowing mirror nailed to the far wall. Missing from the scene were June Bug Tate, Willie Locklear, and Granger Baldwin.

The lights of a police scanner glowed on the mantelpiece above a boarded-over fireplace. So they were listening. Shit.

"Might as well shove another one through," Deever said, not turning from the window. "Just be less for us to do after we take care of him."

"Yeah," Tom said, and grabbed George Mercer under the armpits and dragged his unresisting body across the floor to the mirror.

Eric had an idea. He dropped down, pressed his back against the house, and got on his radio.

"Pete," he said, keeping his voice quiet so that only the radio would be heard in the house, "I am still 10-17 my previous destination—I've got a 10-68 blocking Scraggs Road."

"10-68? You're kidding."

"Wish I were. Scraggs's whole herd is standing right in the middle chewing their cuds, and Scraggs isn't going to be able to get them off the road by himself. They keep breaking away from the fence. We're going to have an accident if we don't get them out of the way, so I'm going to be a while helping him. You get out to Tucker Farm and tell Ernest I'll be along fast as I can."

"10-4. What do I do with our . . . guest?"

"Lock her up and throw away the key. She's killed two people already. Let's not make it three. Treat this as a signal twenty." Signal twenty was his and Pete's private code. It meant, "Everything I just said is bullshit, I am in real trouble, and get here as fast and as quiet as you know how."

Pete was quiet for a second. Then he said, "Signal twenty . . . got it. I'm 10-4 on that and will be rolling in about two minutes. Where should I go?"

"Just go in the front way. Ernest will be looking out for you there."

"You sure about that?" Pete would take that to mean go in the back way.

"Absolutely. I'm 10-7 until I finish chasing cows. Over."

He turned the radio off and reviewed the layout of the room the hostages and their captors occupied. One door led directly to the front. The other led to the back, but through the kitchen and a back porch. It would be easier to be sure of the element of surprise if he could just get across the front porch without being seen and kick in the front door—but Deever was watching out that way.

The back approach made him nervous. Old doors creaked, and even though the back door had been used, it was closed and might be locked. He would almost certainly make some noise getting it open. And once he got past it, he still had to get through the kitchen without being detected.

Front door? Or back door? Tom was shoving Sentinels through the gate. Presumably Willie and June Bug were already in Oria with George Mercer. Granger was a question mark, but since his car wasn't hidden with the rest, Eric figured that for one reason or another, he wasn't around. And he'd accounted for everyone else.

Front door? Or back?

"Any chance you know your way around a gun?" Pete asked Lauren. He handed her a bulletproof vest and said, "You're going to have to go with me. You might have to help."

"I have a Mossberg 20-gauge shotgun at home, and a

Browning High-Power, and a Remington 30–.06. I'm reasonably accurate with all of them—best with the Browning."

"Nice collection."

"They were Brian's. I got plenty of practice with them, though."

Pete stared down at Jake and said, "I hate taking you two into this, but Eric was clear about wanting you to come with me."

"I didn't catch all the numbers, but I know I heard him say you were supposed to lock me up and throw away the key."

"That was signal twenty. He meant that I should do the opposite of what he said. He's in trouble out there, and by the time I get backup from Laurinburg or the SBI or anyone else, he could be dead. I'm going to have to handle this, and I can't leave you two behind. He's afraid that whoever is behind this might break in and kill you and Jake. Besides, if I can count on you to stay by the radio with a gun in hand and watch my back, I'll feel a little better."

Lauren nodded. "I can do that. I don't know any of the codes, though."

"You don't need to. When we get out there, we'll see what we've got, and I'll put you on the Laurinburg dispatcher frequency. You tell the dispatcher you have an officer requesting assistance, and the only other thing you'll have to tell them is where you are."

"Okay."

He was pointing her toward the door. "We don't have time to stop by your place for your weapons. You're going to have to make do with one of our shotguns."

Lauren nodded and finished tugging Jake's jacket on him, and swung him up to her hip. "I'm ready."

Pete gave her a thin smile. "You're all right."

"If the damned deputy is coming instead of him, we might as well just kill all of these and go on through," Tom said. "We get the same reward whether we give them everyone or just a few—and it will be easier to transport just a few."

Deever said, "I figure that's what we ought to do anyway.

Would have been convenient to be able to hold them hostage and make him give us the access codes, but there's no way of knowing he would have given us the right codes anyway."

"You want to just kill them, then?"

"Ah, shit." Deever snorted, and Eric heard him walk away from the window. "I hate that sort of mess."

"It's less to drag with us, Deever."

Back door, Eric decided. And fast. The covered porch looked pretty solid, and the door's hinges didn't look that rusty. If he could time it so that Deever and Tom were talking, their conversation—and the fact that they figured he was chasing down cows nearly five miles away—might give him the element of surprise. He'd roll a tear-gas grenade into the living room from the kitchen, run in behind it and cuff Deever first, then Tom. He tightened his mask and swung onto the porch. He moved as fast as he could while keeping quiet, almost not daring to breathe. His assessment of the back porch had been sound, though. He made no noise at all.

And the back door was unlocked. Sweet. He squeezed into the kitchen, only making the slightest of squeaks. One door in the kitchen led to other rooms—probably the dining room, he thought, and through that most likely the downstairs bedrooms, if there were any. The other went into the living room, where the hostages and their captors waited.

He pulled the pin on the tear-gas grenade, tossed it into the living room, crouched, and jumped into the room behind it shouting, "Hands up, drop your weapons and don't move or I'll shoot."

Deever and Tom were coughing. Through the yellow haze, he saw their hands go into the air. Tom dropped his gun, doubled over coughing, and started to hobble for the door. Deever, swearing and yelling, beat him to it. Eric ran after them.

He only half heard another door open behind him. Only had a hundredth of a second to realize that there had been a third conspirator. "Son of a bitch," he heard Willie Locklear say. Then he simultaneously heard the sound of the gun and felt the fire in his back, his spine, his lungs—the impact threw him forward and then he was falling, and the world turned red and then gray, and his vision behind the gas mask telescoped, and everything started to sound like it was happening underwater. And then he felt wonderfully warm and buoyant and surrounded by fluffy white cotton, and nothing had any sound at all.

CHAPTER 12

Graywinds, Ballahara

RESTLESS DREAMS—she was bathed in green fire; a delicate, winged woman in a glittering gold dress fleeing down the hallway of Graywinds, and turning at the end of the hall, she flung up her arms to ward off the blows of . . .

Flash forward . . .

She lay in the dark, strong and feminine and sated, nestled next to a man whose body was as familiar as breath itself, seeped in warmth and the wondrous smells of soap and sun and the promise of sex, with the fire crackling in the hearth, when out of the darkest corner of the room a shadow bathed in shadows stepped forward, and dry scales rattled and something hissed . . .

Flash forward . . .

A glade, dappled sunlight on tall grass and wildflowers, and she was a child playing behind her mother, and overhead a dark shadow soared. Her mother screamed and picked up her baby brother, her younger sister, and screamed her name, and all the while she stood in the heart of a shadow that grew larger like a black sun exploding . . .

Molly, throat dry and tight from trying to scream, fought free of the nightmares into terrified wakefulness and the sen-

sation of purring—heavy and catlike—vibrating her chest.
She struggled to sit, and tried to shove away the thing on her
chest, and discovered that nothing held her down. She
needed a moment to orient herself; she lay in the bed in
Graywinds, dressed in the too-big pajamas she'd put on the
night before and still wearing the medallion Seolar had
given her. Silence held the house in thrall, and blackness at
the windows told her she had woke before the rising of the
sun. Her fire had died down to embers. Her door, when she
padded across the cold wood floor in her bare feet to check,
was still locked from the inside, as she had left it.

At her window, a sudden soft, erratic scratching.

Her heart clogged in her throat and she suddenly couldn't
breathe. She jumped across the room to land on the floor beside her bed, belly down, and crawled under it.

More soft scratching, and now that she listened carefully,
the sound of the wind, too. She felt a tiny draft of it down the
flue of the chimney—sharp cold that made her wish she was
safely tucked in her blankets.

Soft scratching. She stared up at the windows, willing her
eyes to make out what was there.

A thin, crooked shadow. The line of a branch from a shrub
or small tree that evidently grew beneath the window, then.
The wind had given it movement, and her mind, still shaken
by nightmares, made the sound a threat.

She didn't laugh at herself—she was still too shaky for
that—but she did climb gratefully out from under the bed.
She placed small sticks and a couple of logs on the embers
in the fireplace, and smiled a little as the fire came back to
life. And she crawled back into bed, and pulled the covers
over her head, and ignored the sound of the branch against
the glass.

Eventually she found her way into sleep again, and this
time she found nothing there but rest.

The evil that followed Molly could not touch her—that was
thanks to the magic of the amulet she wore. But it followed
her nonetheless; it waited for opportunity; it waited patiently, unable just this time to create its own opportunity. It

was old—very old—and luck had always fallen its way
eventually.

Seolar, standing outside the window of Molly's room,
stared at the single iridescent scale that lay atop the snowdrift, and with trembling fingers reached out and picked it
up. He had known when she told him of her dream and of
the branch that had so frightened her. She had laughed, and
he had managed to smile as if he were amused, but he had
known—for within the walls of Graywinds there were no
trees, no shrubs, not even any tall plants. The ground was
kept clear to provide a clear field of fire should the keep's inhabitants find themselves under attack. Trees and bushes
would provide shelter to the enemy.

Molly did not know. Nor would anyone tell her—this secret Seolar would keep to himself alone. The rrôn could not
touch her; but if they frightened her, she might insist on going back to Earth. And then the rrôn would win, and the
cities of the veyâr would fall to them—and after them, the
cities and lands of the rest of Oria's people.

"There aren't any bushes or branches outside my window," Molly said from right behind him.

He jumped and turned, dropped the scale, and stepped on
it quickly so that she would not see it.

"You—startled me," he said, and laughed. His laughter
sounded false in his own ears; he hoped she did not know
him so well that she would catch the falseness.

She smiled. "I noticed that."

"Well—I only came outside to see if we could travel today . . . but you can see that we've had far too much
snow . . ."

She raised a hand to stop him, shook her head. "Seolar.
I've picked up a few things in my life. A few bits of wisdom,
if you will. First, don't confuse adversaries and enemies.
You and I are, I suspect, adversaries. There's something you
want from me that you're not telling me, something that I
have the power to withhold, that you think I'll want to withhold—and that's putting us on opposite sides of a big fence.
But I'm not the enemy. I'm not the one you hide things
from. And second, just because they're out to get you

doesn't mean they're always out to get you. Whatever you're hiding under your foot there might be nothing of any real importance."

He said, "I'm not hiding—"

She cut him off again. "Lying doesn't improve your negotiating position." She shoved her hands inside her jacket and held them under her armpits to warm them, and only then did he realize that she'd come out without a hat or gloves or even with her coat properly buttoned. "I'm going to be honest with you. I like you. I like the veyâr, I like this world, and I'm a hell of a lot happier here than I ever was on Earth. I even think there may be some . . . some chemistry between you and me, though I've got a few issues to work through where that's concerned. My first instinct is to stay here, to help you, to do whatever it is that my parents planned for me."

He started to smile at her, but she shook her head.

"That's my *first* instinct. But," she said, "you're hiding things. Big things. There's something going on with this necklace you gave me, there's something going on with that thing under your foot, and there's a reason why you decided to go riding on a day when the weather turned so nasty— and a reason why you took us away from Copper House in the storm instead of toward it. Graywinds was farther. Wasn't it?"

He stared at her, trying to find a corner to duck into—an evasion that would let him keep the truth from her without outright lying to her. Nothing presented itself. So he nodded. "It was a great deal farther."

"Thank you. I thought so. I think you owe me the truth."

"I suppose I do." He glanced up at the sky, nervous, but nothing moved there except for clouds. Still, he would be happier under a roof. A copper-lined roof. "Walk with me," he said, and led her toward the barn. As they trudged through the snow, he said, "I don't really know where to begin."

"This necklace," she told him. "It's been giving me nightmares. And daymares, too."

He sighed. "I'll tell you what I know. One of the Old Gods created it for a child that she had with a man of my people—

about seven thousand years ago, from all accounts. I don't know precisely when; I don't think anyone does, except perhaps for others of the Old Gods, and they certainly won't tell."

"A long time ago, in a universe far, far away . . ." she muttered. "Got it. Go on."

"It protected her. While she wore it, the Old Gods could not kill her, or hurt her, or work any sort of magic against her. And so long as she wore it, it would always bring her safely back to Oria."

Molly said, "She was like me? Half veyâr and half something else?"

"Half veyâr, half human. The Vodi have all been half veyâr, half human. There have been crosses between the veyâr and others of the Old Gods, and between the Old Gods and others of the True Peoples, but none of them have become Vodi. I don't know why." He shrugged. "It's magic, and of magic I know only the stories."

"So this was created specifically for the first Vodi, by her mother."

"Such is the story. The first Vodi stood as mediator between the veyâr and the Old Gods. She buffered their curses, but she also spoke for the veyâr in their courts and councils."

"And after working as Vodi productively for—what, hundreds of years?—she died in her bed at a ripe old age, having lived a fulfilling and wonderful life."

Glancing over, Seolar caught the narrowing of her eyes and the cynical smile on her lips.

"Not precisely."

"Oh, gee. How did I know?"

They walked into the barn, and Molly picked out a bale of hay and settled on top of it. She glanced at the horses in their stalls, at the guards at the doors, and then at Seolar.

Seolar stood facing her, not willing to sit and face her eye to eye. "Different stories of her death exist. Some say she froze to death, some that she was murdered in the first building that stood on this site, others that she died on a world a long way from home. Most of the stories, though, say that one day she put the necklace in a box, and locked the box,

and put it in the deepest storeroom in Copper House, and
locked the storeroom, and walked away from it."

"And was never heard of again."

"Not exactly. The stories say that she then walked out into
the forest outside of Copper House and was immediately
murdered by the . . ." He glanced around and whispered the
word. ". . . the keth."

"How nice."

"The necklace has been worn by seven other Vodian since
then. All seven lived long lives."

He watched Molly run her fingers over the smooth, heavy
gold and stare off into space. He prayed that what he had
told her would not send her fleeing back to her own world.
She didn't know the keth—she didn't understand what being
the liaison between the Old Gods and the veyâr would be
like. But he knew she would already be figuring out that it
wasn't a safe job.

"Any of them die peacefully?" Molly asked at last.

Seolar wanted so much to lie to her. But nothing he could
do would keep her if she did not choose to stay—and he felt
sure that if he lied to her and she discovered the truth, that
would drive her away faster than anything else. "No," he
said, and did not elaborate.

"Well." She took her hand away from the necklace and
stared down at her feet for a long time. "All right. I have a
better idea of what I'm up against now. So . . . why did you
feel it was necessary to drag me away from Copper House
with a snowstorm coming on?"

"If you are to stand between the veyâr and the Old Gods,
you must stand on equal footing with them. You must know
magic—not just how to heal, but how to fight, how to
change things, how to undo whatever they may throw at you.
If you can stop their magic, they can't intimidate you."

"That makes sense."

"I don't know how magic works, Molly. None of the
veyâr know. I know that it is something I would be able to do
downworld from Oria. I know it is something you especially
are capable of doing here. Since I can't teach you what you

have to know, I . . . acquired . . . teachers for you."

"And the teachers are coming here?"

"No. The teachers will be going to Copper House."

"Then why are we here instead of there?"

"Because I did not want you anywhere around the people who were bringing your teachers to you. I don't want them to know you exist—and because they're . . . Old Gods. If you were in residence in Copper House when they arrived, I was afraid they might somehow know you were there."

He felt her staring at him as he talked, but he couldn't meet her eyes.

"That's true as far as it goes, I think," Molly said after a moment of silence. "But you're not telling me everything about the teachers, either, are you?"

He looked up at her and laughed. "I would hate to have my life depend on keeping secrets from you."

"What's the secret?"

"I hired some very bad men to kidnap your teachers from Earth. They're Sentinels—both the men I hired and the people they are bringing to you. I'm ashamed of what I have done—but my people and my world depend on you. You must have teachers who can truly teach you. You cannot be unprepared when you face the worst of the Old Gods. Many Old Gods can be difficult. Some are bad. But the rrôn . . . and the keth . . ."

"You're just full of surprises, aren't you?" Molly said. She watched him with eyes he could not read. He wondered what she thought of him. He wondered if she would stay, or if she would be so disgusted by his dishonorable behavior that she would go. He dreaded finding out—but he wouldn't find out anytime soon, because she stood and said, "I think I need lunch and a nap."

Cat Creek

Sitting in the car, clutching the shotgun with one hand and Jake with the other, Lauren watched Pete disappear into the ruined old house. She tried to look everywhere, tried to make sure that no one would be able to come in behind Pete and Eric and trap them in the house—and that no one would rise up out of the weeds and kill her or Jake. She waited—heartbeat hammering in her ears, scared so bad she wanted to cry. And then the radio in the car came to sudden, panicked life.

"Dispatch! Dispatch! This is Deputy Pete Stark, 10-20 to Tucker Farm, west of Cat Creek on 79. Officer down! Repeat, officer down! Signal 102, CPR in progress. Requesting ambulance and backup." Through that, his voice remained steady. But Lauren heard his calm break with his next words. "Get me some help out here fast!"

CPR? Lauren looked down at Jake, at the shotgun she held, and back up at the house. She needed to be in there, not out here. She could free Pete up to do cardiac compressions. She knew rescue breathing—that ought to be worth something. And Jake . . . she would find something to do with Jake.

Pete was doing CPR on Eric. She sat there staring at the mike, realizing that the one person she could truly trust in Cat Creek—the one who knew who she was and also knew that she was innocent of the crimes that someone had attempted to pin on her—the one person she could have counted on, was in there dying.

Because if Pete was doing CPR, then Eric was dying. Oh, God. Eric couldn't die on her. He couldn't leave her alone in Cat Creek with people who wanted to kill her and her son.

She grabbed Jake under one arm and slid out the door. With the shotgun tucked under her other arm and the safety on, she sprinted for the house. She bolted up the stairs, charged inside, and found Pete kneeling over Eric, fighting to remove a bulletproof vest that hadn't been, with a bloody gas mask beside him on the floor.

She swung around, panicked, thumb on the safety—but she and Pete and Jake and unmoving Eric seemed to be alone in the house.

"I can breathe him for you," she said. She tried not to see the pool of blood beneath Eric. She had never in her life seen so much blood at one time.

Pete, fingers interlaced, pressing on Eric's chest, just nodded. He was counting under his breath. "Thirteen . . . fourteen . . . fifteen . . ." He switched position, checked for Eric's pulse, blew several breaths into his lungs, then returned to Eric's chest. "Settle Jake. Then come help."

She looked around the room, placed the shotgun on the mantel well out of Jake's reach, and told Jake, "Baby wall." She dragged the couch out from the wall, sending clouds of dust into the air and disturbing a mouse—which shot across the floor and under the door into the kitchen—then she jammed the two armchairs into the spaces on either side of the couch and the wall. Instant playpen.

"Sit right there," she told Jake, dropping him into the enclosed area. "Play. Look out the windows."

She did a quick check for anything that might hurt Jake—dangling cords, stray mouth-sized objects, electrical outlets and things to stick in them—but she didn't see anything. Praying that she hadn't overlooked something lethal, she hurried across the room and dropped to the ground beside Pete. She felt warm fluid soaking into the knees of her jeans, and did not let herself think of where that warmth and wetness came from. She and Pete would save Eric. He would live. He *had* to live.

"Count of four. You breathe when my hands come up on four, move back when they go down on one," Pete said, running his fingers over Eric's chest to find the right spot on the sternum. He rested the heel of his left hand on the sternum, the heel of his right hand on top of the left, and interlaced his fingers. "You ready?"

She nodded, tipped Eric's jaw back, clamped his nose closed, and opened his mouth. He was still warm. His skin was a horrible blue-gray and his eyes, half-open, stared at nothing. But he was still warm.

He's going to live, she told herself, and breathed into his lungs, and felt his chest rise, and resolutely did not allow herself to dwell on a day with dappled sunlight, and a single teenage kiss. He's going to live.

You have to live. You can't leave me here alone with Jake—not in this town where someone wants us dead.

You're supposed to protect us. You have to live.

She heard Pete's voice droning, "One one-thousand . . . two one-thousand . . . three one-thousand . . . breathe one-thousand . . ." over and over. She breathed. In between breaths, she looked over her shoulder to where she could see Jake's legs and feet moving around behind the couch. She listened with everything in her for the first faint scream of the ambulance siren.

She prayed. Endlessly, she told Eric he was going to live.

And then, before she really comprehended what was happening, the rescue squad arrived and strong men and women were pulling her back and out of the way; they put a tube into Eric's airway, started IV lines, shocked him with a defibrillator, injected drugs into their IVs, and strapped him onto a gurney.

And then they and he were gone, and she and Pete were left staring at each other, both covered with blood, while the Laurinburg cops poured into the place and started asking questions neither of them had answers for. The only one who knew what had happened—the only one who had even the faintest idea what he'd found at the farm—was on his way to Scotland Memorial Hospital at that very moment, with a woman squeezing air into his lungs with a big blue-plastic bulb and a man pressing on his chest to do the work his heart would have been doing if it had still been beating.

She wandered away from the cop who was asking her questions, gathered Jake into her arms, and held him close to her. Clutching him, she dropped onto the couch and shut her eyes tight. She felt the tears burning their way down her cheeks, she tasted salt at the back of her throat, and choked around the lump there. She hadn't felt so alone in the world since Brian's death.

Graywinds, Ballahara

Seolar stood in the doorway for a long while, watching Molly sitting in the sunroom, the firelight highlighting her hair with brilliant red-gold. She sat watching the snow falling; she'd been so still and silent that he began to worry something had happened to her. Then she turned and said, "You might as well come in here."

"I did not wish to disturb you."

"I'm just thinking. Nothing much to disturb." She smiled, but her eyes still looked somber.

Seolar walked over to her side. "I am sorry for the distress my actions have caused you—"

Molly held up a hand to stop him. "Not that. Not now. I've considered the bitterness of life and the unfairness of the choices each of us are forced to make until I can't stand to think of it anymore. We'll talk about the state of our two worlds, and what they both need, and what we must do. But later. Not now. Right now, I'd really just like to have your company."

He touched her, resting his hand on her shoulder, and trembled with the audacity of it. "Truly?"

She smiled at him, and did not pull away from his touch. "Truly."

They stood so close that he could feel her warmth, so close that he could smell the sweet scent of her skin. He smiled at her, and felt his face grow warm with his nervousness.

She took a half step closer to him and said, "What do the tattoos on your face mean?" She touched a finger to his *karayar.*

"*Karayar,*" he said. "They chronicle my life from the time I reached the age of choice; each rank, each honor. A few other things."

She stroked the finger along the line of his cheek. "They're pretty."

He laughed a little; when he thought of them, all he ever thought of was the pain he underwent each time a new one was added. "They're words in an old, old language—the first written language of the veyâr. We don't use it for anything else anymore." He started to tell her more about the *karayar,* but stopped. Out of nerves, he babbled; he felt foolish. He didn't know what to say to her, but he didn't think a lecture on veyâr facial tattoos would accomplish . . . what?

What did he hope to accomplish? He looked into her
eyes—not veyâr eyes, but not truly human, either. She was
exotic, but beautiful. He slid a hand around her waist and
stepped a little closer to her. Not close enough that their bodies touched, but so close that he could feel the heat between
them as pressure.

"Molly," he whispered.

"Seo." Her hand moved from his cheek to the back of his
head, and she pulled his face close to hers, and touched his
lips lightly with her own.

He kissed her slowly. She closed her eyes, and he ran a
hand through her hair and pulled her so close that their bodies touched along their length; in that instant, he could imagine her beside him in his bed. He wanted to experience the
union of their flesh. He wanted to undress her, to claim her.

Behind them, at the door, someone cleared a throat.

Molly pulled away, startled, and Seolar turned, wanting to
kill whoever had interrupted them.

Birra stood with his back to them.

"What?" Seolar asked.

"We have a break in the weather at last. We need to leave
now."

Seolar turned back to Molly. She gave him a tiny smile
and an even slighter shrug. "Ah, well. There's always Copper House."

With his body aching from denied passion, Seolar bowed
to her and said, "Then we shall find another time. Soon."

"You promise?"

"I do."

Scotland Memorial Hospital, Laurinburg

Lauren sat beside Pete in the ICU. Freshly showered and in
clean clothes, she still felt like she was wearing Eric's blood.
The news was uniformly bad—the doctor had Eric on a ventilator, Eric had never regained consciousness, the staff was
trying to track down a family member to tell them whether

they wanted to remove life support or not.

Lauren, holding the finally sleeping Jake in her arms, thought of Oria. If this had happened in Oria, she could have done something to help Eric. She could have tried magic. She couldn't bring Brian back from the dead, but Eric wasn't dead yet, and she sure could have magicked a bullet hole out of existence.

But the only gate she knew of lay in Cat Creek, and she didn't think the ER staff would let her drag Eric and his life support to Cat Creek so that she could shove him through a magic mirror.

She looked sidelong at Pete, who had been in and out of the ICU since they'd finally finished up with the Laurinburg police.

"Pete?"

"Yeah." He'd been staring in glum silence at the floor for a long time. He barely raised his head when she spoke to him.

"Are there any mirrors in Eric's room?"

He shrugged and glanced at her, a little curious, but still clearly focused in his own world. "Mirrors? There are . . . two, I think. The one over the sink and the full-length one on the bathroom door."

She knew how to get to Oria. How to find her parents' house there. She could feel it calling her even as she sat on the couch. If she had a mirror, any mirror big enough to pull a human being through, she could make a gate. She hadn't done it since she was ten, but she knew that she *could* do it.

The problem would be working around the ICU staff, their glass-walled rooms, their cautious watchfulness.

"Pete?"

Now, sensing something from her shift in position or the tone of her voice, he watched her, unblinking, and said nothing.

"I can save his life."

Those cool, intelligent eyes assessed her. "This have anything to do with Eric's big secret?"

"What do you know about that?"

"Not enough. But you don't live most of your life in a town as small as Cat Creek without getting the feeling sometimes that there's more going on than anyone is willing to admit to. So this is about that."

"Yes."

"You have to let me help."

She nodded. "There's no way I could do it without you."

"And you have to let me know what the secret is."

She managed a small smile. "There's no way you won't know. Just . . . promise me you won't . . . um, freak out. Or get scared. Or . . . anything."

"Not my style."

"No. It isn't." She cleared her throat, looked down at Jake, who was so beautiful asleep, and dropped her voice to a near whisper. "You have to get all three of us into his room. And you have to figure out a way to get the nurses and the doctors and everyone out of his room for . . ." She frowned, trying to guess how much time she would need. ". . . for ten minutes. Maybe more. When we get ready to move . . . er, to fix him, you're going to have to keep the door shut against them. Because the alarms on the machines are all going to start going off."

He looked at her, nodded thoughtfully, and stared down at the floor again. Now, however, he didn't seem lost in despair. He just looked like someone who was thinking.

After a moment, he nodded. "Got it. Bring Jake and come on."

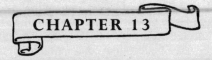

CHAPTER 13

Scotland Memorial Hospital

THEY HID OUT in the cafeteria until shortly after Pete knew the shift change would be complete. Then he took Lauren and Jake upstairs, presented them and his badge at the door, and told the nurse who answered, "Found his fiancée and their little boy. You got any of the rest of the family yet?"

The nurse who answered the door gave Lauren and Jake a pitying look. "We haven't managed to get in touch with anyone. We're short-staffed because of the flu, and all our beds in all our units are full, so the supervisor is having to do a lot of relief. If she was his wife, we could let her sign papers but . . . they're not married, so she can't . . . but if you or she could call a family member . . ." Her eyes kept straying back to Jake. "You're his fiancée?"

Lauren nodded.

"Aw, honey," the nurse said, "you'd better come on in and see him."

Lauren nodded again, not saying anything.

Still the nurse blocked the way in, obviously struggling with something. At last she said, "We shouldn't let the little boy in. Children aren't allowed in the ICU."

"His son," Pete said, his voice thick with emotion.

The nurse winced. "Screw it. Supervisor's tied up with flu cases down in the ER. She won't be able to get back up here for ages. Fifteen minutes, and I didn't see anything."

"Thank you," Lauren told her. She didn't have to feign the anguish in her own voice.

Eric looked like hell. His skin was still gray, in spite of the IV fluids and the unit of blood running in via controllers. He had a big plastic tube shoved down his throat, taped in place and connected to a machine the size of Lauren's washing machine with a bellowslike contraption inside a clear plastic casing that sucked in and out in rhythm to the rise and fall of his chest. Its display blinked and flashed like cheap Christmas ornaments, and it hissed and clicked and beeped and bubbled. Over Eric's head, a wall unit displayed a green line that she could identify as a heartbeat, along with a number of other scrolling green lines that she couldn't even begin to guess at. His eyelids were padded with white gauze and taped shut. His big, strong hands lay limp on top of the smooth, neatly turned-down covers. A thick pad of white bandages, blood-stained at the very center, and with ballpoint-pen lines marking the periphery of the bloodstain, with the date and time neatly inked by an arrow connecting to the line, covered his chest and belly.

"His doctor is in surgery right now—we had another case come in through the ER," the nurse said. "We have another doctor on call for emergencies, but I know that Dr. Sakamurja would prefer to talk to you when he's free. If you can wait."

Lauren nodded. "I'm not going anywhere. What can you tell me about him? About all of this?" She pointed to the machines, the monitors, the IV controllers.

The nurse licked her lips. "He's not good. We have a ventilator breathing for him—he isn't doing it on his own. His heart is beating pretty well at the moment, but we had an awful fight earlier just to keep it going. The drugs going into his IVs seem to have stabilized that, but I can't promise you it will stay that way." She took a deep breath and said, "There's more, too. One of the two bullets went through his spine at the third thoracic vertebra. It . . . damaged the spinal cord."

"How badly?"

"The doctor will have to give you the full details of the

damage, but it was severe. Leaking of the cerebrospinal fluid and swelling of the tissue are complicating our attempts to treat him."

"But he won't be able to walk again, even if he ever does wake up, will he? He'll be lucky to be able to feed himself, or say his own name. Right?"

"Well . . ." Lauren could see the nurse fighting with herself—trying to figure out how much to tell, how much to hold back. She was searching for a way to sugarcoat the bad news. Lauren decided to make it easier for her.

"Um . . . Ms. Baldwin . . ."

"Just call me Nancy."

"Nancy . . . Deputy Stark told me he was pretty sure Eric was going to die. I just want to know, if a miracle happens and he doesn't, how much of him is going to be left?"

The nurse nodded. "Neural injuries are . . . are difficult to assess at best. But the damage to his spinal cord was . . . well, severe. I saw the X-rays—the . . . um . . . injury . . ."

"The bullet," Lauren said quietly.

"Yes. The bullet. It severed the spinal cord completely, tore the sheath that covers the cord, shattered the bones that are supposed to protect it, and badly damaged one of his lungs, his liver, his gallbladder, and portions of his intestine on its way through and out. The other bullet nicked the aortic artery and hit his left kidney, and got more of his intestine."

Lauren closed her eyes. "The bastard," she whispered. She turned to Pete. "Why didn't his bulletproof vest protect him? He was wearing it. You had to take it off him to do CPR."

"Plenty of bullets go right through body armor," Pete said. "Any bullet shot from most any rifle, or armor-piercing bullets shot from just about anything . . . Armor can help you. But it's no guarantee."

"Bastard," Lauren said again. She touched Eric's hand. It was cool and lifeless. She closed her eyes. The tears she'd been trying to block escaped anyway. "He deserved better than this."

"The odds aren't good for him," the nurse agreed, trying to be tactful. "I mean, miracles happen. You can always hope

for a miracle. God knows, I've seen a few people that I
would have thought—"

"I'd like to be alone with him for a few minutes," Lauren
said, interrupting the nurse's pep talk. She looked at the
nurse, not bothering to wipe at the tears that streaked down
both of her cheeks. "Just a few minutes of privacy for Jake
and me . . . well, and Pete. Eric wouldn't be alive at all if it
weren't for Pete."

"I can give you a few minutes," the nurse said. She nib-
bled the corner of her lip and glanced over her shoulder, out
the huge glass wall to the nurses' station where other nurses
sat, watching monitors, filling out charts, and talking to
other hospital personnel who moved hurriedly through the
wide, brightly lit unit. "It won't be long because we have to
do meds and things, but . . ."

Lauren nodded. "Thank you. Anything we can have."

The nurse pulled a hideous green-and-blue curtain across
the window and stepped out of the room, closing the door
behind her.

Lauren immediately handed Jake to Pete and said, "This
is going to get weird, Pete. Just don't freak on me."

"I'll be fine. Just . . . save him."

"Yeah. Pray, okay?"

Pete said, "I've been doing nothing but since this happened."

"Me, too." Lauren walked to the full-length mirror on the
bathroom door. It was narrow, but she thought Eric would fit
through it sideways. The thing that really concerned her was
how long she would have from the time she pulled out his
IVs and disconnected him from the ventilator until he died
on her. In what she guessed was going to be a narrow window, she had to get him, Jake, Pete, and herself from the
ICU into Oria and do whatever magic she could to erase the
damage the bullets had done to him.

He wasn't dead yet. That was her only comfort. Brian's
otherworld twin had said that she couldn't call anyone back
from the dead. But as long as Eric wasn't dead, she was willing to bet that what she could do for him in Oria was going

to be better than what doctors and medical technology were going to be able to do for him on Earth.

Time was what had her spooked. It was always the enemy, wasn't it? She rested her palms flat on the mirror, staring into it, willing herself to see the snow-covered glade that surrounded her parents' house in Oria. She was feeling for that connection, the familiar shape, for a spark that would connect her to the place she knew best there. She breathed deeply, and in a moment, saw the first flash of green lightning, and felt the shivering thrill of power down her spine that was her connection to the wild storm that linked the worlds.

She pulled the storm closer to her, welcoming the thunder, the lightning, the slashing rain, and in the heart of the storm, she began to make out the outlines of the old house, shrouded in the darkness of night, the ancient trees grasping at it with branches weighted and limned in a tracery of white, the small clearing now drifted high with more snow. Moonlight gleamed through patched clouds. She pulled the image closer yet, and was staring into the kitchen, where everything still lay in awful disarray.

Behind her, she heard Pete making funny little squeaking noises. She didn't let them distract her. She fixed the image, forced a road to open between the ICU and the little house lost in snow and darkness, and, with the energy of worlds humming in her veins, turned to Pete.

"Got it," she said. "You're stronger than me. You're going to have to do the next part."

He nodded. Handed Jake to her. Grabbed one of Eric's thick-soled work shoes that were stacked on the windowsill with his few other personal effects, slid the leg of one of the room's sturdy visitor chairs into the shoe, and shoved the wooden back of the chair under the door handle. With the shoe wedged in place to keep the chair from sliding, he gave the makeshift jamb a couple of quiet kicks and said, "That'll hold for a few minutes. If this doesn't work, we're going to go to jail for attempted murder. You know that, right?"

"I know."

Pete nodded. Hurried to the bedside. Grabbed one of a couple of rolls of white cloth tape left lying on the ventilator and two gauze pads, and with a neat efficiency that surprised Lauren, tore strips of tape, put pressure over one IV with his thumb and a gauze pad, yanked out the IV, and taped the gauze down. "Keep them from bleeding," he said in explanation. "I figure he doesn't need to lose any more blood than he's lost already."

Lauren nodded. "Where'd you learn to do that?"

"I got some medic experience . . . overseas. I still have a few skills." He pulled out the other IV in the same fashion. "Long as we let the pumps keep dripping this stuff into the bed, the alarms won't go off. Nothing going to keep the damned ventilator quiet, though." Then he smiled. "Stupid me. Forget I said that." He glanced over at her. "We're going to shove him *through* the mirror. You're sure."

Lauren slid her hand up to the elbow straight into the green-glowing mirror in reply. On the other side, she felt Brian's fingers tighten around hers—a single quick squeeze that told her he was there for her. She blinked away tears and tried not to think of Eric joining Brian in that lost place between the worlds. "I'm sure," she said.

Pete nodded, and she saw him swallow hard. "Yeah. Okay. Well, this is going to have to be real quick. If he's not breathing on his own, we're talking four minutes from off-the-ventilator to dead, and probably with brain damage setting in before that."

Lauren swallowed hard. Four minutes. That was a worse window than she'd imagined. But it was what she had. She nodded.

Pete walked around to the side of the bed closest to the mirror, then reached across the bed and hit a switch. The ventilator fell silent in mid-gasp, its lights suddenly dark, its bellows still. Pete grabbed the blue accordion tube that connected Eric's white-plastic tube to the machine and disconnected it quickly. Then he blew once into the now-open end of Eric's tube and Eric's chest rose, then fell. "Best I can do until we get there," Pete said. He lifted Eric up in a bear hug and dragged him the short distance from the bed to the bathroom door.

"Push him in, don't let go of him, and hold your left hand out for me," Lauren said.

"I remember." Pete looked weirdly pale and scared in the green light. Behind them, the heart monitor, now connected to nothing but dangling electrodes, started screaming. "Gotta be quick."

He angled Eric's limp body sideways and shoved him into the green fire. Wide-eyed, he stepped into the mirror himself, having to turn completely sideways, and sucked in his chest to get through. His left hand stuck out of the glass. Behind them, Lauren heard people pounding on the door, kicking at it, shouting. She grabbed Pete's hand and, with Jake clinging tightly to her, stepped through herself. She felt the wondrous hum of energy suffuse her, and Brian's arms around her and Jake, and behind her she heard the door smash open, and heard, too, a final wail of disbelief and shock and fear. And then she was standing on her parents' floor in the ice-cold house in Oria, with Eric lying at her feet and Pete kneeling over him, breathing into the white tube and checking the pulse at his throat.

Behind her, with the connection between the worlds broken, the gate closed.

"Hurry," Pete said. "His heart isn't doing right."

"Light," Lauren said. And there was light.

Pete made a whimpering noise, then resolutely turned to Eric and breathed for him again.

Lauren dropped to her knees and, with a squirming, kicking Jake locked tight to her chest beneath her left arm, splayed the fingers of her right hand over Eric's chest. "Be ready," she said. "If this works, he's going to wake up fast, and he may panic."

Pete just nodded.

"Heal," she said, and closed her eyes and visualized Eric whole again, alive and standing and talking, with no scars, no blood, no damage. She felt her arm lock up, felt the space between her palm and Eric's chest fill with an electric tingling, and for a moment she couldn't move.

"Oh, my God," she heard Pete whisper.

She dared to open her eyes.

The green flames of magic blazed across Eric's body, which had gone rigid and now began to arch wildly—his head, heels, and the palms of his hands touched the floor, but his torso bent so hard she thought his spine might snap.

"What's happening?"

Lauren, her hand still locked to his chest, with fire flowing between them, couldn't make her mouth form words or her throat form sounds. She could barely breathe. She held her position, concentrating on willing Eric back to health and full life.

And suddenly the fire went out and he collapsed on the floor and his arms shot to his eyes, clawing at the pads, and his knees came up and his feet kicked out. Lauren scrambled back. Pete, either braced against such an eventuality, or more prepared by his experience as a medic, moved in and ripped the end off a tiny tube that protruded from the side of the airway. When Eric coughed, the large tube slid out smoothly. And then Pete was pulling the tape off Eric's eyes, saying, "Man, I'm right here, hang on, don't kick and don't hit me; it's Pete, just hang on, just hang on and everything is going to be all right."

Tears were pouring down Pete's cheeks.

Eric, coughing desperately, clutching at his throat, sat up.

"Where the hell are my clothes, and what is going on and what am I doing in this . . . this bare-assed *thing?*" he demanded.

Pete, weeping, hugged him.

"And what the hell is the matter with you," Eric shouted, pulling back. And then, looking around, "And where are we? . . . And, good Christ, why is it so cold in here?"

"Warmth," Lauren said.

Suddenly it was no longer cold.

Eric's head snapped around, and his eyes met hers, and in a low and dangerous voice, he said, "What the hell have you done?"

"She saved your life," Pete said quietly.

Eric looked down at the blue hospital gown that covered him only to mid-thigh, and rested his hand on his stomach. Another hand crept around to his back, where even more heavy bandages covered him from just below his neck to just above his buttocks.

Gingerly, he lifted the gown front. "Whoa!" He turned beet red, yanked the gown back down, and said, "Where'd my underwear go? And what are all the bandages for?"

Lauren said, "What is the last thing you remember?"

Eric grew still. "We were in the station. And then I got the call—Debora's body. No . . . it was Molly. And I went out to the old house. And all the Sentinels were there—tied up on the floor, and Tom Watson and Deever Duncan were shoving them into . . ." He glanced quickly at Pete. "Into Oria. And they talked about just killing the ones who were left, and I went charging . . . in."

A long, horrified pause.

"And I was careless. Thought I knew where everyone was. But I'd missed one—he came out of the kitchen behind me and shot me in the back . . ."

"Who was it?" Pete asked.

"Willie," Eric said. He shook his head like he couldn't believe his own words. "Willie Locklear. And then everything went black, and I woke up here."

"You were going to die," Pete told him. "You were on a ventilator, your spinal cord was severed, your heart wasn't working right, and the ICU staff was trying to get hold of your next of kin because no one was expecting you to pull through."

Eric looked at Lauren. "Where are we now?"

"This is my parents' old place in Oria."

"How much did you tell him?"

"Not much. He already had his suspicions."

Eric looked back at Pete, startled. "You did?"

"You were very careful. But even that sort of care becomes a flag after a while. I never guessed you were into anything this weird. But I knew something was up."

Eric nodded. "Clothes," he said, and a rumpled pile of clothes appeared in front of him.

Lauren said, "I would have at least created clean clothes."

"Didn't create these," Eric said. "I just moved the pile from beside my bed to here. It disturbs things a lot less that way." He said, "Would you mind turning around for a minute?"

Lauren turned, and Jake kicked her and yelled, "Down! I . . . DOWN!"

"Not yet." She shifted him over to her hip, though he fought her like a wolverine, and did a spell that cleaned up the mess inside the house, putting everything back in its proper place and restoring it to its undamaged state.

"Don't *do* that!" Eric yelled. "Do you have any idea what that sort of power wastage can do back on Earth?"

Lauren said, "No."

"Shit. Don't do it. Let me change, and we'll figure out what we're going to do, and I'll see if I can show you why excess magic is such a bad idea."

"I wish I could do that," Pete said wistfully.

"You could," Eric said, "but please don't. The problems we're facing right now will just get worse—a whole lot worse, with the effects of a lot of amateur magic bouncing around. She's bad enough." Lauren knew he'd indicated her.

"Never mind you'd still be dying—or maybe already dead—without me."

"I didn't say I wasn't grateful."

"You didn't say 'thank you,' either."

Silence. "Thank you." She heard bandages ripping off, and an appreciative murmur from both Pete and Eric.

"Not even a trace of a scar," Pete said. "Damn, that's going to be hard to explain."

"I'm assuming my sudden disappearance from ICU is going to have caused a bit of a stir, too."

Pete was chuckling. "I'm betting they're raising holy hell back there right now."

"That's bad. The world's continued survival depends on people *not* suspecting there's a way to walk through mirrors or disappear out of intensive care units." Lauren heard him stand, and heard thumping as he got dressed.

"All right," he said at last. "I'm done. Now we need to figure out what we do from here."

As they walked to her parents' old table, she did one tiny

little additional spell; she made sure each of them was
healthy. That talk of flu in the ICU, and the sight of hospital
hallways lined with beds filled with gasping, coughing people had made her nervous.

Natta Cottage and Cat Creek

Pete didn't settle for being brushed off. He wanted an explanation of Oria, and he wanted to know what the Sentinels
were and what they did—and when he had that, he'd wanted
a good long explanation of why exactly Eric hadn't recruited
him. He was polite about it, but he pushed hard.

Lauren, on the other hand, wanted to know why she
wasn't supposed to use the magic she could do in Oria. As
Eric told her about the properties of magic flow between the
worlds, and how any act of magic carried out in Oria sent
waves of energy that influenced events on Earth, she began
to regain vague memories of her parents discussing that issue with her—but along with their explanations of the dangers, she started remembering them telling her that
rebounding was not the terrible problem that everyone kept
thinking it was. That *intent* was the biggest director of rebound. She could almost recall seeing that written as a rule
somewhere in her parents' notebook.

"So you're saying that the world as we know is going to
end in about a month," Pete said. "But that you don't know
exactly what is going to end it?"

Eric leaned his elbows on the trestle table and nodded.
"And now the rest of the Sentinels in Cat Creek are either
traitors, or kidnapped and possibly dead, and my chances of
finding the problem and fixing it without them are nil." He
winced and muttered, "Shit. And Willie said he'd called for
backup from some of the other Sentinels nexuses, but he was
one of the traitors. And so was Deever. So there isn't going
to be any backup coming unless we call again." He rested his
head in his hands, and said, "Son of a bitch."

Jake, playing on the floor with pens and a notepad from Lauren's purse, looked up. "Son of bits!" he said. "Son of bits! Son of bits! Son of BITS!"

"Thank you, Jake. Very nice. That's enough now." Lauren managed a weak smile. "What about my parents' notebook?" she asked. "Did you have a chance to look through it? Was there anything in there that might help us?"

"I don't know. They had some truly strange stuff in there. And notations that I really didn't have a chance to decipher—I get the feeling that we're going to have to go through the whole notebook to get an idea of what exactly they were working on. It might have something in it that could help us, but do we have the time to go through it and look at everything, only to find out at the end that it doesn't?"

"Can we take the chance that it does have an answer in it, and not research it?" Lauren asked.

"Not really, I suppose. We have a few things we have to do fast—we have to find the traitors. We have to discover what they've done so that we can undo it. We have to rescue the missing Sentinels if they're still alive. Once we've gotten our people back, *then* we should go through your parents' notebook to see if anything in it could help us."

"Have poopies," Jake, from his position on the floor, announced suddenly and loudly.

"And we have to get some diapers and diaper wipes and winter clothes and food and other supplies if we're going to work from here. Or are we going to work from Cat Creek?"

"That would be awkward," Eric said. "Considering the last anyone heard of me, I was dying. We'll have to deal with the fact that I'm alive and unscathed eventually, but I'd rather not deal with it now. That will just get in the way of our real problems."

"But you don't just want to create the supplies, or make them appear from somewhere over there, do you?" Lauren asked.

Eric shook his head. "I want to keep our presence here as light and low-magic as possible, if for no other reason than that the traitors could pick up large magic signatures and trace them back to us. I don't want to tip them off that I'm alive, or that we're coming after them."

"Agreed. Then we need to go back and get some supplies."

"I'm staying with the two of you and helping out," Pete said.

Eric looked at him, then sighed. "Yes. We'll need you. But you're going to have to be careful; this place is a lot more dangerous than Earth. I'll have to figure out how to protect you from magic and keep you from inadvertently setting off any spells of your own." He frowned off into space for a moment, then nodded sharply. "I'll figure out something that will work. Meantime, let's go back and get what we need. Lauren—the gate leads into your house, doesn't it?"

She nodded. "It does, but I can use the mirror to take us someplace else if you don't want to go there first."

"Let's head to the office. The notebook is locked up in the safe, and I definitely want to get hold of that before anyone else beats us to it."

Lauren sniffed the air. "Second stop is going to have to be my house, though. Jake's diaper definitely needs to be changed."

Lauren got as far as the second step in creating the gate— she'd summoned the magic and focused the view in the mirror on the inside of the sheriff's station. But the place was full of men in uniforms.

"Trouble," she told Eric.

He walked over behind her, looked at what she was seeing, and said, "That's County. Hell's bells. They're all over the place."

"Had to kind of figure that," Pete drawled.

"Oh?"

"Town sheriff is shot and rushed to the hospital. His deputy and putative fiancée and son appear at his deathbed, and only minutes later, deputy, fiancée, child, and man in coma vanish into thin air from behind a locked door. That's bound to raise some eyebrows. But by this time, somebody has probably noticed the other people missing from town, too. County boys could be checking up on that."

"Well, we can't go back to the office."

"I'd say not."

Lauren said, "I don't want to leave that notebook."

"County boys won't be able to get into the safe. Only Pete and I have the combination, and it isn't written down. They'd need to have something pretty extraordinary to get an order to break it open."

Both Lauren and Pete simply looked at him.

"They probably already have a guy with a drill there," Eric conceded.

"Got poopies NOW," Jake complained.

"Home," Lauren said. She refocused the view in the mirror, and when she was looking out her own foyer—which was *not* full of men in uniforms, to her infinite relief—she opened the gate, and everyone stepped through.

She felt Brian encouraging her and touching Jake, and then she was through, strengthened and relieved. For a few minutes, while she busied herself with getting Jake cleaned up and, when that was finished, putting together supplies for the trip back to Oria, she let herself simply enjoy the cozy domesticity of the place. But she felt pressure, too. The people who had tried to kill Eric, and who had, perhaps, had something to do with her parents' murder, were somewhere in Oria; they had prisoners; the clock to an as-yet-unlocated Doomsday bomb ticked ever closer to explosion; and the world could never again be the sane, explicable place she'd believed it to be when she and Brian had made all their hopeful plans. As much as she wanted to pretend she was safe in the old house, she didn't let herself. Instead, she packed with the quick, ruthless efficiency of a military wife faced with an abrupt change of orders. She knew the drill and let old practices and old ways of thinking return to act as guides.

Warm layers of clothing, weapons and ammunition, light dried foods, matches and snares. Brian's personal survival kit, packed at the time of his death, remained. She took that.

She worried about the things she had for Jake; North Carolina winters couldn't begin to compare to the brutal cold that she'd witnessed in Oria. But she decided that, Eric's moratorium on magic or not, if they ran into trouble she would do whatever she had to do to keep Jake safe and warm and dry. And she and Eric and Pete—and the world—would simply have to live with the consequences.

When she went downstairs, she found Pete sitting on the floor crashing cars with Jake, while Eric stared into her mirror. He was looking at the men in his office again. "Not gone yet, I see," she said.

"Not yet. And they're digging through the files. And the guy with the drill has just arrived. The only thing in the safe that could cause us any problems is that notebook. Think you can get it?"

"What do you want me to do—walk up to them and say, 'Excuse me, nice officers, but when Sheriff MacAvery took me in for questioning, he impounded my notebook, and I'd like to have it back?' "

Eric shook his head. "Of course not. I want you to steal it."

Lauren laughed.

"I'm serious. You can see the safe from here." He pointed to an in-wall safe behind his desk. "Just create a little gate into the side or the back of the safe that isn't visible from the front, and pull the notebook out."

Lauren looked at him, realization dawning on her in one wild rush. "The temptation just to take whatever you want must get to be overwhelming sometimes."

"That particular temptation only exists for gateweavers," he said blandly. "Most of us can't create gates, we can just use and maintain ones that have already been created."

"Ah. And I'm a gateweaver. And Willie Locklear is a gateweaver. Why did he turn traitor?"

Eric shook his head, his expression bleak. "I don't know. I can't stop wondering about that. He saved my life a few times; he's a genuine hero. And yet he shot me in the back. How did he do that? He's been my friend all my life."

"Not anymore, I guess," Pete said.

"No. Not anymore." Eric watched the men moving around his office, sitting at his desk, rummaging through his papers, reading a newspaper, eating doughnuts and drinking the coffee from his machine, laughing and talking with each other as if they owned the place and had a right to be there, and

Lauren saw his face darken. "Just make yourself at home, why don't you?"

"Let me get the notebook, why don't I?" she said.

She kept the operation neat and quick, only adding one opportunistic little frill. While the gate was open, the officer who'd been reading the newspaper put it down. Lauren, overwhelmed by curiosity and a puckish sense of revenge, created a tiny secondary gate beneath the newspaper, and snatched the newspaper into it. From her vantage point, it looked like the paper had blinked into thin air. Since none of the men had been watching it, the magical disappearance didn't matter. But the momentary confusion and sharp annoyance of the man who'd been reading it gave her and Eric a good laugh. They could see him accusing the men with him of taking it, and could see all of the genuinely innocent cops denying having any part in its disappearance—and looking at each other to see which man had secretly played the prank.

"You have a wicked streak," Eric told her, grinning.

"I do. But mostly I wanted to see if there was anything about you in here."

"Ah. Hadn't really thought about reading my reviews."

"Want to take a look?"

He nodded and skimmed the front page of the stolen *Laurinburg Exchange*. "Just below the fold. **Wounded Sheriff, Deputy, Mystery Woman Vanish.**"

"That's below the fold? Wow. What was the really big news?" Lauren asked.

"Two stories. The first is **11 Missing from Cat Creek, Abandoned Cars Offer First Clue.**

"I can see that," Lauren agreed. "Big news day for Laurinburg." She laughed. "What's the second?"

"Local Flu Death Toll Mounts as Bodies Found."

"Wow. Really? I didn't realize it was bad enough this year to make the news."

Eric didn't answer her. He was reading the article. She watched as his lips pursed and his face paled. "Oh, my God, this is it," he whispered as he turned the page. And a moment later, "Well, I guess this time *he* didn't go out of town." He put the paper down.

"What? Who?"

"More than a hundred people have died of influenza in Scotland County in the last twenty-four hours. In the same time period, several thousand new cases have been reported. Tens of thousands of cases are cropping up all over the U.S., and apparently in foreign countries, too. The names of those known dead in the county are listed in a separate sidebar, because in a couple of instances entire families have died and no next of kin are known. Granger Baldwin is listed as one of the dead.

The note next to his name guesses him as dead for the last few days."

"You didn't notice he was missing?"

"Granger went off on his own a lot. He never quite fit in with the good old boys, and he didn't want to pretend. So he made friends up in Fayetteville or somewhere, and spent most of his free time up that way."

Lauren said, "So you think that the thing that is going to destroy the world as we know it is . . . the flu?"

"It won't actually be the flu. I'd bet anything the CDC is completely bewildered that they can't culture out any viruses from the bodies of the dead and dying."

"But it looks like the flu."

"Lots of things look like the flu. This is of magical origin, though, and not all the vaccines and antibiotics in the world will cure it. If we cannot find the spell that will reverse it, more than half the world will die at its first blow."

CHAPTER 14

Mourning Forest, Ballahara

Console yourself not with the lie that your foe is weak, or stupid, or evil. Sometimes the enemy is worthy. Sometimes his cause is just. Sometimes both sides are right in their own ways—and in the hour that just causes collide, good men will rise up and leap into the fray, and the clash of their meeting will shake the heavens. And their blood will flow like rivers.

SEOLAR FINISHED QUOTING and looked over at Molly, his eyes curiously devoid of emotion.

"Well, that's a grim thought," Molly said. The two of them and the guards rode back to Copper House beneath sunny skies, through rapidly melting snow. "Who said it?"

"The warrior Tarmin. He led the army of the Wind Veyâr against the Iron Veyâr, during the War of Three Fish. In all of our history, there has never been another battle so bloody, or with such high prices paid by both sides."

"Because both sides were right?"

"Yes. Sadly. Each side fought for its own freedom, for its own right of passage through necessary terrain, for access to vital fields, fisheries, and forests—and because of this, for its own survival. Each side had every right to want the limited resources that would give its people sustenance in a brutal environment. Both sides knew that the resources of the area could not sustain everyone, and that the group which lost would surely perish—man, woman, and child. There could be no truce, no sharing, and no surrender. The side that won the war would survive, the side that lost would perish either at home or in exile, hounded by the hostile forces that ringed the area."

"Oh, God, how awful. Who won? What happened?"

"No one won. Or rather, both sides lost equally and completely. The warriors fought a series of terrible battles, first one side winning, then the other side making up for their loss, until the strength of both camps fell to nothing. The surviving generals threw old men, childless women, and children into the fray, resorted to desperate tactics, and slaughtered each other wholesale. At last, none remained to defend the land from outsiders but the wounded, the crippled, and mothers with babes in arms. Then the keshak, the greatest True Peoples enemies of the veyâr, swept down from the hills and scoured the land clean of life. Not a single survivor of the Winds Veyâr or the Iron Veyâr escaped from the killing fields. And the Three Fish territory fell to the keshak, who inhabit it to this day."

"God," Molly murmured.

"History is a dark and bloody place," Seolar said. "To avoid repeating it, we find ourselves doing things we do not like, and do not view with pride."

"You're trying to save your people, Seolar."

They rode in silence for a long, uncomfortable moment. Then Seolar said, "My falcon reached me this morning bearing a message. The traitors await me at Copper House."

"You knew they would come."

"Yes. But I consort with the evil and harm the good for my own personal gain. These men I hired to perform this foul task for me have performed it brilliantly. For their services, I will reward them richly. But they are evil men, and by dealing with them, by rewarding them, I become like them and a part of what they have done."

Molly twisted her fingers through the long, coarse hair of her horse's mane and considered what he'd said. "You're a good person, Seolar. You're doing what you have to do—

and maybe it isn't pretty, but if these Sentinels were any
kind of people, they would have helped the veyâr long before this."

"Perhaps. And perhaps not. What if their cause is as just
as mine? What if helping the veyâr will endanger the survival of *their* people, and *their* world?"

Molly laughed. "There are billions of humans, Seolar—
and we . . . *they* . . . have technology and vast resources on
their side. There's nothing the universe can throw at them
that they can't take. Humankind isn't going anywhere."

Seolar glanced over at her and tried to smile. "Your reassurance is a blessing. I have fought with this dilemma for so
long—and I still don't know if I can countenance my own
choices. My people are dying, and my duty is to save them.
I can die with my honor intact and my people will die with
me—and I will have failed in my duty. Or I can shame myself and give them a chance to live. History is full of honor-
able dead men who failed to protect those under their care."
He looked straight into her eyes this time and said, "I must
choose dishonor. But I hate myself for being the kind of man
who can do so."

Molly considered that for a moment. Then she said, "I
don't hate you. And I'll join you in dishonor. You're doing
the right thing. My parents believed in your cause. The man
I thought was my father believed in it so much he let a man
from another world father his wife's second child. I'm
here—I was born to be here. And I belong here." She sighed.
"I've never belonged anywhere before."

She could see the relief in Seolar's face, in his body, even
in the way he breathed. "If I can have your willing aid in our
cause, I will ask for nothing else."

Molly felt her heartbeat pick up. She smiled at him nervously, and said, "You could ask. I think I might say yes."

For a moment, he looked bewildered. Then his expression
cleared as he realized she referred to some possible shared
future for the two of them. "If I could have the honor of your
love, what other honor would I ever need?" he said at last.

"We'll figure that out as we go."

Copper House, Ballahara

Seolar did not permit Molly to be present when he paid off the traitors. The traitors did not know why he wanted a host of captive Sentinels, and they didn't care—and he didn't want them to know about Molly, who would surely be a matter of some interest to them if they discovered her presence. Fortunately, the three humans focused entirely on their own desires; they wanted their castle, their servants, and their rights and privileges as landed masters of their own realm— and that they got.

"Are any of them injured?" Seolar asked.

The youngest of the three said, "No. Unconscious, at least for another few hours, but all healthy. We were careful."

"I will inspect them with you and make sure each is confined adequately, and then you will receive your lands and titles."

"And the castle, right? Cold Starhold."

"You have already been using it," Seolar said. "I wouldn't think of changing the terms of our agreement at this late date."

He rose and signaled his guards, and the guards took up their places to the front, sides, and back of Seolar and the traitors. He might have allowed the massive amounts of copper that lined walls, ceiling, and floors of Copper House to serve as his protection, but with these humans, he did not think magic would be the only threat they might offer him should they decide to betray him, too.

The men made him nervous. Any number of times Seolar had thought that he could order them killed when the moment came; that traitors who would betray their own people and their own world deserved nothing better. But what little honor he could still lay claim to would not permit such facile excuses; he had given his word, and he would keep it—even with men whose own oaths clearly meant nothing.

He would, however, make sure that he kept his back covered at all times.

If the traitors objected to the overwhelming presence of the guards, they gave no sign. They merely marched with Seolar, following him to the suite that Molly had once occupied.

In it, unconscious men and women lay on the floor. All clearly breathed, none bore any signs of hurt.

"How have they come to be in this state?" he asked.

"We gave them a ... medicine," the oldest man said. "They will recover from it in several hours. They may be a bit sick at first—sometimes people vomit or complain of confusion or dizziness, but that passes quickly enough."

"Very good," Seolar said. "When they are all awake and demonstrably in good health, I will give you the deeds to your land, and the servants who will accompany you to your new domain. In the meantime, you'll receive accommodations in a fine suite, and we will see to your every comfort."

The third man, who had said nothing until this point, said, "I thought we were going to be on our way as soon as we gave you the people."

Seolar said, "Our agreement was that I would receive them in good health. They may or may not be in good health—I cannot verify this while they lie like the dead in my chambers."

"We tell you they're healthy."

"You also told *them* you served the same cause. I must know that they will wake and live and be able to do what I want them to do. Some of them may have reactions to the medicine they were given that would require your intervention or at least your assistance. Until I can be sure that all of my ... property ... is in our agreed-upon condition, I would prefer for you to be my guests."

"We don't want to be your guests. And I would remind you that we will be your neighbors—our goodwill in the future will matter greatly to you."

Seolar considered that for a moment. "Indeed," he said, "the goodwill of my neighbors has always mattered greatly to me." He studied the three traitors, bowed slightly—so slightly that any veyâr would have been mortally offended—and said, "Let us gather your servants. Your word will, after all, suffice."

He turned to the captain of the guards and said, "Please

take them to the Great Hall, and introduce them to Tonnil. Tonnil is head of the servants who will accompany you to your new domain," he added, glancing at the oldest traitor. He told the captain of the guards, "Meanwhile, I will gather the deeds and seals of the land. I will join you in the Great Hall with the rest of the servants, and formally invest them with their new domain."

The captain said, "This way, please," and he and the rest of the guards re-formed their column around the traitors. The three humans moved down the corridor.

Seolar did not for a moment believe that they would honor any promise of goodwill. They had no honor—they were wild dogs, and he would have to watch them the way a man watched such creatures.

But he had his own secrets in his dealings with them. Their domain lay just on the near side of the most recent influx of rrôn. Once the traitors took up permanent residence in their new abode and started stirring things up, they would discover that they had bigger problems than any dislike they might have acquired for him. He thought they would serve as a good buffer for him—three oath-breaking Old Gods and the larger part of the prisoners from Seolar's dungeon standing between his good land and his worst problem.

Birra, who had the duty of watching the Sentinels until they regained their health, joined him as he headed for the library. Birra waited until humans and guards were out of earshot, then said, "You're sending Tonnil with them?"

"They're taking Blackleg House, right at the edge of the new troubles. They've named it Cold Starhold. I should have sent *you* into that place?"

"Gods forfend! But . . . Tonnil?"

"He will keep track of the rest of the prisoners. Each prisoner who accompanies those traitors volunteered for the position in order to win a reprieve from execution. If they do us other services, they may win full pardons."

Birra smiled faintly. "And do our three future Imallins know they'll be served by the basest and most evil of criminals?"

"No. But the criminals know they'll be serving traitorous wizards, and that they'll be serving them in Blackleg House. They know that any misbehavior on their part is likely to see them turned into little smoking spots on the floor, and that at all times they will be in the power of the basest and most dishonorable of Old Gods. And that, should they consider fleeing, they will flee into the hunting grounds of the rrôn. I informed each man and woman who requested this opportunity of the inherent dangers. Quite a few were willing to take a chance on the rrôn and . . . well, *worse* . . . and on the whims of treacherous wizards, in spite of the circumstances. Better a dubious fate with traitors than a certain one with the executioner, they seem to think."

June Bug Tate woke first, and badly. She dreamed that she swam desperately to escape the maw of some enormous, toothy sea monster, and that no matter how hard she swam she couldn't reach the surface and air and safety. She couldn't breathe, and couldn't breathe, and couldn't breathe . . . and then suddenly she could, and the sharp pain of air in her lungs and the agonizing jolt into blinding light and unbearable heat proved more than her stomach could take. She leaned over, retching and heaving, aware that the awful sounds she heard came from her, washed by terrible stenches and the feeling of embarrassment that always came from losing control of her body's functions.

Something cool and damp materialized on the back of her neck, and a soothing voice said, "You were given some medicine that made you quite sick. But you'll be feeling better soon. We'll take care of you."

"Thanks," she gasped in between heaves.

She tried to remember medicine. She couldn't remember much of anything. She knew who she was, and what her place in the world was supposed to be. But how she had come to take medicine that made her sick, when she took no medicine of any sort—ever—left her baffled.

Her vision cleared and her stomach emptied, though, and she found herself awake among sleeping Sentinels, in a beautiful if overdone room, with one of the natives of Oria hovering over her, looking overdressed and fussy and entirely too tall and blue. Something about that stirred her drugged memory, and she recalled the desperate summons for all of the Sentinels.

"Oh, shit on a shingle," she muttered. "We were had."

The Orian, obsequious and prompt, had already cleaned up her mess. Now he turned to her, and said, "Had? What do you mean?"

"The bastards set us up. There wasn't any gate rip. There wasn't any influx from sideways. We got out there, they gave us all coffee while that son of a bitch Willie pretended to tinker with a gate to take us to the crossrip, and as soon as we swallowed the coffee, we fell off the face of the goddamned Earth."

"You were most certainly betrayed," the Orian agreed. "But here you are our guests, and I know the Imallin has already made provisions to return you to your own world and your own places."

Her head throbbed. "Good. Now would be a good time for your Imallin to do that. We have big problems back home, and if we don't get back there fast, we may not have a home to go back to at all."

"I'll send for the Imallin," the Orian said politely. "He is in a meeting now, but as soon as he is finished, he can explain our situation to you."

Our situation, he said. Not *your situation.* Which meant, June Bug thought, that no one was going to be sending anyone home promptly. *Our situation* meant these Orians had some need, that they'd found a way to bribe a couple of Sentinels in order to have their needs met, and that she and her people were supposed to be the next Great Hope to these lost and downtrodden aliens. She and her people had been kidnapped, and they would most certainly have to deal with ransom demands of some sort.

Well, the hell with that.

She focused her intent on locating the nearest Earth-linked gate, and centered her thoughts on immediate success. She intoned a single spell-word—"Seek"—visualizing a map that would appear in the air before her which she could use to lead everyone to whichever gate her spell located.

Nothing happened.

"Seek," she commanded again, making sure that she had concentrated on each key point in the spell.

Again, nothing happened.

Behind her, the Orian cleared his throat. "What would you have me seek?"

"A goddamned explanation," June Bug snarled. "There's no reason why that spell shouldn't have worked."

"Well . . . actually," the Orian said. He cleared his throat deferentially and waved an arm at the room around her.

Then and only then did she realize how deep in trouble she and the rest of the Sentinels were. She'd noticed that the place was pretty, but she wasn't impressed by pretty, especially not when she was sick. Frills didn't take her fancy, and this place had looked to be all frills to her. She supposed she could blame the medicine, or her own old age, or sickness, but the fact was, she'd been sloppy. She was a warrior first and foremost, and her place as a warrior demanded that she be alert to her situation. The fact that she sat in the center of a solid copper room—where no magic she would ever try could hope to succeed—should have been the first thing she noticed upon waking.

"Maybe I'm too old to be doing this," she muttered. "Time to train my successor and get the hell out while the getting is good. Move to South Florida, get a condo, learn to play shuffleboard. They haven't been able to keep a gate open in South Florida for more that half a second in the last twenty years." She glared at the copper walls, the decorative copper grillwork on the windows, the copper ceilings, the copper floors, the massive, vaultlike copper door, and she swore vigorously and with fine control. She stood, glared at the Orian, and snapped, "But I'd hate shuffleboard, and I'd hate polite little blue-haired old ladies, and I'd hate whiling away the rest of my life being useless."

The Orian backed up a step, wary in the face of her vehemence. "Yes, Narra."

"My name isn't Narra. It's June Bug."

"I request your pardon. *Narra* is a term of respect—it is reserved for the living gods."

"Right. I'm not a god, I'm a Sentinel. We aren't allowed to become gods—it's written into the bylaws."

He looked at her with an expression that suggested he was struggling over his response—laugh politely at a joke he didn't get, or agree politely to a reference he didn't understand. She sighed.

To spare him the struggle, she asked, "Any idea when the rest of them will be awake?"

"No. Your kidnappers suggested that we might have to wait several hours, and noted that you were all likely to be rather sick upon awakening."

"Bastards."

"Yes, Narra."

"June Bug, goddammit. I've never liked those damnfool titles."

"I . . . understand." He clearly didn't understand. He seemed to June Bug to own stock in polite. He said, "Is there anything I can bring you, or do for you, or offer you?"

"I'm assuming that doesn't include opening the door and letting me walk out of here."

"No, Nar—no, June Bug. But anything I can bring that will make your stay more pleasant . . ."

She nodded. "A cigar. Some toothpaste and a toothbrush. A good hot cup of coffee, extrastrong, straight black, and with the caffeine still in it." She looked thoughtfully at the ceiling for a moment, then added, "And a shot of whiskey to add to the coffee would be nice, considering this damned situation. After that . . . we'll see."

He nodded, walked to the door, opened a little panel in it, and whispered through to whoever stood outside. When he returned a moment later, he told her, "It will take a few minutes. But we will have what you requested as quickly as it can be brought to us."

"Thank you. Meantime, I'm going to see if I can wake everyone else up."

She tried shaking her fellow Sentinels, and when that

didn't work, tried pinching them and shouting in their ears. Eventually, Mayhem woke up and promptly threw up all over everything—June Bug, with reflexes that surprised her, got out of the way and missed even being spattered.

Nancine Tubbs was next—she complained of a headache, but didn't throw up on anyone. After her, most of the rest of the Sentinels started to stir. Ernest Tubbs and George Mercer woke up more or less together, and though both were disoriented, neither was particularly sick from the experience. The same couldn't be said for June Bug's sister Louisa, who vomited until she had the dry heaves, or for Jimmy Norris, whose amazing noises when he threw up were so awful that he started a chain reaction among the rest of the Sentinels.

But June Bug's other sister, Bethellen, didn't wake up at all. Her breathing got deeper and deeper and slower and slower, until finally June Bug realized that if the Sentinels couldn't get her to a place where one of them could work magic on her, they would lose her.

June Bug grabbed the Orian. "You have to let us get her away from the copper now. We're going to have to do magic on her or she'll die."

"A moment," he said. "The Imallin is on his way to us, and I believe the Vodi comes with him . . ."

The massive double doors opened, and a contingent of well-armed Orian guards filled the doorway. They made way for an Orian man in an incredible getup, and a woman that June Bug thought was also Orian . . . until she got a better look at her face. Then she realized that she was looking at either the missing Molly McColl, or her kissing cousin—but this girl had been changed by her time in Oria.

"Son of a bitch. Molly?" June Bug asked.

The young woman turned to her and nodded. "I . . . know you. From . . . from the library."

"June Bug Tate. I'm glad to see you aren't dead. But what the hell are you doing here?"

"I . . ." Molly shrugged. "It's a long story, and I heard that one of your, um, Sentinels is in trouble."

"We need to get her out of here," June Bug said. "Tell them—"

"I'll heal her," Molly said softly. "It will only take a moment."

Some of the guards had marched into the room and lifted the dying Bethellen, cot and all, and were marching her toward the door.

"She needs someone who knows how to do this," June Bug said. "Not someone who will practice on her and screw things up."

But Molly simply nodded and said, "That's why I'll do it." And then she stepped out of the room with the phalanx of guards, and the door closed, leaving the larger batch of guards and the elaborately dressed Orian man behind.

"I am Seolar, Great High Imallin of Copper House and the Sheren River Domain. The Vodi, whom you know as Molly McColl, will heal your associate, and they will rejoin us as soon as they can. In the meantime, please let me explain both our situation and yours to you."

He took a slow, steadying breath and looked from one Sentinel to the next. "I paid a high price to bring you here. I apologize for the necessity, but I simply had no choice. Had I tried to pay you to teach our Vodi what she needs to know, you would have refused. Had I threatened, you would have laughed at me. Had I appealed to your compassion, you would have expressed your sorrow and turned away. I know these things because for years, I and my predecessors have tried all these methods to enlist the assistance of the Sentinels, and we have received only those responses."

"So you paid our own people to turn traitor on us, and had us drugged and dragged here against our will."

"I will apologize again—I would not have chosen such methods, and certainly I would have done nothing to endanger any of your lives. The men who brought you to me chose their own methods, and I am displeased with the lack of respect that they showed for you and your care, and unhappy with your condition upon arrival. They will find their own justice in the fullness of time, I suspect. Such people usually do. I cannot apologize for bringing you here, though. My people are dying out, and we have at last regained the person who was born to save us, and she must learn what only you can teach her in order to do that. When she knows what you know . . . then you will be free to go. The faster and more efficiently you teach her everything you can about how you create magic in this world, and what she must do to control it and use it safely, the more quickly you will be back in your own world, doing whatever it is you need to be doing. I have been told by the traitors that there is, in fact, a matter of some urgency that you will wish to attend to. I suggest that you keep that in mind when dealing with our Vodi."

"So to kidnapping you add blackmail."

"Not at all. I merely add a voice of reason to our discussion; you wish to be somewhere else, I tell you what you must do in order to get there."

"The soul of reason," June Bug muttered. "And we're to teach . . . Molly?"

"Yes."

"What happened to her? Why does she look the way she does?"

"Because," Seolar said, "she is partly of your world, but she is also partly of ours. Her mother was one of your Sentinels—Marian Hotchkiss. Her father was one of our Imallins: Nerâmi, the Imallin of White Hold."

"That's impossible," Nancine Tubbs said. "You can't just mix and match like that. Horses can't father babies on cats, and Orians can't father children on humans. And Marian would never have done that, anyway. I knew her. She was as straight-laced as . . . as . . . Good Lord. The idea! And Walt would never have let such a thing happen—and the two of them loved each other—no one ever doubted that . . ."

Seolar held up a hand, and Nancine sputtered to a stop.

"I did not know Marian Hotchkiss, but I know of her. She and her husband are heroes to the veyâr, because they saw that we needed help, and when they could think of no other way to save us, they gave us a child who would be able to do what had to be done. Molly was conceived by magic, with intent. Her conception was carefully planned, and her gestation and birth equally carefully planned. The only thing no one planned for was having her mother die before Molly could be raised, trained, and brought here to help us."

"She didn't look like that on Earth," June Bug said. She couldn't get the picture of this new Molly out of her mind . . . but then, she'd never been able to free herself from the image of the old Molly, either—who had been a mirror of her dead mother.

"She did not. As long as she remained in your world's thrall, only her human side could express itself. Her veyâr side was . . . I don't know. Too weak? Invisible? If not invisible, then at least hidden. But her veyâr strengths have always been with her. She could heal on Earth, too. There she paid a terrible price, but because she had veyâr blood and ties to this world, she could still do magic. Here . . . here, she can do anything, and her magic has no price. No backlash. She is from your world *and* from our world, and here, she is the best of both."

June Bug, older than the others with her, knew something of what Molly was. The Sentinels forbade contact with the indigenous peoples of the other worlds they came in contact with for a very good reason. The Orians were not the first to discover that the offspring of their own kind and members of upworld races would create magic users who paid no price for their magic. Earth had suffered its share of incursions from Old Gods, too—mythology was full of stories of Old Gods who fell in love with beautiful young humans and created children with them. And the children were trouble.

Sentinel policy for the last thousand years had been to destroy such children before they could wreak havoc in their worlds. The Old Gods had mostly moved downworld to greener pastures as the worlds above Earth died and it became clear that Earth was close to its own self-destruction, so in the last hundred years, June Bug could think of only two cases that made it through the Sentinels' grapevine of the offspring of Old Gods and humans. Both children and their human parents suffered necessary accidents shortly after their births.

June Bug had never known of a case where the human

parent filled the role of "Old God" and the other parent was a downworlder. And she would never have suspected the human parent to be a Sentinel, not even one who eventually fell from grace and was named a traitor for collusive activities. To bring such a crossbred child to Earth and raise it right under the noses of those charged with eliminating all such children . . .

But Marian and Walt hadn't done that, had they? Marian, June Bug now recalled, had vanished about twenty-five years earlier for nearly a year, to care for a dying aunt over in Raleigh. She came back looking worn and bloated, and she'd cried for months. Odd for a woman who'd lost an aunt. Not so odd for a woman who'd had to leave a small and much-loved infant in the care of others.

And that left June Bug in a bad place. According to Sentinel rules, which had been developed over the course of human history to keep the world from self-destructing and to protect the people in it, Molly McColl could not be allowed to live. Because June Bug knew the rules—something the majority of the younger members, excluding Eric MacAvery, probably did not—it fell to her to call for Molly's death.

June Bug had fallen in love with Molly—the image of her mother—the first time Molly had wandered into the library looking for books on lute music and watercolor painting techniques. Now June discovered that she was in love with a woman whose death her honor required her to order. The rest of the captive Sentinels would not know if she had failed to do what she was required to do, but if Molly destroyed their world because June Bug had failed to carry out her sworn duty, the fact that only she would know the truth would be of no consolation.

She sat on her cot with her head buried in her hands, and closed her eyes. She wanted nothing more than to sink through floor and earth and stone and molten lava into the fires of hell. Then at least she would feel she'd fallen into the right place.

I'm an old woman, she told herself. Can I not die with *one* love intact, pure and unsullied? Am I doomed to see everyone I've loved die before me, and one by my hand and word? Is this God's punishment for my being who I am?

Molly returned, with Bethellen at her side. Bethellen— looking bright and fresh and completely well.

And now I owe her for my sister's life, as well.

If there was a God, he had a perverse sense of humor, June Bug decided.

CHAPTER 15

Cat Creek, North Carolina

ERIC, LAUREN, AND PETE gathered around Lauren's kitchen table. With the blinds drawn and taped in place to keep stray light from revealing their presence and their nervous leaps at every creak of the old house or thump from Jake, Lauren felt like they were thieves instead of people with a right to be where they were. All of them breathed small sighs of relief when Jake finally fell asleep in a little nest of towels that Lauren made for him beneath the table. With him quiet at last, they only had to deal with the jitters caused by the house settling and by traffic on the street outside.

Those, however, were bad enough. They weren't having any luck rescuing the Sentinels. Eric, crouched over a small hand mirror he'd liberated from Lauren's dresser, searching magically throughout Oria, had grown more frantic as the hours passed. "Nothing," he muttered. "Even if they were dead, I should be able to find their bodies—but it's like they've been erased."

Lauren said, "I know this isn't my specialty, but if you'll just tell me what you're trying to do, maybe I can think of some way to help you."

"It's very simple," Eric said. "I'm trying to locate any of the kidnapped Sentinels. Or even the traitors. I've searched for all of them, one at a time, in groups, and even all together, and they *just . . . aren't . . . there*."

"Have you tried looking for where they last were? Maybe that would at least give you a jumping-off point."

Eric snapped at her. "No, I haven't. If I can't find the place where they are, why would I be able to find a place where they aren't?"

"I don't know. It was just an idea." She shrugged, hurt, and asked Pete, "You want something to drink? I have soy milk, some decent wine, or I could juice a cantaloupe or some oranges for you."

"Got a beer?"

"No. Sorry."

"Could you get a beer?"

She glanced sidelong at him, saw the grin on his face, and after a minute said, "Yeah. I could . . . get . . . a beer. I guess."

"You know where my apartment is?"

"No."

"Know where the old Baptist Church on East is?"

"First Baptist with the pillars?"

"Right."

"Sure."

"My apartment is the top floor of the old house that used to be the parsonage—right next door to it. I have some good beer and a couple of wedges of nice cheese in the fridge there, and I'd hate to waste either."

She led him to the mirror in the hall, and while resting her palms on it, summoned up reflections of the Baptist Church, the old parsonage, and then the top-floor apartment and the inside of Pete's refrigerator. "You know where things are in there. I can't make the light go on without us actually stepping through and opening the door, and the SBI guys might be staking out your place, too. So I'll just hold the gate open, and you reach through and get your beer and your cheese and whatever else you want."

He nodded, she summoned the green fire, and he reached through into his house and pulled out a cardboard box with beer bottles with labels and names unlike any she'd ever seen, a variety of cheeses, some homemade bread, and a whole pie.

"Decided I didn't want to share with the SBI, just in case they got around to searching everything in my apartment."

Lauren was staring at the beer. "That's some weird-looking beer, Pete." She was looking at the names—Wychwood Brewery Company Ltd's Hobgoblin Extra Strong Ale, across whose bright blue label a grim, long-nosed, pointed-eared creature trudged through a moonlit village, carrying a ferocious-looking axe; Black Sheep Ale, with a proud ram on a parchment label; Badger Brewery Export Ale, whose label mascot was a badger; Brakspear Special Traditional Ale—lighter in color than the others, with a green shield label that made her think of knights and tourneys; and a couple of bottles whose labels she had to read twice. "St. Austell's Dartmoor Cockleroaster?" she asked.

Pete smiled. "Heady, rich . . . wonderful stuff. You don't, by the way, see this beer. It is not here, it has never been here, there is no such beer as this anywhere in these parts." Pete lowered his voice. "I have a friend who flies to and from England on a regular basis, and he smuggles in some of the really good stuff for me. The St. Austell's is from Cornwall. Badger comes from Dorset, Brakspear's from Henley on Thames. Black Sheep comes from somewhere up north, while the Wychwood brewery is near Oxford." He sighed, his face for a moment wistful. "Ken, a friend of mine who barkeeps at a fine little pub called the White Hart, recommends things he knows I'll like, and my . . . other . . . friend packs them in cases and smuggles it over for me aboard his plane. The Wychwood is one of my favorites—they have a number of ales and beers, and all of them are just lovely."

She said, "Why illegal English beer? Seems like a lot of trouble when you could buy beer at any corner quick mart in the state."

"No, you can't. American beer is not real beer. If it doesn't stand up on its own—and maybe have a bit of yeast in the dregs—it is *not* real beer. I discovered during my time in England that the only place you can get anything worth drinking is on the other side of the Atlantic. I spent my early adulthood there getting potted in pubs as often as I could. Now I sip my very good ale and just *wish* I was getting potted in pubs."

"You can't buy this stuff anywhere in America."

"Let me put it this way—you can't buy this stuff anywhere around *here*. And here is where I am. For now, anyway."

She laughed and helped him carry his loot out to the kitchen.

Eric sat there shaking his head when they walked in.

"It worked," he said.

Lauren raised an eyebrow. "What worked?"

"Looking for the last place they were." He pointed to the mirror, and both Lauren and Pete leaned over and took a look. They were staring at a magnificent fortified town, on a hill at the very center of which stood a massive, metal-clad castle. Eric jabbed at the image of the castle with his index finger and said, "That's why I couldn't find any traces of any of them."

Lauren couldn't begin to guess what the problem was, and said so.

"The whole place is copper-clad," Eric told her.

She spread her hands out, palms up. "Which means . . . ?"

"You haven't had any problems with copper yet?"

"No."

"Copper insulates against magic. If you put copper hand-cuffs on a Sentinel, the Sentinel won't be able to get out of them except by mechanical means—lockpicks, a saw . . . things like that. If you put your treasure in a copper safe, the Sentinel—or anyone else who can use the magic—won't be able to reach through to touch it. And if you stick a whole group of Sentinels into a copper cell, they won't be able to use magic to get out, and their Sentinel friends won't be able to use magic to get in. Or even to locate them." He sighed. "Which means we can't have you just open a gate for them from your foyer. We're going to have to go there physically and get them out."

"That's not good," Lauren said. "That doesn't look like the easiest place in the world to break into."

"No, it doesn't."

Pete studied the image, sighed, and asked Eric, "Want a beer?"

"Sure. Maybe it'll help me think."

Pete popped the top on two, and handed one to Eric. "Lauren, how about you?"

"I'll go with the soy milk, but thanks anyway."

While she rummaged through her cabinets for her favorite glass, Pete settled into the chair to the right of Eric. "You're looking at either dropping us inside the gate, where we're going to be under observation from the second we arrive until the second we leave, or else starting us off outside the city in the forest—maybe right around there . . ." He jabbed a finger at the mirror. ". . . but then we have to get across the moat and the gate and *still* figure out how to get into the castle."

"I know," Eric said, and took a long swallow of the beer. And choked. And gasped. And sputtered. "Holy sweet jumping Jehoshaphat's grandmother, what in the hell *is* that stuff?" he wheezed, and wiped foam from his mouth onto one sleeve of his shirt.

"British beer."

"That's not beer," Eric muttered. Lauren watched him glare at Pete. "That stuff has teeth and legs . . . and hair. Good Christ."

"You should really drink it at room temperature," Pete told him. "I'm doing it wrong by having it chilled, but I've gotten used to cold beer since I moved back here."

"If it thawed out, I'd be afraid it was going to drink me. You manage to sleep at night with that stuff in the house? I'm surprised it hasn't crawled out of the icebox and murdered you in your bed."

"That would be Belfast beer," Pete said. "This is English beer. Slightly better manners. It just starts singing loudly outside your bedroom door at 3 A.M."

"Ha ha."

Lauren poured her soy milk and sat down on the other side of Eric. "So what are we doing?"

"We're debating the merits of getting shot by those fellows with the crossbows walking along the top of the wall, or dropping ourselves into the forest and then figuring out how to talk the nice fellows manning the drawbridge into letting us in," Eric said. "I don't like our odds, no matter what we do."

Lauren asked, "Is there any sort of magical protection that you can see on the outside of the castle?"

Eric said, "No-o-o-o."

"Okay. So if we landed ourselves in the forest, we could work some sort of spell that would get us past the guards."

"Theoretically. We'd still have to get into the castle by nonmagical means, and find our people, also by nonmagical means."

"Well, then we'd need some sort of . . . physical deception. We'd need to, I don't know, maybe look like someone who was supposed to be there. Right?"

Eric said, "But an illusion spell wouldn't hold within the castle. It would break the second we walked inside the gate."

"Is a true physical transformation possible? One that would hold even if magic were blocked?"

"Theoretically. I've never done anything like that. I have no idea the amount of magic it would take, or the amount of rebound we'd incur."

"Do we have a choice in getting your people back?"

"No. Without them, I have no hope of stopping whatever spell the traitors have set loose."

"So we're talking about possible damage versus the destruction of our planet."

Pete took a long, hard swig of his beer and closed his eyes. Eric bit his bottom lip.

"I guess it doesn't matter how much tougher we make it for ourselves when we go to unravel this mess," he said softly. "Since there won't be anything left to unravel if we don't make the jump."

Lauren nodded.

Eric took a cautious sip of the beer, wincing a little as he swallowed. He said, "I can do a transformation spell. I can do a number of other technically forbidden things, too. I can read the minds of the people there and figure out who would be most likely to get into the castle without challenge. If anyone outside the gates knows where the prisoners are being held, I can create a physical map that will take me to them from that knowledge. If we aren't going to worry about the magical cost, I can get them out. We may have hell to pay when they're out—and it may come after us very quickly."

"We'll deal with it," Lauren said.

Pete nodded. "Point me in the right direction and tell me what to shoot. I have your back."

"All right," Eric said. "Let's do everything we can from here, and make it our goal to get in and out of there as fast as we can."

Ballahara

The presence of civilians scared the shit out of Eric. Having to take a little kid along was bad, but that wasn't the worst problem he had. Just by knowing about the Sentinels, Lauren and Pete compromised the security of a group that had managed to maintain its secrecy—and thus its security—for hundreds of years with only a few really bad breaks.

This was a really bad break. Lauren and Pete didn't just *know* about the Sentinels. They had an active, essential part in a desperate rescue mission, and he simply couldn't do what he had to do without either of them, and if he couldn't do what he had to do, most of the world's population was going to die.

But.

Oh, but.

They'd dropped into a clearing as close to the walled town as Lauren dared take them. Now he gave them last-minute instructions.

"It fires just like an automatic rifle," he told Pete, handing him the weapon he'd created so that Pete could stand guard. "Switch left, and you're on full auto. Switch center, and you're in single-shot mode. Switch right is the safety. It will never run out of ammunition—you won't have to reload, and unless I've really screwed the pooch, it will never overheat, either." He took a deep breath. "But use each shot as if you had to make bullets for the damned thing yourself. We're pulling energy from Earth to power it, and the more you use, the more chance that we do something we won't be able to fix when we get back there."

Pete nodded. "Will it kill?"

Eric rested a hand on Pete's shoulder and said, "You're going to decide that."

Pete frowned. "How so?"

"If you only want it to stun whoever is coming, that's what it will do. If you're in trouble and you need it to kill, it will kill."

"How does it know?"

Eric sighed. "Magic. That's the way things are in this place. So be . . . moderate. All right? Because death costs. In terms of the price our world pays in rebound effect, it costs a lot."

Pete held the weapon out in front of him, staring at it as if it might turn into a snake. Eric didn't suggest that possibility; Pete could, if he thought the wrong things, turn the thing into a snake at the worst possible moment, and Eric didn't think he'd be wise to be planting such unfortunate ideas. Instead, he turned to Lauren.

"Just keep the gate open and steady. We're going to have to go through it fast." He looked from Lauren to where Jake, asleep beside her in a big, warm nest of blankets in a wicker basket that she'd created for him, snored softly— that little-kid snore that sounded like a cat purring beside a heat vent. He was a cute little guy, and angelic-looking when he was asleep. "When you hear us coming, shove him through first. Well, make sure it's really us, then shove him through. And we'll go through. And then Pete, and then you."

"What if the traitors are with the prisoners?"

"They won't be. They might be chasing after us, but they won't be with us."

She glanced at the arch she'd formed of two saplings and bound with a silk cord. The green fire of the otherworld shimmered inside of it, and in its shadows, Eric could still see Lauren's foyer. Empty.

Empty was good.

"I'll be ready," she said. "Are you changing into . . . into whatever you're going to be while you're here, or once you get just outside the wall?"

"I'll change here. I want you to see what I look like, because I'll still look like that when I bring everyone back." He closed his eyes tightly and swallowed hard. "If I don't come back . . ." He didn't want to say those words, but he had to. "If I don't come back, you might as well stay here. There won't be anything to go home to within the month. If you dare, and if you have loved ones you can reach quickly, you might bring them over. On this side, even if they're carrying the plague, you should be able to heal them. But don't waste time trying to decide what you want to do. It . . . wouldn't hurt to have your contingency plans already made, so that you can just go ahead and carry them out."

Pete said, "You'll be back."

"I hope so."

Lauren asked him, "If you . . . ah, don't come back . . . is there anyone you want us to rescue for you?"

He thought about his parents, brothers and sisters, nieces and nephews, good friends. He started to say yes. "No."

"No?" Lauren watched his face closely.

"No. That will be my incentive to succeed."

"Good luck," Pete told him.

He nodded. Then he knelt on the frozen ground and stared up at the black sky, at the stars that twinkled in configurations that were almost, but not exactly, the way they should have been and would be in his home sky.

Let me hear what I must hear, he willed. *Let me see what I must see.*

Into the silence of the night sky, images poured. Voices whispered. He studied inhuman faces, forms, and voices; pored through alien thoughts and hopes and fears, willing that all things that would not hand him the key to the castle be eliminated. The babble became a steady, pulsing current, and then a faint trickle, and at last he held the three best images in his mind—three creatures for whom the watchmen would unquestioningly open the gates to the city, for whom the guards would willingly unlock the castle doors, to whom no answer would be withheld, and from whom no command would require the approval of another.

The first creature was the master of the castle—but he was currently in residence. And he never traveled without a retinue. The second was an odd, squat little monster with bat wings and a hellish, Shar-Pei-wrinkled face, who frequently traveled alone and who was fond of dropping in unannounced. He would have been perfect, if Eric hadn't had to worry about the conservation of mass in altering his form. He could fudge a little, but certainly not the sixty to seventy percent of his body mass that he would have to shed to transform into the ugly little monster.

The third was . . . Eric didn't know what she was. A breathtakingly beautiful creature, thin as gossamer but nearly twice as tall as a man, she had the face of a Chinese goddess—huge, almond eyes, tiny mouth, almost invisible nose—and hair red as blood and twisted into ten thousand beaded, beribboned cords. She wore a gown that floated around her as if it were alive. And, according to the thoughts of those who had dealt with her, she never spoke. She merely pointed, or if pointing did not get her what she wished, she placed a thought picture into the head of the person she wanted to obey her . . . and that person obeyed.

That, Eric thought, would work. He could be female for a while. Female *what*, he didn't know. But female.

He brought the magic into himself, and embraced its fire in each cell. He held the picture of the lovely creature in his mind, and wrapped the picture around him, and stretched himself to become it. The pain—

The pain devoured him. Fire burned in his joints, fire burned inside his lungs, fire blazed within his flesh and bone and nerves and brain until he wanted to scream, wanted to die, wanted to bite into himself and devour himself to get at the maddening, enveloping, inside-out horror of it and put an end to it.

Then, sharp as the first frost of autumn, something snapped within him and the pain was gone.

"Good merciful Lord," Pete whispered.

"Oh . . ." Lauren sighed, and mesmerized, rose and began to walk toward him.

"Stay," he said. "I'll be back as fast as I can. This feels . . . really awkward, and I want to get back into my own skin." His voice, to his horror, was his own. A man's voice, purely human.

Well, he hadn't planned on speaking to anyone but the prisoners anyway. And if they heard his voice in this body, maybe they'd believe it was really him.

He said, "Wait until sunrise. If I'm not back by then, I'm not coming."

Lauren and Pete both raised a hand, and he acknowledged their waves before he turned and headed toward the town.

Copper House

Getting in proved easy—so easy it frightened Eric. The city watchmen almost fell over themselves lowering the drawbridge for him; the castle gatekeeper threw open the gate before he even reached it, and as he passed him, said, "Shall I summon the Master for you, Glorious One?"

Eric responded with a quiet *No* placed in the Orian's mind. The gatekeeper dropped to his hands and knees and crawled backward, scraping his forehead across the floor as he did.

Damn. Who, or what, *was* this thing he was pretending to be? He was starting to scare himself.

He stalked through the mostly sleeping castle, and when he came across a guard—who shrieked at the sight of him but managed to stifle the shocked scream almost before it left his lips—Eric touched the guard and placed within his mind the image of the prisoners.

The guard bowed, shuddering at his touch, and, discreetly pulling away, scurried off up a passageway. Eric followed, musing that he had certainly chosen the right disguise for his infiltration of the castle—but he never wanted to run into the genuine article of whatever he was.

Their path meandered through stone corridors, and then along a passageway clad floor, walls, and ceiling with copper. His terrified guide led him to a massive copper door, and with shaking hands opened it for him. The Sentinels, awakened by the sound of the door opening and by the light of the guard's lantern falling across their faces, rubbed their eyes and sat up. They looked bewildered, weary, and scared.

And now Eric came to an obstacle. He needed to have the guard leave . . . but he didn't dare let him get too far. The guard was going to have to show him and the Sentinels through the maze of the castle and out. He couldn't speak into the guard's mind, directing him to what he wanted him to do, because the copper that now surrounded Eric would prevent him from any magical subterfuge at all. Yet he couldn't let the guard remain within earshot, because he had to tell the Sentinels who he was and what he had to do, and the minute he spoke, the voice that came out of him would belong to a human male instead of the inhuman goddess-thing that he appeared to be, and that voice would blow his disguise. From Richmond to Gettysburg, as his father always used to say.

Eric looked at the guard, looked at the Sentinels, looked back at the guard. Dammit. He was stuck.

And then he had an idea. He pointed one finger to a place just outside the massive copper door, and when the guard took the position he indicated, shoved the door almost closed with himself inside of it. And with a finger, he traced out the message, *It's me—Eric. Come with me now. Don't say anything.*

"I'll be damned," June Bug muttered, but she was the only one who made any sound at all. Eric lined his captives up by twos and opened the door and, with Sentinels trailing him like chicks after a mother duck, pointed the guard toward the front gate again.

They were halfway back to the front door when the creature that Eric recognized as the master of the castle—from reading the thoughts of the gate guards when he prepared his disguise—came running up, panic etched on his face and arms waving. "No," the master begged as he rounded the corner at a dead run. "No! I don't owe you *these*! Take something else! Take treasure, take slaves from among my people, take . . . anything else, but don't take my wizards. Without them, we lose *everything*!"

Eric held up one long-fingered hand, palm forward in what he hoped would be a recognizable "stop" gesture. The master of the castle slowed, but he didn't fall silent.

"Who told you I had them? Was it the rrôn? Do they know? Did they tell you I had wizards here so that you would take them, and their destruction of me and my people could be complete? They are no violation of our treaty, and you don't need them. What are you going to do? Feed on them? Make them work for you? You can do your own magic! Leave them with me, I beg of you. I'll give you the terms you've wanted—I'll give you the forest roads. All of the forest roads. Just leave me my wizards . . ."

Eric felt stirrings of sympathy for the creature. His true panic and his clear sense of loss left Eric wondering what horrors the master of the castle and his people had been facing that they had thought their only salvation was the kidnapping and enslavement of an entire team of Sentinels.

He wasn't facing the destruction of the planet of Oria and everyone in it, though, and Eric hardened his heart against the man's plight, whatever it might be, and pointed that bony index finger down the hall the way the master had come.

The veyâr hung his head and turned away slowly. The guard made a sort of whimpering noise in the back of his throat, quickly stifled, and when Eric pointed toward the door again, led Eric and the Sentinels out.

The instant they stepped free of the confines of the copper-warded castle, Eric willed a cloud of blackness into existence, and would have had it swallow them. But as the swirling darkness rose up from the ground, the master of the castle burst out of the castle's front gate, accompanied by a young woman who looked almost human. The woman pointed a finger at him and said, "I can feel inside of him. He's human—a Sentinel—like them."

"Give me back my wizards, false keth! Give them back!" the veyâr howled.

"That thing is no true keth!" shouted the master of the castle. "Guards, your crossbows on the impostor. Kill it! It pretends to be what it is not!"

"Shit!" Eric yelled. He cast the emergency spell he'd readied for use once the cloud of darkness had swallowed him—he'd hoped to make less of a dramatic exit, but now it couldn't be helped. "Sentinels, to the gate!"

Green fire surrounded all of them plus the veyâr guard who had led them through the castle, lifted them into the air, flung them at horrifying speed toward Lauren and the gate, and threw them, breathless and anxious, on the ground in the clearing. "Now!" Eric yelled. "Get us out of here now!"

Pete, weapon trained toward the city, didn't even turn to look at them. "I've got you covered."

Lauren shouted, "Jake's through! Sentinels, to me now!"

One by one the Sentinels ran through the gate, and after each passage Lauren recharged it for the next. She was slower than Willie, but Eric was glad she could work the gates at all. Without her, he, the Sentinels, and the world wouldn't have had a chance.

"Incoming," Pete yelled, and Eric heard the weapon he'd given his deputy go off, first a few shots, and then a steady stream. "About a hundred coming by land. Christ, they're fast! They're going to be in crossbow range anytime now. We need to move faster."

"Gate's doing what it can," Lauren yelled.

"Give me back my prisoners," the veyâr roared, and a blast of white fire erupted from the ground just behind Eric, throwing him forward and to his knees. The unmistakable stink and yellow smoke of sulphur, saltpeter, and charcoal rolled across the ground.

"*Shit*!" he yelled. "They have gunpowder!"

"Son of a bitch!" That had been Lauren.

Eric turned to find her lying on her back fifteen feet from the gate, with her face scratched and peppered by debris and the front of her coat blackened and torn from the blast. Scared—without her they had no way home—he ran to her side. "Where are you hurt?"

"I'm fine," she said through gritted teeth. "Scared the shit out of me, but I'm fine. Let me get back to the gate."

He helped her to her feet, and she frowned. "Who went through? It's shut again."

"Nobody. The explosion must have blasted debris through."

She shook her head. "I hope nobody was in the way on the other side. Come on—let's get out of here."

A second blast blew a tree ten feet from the mirror into shreds.

"They're serious about this. Pete! Put the weapon on full auto, and blanket the area." An identical weapon appeared in his hands in a flash of green fire, and he moved away from the mirror and started firing into the part of the forest behind Pete's back.

Lauren, steady as hell under fire, got the gate back up and shoved the last three Sentinels through in record time. When she yelled "You and Pete next!" Eric wanted to cheer. Pete came running and dove through, while Eric sprayed his stunner bullets into the trees and the bodies of his attackers.

"You and me together," he told Lauren, and sent a few rounds into the forest. He heard screams that told him his shots had hit targets, and he hoped that he'd been willing his enemies stunned, not dead.

"Ready," Lauren said at last, and grabbed his hand, and the two of them stepped onto the path.

In the instant they hung between the worlds, he felt a cold, angry presence push itself between him and her, prying his fingers loose from hers. A voice whispered in his ear, "She isn't for you."

And then, thoroughly creeped out, he reached the end of the path, squeezed through the mirror, and stumbled into Lauren's foyer in Cat Creek, to find the rest of the Sentinels, Pete, and a very cranky Jake waiting.

CHAPTER 16

Cat Creek, North Carolina

L AUREN'S FIRST ACT as they stepped into her crowded foyer was to turn back, reach into the gate through which she'd just come, and shatter the path that she'd walked. She did not know if any of those who pursued her could walk the paths. She did not know what the consequences would be if she destroyed a path with someone on it. But she knew what the consequences would be if she did not. The creatures pursuing her would burst into her house and hurt her, and hurt her child.

So, remorselessly, she twisted, and the spaces between the universes twisted with her, and the path fragmented into a million green-glass shards. The echo of her action blazed along her synapses and screamed into her skull. She yanked her arm free from the mirror and crumpled to the floor, holding her head tightly between clammy palms, rocking, willing the fire behind her eyeballs to die.

At last it did, and she opened her eyes to see a ring of blurred faces staring down at her. As if from a mile away, she heard a voice querying her, the tone insistent and anxious. "Ham eh orh ehery?"

She clutched her head, shook it as little as she dared, squinted up at the blurry white ovals.

Another distantly echoing query. "Da ngor ta ting beah rah?"

She closed her eyes again and breathed slowly. Her ears

still rang, and the thudding of her own heart and the rushing hiss of blood through her veins drowned out most other sounds. Her head howled with a pain worse than any migraine she'd ever experienced. Her own thoughts, fragmented as the green fire that still blazed in spots behind her eyes, scrambled for meaning, logic, a direction, and found none. She felt little arms wrap around her, and tiny fingers patting her, and she managed to hold Jake close while the pain screamed inside of her.

She shuddered and willed herself to stand inside the worst of the pain, to become the pain. She'd learned that trick when coping with the migraines shortly after Brian's death; it served her well again. The pain lessened and receded, a coward challenged and faced. She moved after it, and it fled still farther.

At last she opened her eyes, and the faces were no longer ringed by the haze of a storm moon. She drew a careful, shaky breath and gave Jake a little kiss on the cheek and said, "What just happened?"

"You've been curled on the floor for almost half an hour. Are you okay?"

"I am now. Mostly," she added, for she could feel the headache lurking, almost as if waiting for a chance to attack again when she wasn't prepared.

"You reached into the mirror, your face turned white as a fish belly, and you popped out sweat all over. I thought you were having a heart attack," Nancine said. "That's how Ernest looked when he had his first one."

"I broke the path behind us. They'd followed us in."

"You broke a path with someone on it?" June Bug Tate looked horrified.

"It was that or let them follow us here."

"I wasn't questioning you doing it," she said. "I just didn't think it could be done at all. I'd always believed once any of us set foot on the paths, nothing could turn us away from our destination."

"It . . . hurt," Lauren said. "A lot. I don't think it's something anyone would do except in desperation."

"It's something only a gateweaver could do," Eric said. He reached down and offered her a hand. The Sentinels stared at her.

"She's a gateweaver?" June Bug asked.

"We'll get to that," Eric said. "We'll get to the explanations in a bit. But we need to talk—all of us. We have a couple of serious problems, not the least of which is the possibility of the traitors coming after us and killing us all."

"If we don't stop the plague, they won't need to," June Bug reminded him. "That will take care of everything for them."

Someone had turned on Lauren's television in the living room, and she realized that she could hear a newscast droning on. Statistics—death tolls. She rose, moved through the group clustered in her foyer, and stepped into her darkened living room.

She'd come in at the top of CNN's hourly update. The newscaster was pointing out red dots on a world map— breakout zones, he explained. The first known deaths from what he referred to as Carolina flu were in the Rockingham, North Carolina area—but Lauren had already known that from Eric. What she hadn't known was that the disease had jumped. Not just the Carolinas, which were showing deaths in the high six figures, but California, New York, Canada. Which each had deaths in the high five figures.

In quick succession, the newsman pointed out fresh outbreaks in Great Britain, Germany, Zaire, and as far of as Alaska, Western Russia, and Hawaii.

Any hope of containing the disease had died on the vine. The current worldwide toll of confirmed deaths, the newscaster reported, had already reached a million people, and he noted that this was *only* confirmed dead. The true number had to be much higher, and would continue to climb hourly as new outbreak zones reported in and more bodies came to light.

A cold spot in the room moved through her, and for an instant, she felt lost, and trapped, and an almost as if she were an alien inside her own head, as if she were seeing the devastation through the eyes of another. Then the cold spot disappeared, and with a shiver, Lauren turned off the television set.

Copper House, Ballahara

Seolar could not contain his fury. His captive wizards had escaped to the gods alone knew where; the traitors were out of reach in their castle, though at least watched by their complement of servant/spies; Molly still knew nothing of magic; and all his plans and hopes for the survival of his people and the world he loved were come at last to naught.

But he still had Molly. Molly, who stood now beside him on the ramparts above Copper House, watching the sunrise burn its way through a cold, tearing fog.

"I'm sorry I couldn't stop them," she said.

"You found out that the keth was no keth. That was enough. The burden of stopping them fell on my shoulders, and those of my men. We failed—not you."

"So what do we do now?"

"We wait. I have one last tiny shred of hope. It will probably come to nothing—the veyâr have been begging help from the Sentinels for more years than I can count, and the only humans who *ever* agreed to help us were your parents. But one of my men managed to go through their gate during the heat of the fighting. He's there now, and perhaps he can find something that will help us."

"Who is he?"

"His name is Yaner. He's done special tasks for me for years—he found you. He's very good at not being noticed, and very clever. You met him, actually."

"I did? I don't remember a Yaner."

"He's not memorable. But you healed his daughter in the back of the wagon, when you were on your way here."

Yaner. For whose sole surviving child a hundred men had consequently given their lives. One hundred men whose sacrifices would come at last to nothing if he failed. *There* was a man with incentive to succeed.

She turned to him and said, "So we wait. I'm not going to just sit in my room and paint pictures, Seo. I'll learn magic somehow. I'll find a way to make a difference—to do what I need to do to mediate between the veyâr and the Old Gods."

He was staring at her. "You called me Seo," he whispered.

She nodded.

"If you can help us, Molly, I will be the happiest man on Oria. If you can't—at least I will have found you. Something good will have come of this, no matter what happens in the future." He reached over and touched her cheek with one finger. "You are so brave. So strong. So beautiful. No matter what happens to me, to my people, I will love you forever," he whispered.

She smiled up at him, face radiant and young and full of faith and hope. And love. "It is because I love you that I will find a way to do what I must do." She shook her head, and he could see that she was somehow amazed. "I *love* you. I have never in my life loved anyone. Never. I could never get past the pain of it—but with you, there is no pain. There is only this miracle; that I love you, and that I am free to love you."

He pulled her close, and held her. No matter what Yaner found, no matter what Molly learned, at least he could experience this. He had never been in love before either. Molly McColl was his miracle as much as she was his world's.

Cat Creek

"The plague happened because those people were tampering with magic in the other world," Pete said.

Lauren, still shocked by the news she'd just seen on the television, jumped. She hadn't realized that he'd come in behind her, or that he'd been standing so close.

"I know."

"Eric told me they might not have even intended to do this—that these things could just happen if people were careless with their magic."

She nodded and rubbed her hands over the goose bumps

that had come up on her arms. A draft from somewhere kept finding her, even as she moved around the room, and she felt cold all the way to the bone. "We have to find out what they did." She turned and saw the way he looked at her, the curiosity and the admiration tinged with something else, and she backed up a step.

The thing that she'd seen in his eyes that made her wary vanished instantly, and instantly, he was Eric's loyal deputy on the job again. "It seems like such a ridiculous thing to me," he said. "Even the idea of magic, but the idea that magic could turn around and destroy a world—and not even the world it was used on. A stupid, silly thing. I think of magic, and I think of a white rabbit pulled out of a black hat; of some girl in sequins climbing out of a box after I just saw the man in the tuxedo saw her in half; of cheesy card tricks and silk handkerchiefs and doves flying over my head and me hoping they don't shit on me when they go over. I don't think of touching a dying man and seeing the holes in his chest just close up. And I sure as hell don't think of a million dead and millions more to die. Of our world burned up to ashes because someone somewhere said, 'Abracadabra' the wrong way." His eyes then were bleak and old and haunted.

"It wasn't what I expected," Lauren agreed. "Hell, when I came back here, I didn't even remember any of it."

"No?"

She shook her head. "I almost fell through the damned mirror that first time. Almost—like Alice through the looking glass, but then I didn't wake up." She stared at the blinds pulled over the windows and carefully taped along the edges to prevent any stray light in the house from leaking out and betraying the presence of the Sentinels to the people who sought them. "It's a terrifying feeling to step through the looking glass and find out you're already awake."

He laughed—a small, dry, humorless sound. "Shit. I'm still hoping this is all one big nightmare."

She smiled. When he talked to her alone, his easy Southern drawl fell away, replaced by the sharper vowels and harder consonants used north of the Mason-Dixon line. Touches of the South remained, but they were faint. "Funny thing," she said. "I know you're a local boy, and when you're talking to anyone else, I'd think you'd spent every day of your life around here. But when it's just you and me . . ." She tipped her head and studied him. ". . . when it's just you and me, I get the feeling you've had a whole lot of the Southern rubbed off—and that if you wanted, you could make it just plain disappear."

She watched his eyes, caught the quick flicker of shock and wariness shuttered over fast by gentle amusement. He didn't say anything. He just smiled.

But she knew what she'd heard, and she knew what she'd seen. She shrugged and said, "I'm going into the kitchen to check on Jake and see if those people are going to shoot us, or if they're going to teach us their secret handshake and let us join their club. How 'bout you?"

He kept smiling at her as she brushed past him, but she could feel his thoughtful gaze fixed on her as she went through the foyer and around the corner, out of sight.

"We're going to have to set up our base of operations right in Oria," Eric was saying. "We don't dare stay here—we've already lost Granger to the plague, and as long as we're here we stand the chance of contracting it and dying. And we need every one of us if we're going to win against this thing."

"It seems cowardly to run." Terry Mayhew looked both embarrassed and a little angry.

"It would be stupid to stay here and die," Eric said. "If we die, everyone else dies with us. We can't afford to stand bravely in the face of danger. There aren't enough of us."

"Then the question remains: What do we with do with them?" Jimmy Norris asked. His white-linen Mark Twain suit was rumpled and soiled, but his thick white hair and white mustache had been carefully combed. The result was a sort of down-at-the-heels elegance that Lauren found almost touching. Or would have, if she hadn't wanted to punch the man.

"I really don't like being referred to as 'them,' as if we're inconvenient baggage or some awful mistake," Lauren said stiffly. "I'm the only gateweaver you have, since yours turned traitor. And Pete is with me. Without him, Eric would have been dead a couple of times."

"But you aren't Sentinels." That from Bethellen Tate, who never had liked Lauren, and who hadn't bothered to hide that fact when Lauren was a child. She didn't bother to hide it now, either.

"You want to swear us in or whatever you do, that will be just fine," Lauren snapped. "In spite of what happened to my parents, I'll be a Sentinel. The world is more important than any grudges I might be holding, no matter how deserved those grudges are." She felt she was watching a bunch of bureaucrats fiddle while the world burned, and her blood boiled for a fight. "You want us to say the magic words? Will that clear your consciences?"

"If you aren't Sentinels and you know about the Sentinels, you're supposed to . . . ah, have your memories altered."

"Been there," Lauren growled. "Done that. I'll kill the person who tries it again."

She and Pete, outsiders both, stared across the kitchen at the people who had seated themselves around her kitchen table as if they owned the place. Jake slept tucked into his nest of blankets, blissfully unaware of the tension and the anger and the distrust that crackled through the air around him.

"I vouch for both of them," Eric said. "I've known Pete for years. I knew his family, as did most of you. He's solid and dependable, he's one of ours, he's a good ol' boy like the rest of us. He follows orders, he listens, and he's a reliable man to have at your back."

That seemed to Lauren to be only the surface of what she was beginning to see in Pete, but pointing out that he looked like a lot more than "just a good ol' boy" from where she stood would have been tactically unwise. She kept her mouth shut.

"And what about her?" Bethellen pushed. "Her with her traitor parents, and her gateweaver talents, when according to everyone, she didn't even have the talent to walk a gate, much less create one? Are we supposed to trust her with the secrets of the Sentinels, too?"

June Bug Tate had gotten a funny, almost guilty look on her face at the mention of Lauren's parents, and it didn't go away when she glanced quickly at Lauren and then looked down at her hands. Now, studying her out of the corner of her eye, Lauren realized June Bug had a secret. The old woman knew something about Lauren's parents, or about Lauren—something that she wasn't telling the rest of her precious Sentinels.

Interesting. Lauren resolved to get June Bug alone at her earliest opportunity.

In the meantime, she glared at Bethellen.

Eric said, "Yes. You're supposed to trust her. I'll vouch for both of them. If I vouch for them, you treat them as you would treat me. Unless you want to take an extended vacation in Charlotte."

"We *voted* you to lead us. That don't make you God. We can unvote you at any time."

"Yes, you can," he told her. All of them, really. "You all want to do that?"

He looked around the table, and no one was nodding yes.

"Fine, goddammit. Let me lead."

They caved. They had to, Lauren knew. They had to have her, and they weren't getting her without getting Pete. She was in, Pete was in, Eric still led, and everyone was going to work from a base in Oria.

"We have one other problem, aside from the big ones," June Bug said, and again she was staring at her hands.

Lauren leaned forward, suddenly expectant though she didn't know why.

Eric looked at her without letting any expression leak across his face. "Problem?"

"Molly McColl. We left without her, but we're going to have to go back and get her."

His face bleached white. "She was *there*? She's alive, and she was there, and you didn't tell me so that I could get her out, too?"

Molly McColl, Lauren thought, oddly disappointed. The

woman who'd disappeared right when she'd moved to Cat Creek. Nothing to do with her after all.

"That's not the whole problem," June Bug said, and her head still hadn't come up to meet anyone's eyes. "All of us saw her. She's . . . changed. She, well, she partly belongs there. Seems her mother was Marian Hotchkiss, and her father was some veyâr. Her mother went away to have her, and gave her to some distant relatives or friends or somesuch to raise, and Molly only moved back here when she found out who her real parents were. Her real mother, anyway."

Lauren ran that through her head a couple of different ways, realized what it meant, and sat down on the floor, abruptly too weak and shaky to keep herself balanced on her own two feet. It meant that Molly McColl was her sister—or half sister, anyway. That she and Jake weren't alone in the world. That they had family, and from the sound of things, family that would be happy to meet them, too, because if Molly had nothing better to do than move back to the town where her mother had once lived, just because she'd come from there, she plainly didn't have a lot else going on in her life, either.

I have a sister, she thought, and realized why June Bug had been giving her those odd looks.

Her mother had had a child with an off-worlder.

A lot of unhappiness around their house right around the time that she'd turned ten suddenly fell into place—and with it, her mother's remembered absence, taking care of some old woman up in High Point for months on end. And Mama's inconsolable grief when she came home at last, reporting that the old woman had finally died.

If I'd had to walk away from Jake after he was born, I damn near would have died, too.

A sister. A sister left behind, captive in that castle. And how the hell were they going to manage to get her out? They'd blown their easy chance. They weren't going to be able to just waltz into the place a second time and spirit her out.

"She's a half-breed?" Eric asked, and the strangled sound of his voice brought Lauren back to the present.

"Yes."

"All of you saw her? You're sure of this?"

A scattering of yesses from around the table. "The master of the castle paid Willie and Deever and Tom to kidnap us so that we could teach her magic," Terry Mayhew said. "One of those Orians told me the three of them got a castle, and servants, and a whole mess of other stuff in exchange."

June Bug still stared at her hands. Eric gripped the edge of Lauren's old pine table so hard his knuckles looked ready to pop out of the skin. "Oh, Christ," he said, putting his head down on the table. "Why us? Why now?"

"What?" Lauren asked.

"Doesn't concern you," Eric said. "This is a Sentinel problem."

"I just found out I have a sister," Lauren said softly. "And she's a prisoner in the castle we just came from, and she needs our help. I'd say it damned well does concern me."

Eric looked at her and slowly shook his head. "She's not your sister. She's a disaster of unimaginable proportions—like the volcano that wiped out Pompeii, or maybe the comet that wiped out the dinosaurs."

"From where I'm standing, she's my sister."

Eric pressed his fingertips to his temples and closed his eyes. "The Sentinels have a law dealing with human-offworld crosses. The Sentinels require that every such person—man, woman, or child—be put to death. Humanely, if possible, but immediately. Crossbreeds are chains that tie together two universes that aren't meant to be chained. Their simple existence brings devastation to both the worlds that gave them life—not through any malice or evil intent on their parts—just because they were never meant to live."

"Meaning you intend to kill her."

"Oh, Christ. I swore to uphold the Sentinel laws—to put the good of all humanity above the good of any individual human. To hold life sacred . . . but first and foremost, to protect my world from anything that could destroy it."

"Meaning you intend to kill her," Lauren repeated.

"Meaning I don't know what the hell to do."

June Bug still stared at her hands, and Lauren saw tears

running down the old woman's creased face and falling un-touched to the table.

Bethellen said, "She saved my life." Other Sentinels concurred.

"The Sentinels murdered my parents. I'm not going to stand by while you murder my sister. I don't care what your laws say."

Heads snapped around to stare at her.

"The Sentinels didn't murder your parents," Bethellen snapped.

But now June Bug looked up, her face a crumpled wreck. "Some of them did," she said. "Because they'd brought Orians here, and because they were in regular asso-ciation with them, and because they were doing magic for the Orians, tampering in Oria, just the same as the Old Gods did when they came here. And because Walt and Marian refused to move to a big city where they couldn't keep an open gate once they got caught. I voted against it, but I was in the minority."

All the other Sentinels were staring at her. Pete, standing by the doorway, looked like he couldn't believe what he was hearing. Lauren, still sitting on the floor, felt grateful for its support.

"Who?" she asked. "Who killed my parents?"

"Mostly people long dead," June Bug said. "The old sher-iff, Paulie Darnell. Mac MacAvery." Eric jumped at the sound of his father's name, and stared at June Bug with dis-belief on his face. "Rulan Sweeney, who ran the auto body shop in town back then. Willie Locklear, of course—the last of them still alive. They couldn't have done it without Willie. They didn't know about Molly, or it would have been her, too." She drew a deep breath. "They didn't think you could do anything with gates either, Lauren, or it would have been you as well."

June Bug laid her head on the table and her shoulders shook. "She was the kindest, most beautiful, most generous woman I ever knew, your mother," she said between sobs. "I fought them with everything I had. When I knew I'd lost, I called your parents and told them they had to leave—that the

Sentinels had passed sentence on them. Didn't tell them who I was, tried to disguise my voice, but I figure they probably knew. Best I can figure, Walt and Marian were just doing what I told them to do when they were killed. The bastards had already doctored their car."

"You never turned them in?" Pete asked.

"Sentinel business," the old woman said, lifting her head just a little, wiping her eyes on her sleeve. "Sentinel business stays between Sentinels. Always. No matter what. No matter how we feel about it. It's a damned ugly thing sometimes. But it's the only way."

Pete turned to Eric. "You have people here confessing to being accessories to murder, discussing the possibility of another murder, for chrissake. And you're participating in the discussion. Jesus God, Eric. *You* suggested that maybe you should murder a girl you were tearing the town apart to find just days ago. What kind of insanity is this?"

Eric looked at him bleakly. "I didn't know about Lauren's parents. I don't know *what* to do about Molly McColl. But I know the price we'll all pay—the whole world—if I make the wrong choice." He turned to Lauren. "Have you ever been inside Willie Locklear's house? Could you make us a gate to it?"

Lauren, still trying to get her mind around the fact that her parents' murder had been sanctioned by the then-ruling body of these people, just stared at him, disbelieving.

"You're going to ask *her* to do you a favor?" Pete asked. "If I were her, I'll kill the whole damned lot of you, and good riddance."

"I don't know what the right answers are," Eric said. "But I'm going to show you why it matters. I'm going to take you both to Kerras. But Willie Locklear has the only preset gate to Kerras in the region—*if* he left it up when he bolted. We might get there and find out he's smashed all of his mirrors, or erased all his gates. I don't know. I can't get us there if he's destroyed the path. But if it's there, I'll take you both."

"What's Kerras?" Pete asked at the same time that Lauren said, "You think that seeing this place is going to make me all right with the fact that you people killed my mother and father? That you want to kill my sister? I'm telling you right now, you aren't killing my sister. Not now, not ever. You act like this is an either–or situation, like it's either my sister survives or the world survives. I'm telling you there had better be a third alternative, one that includes both the world and my sister, because if you don't all agree that she's safe and she stays safe—and Jake and me, too, while we're at it—then she'll live and Jake will live and I'll live, and you people can make your own goddamned gates and solve your own goddamned problems. Oh, you can't do that? Well shucks. Too bad for you."

"We don't have to have your help. We have backup coming," Bethellen started to say, and Eric shook his head.

"Willie and Deever and Tom said they'll call our backup. They never called anyone. And now we can't reach any of our contact nexuses. Either our contact people are dead of the flu, or they're in hiding. Either way, folks, it's just us."

Lauren glared around her kitchen at the men and women sitting there. "Molly, Jake, and me—no murder plots, no convenient accidents. Not now, not ever. Are you all agreed?"

They looked at each other and nodded reluctantly.

"Oh, that's convincing," Lauren said.

"They'll keep their word," Eric said. "I swear it on my own life. But let me show you what you're fighting for. Let me show you why this matters. Because until you've been to Kerras, you cannot hope to understand."

Cat Creek to Kerras

Since Lauren had never been inside Willie Locklear's house, she had to creep up on it—first forming the gate on the street, then focusing it on the front porch, moving through the front door, and finally locating the parlor. The front parlor had plenty of room for her to bring everyone in, and the mirror there was just a mirror—at least until she finished with it.

She and Pete stepped through first, lugging the sleeping Jake in his basket between them. The eastern edge of the sky had turned pale silver; true day would be upon them soon, and with it, an increase in their danger as long as they were in Cat Creek. No one watched Willie Locklear's house, though. Unless he unexpectedly returned from Oria, it would make a safe enough hiding place for the next few hours.

Once the Sentinels had gathered in the parlor, Eric turned to Lauren. "You and Pete come with me. They can wait here until we get back. They all know what Kerras is like."

He started toward the back of the house, Lauren picked up one side of Jake's basket, and Pete picked up the other.

"You can leave him here with us," June Bug said.

Lauren stared at her, then laughed. "Leave my child with Sentinels? When I skate on the ice in hell," she said, and followed Eric into Willie's workroom, still lugging her half of Jake's basket.

Eric ran his fingers over each of a dozen full-length mirrors that lined the one wall in the workroom. As he did, green fire flickered behind the glass and images briefly sprang to life, then shimmered back to nothingness as he moved on. "He doesn't seem to have done anything to any of them," he said. "They all go where they're supposed to."

"Then lead on," Pete said. "Unless this is just some trick to trap us someplace and rid yourself of a problem you can't deal with in any other way."

Lauren said, "I could get rid of him a lot more easily than he could get rid of me. I can make gates; he can't."

Eric nodded. "I'm not trying to trick you or to hurt you. But you can't understand what we're fighting until you see Kerras. Then you'll understand." He stood before one mirror that looked like all the rest, and said, "The place can't hurt you. You'll be there physically, but you won't have, well, substance, for lack of a better word. Kerras is our upworld, in the same way that we are Oria's upworld. Our most recent Old Gods came from there. It was a beautiful place once. Not all that long ago, in fact." He splayed the fingers of his right hand on the glass, and in the distance the green fire began to build.

Lauren watched the mirror for images, trying to brace herself for whatever Eric planned to frighten her with on the other side, but she could see nothing. Aside from the green fire that would form their path, the mirror reflected nothing from the world beyond.

"Pete, Lauren, since you're lugging the basket, you might as well go first. I'll follow after you."

Lauren shrugged. She knew she could get home from anywhere. She had no worries about being trapped. Pete seemed to draw from her confidence; when she pressed a hand through the yielding glass and hoisted Jake's basket one more time, he was right behind her. They flowed between the worlds, but this time Lauren felt no exhilaration, no breathless wonder as the energy of eternity flowed through her— and no touch from Brian. Wherever he was . . . he was not here. Instead, she felt a subtle poisonous horror that grew stronger and more insistent the farther away from Earth and the closer to Kerras she moved. Long before she stepped off the road, she knew something had gone horribly wrong; she felt sickened, drained, sapped of all her vitality, and she felt a frightening rage that came at her from all directions and seeped into her flesh and touched her bones and her blood and her mind.

From far away, she heard Pete shouting, "Something's gone wrong! We need to turn back!"

She felt the same way—but the path flowed in only one direction, and when it deposited her in Kerras, she could neither stop it nor fight it.

She landed in darkness, in the midst of a silence so absolute that she could not hear even her own breathing. She had the impression of horrible, unthinkable cold, but she could not feel the cold. She sensed emptiness, but she could

see nothing. Her hand still gripped Jake's basket, as did
Pete's. A moment later, she felt Eric join them.

They couldn't speak to each other. Sound simply didn't
carry. If she had screamed at the top of her lungs, she would
have looked like an actress in the era of silent movies.

She turned slowly in a full circle, and in that circle, she
saw nothing, and nothing, and nothing but the cold white
brilliance of a billion distant stars that hung over her head,
illuminating more nothing.

Then a sharp flash of white erupted over a suddenly
marked horizon, and in an instant, deformed shadows
crawled across the world toward her. She could see that she
stood on a plain of tortured glass, twisted and boiled and then
frozen by some hell-spawned demon or the actions of
demon-driven men. In the distance, she made out twisted
metal skeletons that clawed skyward or bent double to touch
the earth, defeated by gravity and forces she could not imagine. They stood in greasy snowfields, but as the sun rose
higher, those snowfields began to steam and boil, and a low-
lying fog began to creep across the ground. That groping fog
offered the only movement visible anywhere on the slice of
planet that she could see. And with loathsome certainty, she
knew that what she saw was a fair representation of the whole
planet. She had come to the end of a world, to the terminus of
a planet's existence and the crematorium for the life, the
light, the hopes and aspirations of countless species, countless sentient creatures.

In the silence she could feel their frantic flight toward
hoped-for escape. She could hear the ghostly voices of the
dead pleading absolution and a second chance. She could
see the shades and specters of green life and blue sky and
fecund fertile air and water burned and boiled and raped
and slaughtered, and in the bones of the world itself the
rage of unjust death, and the rage of the madness that had
summoned that death commingled, birthing a blight on
soul and hope and spinning that blight out in every direction.

Hell, she thought. I'm in it—and if I looked around I

could find a patch of ice and skate here, and bring a million oaths and curses home to roost.

She didn't know how this place had come to this evil end. But she knew that she would do anything to keep her own world from such a fate.

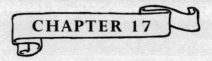

CHAPTER 17

"We interrupt your regularly scheduled programming . . .

". . . for a message from the president of the United States of America."

"My fellow Americans, friends, neighbors. This epidemic that is ravaging our nation must be stopped, and we have within our grasp both the understanding and the means to stop it. In order to halt its spread, we must temporarily suspend all unnecessary travel. With that single clear fact in mind, I am declaring a state of emergency and imposing martial law and a nationwide quarantine until, together, we bring this terrible disease to an end. Let me reassure you that your cities and towns will do everything within their power to maintain emergency services. The delivery of food, medicines, and other essentials will continue uninterrupted. However, private travel will be halted, and the National Guard will be deployed to ensure that the quarantine is obeyed.

"I remind you that what you do now, you do not just for others but for yourselves and your families. The Surgeon General will now join us to give you health guidelines that you can follow to help keep your families safe . . .

Kerras to Cat Creek

Jake was sobbing when they stepped onto the path back to Cat Creek—Lauren wondered if he'd been crying while she stood stunned on Kerras—if she simply couldn't hear him because sound didn't carry there. No atmosphere left, she thought. It had been hell man-made, the postapocalypse that never made it into novels because you had to have characters to write about—and on that blasted surface not even bacteria could live. She wished she hadn't taken Jake with her. She feared that the poisoned energy of the place would affect him. Still, promise of safety or not, she wouldn't have left him with any of the Sentinels for the world. She still wouldn't.

Lauren picked him up and held him and hushed him, and he cuddled against her chest, arms wrapped tightly around her neck. "It's okay," she told him. "It's okay. We're safe, and everything's going to be all right."

Mothers have been lying to their children since the beginning of time, she thought. Nothing was okay, and nothing might ever be okay again—but this certainly wasn't the time to start telling the truth.

He looked at her, wide-eyed and wordless, with tears running down his cheeks, then shoved his head into the curve of her shoulder and her neck, and his whole body shook with his sobs.

She knew exactly how he felt.

"It's all like that," Eric said. "The whole planet—the atmosphere is frozen on the ground when it's dark, and some melts off in sunlight, but nothing could live there. Nothing will ever live there again. And if you go to Kerras's upworld, it's just the same. Another blasted planet that used to be green and wonderful. And upworld of that . . . another cinder. As far up as any of us have been able to go, that's all we've found. Dead worlds." He looked at Pete, then at Lauren, then at Pete again. "You know when Kerras stopped being a beautiful green world and became a cinder?"

Without waiting for them to answer, he said, "October 22, 1962. Within your parents' memory. Almost within yours."

"That date sounds familiar," Lauren said, frowning.

Pete was staring at his shoes. "It is. It was . . . ah . . . yes! Cuban Missile Crisis—the date that John F. Kennedy announced the naval blockade of Cuba to prevent the USSR's delivery of more missiles."

"Yes," Eric said. "Sentinels around the world held their breath—the crisis had been fed not just by Cold War politics, but by the poison that was pouring down to Earth from a world war in Kerras. When the Kerrans set off their nukes and their even-higher-tech weapons and annihilated life on the planet, the reverberation here was nightmarish. We were sure the people in our world with their fingers on the triggers were going to twitch, too, and that was going to be it for us."

"Then each falling world shoves the next toward oblivion?" Pete asked.

"Dominoes," Eric said. "They're dominoes, and we're next. It's just a matter of time. We can't evacuate the whole planet. We could save ourselves, a few of our family and friends . . . but that isn't our job. Our job is nothing less than to save the world, and if we fail at that . . ." He shrugged. "That's our job. It can be harsh, but we've seen what will happen if we fail, and next to that, individual lives can seem very small and very insignificant."

Lauren watched him, and felt the bleak, dead horror of that place, and felt its echoes moving through her even yet. The poisons of Kerras seeped into Earth still—pushed it ever closer to inevitable doom. And against the weight of worlds stood a few people scattered throughout little towns all across the planet, isolated from each other, dedicated to holding the line on their own little patch of ground until the last man fell.

Like Chamberlain at Little Round Top in the Civil War, she thought. The Yankee schoolteacher whose men had stood in a line and held back charge after Rebel charge, and when half of them were dead and they had no ammo left, they still held. They more than held. They fixed bayonets and charged down the hill and the Rebels broke, and some ran, and some surrendered and sat out the rest of the war.

Her family had fought on the Southern side of that Past

Unpleasantness—a bunch of landless, dirt-poor tenant farmers fighting to protect their homes and families from an invading force. Her father had told her, "It was the finest war ever fought, and for the worst damn cause—heroes and honor and tragedy on both sides, and if we'd been smart, we'd have freed the slaves first and then seceded. Spiked the Yankees' goddamned cannons, that would have." He'd told her about Little Round Top at Gettysburg, told it almost like he'd been sitting there watching it. And the way he told it, there were heroes on both sides, and honor, and sacrifice, and the whole thing was a tragedy and a waste of better men than you could find in this day and age. More than fifty thousand had died in that one battle alone.

Individual lives can seem very small and very insignificant, Eric had said.

And Lauren thought that against the weight of a world, her sister's life didn't amount to much. But she still wouldn't bargain with it.

"I'll do the gates," she told him. "I'll help you. This matters—this stand, this moment, this choice. But Molly lives, and I live, and Jake lives. I won't change my mind on that. I'm going to forget about the fact that if you'd known I was a gateweaver, you would have murdered me. I'm going to put the fact that you—or your people, anyway—murdered my mother and father. But I'm not willing to accept a reluctant nod of agreement from you people. I'm not willing to trust you—you haven't earned my trust. So you and every other Sentinel here is going to both swear an oath and sign a piece of paper promising the safety of my sister's life, and Jake's and mine. The three of us are sacred and untouchable for the rest of our lives."

"They'll sign. We'll all sign."

Copper House, Ballahara

The veyâr Yaner appeared in the little solar where Molly and Seolar were having their meal. He was pale and disheveled, breathing hard, and clearly terrified—and Molly would not have recognized him from their meeting her first night in Oria, except that Seolar half rose from his seat and said, "Yaner! What ails you?"

This, then, was the man whose child she had saved at such cost.

"I have news," Yaner said. "Urgent news."

Molly put down her glass and waited. Her gut tightened—the way Yaner looked at her frightened her.

"What have you found for us?" Seolar asked him. He pointed him to a seat, then waved one of the servants over to bring him a drink.

"They were going to kill the Vodi," Yaner said. "But your sister intervened in your behalf. She said she would let their world die rather than let them kill you."

Molly's pulse fluttered and raced, and her breath suddenly went tight in her chest. "My sister?"

"She's in Cat Creek. In your family's old house—it's her house now. And she's a gateweaver. She and the man in charge didn't know you were here, or they would have tried to get you when they stole the prisoners away—but she knows you're here now, and after they take care of the traitors and some disease they caused, your sister and the Sentinels intend to come back here and get you. They think they're rescuing you."

Molly wasn't really hearing what Yaner was telling her. "My sister?" she whispered. "She is coming here?"

"She has other things she must do first, but—yes. But . . ." Yaner held out a beseeching hand. "You fail to see what I am saying. She and those people wish to take you away from us. From here. You must not be here when they come."

"My sister," Molly said, turning from Yaner to Seolar, "is going to be here in Oria. I have to see her. I have to meet her."

Yaner said, "The people she is with wanted to *kill* you. Lauren got them to promise that they wouldn't—but you can't let them get near you. Perhaps they told her the truth, but what if they didn't?"

"I have to go to her. Where will she and the Sentinels be going first?"

Seolar said, "He can't tell you that, Molly. If you went to them, you would be putting yourself in danger. And we need you. *I* need you. You must stay safe."

"He's right," Yaner said. "These are the people who murdered your mother and father—well, not *your* father, but . . . you know what I mean. They can't be trusted."

Molly froze. "My mother and, well, her husband were murdered? They were in a car accident."

"It wasn't an accident. I heard an old woman admit it— she said she warned them so they could get away, but it was too late. Those Sentinels are evil, evil people."

But her sister had fought for her. Had won against those people. Molly stared down at her hands. Changed hands, the fingers long and slender. She'd known about her sister, but had never tried to find her. She'd imagined the child her parents kept would think nothing good of the child they'd given away. Apparently she'd been wrong. She and her sister shared a bond. They shared blood and birthright. And this sister, Lauren, held a portion of Molly's past that she would never know and never understand otherwise. This sister had actually known her mother. She would have stories to tell. She could answer questions. Molly had burned with questions her entire life—and now the answers to at least some of them would be within her grasp.

She turned away from Seolar and stared at Yaner. "You told me that when I needed you most, you would be here for me."

Yaner blanched, but nodded. "I owe you more than my own life."

"I need you now."

Seolar said, "I forbid you to tell her what she wants to know. They'll kill her if they find her."

But Yaner said, "Imallin, I gave my oath to her, and it is my life if I break it. You may kill me if you must, but if I live, I will do as she commands." He dropped to one knee and bowed his head. "I am yours to command, Vodi. I am yours, body and soul. Ask of me what you will." Molly saw tears glistening on his cheeks, saw the trembling of his shoulders.

She felt guilty for what she had to ask him. "You know where they're going."

"They're going to the traitors' castle."

"The rrôn are there," Seolar said, his voice edged with horror. "It's at the edge of their hunting grounds. Good gods, of all the places in the universes for you to go, you cannot think of going there."

Molly kept staring at Yaner. "If I can find the magic to take us there, will you guide me to the right place?"

"Please, Vodi," Yaner whispered. His head hung and he sobbed without sound. "Please do not ask this thing of me."

Molly closed her eyes and clenched her fists. "I must go to her. The Sentinels cannot return here—they might try to hurt Seolar for taking them prisoner. They might do something to hurt the others here. I *must* go to them, and I must do it now. I have to tell my sister that I want to stay here—that I don't need to be rescued. That I've found my place in the universe. I have to make sure that they understand that—all of them. I *will* find the magic to take us there. Will you guide me?"

"You know I will," Yaner said, his voice so soft that Molly almost couldn't hear it.

"Then come with me. We have to go outside." She turned to Seolar and kissed him. "I'll be back," she told him. "I promise you, I'll come back to you. I can't explain how I know this, but I do. You and I were meant to be together."

"Murderous wizards and rrôn and traitors and spells run wild, with you heading into the heart of this when it will be at its worst, and you think to reassure me that you won't get hurt."

"I'll be fine. When I talked to the old woman—to June Bug—she said that magic was nothing more than focusing your will on the thing you wanted, and creating it as a real thing in your mind. I know how to do that with healing. I can figure out how to do it with traveling, and with protecting myself, and whatever else I have to do." She laced her fingers through his and smiled up at him. "I'm your Vodi, right?" She tapped the necklace that hung around her throat and said, "I did not come this far to lose now."

"Go, then," he said. "But if you die, know that a people and a way of life die with you."

She nodded. "I'll remember." She kissed him again, then pulled away. "Yaner, we need to get out of doors, away from the copper. How much time do we have?"

"Not much. I had to go a long way from the gate I used to get to you."

"Then let's hurry."

Cat Creek to Oria

While Lauren entertained Jake, Eric, Pete, and the Sentinels spent the morning working out battle plans, tactics and strategies, orders of priority, and lists of supplies. They kept Lauren busy opening up gates into all sorts of places so that they could steal what they needed.

"Not the way we usually operate," Eric told her, "but if we walk out the front door, we're all busted, and we don't have the time to explain right now why we disappeared and how come I'm not dead."

Their first order of business would be the reversal of the spell that had transmuted into the Carolina flu—according to Eric, the second they tracked it down and neutralized it, the deaths on Earth should stop. By last count, deaths had risen to two million. Nothing could save those people already dead, but they had to do everything they could to save the billions who remained. Only these few people could save those still alive. And the clock of dead and dying ticked ever faster.

For the size of the task that faced them, and the endless list of unknowns they had to plan for, they made good time. At just past noon Eric said, "That's it, then. We're as ready as we can get."

Lauren finished their first gate. It would take them to the grounds outside the castle where their three traitors had taken up residence. June Bug said the few traces of plague-related magic that she could find centered there. They would undo the plague spells, then go after the traitors. And when that was done, they would use one of the two self-standing full-length mirrors they'd stolen from an antique shop in Laurinburg to set up a temporary gate to Copper House so that they could retrieve Molly. Lauren would create a gate back to their base of operations in the second one, which the rescue team would take with them.

Lauren sent Eric through first, then all the supplies, then the rest of the Sentinels, and finally Pete. She stood there holding her squirming son, who was delighted to be going through the gate again, and stared at the green fire and the lovely valley, the castle, the forest, and the river that waited for her on the other side. She was taking Jake into what was nothing less than a war zone—but if she stayed, the two of them would face the plague. At least in Oria she could use magic to protect them from plague and whatever else they would face. And for threats that magic couldn't handle— whatever those might be, she had Brian's Browning High-Power in its shoulder holster beneath her jacket.

Safety is an illusion, she reminded herself.

She hugged Jake tight to her chest and stepped into the cool, energizing fire, and for that instant while she hung between worlds, Brian was with her again, whispering, "I love you; I will always love you," in her ear.

And then she and Jake stood at the base of a rocky promontory with the Sentinels and Pete. A broad river rolled past her; a fine, tall stone castle guarded the passage downstream from its place on a bluff. Nothing moved except the water—not in the castle or on the land. The stark trees stood black against a field of melting snow, with black earth showing through in several places, and the blood-red heads of tiny flowers peeking out from the edges of snowdrifts in the midst of the understory.

Nothing moved. And then something did.

A gaunt wolf loped out of the forest to stand on the opposite bank of the river, staring at the humans with hungry yellow eyes. It licked its lips and made a low, coughing sound, and more wolves materialized.

"They're usually terrified of humans," Eric said.

"At least wary," June Bug added. "I saw a *National Geo-*

graphic special on them once—they only go around humans if food in the wild is scarce."

"Those fellows don't look like they've had a decent meal all winter," Lauren said.

"Mama . . . doggies," Jake murmured, pointing and grinning.

"Not quite, baby," Lauren said, and created a spell which she held in her mind that would turn the whole pack to dust should they decide people looked like a good bet for lunch.

But they didn't. Instead, the leader coughed again, and the pack melted back into the forest.

June Bug had her mirror out, and stood staring at what looked to Lauren like a green-glowing map drawn by earthworms. Endless, constantly moving squiggles that started and stopped, bisected each other's paths, and kept looping back to their starting places. Three of the trails turned red as she looked over June Bug's shoulder.

"Willie, Deever, and Tom are in the castle right now—but they aren't alone," June Bug said. "Not by a long shot. Looks to me like twenty or thirty others are in there with them."

"What are they doing now?" Eric asked.

"Can't tell. They've muddied things up royally—scrubber spells and false trails going at the same time, and very low-level white-noise generators scattered all over the place to lead us away, and a handful of other things I can't pinpoint. But they've shielded the castle. I can tell you they're there, and they aren't alone, and not much else."

Eric turned to Lauren and said, "I'm going to put a shield around Jake, and around the mirrors. That way once you get them made, our gates will be protected. I can't shield you or Pete—you're going to have to cover us if we start taking fire from the castle."

Lauren looked at Jake, and then back at Eric. "I don't like that. What if something happens to me?"

Eric said, "We don't have any good alternatives. If we don't fix this, it's all over for everyone. I don't know what to do about Jake. He shouldn't be here, but the way things are . . ." Eric shrugged. ". . . the way things are, you can't be sure he'd be better off back in Cat Creek."

"I know."

"Keep him out of sight and hope for the best."

"We'll manage," Lauren said. "I'll have the gates ready before you need them."

The other Sentinels had formed a half circle around June Bug, facing each other and the high stone walls. They each had something in hand—Lauren could make out some of the objects, but couldn't figure out what purposes any of them might serve.

When Lauren and Jake joined Pete, he said, "He gave us each one of these." He held up an energy weapon like the one he had used to slow down the veyâr when Eric led the Sentinels out of Copper House. "Yours is with the supplies." She retrieved it, and he showed her the safety, the single-shot setting, and the automatic-weapon setting. When he was confident that she could use the weapon, he watched Jake for her while she set up the gates. She created one to her foyer in Cat Creek, and one to the clearing in the forest near Copper House.

Jake needed something to do. He wanted to run, and Lauren put him to work gathering sticks and twigs out of the castle's line of sight. This wasn't entirely busywork—the air had not lost its bitter winter bite, and Lauren thought a fire would feel good. Having Jake gathering firewood was only twice as much work as doing it herself, because he would lose interest for a few minutes and have to be shown where he left his sticks so that he could go back and pick them up. But at least he was focused on her, and not on the half sphere of light that shimmered around him like a grounded bubble, or on the scene closer to the castle, where the Sentinels looked like they were setting off fireworks. Lauren's skin tingled from the flow of magic that coursed through the area.

"Wish I knew what they were doing," Pete said when he saw where she was looking.

She nodded. "Wish I could help."

Pete snorted. "If I were you, I'd wish I could blow them all to kingdom come."

"That too."

Outside Cold Starhold

With shields cast around Jake and the gates, and with Lauren and Pete acting as backup, Eric and the Sentinels got to work tracking down the spell that plagued Earth.

"We're working without shields this time, y'all," Eric said. "Watch your backs. Pete and Lauren have weapons and will do what they can to cover us, but we're going to be wide-open to any spells cast our way. Keep a protective buffer for yourself ready."

Nancine held out her watch and said "Clock," and the glowing time readouts appeared in the air in front of each Sentinel. Timing would be less critical for this operation, because the Sentinels couldn't leave; when they'd unraveled the spell, they still had to deal with the three traitors who had cast it. Still, the quicker and cleaner they kept their operation, the less unwelcome attention they would be likely to draw and the better off they would be.

Ernest rested a hand on his tripod and said, "Light feet." Eric could feel the magic being channeled into Ernest's funnel and kept under tight control, and he breathed a little easier. As long as Ernest could keep their work tightly funneled, they should avoid making the situation worse.

With their timer running and the magic carefully channeled, George Mercer set his slide rule spinning in midair. He would take over in Debora's specialty, setting perimeter guards. It wasn't what he did best, and it wasn't what he liked, but the full circle had lost a lot of people. He would do what he had to do. "Set watchdogs, circle times two."

Little sparkles erupted around the perimeter of their work area. Even if they couldn't be shielded, they would have advance warning of anything coming at them. George's "watchdogs" spun and zipped like fireflies on speed, racing each other around the work circle, zipping out to about twenty yards in every direction and swarming back in—very pretty, a bit gaudy—not as elegant, as unobtrusive or as carefully conservative of magical energy as Debora's would have been. But they would do the job.

Terry Mayhew stepped to the center of the circle beside June Bug and held the tiny mirror on his key chain in the palm of one hand. It grew to the size of a saucer, and as he traced his finger across its surface, green fire shimmered in its depths. Terry had studied tracking with June Bug, and he would work with her to try to locate the source of the plague that was wiping out the Earth's population.

He looked at June Bug, and she held out her right hand. He took it with his left. They stared into the surfaces of their own mirrors, and June Bug said, "Show the source of the rebound plague."

Mayhem waited for a moment to let her spell clear, then said, "Draw path, disease vector."

The Sentinels' circle waited, holding its breath. When they had tried this before, Lauren's massive redecorating spells had completely overshadowed any tracks Willie, Deever, and Tom might have left behind. This time, the Sentinels were as close to their targets as they dared get, they were pointed in the direction of the enemy, and they'd canceled or blocked magical sources from other directions.

They should be able to get a read, Eric thought. Even if the spellcaster had put a heavy shield over the spell that was causing the problem, they should still get a direction, an indication of the source, and from both of those, an idea of what they could do to counter the problem.

Eric wanted to see something good happen—he had to fight his natural impulses to keep from *willing* something good to happen. That would just cast another spell, and screw things up. He tried to think of nothing but the integrity of the shields he'd cast around Jake and the gates, and the backup shield he kept on ready for himself, and the steady movement of air in and out of his lungs. That was the hardest part of doing magic as a team—keeping metaphorical fingers out of somebody else's part of the spell. All of them struggled with it. Sometimes someone, too eager for results, slipped.

But this time everyone held. They all apparently kept their urgent desire for results in check by remembering how dire the fallout would be if they screwed up. They didn't screw up, and finally, Mayhem said, "I've got a mouse here," at the same time that June Bug blurted out, "I have a complete spiderweb of trails, and all of them link to other trails, and then most of them die off to nothing."

"A mouse?" Eric asked, looking from Sentinel to Sentinel. "A mouse? What does a mouse have to do with the end of the world?"

Inside Cold Starhold

"They're out there," Willie said. He leaned against the parapet and pointed down at the river.

Tom and Deever both looked. "Don't see them," Tom said.

"Look for a tiny 'divert attention' spell attached to the area straight ahead and down. Then look for a couple of small shields back of it, that it's been anchored to."

Tom wove a little spell in the air, and suddenly held a tiny circle of clear glass. He angled the glass in the direction Willie had been pointing, and suddenly two brilliant green bubbles appeared: one fixed, one moving. He looked for the "divert" spell Willie had mentioned, and when he finally got through it, noticed the semicircle of Sentinels pointed toward the castle, shieldless. Easy targets. "They must have gotten reinforcements."

"They came directly here—not overland. Which means they have a gateweaver," Willie said. "So, yes, they've brought reinforcements. And that means we have a problem."

He paced along the parapet. He didn't look much like the old Willie Locklear anymore. For one thing, he appeared to be no more than thirty. For another, the etching of constant pain that had deepened the lines on his face for the last two years was completely gone. When he finally made his break with Earth and the Sentinels permanent, he erased the cancer he'd been secretly fighting; he'd felt the awful gnawing that had eaten halfway through his spine and deep into his liver and his bones just melt away, and he had rejoiced. And in the same breath, had cursed the Sentinels for refusing to let their own take advantage of the wondrous powers that they controlled. He would never have been permitted to use magic to eliminate his cancer; nor would the Sentinels ever have allowed him to reclaim lost youth. Those were, in their eyes, unnecessary and deadly expenditures of magic, and, timid creatures that they were, they dreaded the slightest divergence from their narrow, chaste path.

"We could attack them," Deever said.

"Could. But I don't think we should. They're not after us right this second, though they surely will come after us sooner or later. They're trying to track down the spell that's killing Earth. They'll have their hands full trying to deal with that; they won't have anything left over for us for quite some time."

"Then now would be the perfect time to hit them," Tom said.

Willie turned and studied his protégé with narrowed eyes. "You think so?"

"Of course. While they're completely focused on something else—"

"They're trying to save your world, you ass. They're trying to save the lives of all the people you've ever known. You're going to interrupt them in the middle of that?"

"What do we care? We aren't ever going back," Tom said.

Deever shook his head and turned away, disgusted. Willie said, "Did you mean anything you said when you took the Sentinel oath?"

"Of course. But I'm not a Sentinel anymore." Tom didn't seem to see that he'd suggested anything wrong.

"The values you hold as a Sentinel don't go away when you cease being a Sentinel," Willie said. "If your world and your people ever mattered to you, they still do."

"And that's the reason you sold your friends and colleagues to an Orian? That's the reason you broke every rule in the Sentinel book about contact with natives, about the use of magic for personal gain, about making yourself one of the gods, for the love of Jesus . . ." Tom looked from Willie to Deever. "And you, Deever, have a lot of room to talk—turning yourself into a golden-haired Greek god and planning on sneaking back to Earth while there's still something left to pick up women for your harem. I'm not the one who decided I needed a wang like a flagpole, am I, or a whole bunch of new hair, or muscles on top of my muscles? I haven't done a single spell for myself. But you two are sure enough quick off the mark to tell me what a bad boy I am."

Willie had the good grace to flush. Deever just scowled and kept staring at a fixed point at the far corner of the tower on which they stood.

Willie finally noticed where he was looking. "What do you see, Deever?"

"A mouse."

"Dead?"

"Looks real damned alive to me." He pointed, and both Willie and Tom looked where he was pointing. "I thought we got rid of all the mice."

"Might be the last one," Tom said. "If it is, it could live a long time. I set the spell so that each mouse would only die after it had infected at least one other mouse, so if it's the last one, we ought to catch it and throw it over the side."

"You limit that spell?" Deever asked.

"Limited it to mice."

Deever considered that, then shrugged. "That ought to be good enough." He took a deep breath and returned his attention to the encampment of Sentinels below the castle. "So what are we going to do about *them*?"

CHAPTER 18

Copper House

MOLLY SAT CROSS-LEGGED on a stone bench in the center of one of Copper House's many gardens, with Yaner twitching and squirming on the seat beside her.

The tips of her middle fingers rested against the pads of her thumbs firmly enough that she could feel her own pulse beating steadily; she matched her breathing to her pulse. Breathe in for six heartbeats, hold for six heartbeats, breathe out for six heartbeats, and hold again for six more. She concentrated on slowing her heart rate, on driving her breathing deeper and deeper into her belly, on erasing everything but the calm, cool center that she had first found in the Air Force M-16 training. The staff sergeant watching her shoot told her that if she controlled her breathing, she would be able to keep her pattern tighter. He'd been right—when she controlled her breathing, everything about her relaxed and steadied and she seemed to move into a universe that only she inhabited—a place where she and she alone made things happen.

She needed that control now. Seolar had stayed behind at her request, but she could still feel his panic at her departure. He was certain his people were going to die out, and he was terrified that he would lose her.

But the Sentinels could not come to Copper House as a rescue force. The veyâr would die trying to save her, and they couldn't hope to survive against Sentinels who commanded the powers of gods. She would not let them die for her.

She wanted—needed—to meet Lauren, too. The compulsion was as strong as the one that had driven her to find out who her family was, as the compulsion that had finally pulled her back to Cat Creek to live. She *had* to do it. And she had to do it immediately.

Which meant she had to figure out magic, and do it well enough on her first try that she could transport Yaner and herself to the place where Lauren and the Sentinels prepared for their battle.

Aim high, she thought, smiling just a little. And, with her eyes closed, she stared at the spot inside the center of her forehead, counted her breathing, and willed herself to go with Yaner to the place where her sister was.

She seemed, after a time, to grow lighter, to slide away from the reality of her body. She seemed to become a creature less than flesh, yet more than spirit. She became aware of the energy that flowed through her, energy that came from the movement of the world, from the radiance of the sun, from the pulsing of distant stars. All of that energy was hers if she chose to use it. She could fly with it. She could move mountains and redirect rivers and summon storms with it. All she had to do was . . .

. . . was . . .

. . . all she had to do was . . .

. . . *want* it.

Yes.

I want to take Yaner with me to join my sister Lauren, she thought. But she did not just think it. She willed it, creating the image in her mind and feeding the image with the music of the stars and the fire of the sun and the slow, solid force of the dark, cool earth. *I will go there.*

She settled into her body again, and it felt the same as it always had to her—solid and firm and real. But when she opened her eyes, she no longer sat on the stone bench. She rocketed through the air, surrounded by a blaze of palest, sparkling light—and beside her Yaner floated, rolled into a fetal ball with his arms wrapped tightly over his face. He mewled like a new-born kitten.

"Oh, my," she whispered.

The force of her own will, of her own desire to shape her existence, had become a solid, immediate tool. Beneath her, trees and hills and rivers rolled away like an undulating carpet of brown and black and white. She had a sense of movement faster than anything she'd ever experienced in her life, including the incentive flight in the F-16 when she was working engines at Moody. But she heard nothing from outside the sphere of light, felt no breeze, smelled nothing. The light sealed her off from the outside world as effectively as any cockpit.

"You have to open your eyes," she told Yaner.

"We're going to die," he squeaked, not moving a muscle.

"You have to let me know if we're going in the right direction."

"I thought you were going to make us a gate and we'd just step through it! You made us *fly*, and we're going to smash on the rocks or end up skewered on the branches of trees, or the Old Gods will blast us from the sky for our impertinence."

"We're not going to die. We're doing great. I just need to know if we're going in the right direction."

Yaner moved one arm fractionally—one eye peered at her from beneath its shield. "You promise?"

"Promise what?"

"That we won't die."

"We aren't going to die. At least not from this. When we get where we're going, I'll land us. No problem."

Yaner shuddered but pulled his arms away from his face and unrolled. He looked down at the ground racing beneath them, mewled again, and closed his eyes tightly. "We're going in the right direction. You'll see a large black-stone fortress ahead of you soon. That's Blackleg House, where the traitors went and where the Sentinels plan to go. I don't know if your sister is there yet or not, but we're at least going where she will soon be."

"That's all I needed to know," Molly said.

"Good." Yaner rolled himself back into his little ball and covered his eyes again. "Let me know when it's over."

Outside Cold Starhold

"Oh, no," Lauren said, and pointed to a huge bubble of light that raced toward them just above the tree line. "Look."

"I see it," Pete said.

Lauren looked frantically for better cover for Jake, but she had her choice of clearing—in clear view of the castle; forest edge—where the gates sat and where they currently waited; and deep forest—where she wouldn't be able to keep an eye on Jake or the Sentinels. "Screw it," she muttered, and created a little tent around the mirrors and the gates, a replica of the *Blue's Clues* tent Jake had in the playroom, with bright blue puppy-head door, paw-print décor, and appliquéd picture of the show's host in his green-striped shirt. Only bigger. A lot bigger. Big enough to serve as cover for more than Jake if necessary. If she got in trouble for the magic use, she got in trouble. Her little boy was her first priority.

"Jake. Into the tent, puppy-boy. Quick. Run." Jake laughed when his plaything appeared, and raced toward it as fast as his short legs would take him, liking this game and its urgency. He squealed as he ran—that happy squeal that Lauren usually loved to hear. This time she shivered, not from the cold. Trusting—he was so trusting, so incapable of imagining the nightmares that life could pour on him in an instant.

She swung her Oria-rifle to ready and switched off the safety. To Pete, who also had his weapon ready, she said, "He told you these things would stun or kill, depending on what you wanted them to do, right?"

Pete nodded. He was watching the bubble getting closer and bigger at an alarming rate. "Yep."

"Do we shoot?"

"Stun," he said with a nod. "No damage from a stun."

They both fired together, and flung themselves out of the way of the shots, which ricocheted off the shield that surrounded the oncoming bubble and bounded back at them. Pete got away unscathed. Lauren took a hit in her right leg, and discovered two things. One, she couldn't get back up, and two, those stun shots might not do any permanent damage, but they hurt like hell. She lay there with her eyes watering from pain, gripping her leg, fighting back a howl because she didn't want Jake to be scared.

Pete dropped to her side. "Oh, shit. Thank God we were just shooting to stun."

"We can't shoot it, can we?"

"Looks like no."

The bubble was slowing. Lauren sat up. Now that it was closer, she could see through the radiance to a woman and a man who knelt inside. Not human, either of them. But dressed in fine clothes, and not bearing anything that looked like weapons, and both waving wildly at her and Pete, as if they were all good friends.

Lauren said, "Maybe we shouldn't shoot them—if we get the chance."

"Maybe not."

The bubble settled to the ground outside the shield, and Jake burst out of his tent and ran to Lauren yelling, "Oz witch! Oz witch! Oz witch, Mama!"

Lauren's leg remained numb. She wanted to stand, but it wasn't going to happen. So she sat there on the icy ground, with pebbles digging into her rear end and snow melting into her jeans, and watched the beautiful woman and the man stand up, and watched the bubble shimmer away into nothingness, and watched them walk over to Eric's shield, stop, then walk right through it.

Jake was giving the woman the fishy eye. "Good witch? Or bad witch?" he muttered. "Good witch, or bad witch?"

"Not a witch at all," Lauren told him. He would have liked the woman better if she'd been wearing a pastel pink ball gown with huge puffy sleeves, Lauren suspected. And a huge crown.

"Hey," the woman said, and she had a Southern accent. Lauren's sort of Southern. It didn't sound right coming from someone with slanted eyes and faintly gold-tinged skin and metallic copper hair that nonetheless managed to look natural. "Lauren, I know this is awkward, but we really don't have a lot of time, and I had to meet you. I'm Molly. Your sister."

* * *

Molly found herself looking into a face very much like her own—or at least, very much like her face had been when she'd been on Earth.

Lauren stared. "Molly? They said you'd changed, but . . . You're really Molly?" She struggled to rise, and Molly noticed that her right leg wasn't moving at all. "I'd stand up and say hello, but I can't." She managed a smile.

"What happened?"

"I was trying to shoot you and the shield that's surrounding you sent our shots back at us. I didn't get out of the way fast enough. When they ricocheted, one of them hit me."

It was Molly's turn to stare. "I . . . I'm afraid I don't quite know how to take that."

"Not too badly, I hope. We were shooting to stun, which is why I'm still alive to say hello, and we had no idea who you were, but with everything going on around here, we assumed you were something on its way to kill us." Lauren hugged the little boy who was using her to shield himself from Yaner and Molly, and said, "We aren't in a position to give everyone the benefit of the doubt."

"You aren't going to shoot us now, are you?" The man standing at Lauren's side had lowered his weapon, but hadn't removed his finger from the trigger or taken his eyes off them once.

"You here to kill us?" he asked.

"No."

"Then we won't shoot you."

"He's one of the reasonable ones," Yaner told her. "I think his name is Pete."

Lauren and the man gave each other wary looks, and the man said, "My name is Pete. You seem to have the better of me, sir. I would have said we'd never met."

"We haven't," Yaner told him. "I followed you through the gate back at Copper House and spied on you in Lauren's house. That's how I found out that Molly had a sister, and that . . . those *people*"—he pointed to the semicircle of men and women who all stood facing the traitors' castle—"wanted to kill her."

"They aren't going to," Lauren said, her face abruptly grim. "They aren't going to touch you. I made them swear and sign a paper." She held out her hand to Molly. "Give me a hand up, will you. I feel like an idiot sitting on the ground—maybe I can make myself a chair or something, so that we can talk comfortably."

Molly reached down a hand to Lauren . . .

. . . and their palms touched . . .

. . . and light erupted behind Molly's eyeballs, and pain screamed into her head like a heat-seeking missile that had found its target.

She thought she screamed, but she couldn't be sure; the deafening roar inside her skull drowned out all sound. She knew she was falling, but her body no longer seemed to belong to her; she couldn't throw out her arms to stop herself. But someone caught her and lowered her to something soft. And someone pressed a warm cloth to her forehead and held a cup of water to her lips. She couldn't see. The light behind her eyeballs blinded her as effectively as complete darkness would have.

Couldn't see.

Couldn't hear.

Couldn't move.

Couldn't speak.

Almost couldn't think.

And then the pain began to ebb away, and like a high tide, it left things behind.

Memories.

Memories that didn't belong to her. Her mother and stepfather were suddenly inside her head, and she knew. She knew them as well as if she'd spent her whole life with them. She knew what they'd planned for her. She knew what they'd planned for their magic, for the world. She was part of something big—bigger than she could have ever imagined.

Her eyes cleared, and she looked at Lauren, who was sagging forward, her skin pale and beaded with sweat. Their eyes met, and Lauren said softly, "You got that, too, didn't you?"

Molly nodded, and the two of them hugged, and in Molly's ear Lauren whispered, "Sweet Jesus, are we in trouble."

They pulled apart, and both Yaner and Pete were at them immediately, wanting to know what happened.

Lauren shook her head at Molly, the tiniest possible "no."

Molly looked up at Yaner and said, "That was a spell left for us by our mother. To make sure we knew each other."

Lauren agreed. "Gave me back memories of my parents and Molly when she was born, told me she was my little sister and I'm supposed to take care of her." Lauren rubbed her temples. "Loudly, too. Feels like the top of my head is still going to blow off."

Molly looked at Yaner and Pete, wishing she could get rid of both of them. She and Lauren needed to talk. Badly. Some of the plans her parents—her human mother, her human stepfather, and her Orian father—had made for her and Lauren didn't mesh well with the plans she'd made for herself since coming to Oria. She could feel the importance, even the urgency, of her parents' carefully designed plan. She could see the necessity. But she had found a life for herself now, and she needed to discuss how she could keep the life she'd found and still carry out the enormous duties that waited for her.

But neither Pete nor Yaner was going anywhere. They were, instead, looking toward the Sentinels' circle, and they looked worried. Scared, even. So her talk with Lauren was going to have to wait for a time when the two of them could find a moment's privacy.

Lauren did a lovely job of moving the conversation in a safe direction. She said, "I'm thrilled to meet you, but, honey, you have to get out of here. There are people here who want to see you dead, and even though they promised that they wouldn't hurt you, I'd rather trust a flock of politicians than the lot of them." Lauren rubbed her right leg and winced. "We'll get you out of here as fast as we can. But, damn . . . I really am happy to meet you. I found out about you just yesterday—I can't believe I have a sister. I've been alone for a while."

"I know the feeling," Molly said, and meant it. She gave her sister another hug. "I'm glad I came here."

The little boy said, "Mama . . . biteys. Please, biteys. And truck."

Molly looked down at him. "Your son?"

Lauren nodded. "Jake."

"He's beautiful. And that's his father?" She nodded toward Pete.

Lauren said, "His father is dead. On his way home from Pope Air Force Base, took the wrong bus . . . he was in the wrong place at the wrong time."

Molly winced. "I'm sorry. I was in the Air Force for a number of years. I lost a few friends. It's . . . ah . . . there's just no way you ever can make that sort of loss right in your mind."

"Brian was a wonderful man, and he deserved better than what he got," Lauren said. "And I don't think I'll ever get past feeling like the place where he's still supposed to be is this giant hole in my life."

"Jake has to be a blessing. He's a darling little boy."

Lauren said, "He's everything I have left of Brian. And he's wonderful all on his own . . . even if he is a huge pain sometimes." She smiled and ruffled her son's hair, and Molly felt a quick stab of envy that transformed itself into a sense of wonder. Perhaps someday she and Seo would have a child. Or children.

Molly realized Lauren was scrutinizing her closely.

"I can see a resemblance between us, even now," she said. "They—the Sentinels—they told me a little bit about you. About the fact that you were Mom's daughter, but also the daughter of one of the Orians here."

Molly nodded.

"You didn't look like this on Earth."

"No. I didn't tell anyone in Cat Creek who I was, because . . . well, my parents gave me up for adoption. That's not the sort of thing you want to go back and broadcast. But the librarian told me I looked exactly like your . . . our mother looked when she was young."

"Makes sense," Lauren said. "If only Earth genes could

express themselves on Earth, then it would be the same as if you just had Mom's genes. I'll bet you did look just like her." Lauren said, "I wish I could have seen you there." She smiled sadly. "I miss her."

"I never knew her. She and your dad had been dead for a number of years before I even managed to find out that they were my real parents. Well, my parents of record, anyway. I still haven't met my actual biological father."

"Mama and Dad were good people."

Molly smiled. "So I've heard. According to the veyâr, they were practically gods."

"Mama!" Jake yelled. "Biteys! Play! Truck! Water!"

Lauren rubbed her leg hard and wobbled to her feet. "Damn, that hurts," she said. But she gingerly put her weight on the leg that had been hit and didn't fall over. "Please excuse me," she said. "I have to do mom things for a little bit. And Pete and I have to watch the Sentinels over there to make sure nothing takes a shot at them while they're undoing the traitors' spell. But we'll talk later."

"Count on it."

"Track the mouse lead," June Bug suggested. "There has to be a reason for it showing up. It has to be tied up with the spell that's causing the problem somehow."

"It seems so . . . irrelevant."

"Insignificant," Bethellen said.

"That could be the reason why we haven't had any luck finding it until now. Maybe even little spells have been big enough to hide it."

Jimmy Norris said, "I've been working on my disentangle spell. I think I can handle this."

None of the Sentinels mentioned how much they missed Granger, with his quiet confidence and unquestionable competence at unraveling even the most complex of spells. That sort of comment would only make Jimmy's work harder, and decrease his likelihood of success. But Eric thought it, and he would have bet that every other Sentinel in the circle thought it, too. Most likely, Jimmy was thinking it harder than any of them—he'd been only too happy to relinquish that particular duty back when Granger and Debora had first joined the Cat Creek nexus.

Now he pulled the autographed copy of *Tom Sawyer* that was his talisman out of his kit bag, and held it in front of him, closed. He slid his thumbs back and forth across the worn leather cover as he closed his eyes, licked his lips, and began to focus. When the book glowed green, he said, "Mouse. Unravel."

The Sentinels braced. The spell would go out and start undoing whatever the traitors had done—and as it did, the magical backlash would start to build. Everyone was ready to ground the energy that hit them; Ernest had his tripod-mounted bit of pipe going so hard it glowed white.

Nothing happened. The wait grew agonizing, because the longer it took to unravel and the longer it took to come back, the worse it was going to be. Nancine's clock ticked in front of all of them, and one minute became two, then three, then four, in appalling slow motion. Eric's gut knotted watching-a-train-wreck tight. Five minutes. Six minutes. Good God, he'd never seen a spell take this long to unravel. Seven minutes. Eight. If they had twenty Sentinels, they wouldn't be able to absorb the rebound from this thing safely. What the hell was it? What had the traitors done? Nine minutes.

"Oh, God," Jimmy whispered. "Here it comes."

Eric tasted ashes, smelled his own rancid sweat, shivered from cold and dread, and suddenly, desperately needed to piss.

The first part of the rebound slid into them all—a soft, light, pillow of a crash that almost caused them to fall over. It was nothing—nothing. They'd been ready for the sun to fall blazing on their heads, and instead, someone started pelting them with paper cups.

"Mousetrap," Jimmy said, but unnecessarily. They could all feel what the spell was. A tiny little steady-stream spell to rid the traitors' castle of mice; a throwaway; a piece of nothing. It used almost no energy, almost no magic—all it did was give a single mouse a disease contagious only to other mice, and then keep him alive until he had infected at least one other mouse.

Eric would almost, almost have thought that they'd tracked down the wrong spell; that this little bit of fluff couldn't be the thing that had already snuffed out more than two million human lives back home, and that stood, within the next week or two, to eradicate half of the species from the face of the planet. Almost.

But for all that it was tiny, the spell had one inescapable bit of poison in it. It was a spell anchored in death. It killed—and magic that killed on the way out killed on the way back. No one, to his knowledge, had ever devised a spell based on death that didn't move out of the channels that had been devised to keep it in bounds.

And it wasn't finished with them. The second part of the rebound, the tiny twist that made the spell lethal to mice— the part of the spell that had metamorphosed into something massive and deadly and ugly to humans in Oria's upworld of Earth—came slipping in then, point first, like a dagger between ribs, and even though they thought they were ready, even though they had braced themselves and grounded their magic, it caught them unprepared. They thought they would be facing the blow of a mace—a loutish swing that would be the logical rebound to level Earth's human population. They were braced for the big blow, so the stiletto was through their magical chain mail and into their ribs before they knew it had arrived.

Lethal. Bethellen Tate had prepared least. Her son Tom had cast the spell, and she had read his touch in the magic, and she had been unable to believe that anything her boy would do could come back to haunt her. The rebound hit her, and she gasped once, eyes flying open wide in horror and dismay, face a picture of betrayal realized at last. And she dropped to the ground, stone dead.

Lethal. Nancine Tubbs, plump and still rather pretty at fifty-one, the cheerful owner of Daisies and Dahlias, whose main magical contribution, aside from keeping

track of the Sentinels' time on site was simply to act as a
buffer for rebound magic, never saw the rebound coming.
The gentle strike of the first half of the spell had put her off
her guard. She'd let herself believe "mousetrap," even
though she knew in her heart that the spell's big brother,
turned loose back home, had already killed millions. She
was thinking they were unraveling the wrong spell—such a
simple bit of self-deception. And the second half of the
spell dug into her and dropped her to the ground so fast she
didn't have time to cry out. One instant she stood there
checking the Sentinels' running time, and the next she was
dead on her feet. She toppled to the ground with her eyes
open, flopping.

Her husband, Ernest, had been better braced, better
grounded, less put off his guard, but he saw her fall, lost his
focus, and lurched forward to catch her, and the rebound
took him in the space between breaths, between heartbeats,
and he crashed to the ground beside her.

"Steady," Eric shouted. "Steady! Ground it. Channel it.
Don't let it get away from you!"

With Ernest dead, his energy-channeling spell died, and
suddenly the rebound wasn't even coming in at them from a
predictable direction. It swirled like a dervish, buffeting
them from all directions, while they stood with feet planted
in the ground, arms outstretched, trying to make themselves
the lightning rods that would conduct it through their bodies
and harmlessly into the earth.

George Mercer held. Battered, scared, he nonetheless
stood his ground. He'd seen action in Vietnam—he'd survived too many firefights in his two years in the jungle, had
watched men to either side of him blown apart time after
time, had, one very bad night, taken a bullet through the
thigh. Had kept firing, laying down heavy cover that let his
surviving buddies regroup, and had put the fear of God into
the enemy; had, when the enemy backed off, wrapped a rag
around his wound and pulled his wounded and dead buddies
to a staging area, where the choppers could get in. In his
drawer, a purple heart in a box attested to his courage. As he

watched his friends and neighbors fall, the man who loved numbers, who delighted in the steadying influence of the accountant's life, fell away, and the warrior who had stood his ground shimmied out of the shed skin of quiet respectability and fought.

Louisa Tate, spinster, who had lost her only love in the same war, but in a different battle, held her ground. She embraced the rage of her loss and remade herself into an avenging Fury. Without the steadying influence of Ernest Tubbs and his protectively narrow pipeline to magic, she drew what she needed, and swelled from gaunt, gray-haired mouse to towering, howling Valkyrie. The rebound magic slammed into her, and she absorbed it and transformed it— fed on its energy and shed its poison into the ground. Eric saw lightning crackle from her fingertips and clouds gather around her head, and had to fight the urge to break and run from her.

Eric held. He'd accepted his own death in the line of duty long ago; he should have already been dead, and would have been without Lauren's intervention. He figured every extra minute was borrowed time. So, accepting that he was dead already, he released his fear and took the magic that hit him, and bent with it. The great tree breaks in the flood but the reed survives, he thought. Like a reed, he bent beneath the storm of the rebound, and accepted everything that it threw at him, and passed the shock of each blow through his body to the ground beneath.

June Bug Tate held. Her secrets frightened her more than any death by magic she might face, and so she did not quaver when the taint of death drove into her. She accepted it, channeled it, let it use her without letting it destroy her.

Even Terry Mayhew held. He thought himself a coward, but he discovered that being afraid didn't mean being unable to fight. He shook with fear; his mouth cotton-dry, his skin soaked with the stink of his own terror-born sweat. He felt his muscles clench and his bowels churn. But something inside of him kept him in place, feet welded to the ground, arms raised to the storm that slammed into him. He thought of his nieces, five and seven years old, with their silly laughter and their delighted shouts every time he pulled into the driveway of their house and hurried up the walk to see them. They deserved another day, another week, another seven or eight decades. And only if he held would he know that he had done what he could to give that to them. If he survived by running, he thought, he would never be able to face them again.

Jimmy Norris broke. He made a brave show when first his spell untangled the mess the traitors had left for them; but when Ernest and Nancine and Bethellen dropped dead, he screamed and dropped his beloved book and fled.

He got no farther than the outer edge of their work circle. As his feet cleared the perimeter guarded by George Mercer's firefly "watchdogs," a bolt of fire from the parapet of the castle lanced down at him and charred him to powder. The attack was quick, soundless, as cold and fast as the bite of a rattlesnake.

Eric had the best position to see what had happened, and he groaned; Jimmy's death proved the traitors watched and waited. They would let the Sentinels undo the destruction they had caused, perhaps, but if the Sentinels survived the rebound of the deadly magic, all three traitors would be waiting to take them on. And with both time to prepare and the vast advantage of ready-made fortifications on their side, Eric thought the odds in battle favored the traitors.

He could have done nothing to help Jimmy, but he wanted revenge for his murder. He wanted revenge for Bethellen, and Nancine and Ernest, too. And Debora and Granger. And the faceless millions dead for no reason, dead from stupidity and carelessness and a simple disregard for the tenets of the Sentinels—that each rivulet of downworld magic released an upworld river; that good begat good and evil begat evil; that Sentinels protected life; and most of all the Sentinels did not interfere with the natural workings of the worlds below and beside them, but worked only to stabilize the flow of magic between the worlds and maintain the steady state of the universes.

He could not seek the revenge he wanted; he could only stand, taking the blows that rained down on him, channeling them downward.

Each death struck the surviving Sentinels. The deaths of uncounted mice—tiny individually, but like the pelting of hail that, massed and concentrated, could pound men flat, destroy mighty trees, crush and rend to a pulp everything beneath its rage. And mixed in with the deaths of mice, the millions of deaths of humans—men, women, and children who were ripped untimely from their lives and cast between the worlds. Those deaths brought with them rage and shock and dismay and grief, yearning and despair, madness and desperation. If the deaths of the mice were hailstones, the deaths of the humans were comets hurled at the Sentinels from space—a rain of two-million-plus comets, to be borne by five trembling mortals.

They stood, arms and faces lifted skyward, absorbing, suffering, and though the hellish rain tore them and battered them and scarred them body and soul and bent them to the ground, they did not break.

And at last the poison leached into the earth beneath their feet, and the furies of the dead abated, and they dropped, one by one, to hands and knees. Eric managed to keep the shield around Lauren and Pete and Jake in place. He strengthened it as best he could against magical attacks. He created a tiny shield around the fallen Sentinels, living and dead. But he could no more stand against the traitors at that moment than he could walk across the surface of a sea back home on Earth. None of the five survivors would be able to stand and fight—they had nothing left.

Eric, weaving on hands and knees, stared up at the castle, knowing that now his enemies—who had once been his allies and friends—would approach. And when they did, he would be helpless to lift a finger against them.

With the last of his energy, he rolled to his back so that at least he would see the end coming, so that he would not die unaware of the fate that would claim him. He stared up at the crisp blue sky, at the crystalline perfection of the white mares' tails that swirled across it, and he thought, At least perhaps my world will survive. At least I can hope that we accomplished that.

CHAPTER 19

Outside Cold Starhold

Lauren cuddled Jake against her chest and crouched behind a tree; she held the energy weapon tucked against her hip, safety on and still set to stun.

Pete dropped to one knee beside her. "They're in trouble."

"But not from the traitors. This is the plague on Earth they're fighting. This is what they came to do."

"I can feel it."

Lauren looked at him, surprised. "Really?"

"Yeah."

"I don't know how to help them. I'm not sure we could if we tried; I have the feeling that if we did, we'd just foul things up."

"We have to sit and wait," Pete said. "They aren't done, and neither are the traitors. Our turn is coming pretty fast, I think."

Lauren saw movement along the castle parapet, and came to a decision. "This is nothing I want Jake to be around," she said softly. She hugged him; he was, uncharacteristically, hanging on to her as tightly as he could. He felt the magic, too, and didn't like it.

Molly and her companion sat on a fallen log just behind Lauren. Lauren turned to her new-found sister and said, "This is bad, but it's going to get worse. I can't leave. I have to be here to run the gates."

Molly looked scared. "What's going on here is making me sick. I've never felt anything like this. It's evil."

"As I told you," Yaner said. "We need to go home. Now. Seolar would be frantic if he knew the danger you were in."

"Don't go," Lauren said. "You're my sister, right?"

"Of course."

"You and I . . . know . . ." She paused. "We share a past. A future."

Molly nodded.

"You have to take care of Jake for me. You have to get him back to Earth before the next trouble comes." She pointed to three men who stood on the parapets atop the castle and stared down at the circle of fallen Sentinels. "Pete and I are going to have to get the Sentinels out of there and deal with the traitors, and I don't want Jake here." She picked him up and shoved him into Molly's arms and said, "There's a gate already waiting in the tent over there. Please, take Jake and go through it. Wait for me on the other side."

"Where will it take us?"

"Back to my house in Cat Creek."

"No."

"What do you mean, no? It's not perfect, but it'll be safer there than it is here."

Molly, holding Jake in her arms like she'd never picked up a little boy before, looked terrified. "I can't go back to Earth," she said. "I've changed. The veyâr part of me will—dissolve or something if I go through the gate. I have to stay in Oria."

Lauren put her hands on her sister's shoulders. "Please. I know we don't really know each other—not yet. But Jake is all I have, and he can't stay here. You can come back here after. If you changed once, you'll change again. But you have to go . . . and you have to hurry. Promise me that you won't let anything happen to Jake."

"Everything I ever wanted is here," Molly whispered.

Lauren clasped her son's hand and said, "And everything I have left is here. Promise me. Please. If you go now, you can come back when this is over. I can make a gate for you to anywhere. But the shield around Jake and the gates is collapsing and those men on top of the castle wall have already killed Sentinels—and they're going to kill us and anyone else who isn't already dead unless Pete and I can find a way to stop them." She stared into Molly's eyes. *"Promise me."*

Molly paled and bit her lip, but she nodded. "Go. Do what you have to do. Jake will be safe with me. I swear it."

Yaner stood, trembling. "Vodi, you must leave. You cannot stay here—cannot take the child through to Earth—cannot abandon us. We *need* you. The veyâr need you as the humans do not and never can. And you are ours now."

But Molly pressed a finger to his lips and said, "She is my sister. I've waited my whole life to have a sister. My whole life. I have to do this for her."

Lauren glared at Yaner and, uneasy, turned to Pete. "One of us is going to have to fire on the traitors while the other one drags the Sentinels back and pushes them through the gate."

Pete said, "Can you shoot someone?"

"These things are set on stun."

"I know that. But if stun doesn't work, *can you shoot someone?*"

Millions of people back home were dead—and their killers stood on the castle parapet, threatening her, her child, and her future. To save themselves—or maybe just because they wanted to—the traitors would kill Pete. The Sentinels. Her.

Lauren remembered Eric's warning—that using magic to kill in the downworld would have serious repercussions in the upworld. If she took the weapon off stun, people back home were going to pay with their lives. They might be strangers. They might not. She looked at Jake, clinging to Molly.

Any magic the traitors used to kill would have the same effect. If they attacked the Sentinels, or her and Pete, she would have to act quickly to stop them. But she wouldn't kill them unless she had no other alternative. She didn't dare.

"I can if I have to," she told Pete. "But I'm keeping this on stun unless there's no other alternative. The price we pay back home may be too great otherwise."

"No easy answers," Pete said. He glanced over his shoulder, cringed at what he saw in the Sentinels' circle, and hoisted his weapon. "Get me home safe if you can," he told her. "I've got to go. You cover me—I'm going in there and pull out the ones that are down. I'm bigger and stronger and will be able to move dead weight a whole lot easier than you could." He looked over at Yaner. "And if you help me, we can get your Molly back where she belongs a whole lot faster."

Yaner started to beg off, but Molly leaned over and whispered softly enough that Lauren almost couldn't hear her, "Go. Help him. Doing so will help me."

Yaner seemed to pale, but he said, "I will assist you."

"Good." Pete turned again to Lauren. "Don't miss, all right? I've never liked the idea of being toasted by friendly fire."

Lauren said, "I'm a good shot. I've got your back."

"Just make sure you leave it in one piece. You have any actual idea how to cover someone against several enemy positions?"

"Shoot at them when I see them?" Lauren asked.

"No. You have unlimited ammunition, and the weapon won't heat up or jam. So you just send a steady stream of fire at the wall. Spray the whole thing from one side to the other. Irregular sweeps, so they don't get a feel for a pattern and pop up where you aren't to take me or Yaner out. Or more likely, you. You're going to be their first target."

"I know."

They stared up at the shield that glowed around Jake, which faded and strengthened, then faded again. "I don't think it's going to last much longer," Lauren told him. "And that's our protection for the gates, too."

"Before everything goes, I'm running. Be ready to cover me."

Lauren nodded and turned to her sister. "Molly, go back to Cat Creek now. I'll be back at the house as soon as I can. And if I don't make it . . ." She blinked back the tears that threatened to blur her vision and said, "You're the only family he has. Take care of him for me. Okay?"

Molly, white with fear, just nodded.

"The gate's set up in that tent." She hugged her sister, then hugged Jake. "Oh, God. There are two mirrors in there, and two gates, but only one is primed. You have to use the one on the right. All you have to do is press your hand against the glass. You'll feel a vibration in your palm, and then the glass will . . . sort of give way. Step through."

Molly said, "I'll . . . um. Yes. I can do that. I can."

"Mama," Jake sobbed, knowing something was wrong but not knowing what. He held out his arms for her as she pulled away, and Lauren's desire to hold him and comfort him at that moment was so fierce it stopped her breath. She thought the pain of letting him go with someone else—even her sister—would kill her. "Go," she told Molly. "Hurry. Please. Get him away from this place."

Molly, with a wailing Jake in her arms, turned and ran for the tent.

Pete took a deep breath and began running along the edge of the clearing, keeping cover between him and the men on the castle parapet. Yaner stayed right behind him. The three traitors hadn't seen either of them yet. When they did, she was going to have to shoot.

Lauren swallowed hard and gripped the weapon in her hand. It seemed to get heavier as she stood there, until she felt she wouldn't be able to hold it long enough to get off even a few initial shots. She wondered if fear always did that. "Tripod," she whispered, willing one into existence. She affixed the weapon to the tripod quickly, sighted on the castle wall where her enemies stood waiting, and braced herself for what she would have to do.

Then one of the men on the parapet shouted and pointed toward the forest, toward Pete and Yaner. Lauren pulled the trigger back hard and pivoted the weapon in a short, fast arc from one side of the castle parapet to the other. She saw the watchers on the wall dive. Her belly was a sick knot, queasy from fear of hurting the three men up there—but she kept the weapon on stun, and maintained a steady stream of fire, spraying the wall in random fast and slow sweeps.

Beneath the spray from her weapon, Pete and the veyâr charged out of the forest and bolted toward the fallen Sentinels, grabbed the nearest, and started dragging her back. Then Yaner dropped his side of the woman and pointed toward the sky behind Lauren, and his face was the face of horror from an Edvard Munch nightmare. Pete dropped the other side of the Sentinel, swung his weapon around to the fire position, and began shooting over Lauren's head.

Lauren saw one of the traitors point behind her, too, and then the traitors were all three firing at whatever was coming.

Lauren knew she shouldn't turn her back on the enemy, but she couldn't help it. She turned . . . and wished she hadn't.

They hung in the air like holes in space—three huge, winged nightmares whose bodies swallowed the light around them, twisted it, and bent it so that they hung in circles of darkness in the middle of the day. Her eyes refused to see the three horrors clearly—she got the impression of teeth, of scales and claws, but the way they bent the light, the way they seemed to pull terror around them like a cloak, set her flesh crawling and made her knees bump against each other for support. Unthinking, she raised her weapon and fired on them. The flashes of energy splashed in the air in front of them, as if she were shooting paintballs at a window, and slowed them as much as paintballs would have.

"The Vodi is here," one of them said in a voice that made the ground beneath her feet tremble. And all three of the monsters, unbothered by her fire, Pete's fire, and the blasts from the three traitors, turned their attention to the tent with the gate.

Molly and Jake were long gone, of course, Lauren thought. But the gate would still be open. She couldn't let them follow. She switched her weapon from stun to kill. Nothing changed.

The three creatures hovered over the tent, and it erupted into flame, and each of them dropped an egg-shaped object. Three explosions tore through the clearing, throwing Lauren to the ground. She lost her grip on her weapon—but she still had the handgun in its shoulder holster. Brian's gun. She pulled it out, switched the safety off, and fired at one of the monsters.

Her first shot, carefully aimed at the head, registered a hit. Screaming, twisting, writhing, the monster fell from the sky. The other two beasts turned to stare at her, and her mouth went dry and her heart pounded in her chest like the heart of a rabbit caught in the gaze of a hunting hawk. She aimed again, for the second nightmare, and her finger trembled on the trigger, but she squeezed.

This time the bullet hit center mass on the monster—it shrieked, and the darkness around it coalesced, and it and its partner vanished. Lauren looked at the ground where the first one had fallen, and discovered that it, too, had vanished.

And then, from behind her, shots that tore into the rocks to the left of her. The traitors, with the bigger threat eliminated, had decided to take her out. She thumbed the safety on and jammed the Browning back into its holster. It didn't have the range to hit the castle. She dove for the magic weapon, came up with it, and had the satisfaction of seeing one of the traitors go down.

And then she realized the weapon was still set on kill.

Molly hadn't gone through the mirror back to Earth. She had been standing there in front of it, trying to convince herself that she didn't really need to leave; that anything she needed to do, she could do in Oria. And then she'd heard Yaner and Lauren's friend Pete coming toward her, and Lauren shouting that she had them covered, and she realized she had to be out of the tent before they got there, because she'd promised.

She had promised her sister—and now she had to keep her promise, no matter how much she didn't want to, no matter how much she resented taking this kicking, fighting, crying kid to a place she never wanted to go to again.

She had promised.

She'd turned sideways so that she could fit herself and Jake through the narrow mirror together, and they were partway into the gate, with the lower half of Jake's body and the

right side of hers still in Oria—with one of her feet still on
Orian soil because she couldn't quite force herself to take
the next step.

And the tent erupted. Fire. Explosions. She felt the blast,
but the necklace at her throat seemed to vibrate, and the heat
and the force of it washed around her.

It didn't wash around Jake. One minute she was holding
a fighting kid, and the next, she was carrying the rags of a
child. He didn't even cry out. He lay limp in her arms, a
bloody, shuddering piecework of skin and bone and flesh,
bleeding everywhere, and she clutched him tight against her
as the path dragged her through green fire, away from Oria,
back to Earth.

He breathed. Against all odds, against all possibility, he
breathed, and she realized that he was not alone. That some
force within the fire itself had embraced him and fed him its
own life, kept him breathing in this place between worlds
where her magic was helpless to save him. She could feel
thoughts around her—"Hang on, Jake. Don't die. Your
mother needs you. Hang on—I'm with you"—but she could
not find the source of those thoughts. To all appearances,
she and Jake slipped between the worlds alone, but she
could hear that voice. She could feel that power. And Jake
lived.

In the instant and the infinity in which she and her sister's
child hung in that place out of time, Molly realized that once
she stepped through the other side of the gate, he would die.
The force that fed him was not healing him—he was still in
tatters, still unconscious, still bleeding. When the two of
them stepped through the gate on the other side, Jake was
going to die.

She had time to think about Seolar. About her promise to
return to him; about her people, the veyâr, who needed her.
She had time to think about her promise to Lauren, to keep
Jake safe. She even had time to hate herself for failing to
move as quickly as she needed to.

But most of all, she had time to think of the boy whose
mother had brought him to her on the last night of his life,
and how she had turned him away. She could still see his

eyes. And the unblinking eyes that stared through her from Jake's shattered body held that same mute plea. "Help me. I didn't ask for this. I didn't deserve this. I am innocent of any act that would make this fate justly mine."

Echoes of her past, the pain of her present, ghosts of a future that might have been hers.

She could not turn back to Oria, where she could heal him without cost. The path carried her in one direction, and no matter how she willed it, she and Jake kept moving in that direction. She would not have time to figure out how to go through the gate again—if it would even accept her a second time. Jake was a breath away from death. She could feel it in every cell of her body, and the closer she came to Earth, the more fiercely she felt it. The being with him held the breath in the child's ruined body by sheer force of will, but she understood somehow that its power and influence would end at the gate, and she and Jake would be on their own.

She could save Jake, but she would pay with everything she had. Her future, her dreams, her duty, and her life. She could let him die, and have the life that was better than anything she could have ever dreamed of—but if she let him die, she would carry not one child's ghost with her through the rest of her life, but two.

And then she was out of time.

The path expelled her into the foyer of a nice old house, and the pain of Jake's injuries consumed her. The choice was upon her. She had only seconds to do what had to be done, or it would become impossible.

Lauren switched the weapon over to stun and kept firing, but she knew she'd killed someone. The air around her changed, and clouds pulled in over the sun, and she knew a storm was building, and felt herself at its heart. Eric had said there would be consequences if they used magic to kill, and she felt those consequences coming.

She clenched her jaw and kept firing, praying that the traitors would stay low, that they would keep out of the way while Pete and Yaner got the Sentinels out of harm's way.

"Is the gate still there?" she yelled to Pete.

"Hang on!" Pete, who had also been thrown to the ground by the explosion, had helped Yaner up, and the two of them were dragging the woman—June Bug, Lauren thought—toward the place where the tent had been.

A moment later he yelled, "Still here. Still open. The frame is charred, but the gate itself doesn't look like it's been touched."

"Hurry, then. We have to get out of here."

She heard nothing for a moment, then he was running past her. "I'm going to grab them all. The only one I can be sure won't make it is Jimmy Norris. There isn't enough left of him to put in a shoe box."

Lauren could have done without knowing that, but she said, "Run, then. We have trouble coming."

"Shit," Pete yelled, taking her at her word, and ran. Yaner, longer-legged by far than any human, was already halfway back to the gate with the next body draped over his back, its arms over his shoulders like handles, its legs dangling. Lauren couldn't even begin to guess who he had.

Pete, though, grabbed Eric next, and got him up onto his back in a modified fireman's carry. Lauren only caught a glimpse of the two of them moving toward her; then she saw a head poking over the parapet, and she shot at it.

Pete and Yaner ran back and forth, and she kept up a steady stream of fire. And then a bolt hit her, and pain seared her, and she toppled to her side and stared in horror at the stump where her leg had been. The pain tried to devour her—but she pulled from the magic, not caring about later price, about the rules of Sentinels, about anything but that she would never get home to Jake if she died on this field, and she healed the stump. Watched her leg re-create itself out of green fire. Stood again, and said, "The hell with caution. Bring on the storm," and switched her weapon back to kill. Come hell or Armageddon, she *would* get home to Jake.

In her hands, the weapon began to change shape. It got bigger, and began doing more damage with each hit. It stretched longer, as well, and became more accurate. She realized her will was reshaping it for her purposes—she wanted to destroy the men on the castle and the castle itself, and she was doing it. The parapets began to crumble, and one dark shape toppled to the ground stories below. She caught movement from both sides as the surviving traitor ran for new cover.

The castle parapet rebuilt itself—and as quickly as it did, she shattered it with a single hit from the weapon that had become a cross between a mortar and a handheld nuke launcher. Two volleys of green fire arced toward her, and she blasted both out of the sky. She became an avenging angel. One of the Furies, bent on the utter destruction of her enemies.

The storm that had been building erupted all around her— lightning and thunder, twisting winds that screamed through the trees and ripped stones from the castle wall and picked up the last of the traitors from the roof and sucked men out of the lower floors and dragged them high into the air. Pete was screaming at her to knock it off, that he still had people to get, but the storm fed deep inside of her. It didn't listen to logic, to reason, to anything but the rage she felt at those people who had tried to take her away from her son. She could not turn off her rage, and so the storm grew wilder. She'd stopped firing—the men hung high in the air, spinning inside the cyclone that she had given life. They couldn't touch her. The cyclone could, though—so she abandoned her weapon and ran with Pete and Yaner for the last of the Sentinels, and dragged them through screaming wind and rocketing debris, pelted by stones and sticks and leaves and branches.

The cyclone held its position on top of the castle—or what remained of the castle—long enough for the three of them to get everyone shoved through the gate.

"Are you going to leave it like that?" Pete shouted above the howling winds.

"No! I have to finish this! There's no telling what it will do on Earth if I let it die down on its own. If magic done here always has echoes there, then I don't even want to think about what this is doing right now. If I walk away and leave it . . ."

"How can I help!" Pete shouted over the roar.

Lauren shook her head. "Go back! Help Molly with the Sentinels and Jake. I'll get there as fast as I can."

"It's coming from you!" Pete yelled. "If you leave, maybe it will die down on its own."

Lauren considered that. Nodded. "Let's go. I'll come back in a minute and see if it worked. If it didn't—I'll deal with it then."

Yaner stepped through the mirror. Then Pete. Lauren followed him.

For a moment she felt the delicious embrace of the green fire that burned between the worlds—but this time she was alone. She couldn't feel Brian, whose touch had been with her every time except when she stepped though to Kerras. She reached for him, tried to find him in the timeless instant when she floated in the fire. The path spit her out into her foyer before she was ready—and threw her into chaos.

She landed in a pile of limbs, and from deep within it, she heard weak sobbing. And a single faint wail. "Mama."

Pete and Yaner, a second ahead of her, were already pulling bodies off the pile.

Lauren started dragging people away from the center of the pile. Warm bodies, and cool ones that she shuddered to touch. Somewhere beneath them lay Jake. "What the hell happened?"

"I don't know. I've yelled for Molly, but she isn't here."

"She didn't want to come back," Lauren snarled. "She shoved Jake through the gate alone—she abandoned a little guy in a house all by himself . . ."

She was tugging at bodies, heedless of whether they were alive or dead, with visible injuries or without. "Mama!" Jake cried again.

And then she found him, and with him, Molly.

Both were covered in blood. Jake's clothing hung in tatters. Molly's, blood-soaked, seemed intact, but she didn't move. "Ma-MA!" Jake howled, and reached up his arms to her.

Lauren snatched him out of the pile and checked him. He seemed fine. Terrified. Bloody. But fine. She clutched him tight, buried her face in his hair, and vaguely realized that tears poured down her cheeks, and that she almost couldn't breathe, she was crying so hard.

Pete knelt by Molly, fingers at her pulse. "She's dead," he said softly, looking up at Lauren. "I don't see any external injuries, but she's bled from her mouth and her ears—I'd say she had bad internal bleeding."

Yaner, a thin ghost of himself, let out a wail and flung himself on the floor beside Molly's now-completely-human body. A mist rose around him, and the air grew icy. His keening set Lauren's teeth on edge and made Jake scream.

Lauren couldn't understand what she was seeing. "Molly could heal. Even here on Earth, she had the magic to heal. Why would she be dead?"

"I don't know. But she is." Pete looked at Jake, and at Lauren, and then at the hysterical Yaner. "You need to get the little guy out of here for a few minutes. Go get him cleaned up, and I'll take care of all of this."

Lauren nodded. Then she remembered the storm. "Shit. I need to go back through the gate to make sure the storm is slowing down. And then I need to take each of the Sentinels who is alive back to Oria to see if I can do anything to heal them."

Pete winced. "Go check on the storm, and then come back and take care of your little guy. Let the rest wait for a minute. The ones who are alive have strong pulses, warm skin, no bleeding—we aren't going to lose them, and the less magic you do over there, the better for us over here. Right?"

Lauren knew he was right. The events of the day—of the past few days—terrified her, and she felt out of control and overrun by things bigger than anything she could have imagined. She wanted to fix everything. To make right all that had gone wrong. Only she couldn't. She couldn't bring back the dead, she couldn't erase the magic that had caused so much heartache and loss, she couldn't save her dead sister, so recently found.

She could check on the mess she'd left behind. And then she could come home.

She went to the mirror, with Jake clinging to her neck. And as she started to hand him over to Pete, he screamed— a wordless high-pitched shriek unlike anything she'd ever heard from him. His arms clamped around her neck like vises, his legs wrapped around her torso, and he buried his head against her cheek.

"He's scared," Pete observed.

Lauren patted and bounced him, cooing, "It's okay, it's okay, everything's going to be all right." But he didn't loosen his grip, and when she tried to force his arms from around her neck, he shrieked again.

She looked at Pete. "He's absolutely panicked. I can feel his heart pounding against me, he's so scared. I can't leave him with you, and I don't want to take him back there again. Not with things so uncertain."

"Hold the gate open for me. I'll go through and check," Pete said. "If there's a problem, I'll come back and tell you, and we'll figure out what to do about it from there."

"Thanks." She held her hand to the gate, and it glimmered to life. "Go. Come straight back. I'll hold it open as long as I have to, but I don't want anything to happen to you over there."

"I'll be fine."

He stepped through the gate, and she watched him shimmer across the fire road, and step out into Oria. She could see him crouch, raise his hand to shield his eyes, and then he was running toward something, leaning over, and after a moment she thought, but couldn't be sure, that he was throwing up. He had his back to her. He stared again, but she couldn't see what he was looking at without disturbing the gate. He pulled something out of his pocket, made a quick move, ran a ways away, did something else—always with his back to the gate, shielding his actions from her sight. Then he stepped away from whatever he'd found. An instant later, he was making his way through the mirror and back to her. When he stepped back into the foyer, he was ash-gray, with his forehead and upper lip beaded with sweat.

"What did you find?"

His mouth formed a tight, grim line, and he wouldn't meet her eyes. "The storm is over. Your leaving did the trick."

"Good. What did you find?"

"The traitors are all dead," he said. "And the natives who were with them." She could see in his face that he would not tell her what he'd found. And she could see in his eyes that she did not want to know.

But he had blood on his hands—blood that she felt sure had not been there when he crossed over. And she saw streaks of blood on his right pocket, as if he'd shoved a bloody hand into it and pulled it out.

She stared at him until he actually looked at her, and she held Jake, and rocked him, and said nothing.

Pete said, "Even rabid dogs deserve a quick, merciful death."

In Lauren's memory, the traitor and the veyâr in the castle spun in the air, caught in the cyclone. She thought about the storm dying away suddenly, as if turned off by the flip of a switch. Maybe that had happened. Or maybe the cyclone had flung each of its victims free before it died away. Ugly. An ugly fate.

Pete turned to Eric and June Bug and the other Sentinels, and Molly, all still sprawled on the floor, and said, "I need to do something useful for a while. Why don't you let me take care of these folks?"

Lauren stroked Jake's blood-matted hair, and said, "I'll be upstairs giving him a bath if you need me."

Jake's diaper—what was left of it—was soaked with blood.

Lauren pulled it off him and settled him into the tub, and stared at the diaper, trying to figure out what had happened. "Her clothes are soaked with blood, but I couldn't see any wounds, or any tears, or anything wrong with her except that she's dead. But your clothes are in shreds, your shoes and socks and the bottoms of your pants are gone completely, the back of your coat and your shirt are gone, and your dia-per has enough blood in it to transfuse someone. The blood on her isn't hers, is it?"

She rubbed shampoo into Jake's hair with shaking hands.

"It's yours, isn't it? That's why you're so scared. Some-thing terrible happened to you. She didn't get you out of there when I told her to, and something awful happened to you, and she died fixing it."

Jake didn't fight her when she washed his hair, or when she scrubbed the blood from his skin. That was so out of character, Lauren wanted to scream. He hated having his hair washed, he hated being scrubbed, and he'd never been still in the tub. Now he sat like a little zombie, shivering in the warm air and the warm water. He seemed like a stranger to her; like someone else's kid.

"Oh, sweetheart," she whispered. "I'm so sorry. I wish I could take back what happened to you. I wish I could make you forget it."

She considered that for a moment. She could make Jake forget it—but what else would he forget in the process? Her memory hadn't been right after her parents' experiment, and they had much more experience with magic than she did. She could very well erase not just his memory, but his per-sonality. She could leave him a drooling, unresponsive lump, instead of the busy, frustrating, delightful little boy he had always been.

"No, I don't wish that. I wish I could make whatever hap-pened to you not have happened, but I can't. And I won't play God with your brain." She kissed his cheek. "We'll get through this, you and I. We'll find our way back to where things are good, and where you can laugh and play. You're young, and you have me. You'll get better. I promise."

She hoped her promise wasn't an empty one.

When she went downstairs, with Jake once again clamped to her like a barnacle, she found Eric sitting on the floor of the foyer next to Louisa Tate. Both looked pale and shaky, but both were talking. Terry Mayhew, already on his feet, helped Pete pull bodies out onto the front porch. June Bug, on her hands and knees, scrubbed blood from the floor-boards. Lauren didn't see George Mercer, but when she got to the bottom of the stairs, she heard his voice coming from the kitchen.

". . . That's right. More flu victims. Right . . . and one we're not sure of. The deputy is here—that's right—Pete Stark. We heard about the Sheriff, but the deputy has been here in town. Nossir—he's been busy as a one-armed paper-hanger. Don't think he's had time to kidnap the Sheriff and disappear into thin air." A long pause . . . ". . . Well, I've heard some nurses are crazy . . . Pete's already checked everything out and released the bodies. . . . An hour or more? . . . That's fine. We'll still be here. I know you have to get the people who have a chance first."

Lauren heard his footsteps in the hall. George was only in his mid-forties, but he looked very old and frail right then. "I need to get home and check on my family," he said. "I tried calling, but didn't get an answer. The flu . . ." He didn't need to say anything else.

"You want me to go with you?" Pete asked. "You shouldn't be going there alone."

"I'll be fine. I . . . don't want to have anyone with me. Be-sides, you'd better stay here. An ambulance will be along to get the bodies when it can, but the dispatcher said they've been running straight for the last twenty-four hours, and they have to get live people first."

"They're outside, and it's cold," Eric said quietly. "They'll keep."

"Doesn't seem very respectful," George said.

"I'll cover them," Pete told him. "I won't just leave them out there that way. Not much else we can do for them."

June Bug said, "That's good enough."

Lauren saw tears in her eyes, and realized that she'd lost a sister, too. She crouched next to June Bug and said, "I'm sorry about Bethellen."

June Bug nodded. "So am I. And Molly. She was so like your mother, it was almost like having her back again." She wrung her sponge into the bucket of blood-red water, dipped it into the bucket of clean water, and went back to scrubbing the floor. "I'm tired. I'm tired of the Sentinels, I'm tired of the pain, I'm tired of life. I don't know why I lived, but right now I wish I hadn't."

Lauren levered herself down next to June Bug, careful not to dislodge Jake, and put a hand on her shoulder, and waited until June Bug looked away from the bloody floor and up at her. "I'm sorry. I'm sorry you lost the people you loved. I know what that feels like. I wish I didn't—I wish I was just saying polite things here to try to make you feel better, but I do know what that feels like. I waited years to find Brian— years in which I made a lot of stupid mistakes because I was looking for something I don't think I had the capacity to find or even to define. Brian found me, not the other way around." She drew her hand back and glanced out at the bodies on the front porch, then glanced away again, because it hurt to look. "There's this pop song where a guy sings that he doesn't want to go to sleep because if he does he'll miss a minute of his time with the woman he loves—and until Brian came into my life, I would have told you that the lyrics of that song were just sentimental bullshit. That no one ever really felt that way." She felt the lump growing in her throat, but she plowed on. "But when he found me—when we first got together—I remember him coming home to the little apartment we shared after a full shift on the flight line, and staying awake all night—and keeping me up, too—because he was afraid that if he went to sleep, he'd miss something. He went to work on two hours of sleep a night for a month, and then he went TDY and I felt like I couldn't breathe because he was gone." She closed her eyes. "We had each other for a few years, and now he's gone forever, and I haven't been able to really breathe since he died. There isn't enough air in the world for me to breathe, and the only reason that I'm alive at all is because of Jake. Without him . . ." She shook her head.

June Bug had tears running down her cheeks. She was staring down at her hand still wrapped around the sponge, her gray hair hanging loose around her face. "It doesn't get better," she said. "A year . . . five years . . . ten years. I wish

I could say that it did, but there's never going to be enough air again."

Lauren felt Jake's cheek against hers and swallowed the lump in her throat, and said, "I know. Real love found me, and I knew it, and I knew how lucky I was the whole time he was in my life. I *knew* it. I always thought it was the people who didn't appreciate what they had who lost it—and I knew what I had and I was grateful, and I thought that because I knew what a miracle Brian was, I would get to keep him. And I lost him anyway." She thought about the place between the worlds, where he had found her again for a while, and how he was now gone from there. Gone. She couldn't find him; she'd lost him again in a different way.

Then Jake raised his head, and leaned over and kissed her on the cheek, and patted her softly on the neck with one little hand. "Daddy loves Mama," he said. "Daddy . . . say . . . love you, Mama." He wrinkled up his face, frowning fiercely, concentrating on something. And then he added, "We okay. Daddy say . . . fings be okay." The frown got deeper. He was fighting to get something, and she could see his frustration, and finally he blew out his cheeks, and shook his head, and said, "Daddy here. Be okay." He kissed her on her cheek again, and laid his head on her shoulder, and wrapped his arms around her neck.

Lauren stood there staring at June Bug. "He doesn't remember his daddy," she said. "He doesn't say anything about Brian except when he looks at the picture I keep of him beside my bed. And that's only sometimes. He's . . ."

What did Jake mean, that Daddy was here? That things would be okay? What was going on?

"Brian?" she whispered, looking around the foyer. "If you're here . . . give me a sign."

Jake, heavy on her shoulder, drifted toward sleep.

"Brian?"

And from Jake's lips, in a voice that was partly Jake's but partly someone else's, came clear, impossible sentences. "I didn't die for nothing. Today it counted. I can't stay. But . . . I wanted to say good-bye, Lauren. There's another side. I'll be there, waiting. For both of you."

"I love you," she whispered.

"Forever," he said. Then Jake's eyes closed completely, and his breathing grew deep. And Lauren knew that her miracle had run its course.

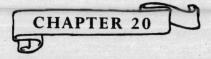

CHAPTER 20

UNSEASONABLE TORNADOES DEVASTATE SOUTHEAST
Reuters—Charlotte, NC

A line of tornadoes running from Kansas down to Florida's Gold Coast erupted without warning yesterday afternoon, leaving 734 dead and thousands injured and still missing, and meteorologists across the nation are left scrambling for an explanation.

"We had a uniform high-pressure front over the entire area, and have for the last week, and we got nothing on radar anywhere until these things just erupted," says Steve Billings of the National Weather Service. "None of our current models offer any explanation for what happened yesterday. 'Freak storm' just about sums it up." Others working in the field were quick to agree.

(**Tornadoes**—continued on 2-A)

FLU ENDS AS ABRUPTLY AS IT BEGAN
UPI

Worldwide reporting of new influenza cases has returned to normal levels and normal demographics overnight, as the Carolina flu that left more than four million dead over a course of mere weeks has seemingly vanished. Hospitals, short-staffed from losses of their own, watch gratefully as their overflowing halls begin to empty, and the weary doctors and nurses who have survived the onslaught look toward the possibility of going home to families and beds they haven't seen in days.

"Viruses sometimes do this," says Dr. Fenton Willoughby, of the Mayo Clinic. "They erupt abruptly, burn through the susceptible population too fast to sustain their own spread, and die out as quickly as they appeared. We can be grateful, of course—as horrible as this was, it could have been much, much worse.

"Which doesn't change the fact that this is the most lethal outbreak of influenza since the epidemic of 1917," he added.

(**Flu** continued on B-4)

ABRUPT CESSATION OF PEACE TALKS— EGYPT AND ISRAEL ON BRINK
Geneva, Switzerland—AP

In an abrupt about-face, Egyptians and Israelis who were rumored close to signing a collaborative agreement just yesterday have walked away from the table. The agreement, which would have paired the two nations in a wide range of health-care, education, and scientific programs, offered what many observers thought was the best hope of stabilizing the region put forward in years.

No definite word on the cause of the schism, but both sides have arrested members of their own delegations, charging treason. Following the breakdown in negotiations, both nations have placed military personnel on alert, troops are massing along both sides of the border, and civilian violence has erupted . . .

(**Middle East Traitors** continued on 9-D)

Cat Creek

LAUREN BURIED HER SISTER, Molly, on a bright North Carolina morning with the first crocuses peeking above the ground. Pete attended the service, as did Eric and June Bug. The rest of the Sentinels stayed home. Lauren was relieved. She and Pete had taken their oaths, but she still didn't feel like a Sentinel, and she didn't feel like fielding the false condolences of people who had wanted her sister dead.

She and Jake stood by the grave after the service, and she said, "Thank you, Molly. I'm going to miss you, and I wish we could have done all the things we were supposed to do together. But thank you for saving my son." Jake turned to her and raised his arms. "Up," he said.

She picked him up and he clung to her again. He still wasn't back to being himself. Unexpected noises scared him, he was suddenly terrified of bright lights, and for the first time in his life, he was utterly terrified of strangers.

"You need some company?" Eric asked her, as they walked through the cemetery, back to their cars.

"I'll be all right. I have some thinking to do—our parents had a plan for Molly and me, and now I have to figure out what I can do about it alone. I'll see you later."

"I'm here for you," Eric said, and she caught the extra nuances in his voice and in his eyes. He would be there in a lot of ways if she gave him the sign.

She said, "Thank you. I appreciate that." And kept her face friendly and her voice neutral. And she hoped that he got the message. They might have once had a chance of being friends, but he'd been willing to see her sister dead, and that would never go away.

"Call if you need me," he said, and turned without another word and walked to his car alone.

Pete said, "That goes for me, too, you know. Say the word, and I'll be there."

She smiled. "Thanks, Pete. Have a really good beer for me, okay? And don't let Eric run you too ragged. That speech of his about one Sentinel doing the work of four until he recruits help didn't sound promising . . . and I saw him looking at you when he said it."

"Me too," Pete agreed. "I'm not sure that signing on was the right thing to do . . . but I didn't see how I could go through all of that and then just walk away. You know what I mean?"

Lauren had taken the Sentinel oath along with Pete. She nodded and shifted Jake from one hip to the other. "Unfortunately."

Pete stood beside her car and watched her tuck Jake into his car seat. "If you need more than just a friend, Lauren . . ." He stopped. "Yeah. I guess I won't make a complete fool of myself today. But if you need anything, you know where to find me."

She nodded, ignoring the fact that her pulse was racing and her mouth was dry. Brian had said that he would be waiting for her on the other side. And she wanted Jake to know that Brian had been his father. She wanted to give him everything she had of Brian. But perhaps he had more of Brian than she did.

She felt lost.

"I'm not really . . . looking, but . . ." She gave him a tiny smile and got into her car. He was still standing by the side of the road watching her as she turned the corner and drove out of sight.

Forever. Brian had come to her from the other side of death itself to tell her that he would be waiting for her, and that he loved her, and he had promised her forever. How could she hope to find another love like that? How could she even consider looking? And if the impossible happened and she found someone she could love as much as she loved Brian, what then? Would Brian still be waiting for her? Would she have to leave behind the other love?

For just a moment, she could almost feel Brian's arms around her, and could almost hear Brian whispering in her ear, "Don't worry. Everything's going to be all right."

She took a steadying breath, and turned into her driveway. *Don't worry. Everything's going to be all right.*

She didn't have to do anything right then. Play with Jake,

make a meal, get some sleep. So she wouldn't worry. And maybe everything *would* be all right.

Copper House, Ballahara

Seolar had draped the whole of Copper House in black and declared a year of mourning—for Molly, for his people, for the future that was no more. He sat in his study at his desk with a book opened before him, and when anyone walked by he pretended to read, but he had read nothing since Yaner brought the news to him. He thought he would never read again. In a single blow, he had lost everything—future, people, world, and love. In his darkest moments, he considered orchestrating his own death.

He was thinking of just that when he heard movement from the balcony, and froze.

Nothing should be on the balcony—only his study opened onto it, and his doors were locked. He looked at them just to be sure. Yes. Locked.

Something tapped on the glass.

Curtains blocked his view—after Molly's death he had blocked light from the room, wanting to see nothing of the hateful sun. Firelight was enough, and sometimes more than enough, for his mood. But now he regretted the window covers. He would have liked to see what waited on his balcony.

Tap. Tap. Tap.

Persistent.

And then a voice. "Seolar? Are you in there?"

He thought he could not be hearing that voice, but it came again.

"Seolar? Seo?"

His hands shook and he thought he might die of fear, but he went to the door, moved back the curtain, and looked out.

Molly stood there. Molly, with the Vodi necklace about her neck, otherwise naked as she came into the world. Her long copper hair whipped around her, burnished fire red by the setting sun. She looked more veyâr than she ever had before, as though most of the human had been purged out of her. But she was Molly.

"You're dead," he croaked.

"Apparently not. Would you let me in? It's freezing out here." Her breath swirled around her in frosted clouds. She rubbed her arms with her hands and stamped her feet, and when he looked at her he could see that her skin was nubby with gooseflesh.

He unlocked the doors with fingers that almost wouldn't obey him, and pulled them open, and she hurried in and rushed to the fireplace. "God, it's awful to be stuck outside in this weather with no clothes. I hope I don't get frostbite."

"You're alive," he said.

She was turning in front of the fire, rubbing her arms still, shivering. "Much to my surprise."

He pulled one of his dressing gowns from its hook on the wall and hurried to her side and draped the gown around her.

"You're alive," he said again.

She pulled the robe tight and cinched it into place with the belt. And then she looked up at him and said, "I promised you I'd come back. I promised you that I wouldn't leave you alone. That I wouldn't let the veyâr die. So here I am."

He nodded. "You didn't die. Yaner told me you were dead. Everyone thought you were dead."

She rested a hand on his arm and looked into his eyes, and a chill ran through him. "I was dead," she said. "I came back. I'm here to be with you, to help the veyâr, to carry out my parents' plan. But I was dead. I came back. The necklace—well, let's just say I found out where all those nightmares I had of my predecessors came from. The necklace doesn't actually keep us from dying—it simply brings us back afterward. And that's a problem."

He pulled his arm away from her, shivering in spite of his wish to appear brave. "A problem?"

"Using magic to bring people back from the dead is bad. Very bad. What comes back is never the same as what was there before. I'm Molly—but, Seo . . . this necklace I'm wearing can never come off. Never. Because if it came off, I don't think I'd *be* Molly anymore."

He nodded. He could not think of a single word to say.

"But I *am* Molly. Right now, right here, I'm the Molly you know. The veyâr are safe. I'll stand between you and the Old Gods. And I love you, Seo. I love you."

She wrapped her arms around him, and held him tight, and he wrapped her in his embrace. She was right. He had his world back. His people. His future. His love.

But he thought of the fact that she had been dead, and was alive again. About the fact that she said coming back from the dead was bad—that if she removed the necklace, she would be someone (or perhaps some*thing*) else. He considered that she was the only woman he had ever loved, and she had cheated death to return to him.

And for the life of him, he could not think of a single word to say.

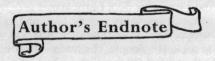
Author's Endnote

I've never done an endnote before, but this book—or at least the existence of the little town of Cat Creek—calls for some explanation. Initially, you see, I'd placed the story in Gibson, North Carolina, a tiny and absolutely charming town where I had the good fortune to live and spend time for a number of years. It was the perfect setting for this tale, and I made happy use of buildings, streets, people, and other things that stuck out in my memory. I couldn't figure out a way to work in either the Firehouse Restaurant, where I painted the sign over the door and played guitar for unsuspecting diners, or the cool old train station, but I still have books to write in this universe, so I'll keep looking in the next one.

However, once the body count started rising and I realized how very many people I was going to kill off, I suddenly couldn't leave the book set in Gibson anymore. I like the place, you see, and the folks who live there certainly wouldn't get that impression if I wiped out half the town's inhabitants in the blink of an eye.

So I created Cat Creek. It's situated exactly where Gibson is. Has many of the same streets (and street names). Many of the same buildings. Even a few folks I adored from the area playing major roles in the novel (but of course with names changed).

If you live around there or are in the area and want to spend an amusing afternoon, here's the gig on people in the book—if you like someone in this book, there's about a twenty-five percent chance he or she is based at least loosely on someone I once knew in the area; seventy-five percent of the good folks are purely imaginary. All of the bad guys are imaginary. I have a firm rule; I don't put anyone I don't like into a book. Why immortalize people you can't stand when there are so many you can walking around? And there you have it. Do a walking tour of Gibson, figure out which of the great old houses is Lauren's, which building is the sheriff's station, and guess who a few of the heroes are based on. And tell 'em I said hey; it's a fine little town.

And as a final note, because I caused my biologist friend Sarah Jane Elliott to beat her head against the wall over this one point: Lemmings do not commit mass suicide by jumping off cliffs. This legend apparently got started when a couple of photographers stampeded a few in order to get some interesting footage. However, Lauren Dane doesn't know this, and thereby may be forgiven for her erroneous metaphor in a moment of extreme stress. You, however, now know better (and so do I), so we have no excuses.

With the hope, then, that you've had as much fun reading this book as I had writing it.

Holly Lisle
April 4, 2001

Interview with a Dragon

One accepts the invitation of a monster cautiously, and with a backup plan if possible. I have no backup plan.

The rrôn faces me, smiling, and says, "I've been looking forward to this chat."

"Why?" I ask. The question the mouse asks the owl, and the rrôn laughs, but does not give me an answer.

Unnerved, I fall back on my questions, scrawled on an index card.

Where did the rrôn come from?

Rrakille. My homeworld hung a hundred worlds upworld of yours, wonderful beyond words. All the races of the rrôn filled it, spread from mountains to jungle to desert. We built great cities and hunting preserves; we sang at night from the clifftops and the city spires; we created art and science and literature and magic. We lived, we loved, we hunted . . . and then the old gods came, caught up in terrible battles they brought with them from worlds above ours.

In a day our shining home died, taking with it most of my kind, most of the warring old gods who used it as a battlefield, and all the joy the rrôn knew.

You fit many of our myths about dragons—are your people the truth behind our myths?

Of course. We are the dragons, bright and dark, from human tales and the tales carried from upworld. Your world lay in our path. We fled downworld ahead of destruction. Some of us stayed, some moved on. Eventually *most* of us moved on, when it became clear that Earth sat on the edge of annihilation. A few still remain, of course. A few always stay until the last.

There are still dra—ah, rrôn on Earth? Where are they now?

[The rrôn smiles, cocks one eye-rille, says nothing. I ask my next question.]

What do you and the other rrôn want?

We want our world back. There is no Diaspora more hellish than the scattering of a handful of survivors from their dead planet. We cannot hope to return; we hold in memory all that exists of the joy and the beauty that once belonged to us. And memory fades. Especially for the dark gods, memory is ever a traitor.

And yet, there are rumors. A plan—tried once before—now resurrected, to revive the dead upworlds and stabilize the chain. We're . . . looking into those rumors. If things go well, I suspect the rrôn will be very busy for a while.

What are the rumors?

Secret. They pass only among the trusted, to those who know how to keep from telling secrets to the enemy. The rrôn want to stop the deaths of worlds—but not everyone shares our sentiments. There are names not even we mention, for fear of summoning evils too great to bear.

[*Things that scare the rrôn?* I switch topics.]

Are the rrôn obsessed with gold?

Obsessed? No. But precious metals have purpose in the hands of those who know how to use them. Copper shields against magic. Silver channels the magic of order. And gold . . .

[He smiles at me.]

Gold channels the magic of chaos. The more gold you hoard, the more discord you bring to yourself. Not a good thing if you don't know about the effect. If you do, though, you can summon tremendous power through a mound of the stuff.

That would mean that gold is . . . bad.

Gold is chaotic. It stirs things up. That isn't necessarily bad—but gold can be used to create truly evil things. [He grins at me, and reaches forward, one talon extended, and I'm sure our interview is about to be cut short in the worst way, but then something glints. A little ring. Silver. Intricate wirework, no stone.] Here's a parting gift. It holds a little magic of its own—it offers a bit of protection, to warn you about the approach of those forces that live by chaos. And it will remind you what's important while you're writing.

Why? What is important?

That you get our story right. Remember—we're watching. We know where you live. And not all of us have moved on.

Then, with an agile twist, he launches himself into the air—the wind from the downbeat of his wing knocks me over. When I get off the ground, he's gone, and all that remains is the rapidly diminishing thunder of his wings.

And a gleaming circle of silver in the palm of my hand.

We hope you've enjoyed this Eos book. As part of our mission to give readers the best science fiction and fantasy being written today, the following pages contain a glimpse into the fascinating worlds of a select group of Eos authors.

Join us as beloved sf author Sheri S. Tepper recounts an intelligent, witty, and deeply human tale of first contact. As fantasy author Sharon Green reveals the true fates of the Chosen Blending, six courageous men and women whose talents stand between the evil and the innocent. As Holly Lisle introduces a magical world so close to our own that both destiny and disaster spill through the world gates. And as acclaimed editor David G. Hartwell brings us the very best science fiction stories of the year.

Spring 2002 at Eos. Out of this World.

THE FRESCO

Sheri S. Tepper

Available in February 2002

Along the Oregon coast an arm of the Pacific shushes softly against rocky shores. Above the waves, dripping silver in the moonlight, old trees, giant trees, few now, thrust their heads among low clouds, the moss thick upon their boles and shadow deep around their roots. In these woods nights are quiet, save for the questing hoot of an owl, the satin stroke of fur against a twig, the tick and rasp of small claws climbing up, clambering down. In these woods, bear is the big boy, the top of the chain, but even he goes quietly and mostly by day. It is a place of mosses and liverworts and ferns, of filmy green that curtains the branches and cushions the soil, a wet place, a still place.

A place in which something new is happening. If there were eyes to see, they might make out a bear-sized shadow, agile as a squirrel, puckering the quiet like an opening zipper, rrrip up, rrrip down, high into the trees then down again, disappearing into mist. Silence intervenes, then another seam is ripped softly on one side, then on the other, followed by new silences. Whatever these climbers are, there are more than a few of them.

The owl opens his eyes wide and turns his head backward, staring at the surrounding shades. Something new, something strange, something to make a hunter curious. When the next sound comes, he launches himself into the air, swerving silently around the huge trunks, as he does when he hunts mice or voles or small birds, following the pucker of individual tics to its lively source, exploring into his life's dark-

ness. What he finds is nothing he might have imagined, and
a few moments later his bloody feathers float down to be followed by another sound, like a satisfied sigh.

Near the Mexican border, rocky canyons cleave the mountains, laying them aside like broken wedges of gray cheese
furred with a dark mold of pinon and juniper that sheds hard
shadows on moon glazed stone, etched lithographs in gray
and black, taupe and silver.

Beneath feathery chamisa a rattlesnake flicks his tongue,
following a scent. Along a precarious rock ledge a ring-
tailed cat strolls, nose snuffling the cracks. At the base of the
stone a peccary trots along familiar foot trails, toward the
toes of a higher cliff where a seeping spring gathers in a
rocky goblet. In the desert, sounds are dry and rattling: pebbles toed into cracks, hoofs tac-tacking on stone, the serpent
rattle warning the wild pig to veer away, which she does
with a grunt to the tribe behind her. From the rocky scarp the
ring-tailed cat hears the whole population of the desert pass
about its business in the canyon below.

A new sound comes to this place, too. High in the air, a
chuff, chuff, chuff, most like the wings of a monstrous crow,
crisp and powerful, enginelike in their regularity. Then a cry,
eerie and utterly alien, not from any native bird ever heard in
this place.

The peccary freezes in place. The ring-tailed cat leaps
into the nearest crevice. Only the rattler does not hear, does
not care. For the others, staying frozen in place seems the
appropriate and prudent thing to do as the chuff, chuff, chuff
moves overhead, another cry and an answer from places
east, and west, and north as well. The aerial hunter is not
alone, and its screams fade into the distance, the echoes still,
and the canyon comes quiet again.

And farther south and east, along the gulf, in the wetland
that breeds the livelihood of the sea, in the mangrove
swamps, the cypress bogs, the moss-lapped, vine-twined,
sawgrass-grown, reptile-ridden mudflats, night sounds are
continuous. Here the bull gator bellows, swamp birds call,
insects and frogs whir and buzz and babble and creak. Fish

jump, huge tails thrash, wings take off from cover to silhouette themselves on the face of the moon.

And even here comes strangeness, a great squadge, squadge, squadge, as though something walks through the deep muck in giant boots on ogre legs, squishing feet down and sucking them up only to squish them down once more. Squadge, squadge, squadge, three at a time, then a pause, then three more.

As in other places, the natives fall silent. The heron finds himself a perch and pulls his head back on his long neck, letting it rest on his back, crouching a little, not to be seen against the sky. The bull gator floats on the oily surface like a scaly buoy, fifteen feet of hunger and dim thought, an old man of the muck, protruding eyes seeing nothing as flared nostrils taste something strange. He lies in his favorite resting place near the trunk of a water-washed tree. There was no tree in that place earlier today, but the reptilian mind does not consider this. Only when something from above slithers sinuously onto the top of his head does he react violently, his body bending, monstrous tail thrashing, huge jaws gaping wide . . .

Then nothing. No more from the gator until morning, when the exploring heron looks along his beak to find an intaglio of strange bones on the bank, carefully trodden into the muck, from the fangs at the front of the jaw to the vertebra at the tip of the tale. Like a frieze of bloody murder, carefully displayed.

DESTINY

Book Three of The Blending Enthroned

Sharon Green

Available in April 2002

"What's happenin' now?" Vallant asked, and there was almost accusation in his tone. "I leave the bunch of you alone for no more than five minutes, and you find somethin' else to worry about as soon as my back is turned. So what is it now, and just how dangerous will it turn out to be?"

"A flux has been keeping me from Seeing more than bits and snatches," Naran said with a sigh. "I'm being surprised by everything but what we absolutely have to know."

"You know, that's exactly the way it *has* been," I said, hit by a flash of revelation. "You haven't been able to see much of anything beyond the completely essential, and that can't possibly be a coincidence either. Someone has to be deliberately blocking you."

"Could the enemy really be strong enough to reach all the way here to block Naran without us being aware of it?" Lorand asked, worry widening his eyes. "If they are, we have even more trouble than we thought."

"It can't possibly be the invaders," I said while everyone else just came up with exclamations of worry and startlement. "Naran's had this trouble since before we left Gan Garee, and if the invaders are *that* strong we might as well just stand here and let them take us over. No, someone else is responsible for blindfolding us, and I'd really like to know who that is."

"Who *could* it be?" Vallant countered, but not in a challenging way. "I'd be willin' to believe that Ristor Ardanis, leader of those with Sight magic, is behind the blockin', but he and most of his people are a long way away from here. Naran, are you absolutely certain that the people in your link groups are workin' *with* you rather than against your breakin' through?"

"Normally I might not be absolutely certain, but once I'm part of the Blending there's no doubt," Naran answered with a nod. "My people are trying as hard as I am, but something is keeping us from breaking through."

"It certainly can't be the Gracelians," Jovvi said, her distracted gaze saying that her mind searched for an answer. "The Gracelians don't *have* anyone with Sight magic, so they can't possibly affect it. Who does that leave?"

"No one but the Highest Aspect," I said, finding it impossible to keep the dryness from my tone. "If the enemy isn't doing it, the Gracelians aren't doing it, and Ristor Ardanis's people aren't doing it, there's no one left."

"But there *is* someone left," Rion disagreed slowly, his gaze as distracted as Jovvi's had been. "We haven't mentioned the fact in quite some time, but there's still a mystery in our lives that we haven't solved. Those 'signs' the Prophecies spoke of . . . We've denied that they ever happened, but they did happen and we still don't know who was responsible for causing them."

"And we don't know who was responsible for bringing us all together," Lorand took his turn to point out. "A minute or two ago we were refusing to accept all those dreams as a coincidence, but we never questioned the even bigger coincidence that we all ended up in the same residence. We are each of us the strongest practitioner of our respective talents, and we all just *happened* to end up in the same residence and made into a Blending? If you can believe *that*, then you must also believe that the Highest Aspect leaves a copper coin under our pillows as a reward for having gone through the five-year-old tests successfully."

"It looks like someone's been makin' a *lot* of things happen around us," Vallant observed, vexation showing on his face as strongly as I felt it inside me. "So there's some group, large or small, makin' these things happen, but we don't know if they're friend or foe. Until we find out just what their aim is, we can't call them one or the other."

"Well, one of their aims *was* to bring us together," I suggested, thinking about it even as I spoke. "If they're friends of ours, they did it so that we could win the throne and get rid of the nobility. If they're enemies, they did it to put us all in the same place so we could be gotten rid of with a single effort. If *we* get taken down, everyone knows that no one else is as strong as we are and so they might not even put up a token struggle. By winning over us, the enemy would win over everyone else at the same time."

"I see a flaw in that logic," Lorand said, another of us almost lost to distraction. "These unknown someones have obviously known about us since before we got together in Gan Garee. Putting us all together just to conquer us at the same time makes no sense, not when they could have killed us one at a time before we knew what we were doing. If they had, there would *be* no 'others' to worry about, only the Middle Seated Blending the nobles picked out. Even an arrogant enemy would never go to such lengths just to best six people."

"I'm forced to agree with that," Vallant said even as Jovvi nodded her own agreement. "What's the sense in havin' almost a dozen more enemies, when killin' a few people will give you no enemies to speak of at all? These invader leaders just rolled over all opposition until it was crushed, and then it took over the people and used them for their own purposes. That means there's definitely someone else in the game."

MEMORY OF FIRE

Book One of the World Gates

Holly Lisle

Available in May 2002

Molly McColl woke to darkness—and to men dragging her from her bed toward her bedroom door. The door glowed with a terrifying green light.

She didn't waste her breath screaming; she attacked. She kicked upward, and felt like she'd kicked a rock—but she heard the satisfying crack of bone under her bare heel, and the resulting shriek of pain. She snapped her right elbow back into ribs and gut, and her hand broke free from the thin, hot, strong fingers that clutched at it. She twisted and bit down on the fingers holding her left wrist, and was rewarded with a scream. She clawed at eyes, she kneed groins, she bit and kicked and fought with every trick at her disposal, with every ounce of her strength and every bit of her fear and rage.

But they had her outnumbered, and even though she could make out the outlines of the ones she'd hurt curled on the floor, the rest of her assailants still dragged her into that wall of fire. She screamed, but as the cluster of tall men around her forced her into the flames, her scream—and all other sounds—died.

No pain. No heat. The flames that brushed against her didn't hurt at all—instead, the cold fire felt wonderful, energizing, life-giving; as her kidnappers dragged her clawing and kicking onto the curving, pulsing tunnel, something in her mind whispered "yes." For the instant—or the eternity—in which she hung suspended in that place, no one held her, no one was trying to hurt her, and for the first time in a long time, all the pain in her body fell away.

She had no idea what was going on; she felt on the one hand like she was fighting for her life, and on the other hand like she was moving into something wonderful.

And then, out of the tunnel of green fire, she erupted into a world of ice and snow and darkness, and all doubts vanished. The men still held her captive, and one of them shouted, "Get ropes and a wagon—she hurt Paith and Kevrad and Tajaro. We're going to have to tie her." She was in trouble—nothing good would come of this.

"It's only two leagues to Copper House."

"She'll kill one of us in that distance. Tie her."

"But the Imallin said she's not to be hurt."

Other hands were grabbing her now—catching at her feet, locking on to her elbows and wrists, knees and calves.

"Don't *hurt* her," said the one closest to her head. "Just *tie* her so she can't hurt us, damnall. And where's that useless Gateman the Imallin found to make the gate? We still have people back there! Send someone to get them out before he closes it!"

Molly fought as hard as she could, but the men—thin and tall, but strong—forced her forward, adding hands to hands on her arms and legs until she simply couldn't move.

When she couldn't fight, Molly relaxed her body completely. First, she wasn't going to waste energy uselessly. Second, if she stopped fighting, she might catch them off guard and be able to escape.

Someone dragged a big, snorting animal through the dark toward her, and rattling behind the animal was a big wooden farm-type wagon. But what the hell was the thing pulling it? It wasn't a horse and it wasn't any variety of cow—it had a bit of a moose shape to it, and a hint of caribou, and some angles that suggested bones where bones didn't belong in any beast of burden Molly had ever seen. And its eyes glowed hell-red in the darkness.

The whole mob of them picked her up and shoved her into

the back of the wagon, and most of them clambered up there with her—bending down to twist soft rope around her ankles, and then around her wrists. When they had her bound, they wrapped blankets around her, and tucked her deep into bales of straw. Instantly, she was warmer. Hell, she was warm. But as the wagon lurched and creaked, and began to rattle forward, she heard lines of marching feet forming on either side of the wagon. She knew the creak of boots and pack straps, the soft bitching, the sound of feet moving in rhythm while weighted down by gear and weapons. She remembered basic training all too well—and if Air Force basic was pretty easy compared to the Army or the Marines, she'd still got enough of marching to know the drill. She had a military escort.

What the hell was going on?

But the people who had come to get her weren't soldiers. They were too unprepared for resistance, too sure of themselves. Soldiers knew that trouble could be anywhere, and took precautions. More than that, though, she couldn't get over the feel of those hands on her—hot, thin, dry hands.

She decided she wasn't going to just wait for them to haul her where they were going and then . . . do things to her. She'd learned in the Air Force that the best way to survive a hostage situation was to not be a hostage. She started to work on the rope on her wrists, and managed by dint of persistence and a high tolerance to pain to free her hands. She'd done some damage—she could feel rope burns and scratches from metal embedded beneath the soft outer strands, and the heat and wetness where a bit of her own blood trickled down her hand—but she wasn't worried about any of that.

Fold and wrap a blanket around each foot and bind it in place with the rope, she thought. It won't make great boots, but it will get me home. Turn the other blankets into a poncho, get the hell out of this place and back home. She could follow the tracks in the snow.

Except there were the niggling details she hadn't let herself think about while she was fighting, while she was getting her hands and then her feet untied, while she was folding boots out of blankets and tying them in place. She hadn't heard an engine since she came out of the tunnel of fire; she hadn't heard a car pass, or seen anything that might even be mistaken for an electric light; nor had she heard a plane fly over. In the darkness, she could make out the vague outlines of trees overhead, but not much else—not a star shone in the sky, which felt close and pregnant with more snow.

She had the bad feeling that if she managed to escape the soldiers that marched to either side of the wagon and succeeded in tracing the wagon tracks back to the place where she'd come through the tunnel of fire, that tunnel wouldn't be there anymore. And she was very, very afraid that there would be no other way to get home.

She listened to the speech of the men who drove the wagons, and she could understand it flawlessly—but if she forced herself to listen to the words, they were vowel-rich and liquid, and they didn't have the shape of English. The hands on her arms had felt wrong in ways besides their heat, their dryness, their thinness. When she closed her eyes and stilled her breath and forced herself to remember, those hands had gripped her with too many fingers. And when she'd been fighting, her elbows had jammed into ribs that weren't where ribs were supposed to be.

When the sun came up or they got to a place with lights, Molly had a bad feeling that she wasn't going to like getting her first clear look at her kidnappers. Because when she let herself really think about it, she had the feeling that she wasn't on Earth anymore—and that her captors weren't human.

YEAR'S BEST SF 7

Edited by David G. Hartwell

The tradition continues! The YEAR'S BEST SF 7 collects the best science fiction stories of 2001, never before published in book form, in one easy-to-carry volume. Previous volumes have included stories by Ray Bradbury, Joe Haldeman, Ursula K. Le Guin, Kim Stanley Robinson, Robert Silverberg, Bruce Sterling, Gene Wolfe, and many more.

With tales from both the grand masters of the field and the rising new stars, the YEAR'S BEST SF is rapidly becoming the indispensable guide to science fiction today.

Praise for the YEAR'S BEST series:

"Impressive."
—Locus magazine

"The finest modern science fiction writing."
—Pittsburgh Tribune

Don't Miss Any of the
ACORNA ADVENTURES

"Good spacefaring fun."
Publishers Weekly

ACORNA
by Anne McCaffrey and Margaret Ball
0-06-105789-4/$7.50 US/$9.99 Can

ACORNA'S QUEST
by Anne McCaffrey and Margaret Ball
0-06-105790-8/$6.50 US/$8.99 Can

ACORNA'S PEOPLE
by Anne McCaffrey and Elizabeth Ann Scarborough
0-06-105983-8/$6.99 US/$9.99 Can

ACORNA'S WORLD
by Anne McCaffrey and Elizabeth Ann Scarborough
0-06-105984-6/$6.99 US/$9.99 Can

And in Hardcover

ACORNA'S SEARCH
by Anne McCaffrey and Elizabeth Ann Scarborough
0-380-97898-9/$25.00 US/$37.95 Can